Where there is SMOKE

Meanwhile, in Montana: Ponderosa Pistons Book 3

By Elle J. Brae

ISBN 978-1-7640873-4-6 (Trade paperback)

Electronic Version 978-1-7640873-5-3 (E-book)

Cover art by Jaqueline Sweet Cover Design

Design elements by Sergio Mayo Art

Editing by The Author's Archive

Interior design by Meet Me in the Pages

Acknowledgements:

A huge thank you to Mr B. My boy, my brightness and my bump in the darkness when I snore too loudly. You snore too, you know!

Woman, I'll take you over my goddamn knee and
stripe that ass until you can't fucking speak.
The only pole you'll be riding is mine.

Call Rae
Bar

CONTENT WARNINGS

Including but not limited to

Ass Play - on page

Breath Play - on page

Intentional Contagion - on page

Degradation - on page

Vehicular Collision/Trauma - on page

Cum Play - on page

ABDL, splash blankets - mention of

Kink Discovery and Exploration - on page

Extreme Religious Views - on page

BDSM, Spanking - on page

Depiction of Cult - on page and past mention of

Domestic Violence - on page

Coarse Language - on page, plentiful

Suicide - on page and mention of

Drug Use - on page

Pegging - on page

Assault - on page

Contents

PROLOGUE - CALLY RAE
7 YEARS EARLIER
Cally with an 'I

Growing up in Texas with a heap of cousins was the perfect childhood for me and my older sister, Jo. Our house was always full of friends, family and fun. Mom would serve up a healthy slice of Southern hospitality alongside her county-famous pecan pie. Days began with a prayer to the Lord, thanking Him for blessing us with another day on our beautiful earth. On each occasion, our best efforts would be directed toward helping and making a difference. Charity was given from the heart, not just the hand. That was drummed into each of us from an early age. Jo and I would help with food drives, pack boxes of books and other school supplies for less fortunate children, and pack the sweet treats Mom baked for the church fair. We had a typical, quiet suburban Christian upbringing until everything shattered like the rose-patterned plate now in a thousand tiny shards on our kitchen floor.

"Callista Rae, please be careful; that's part of a set and very expensive," our mother chided when it had slipped from my soapy grasp. Dish towel in hand, Jo simply stared at me accusingly. If I dropped it, she didn't catch it either. We were too busy standing there in horror with jaws slack. Moving to Utah and away from our family and friends—why?

"Are we moving for Dad's work?" Jo asked, stepping over the broken shards to fetch a broom. As the older of us by four years, her young shoulders held on to a level of maturity I could only aspire to.

"Yes, Johanna, we are." Mom beamed at my sister before turning to scowl at me. Guess that broken plate really was important, huh?

It only took four months of living in Utah for me to realize that the 'work' we moved across the country for had less to do with Dad's paycheck and more to do with his increasingly extreme religious beliefs. Charlton Jenkins worked as a small appliance salesperson; a position he could have accepted anywhere. While the gorgeous state of Utah had an abundance of appliance retailers, Dad didn't punch a timecard at any of them. Instead, he took up a position with a local *church foundation* that—I realized after several years—was more cult than church. Their rhetoric and beliefs leaned towards traditionalism and were closed-off. Over time, as I matured, I understood the scope of what we had moved for. We didn't visit family anymore, nor did they come to visit us. There were no celebrated birthdays or Easter, Thanksgiving or Christmas. Revered occasions centered on dates important to the pastor only. The day he was born, and the anniversary of the day he founded his circle of the righteous. You see, the only people who don't realize a cult is a cult, is the cult themselves. The only way Jo and I could contact our Texan branch was to use the computers in the school library. Then, that became a distant memory.

Harmful messages and depraved teachings were being sent into our home appliances by the government, according to Pastor Rich, Dad's new 'boss' and self-appointed righteous mentor. He had set up his own branch of *the church*, called the Righteous Moonyata Circle. It leaned more cult than church, and according to the RMC, we were all at risk of infectious ruination from these subliminal messages promoting sin. Toasters, coffee pots, rice cookers—all of them were vessels for the devil's message, sent innocuously down each power cord from the sockets in the wall. Once the appliance 'absorbed' the subliminal messages, we too would succumb. Don't even get me started on microwaves! It didn't matter if we ate rice from the cooker, drank coffee from the pot, or ate toast from the toaster; we only needed to be near the appliance for the message to absorb through our skin and alter our DNA permanently. Pastor Rich had sought my father out because he sold appliances. He was *unknowingly dealing the devil's doctrine* to tens of thousands, if not millions of Americans each year. Now, he had his chance to atone, and a whole lot of work to do, starting with our own household.

"Home schooling? Why?" I'd wailed when Mom told me I wouldn't undertake my junior year at the local high school, the one I'd arrived at partway through my sophomore year.

"Not homeschooling, Callista, and *do not take that tone with me*. What does the Lord say about being prideful? Every lesson is a gift. You will learn the pastor's righteous lessons along with your neighbors, our extended family."

And that's where it all turned to shit. We had extended family, real family back in, and around, Brenham. Our new neighbors? They were just as devout as Mom and Dad, only the message of servitude and charity was intermingled with hatred and homophobia, judgment and lies. This wasn't religion; this was oppression, and I couldn't wait to get the fuck out. Yeah, that's a cuss word all right. Only they were said with my *inside voice*; the one hammering in my head behind my rolling eyes.

Lazy days by the pool sipping iced tea in a modest two-piece bathing suit stayed behind in that four-bedroom, mid-century modern home almost midway between Austin and Houston. Joy and laughter stayed there too, refusing to embark on the road trip that was Dad's calling to some whack-job cleric who didn't deserve his collar. Only Dad's journey to salvation included all four of us.

"We can save you from spiritual penalty child, it's never too late," was the first sentence spoken to me when the Jenkins clan arrived on the front steps of this new 'church' I didn't identify with, nor invite into my life. The only thing I need saving from is you fucking weirdos, I thought, as I planned my way out of this tenure of pious heresy and began my life as a porcupine.

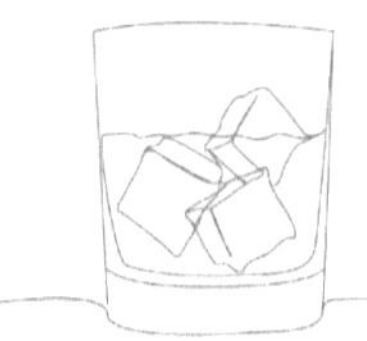

CHAPTER 1 - SMOKE
Dance like no one is watching

The renovations are taking their sweet ass time; this supposedly up-scale bar still looks more like the Chinese restaurant it was for twenty-six years. I've been appointed manager of the place next door, Wildcats Bar. It's owned by the Ponderosa Pistons, the MC I patched into just shy of a month ago, out of Bozeman, Montana. The Pistons are the coveted destination of retired military vets with no place else to go, or places to go that they have no intention of returning to.

Me? I'm here for a new start. A place in a company, team, or military regiment is always spruiked as offering a 'sense of belonging', a brotherhood. Recruiters will wax lyrical about a sense of support and togetherness as we fight common enemies. I felt no such inclusion when I was enlisted; the enemies I fought weren't always through the end of a rifle scope either. Yet here I am, alive and with use of every limb, every faculty. I was able and fortunate if you compared my years as a marine with the statistics of those injured and those who lost their lives. I knew I was fortunate, yet it changed nothing.

The Pistons own and run Wildcats, and bought up the building next door when Fong's was set to fold. No more orange chicken or broccoli beef will surely be a culinary crime, but the building's location was in the perfect position for the Pistons to pounce on desirable real estate, and pounce they did. The only issue was the glacial slowness of the renovation. I can still see paper lanterns hanging from the collapsing ceiling tiles, and more than one round table remains in the main dining space. A vintage cash register lived where there should have been a modern bar, and I can not imagine a stage and sleek stripper pole while looking into a deep fryer and off-white brick painted with congealed grease. I don't have a vivid imagination, but the smell of frying nearly three decades worth of prawn crackers told me it would be several weeks before girls in G-strings graced this establishment.

I'm leaning, arms crossed, against the hole in the wall between the two buildings when a feminine throat clears behind me. We have a host of girls interviewing for positions at the new venue, Kittens. We've seen three already today, and one might work out. Our president has left for more official club business, leaving me to see some guy named Ray coming in for a job in the bar, so I need to move whoever this is, on. I turn slowly to spy a mass of mahogany copper tresses, long legs, and a smattering of freckles around the cutest little button nose. Holy shit. Two club members who work here, Feather and Saint, stand a distance behind the woman, Feather with two thumbs up. Saint strides up and speaks first, his excitement palpable. "Smoke, this here is Carly."

The gorgeous redhead pouts. "Uh, it's Cally R—"

"Sorry, Cally. Smoke, this here is Cally. Let's get this happening. We have stuff to do, right?"

"Right," I mumble, hand scrubbing over my face. Three girls and some dude for the bar. I whip the crumpled piece of paper from my back pocket. Pulling it open and rereading the almost illegible scrawl. Call Rae, and a downwards arrow to the word Bar. Call Rae, and yet there is no telephone number. Maybe this chick is the one the agency sent over? Anyway, she's here now, we're here now, so if she's quick enough, what's one more routine before my time with Ray, or Rae, or however the fuck he spells his name?

"I'm here about the job," she replies, fingers entwined in front of her. She is fresh-faced and timid. Tits are on the smaller side, but they look natural, like the rest of her.

"Perfect. You look good, sweetheart. Like Ariel from the Little Mermaid. You got one of them clamshell bras on?" Feather asks hopefully in his deep baritone rumble.

"Clamshell bra? Um, no," she squeaks. She looks like she's dressing up in borrowed clothes. Nothing fits well, and she's squirming. Perhaps she's one of those quiet library types with a raunchy side once you get a few drinks into them, or the first drumbeats of her signature song play through the speakers.

"Doesn't matter. This is an audition, yeah. We'll see what you've got?" Saint adds, slapping Feather on the back and guiding him to a chair around the small back table. As I'm sinking into the last remaining chair, I hear her muttering under her breath. My hearing is hypersensitive thanks to military training.

"Audition? Isn't this an interview? Same thing, I guess." She's talking to herself. Cally's lips are moving with whisper-soft precision, eyelids blinking across orbs of pure honey and whiskey fire. She looks nervous as hell. Feather is one huge motherfucker, six-nine and almost three hundred pounds. He must've scared the living shit out of this dainty little thing. It's wise that these tiny dancers know Feather heads up our security and will have the welfare of our dancers as his top priority. Grabby hands are par for the course with drunk guys at strip clubs. Patrons at Kittens can look, but not touch, or Feather will spin those grabby hands into fractured ones.

"Do you know a guy called Ray?" I ask Saint while Feather continues the perusal of the fidgeting redhead.

"Nope," he drawls, hand smoothing down his stubbled cheek. "Why?"

"Alpha gave me this piece of paper to call some guy named Rae about the bar. But there is no phone number." I pull the crumpled paper from my pocket and throw it onto the tabletop among the tumblers. Rae, or Ray, is just gonna have to wait until Ariel shows us her whole new world.

"You got music with you?" I ask the woman wringing her hands and sucking her full lips between her teeth. Yep, this one looks the goods. I'm hoping she'll go off like a fourth of July rocket once the beat pumps and the clothes disappear. Those slender porcelain fingers wrapped around the pole as she slides around in come-fuck-me heels and—

"Music? No, was I supposed to supply a playlist?" Her head cants to the side. We can see the cogs turning in time. She forgot her music; I guess it happens.

"Yeah. It's not essential. We can find whatever song you want. Just let us know the title and artist. We need to check the run time, maybe get an extended mix if we need you to fill a longer set, but that's something we can sort out later, right?" Saint adds for clarification.

"Okay." She nods enthusiastically, chin almost at her chest.

"So... your song?" Saint presses, phone in hand, music app at the ready.

"My song?"

I'm thinking this woman might be a little slow. Every question is answered with another question. If she's on drugs, the agency will wish they'd never sent this princess to our place, irrespective of her stunning looks. They know we drug test all of our staff, and there are no exceptions.

"What do you normally work to?" Feather asks, annoyed. "Come on, Jessica Rabbit, we don't have all day."

Cally lets out the tiniest giggle, snapping us out of our frustration. Saint and Feather look to me for guidance, and I shrug. All the girls from this morning turned up in killer heels and skimpy outfits, big hair, and full faces of heavy makeup. They walked in with an air of confidence, almost arrogance, and their music selections were queued up and ready to go. This little rabbit looks so far from cued up and ready to go, I almost want to direct her to the Austrian mountains where the hills are alive.

"What do you dance to?" Saint asks again, sounding out each word like he is talking to a child. His delivery works wonders. The smile that breaks out across her face is the most astounding thing I've witnessed in a long time. Pure joy. Her body vibrates with excitement. Saint is already swiping through a list of songs about fire on his music app before settling on one.

"Dancing, anything!" She beams, and that smile lights up not only her face, but the room. Feather arches a bushy eyebrow and grunts, already bored.

"Okay, Halsey: Angel on Fire. Let's see you move, darlin'. The floor is yours," Saint adds, throwing his phone onto the table and partially obscuring the scribbled note. Her bag is placed on the only other available table near the hole in the wall. While the renovations continue, this back area is off limits to patrons, and there is no point in cluttering the workspace with tables and chairs that will only be in the way.

As the song begins, she pushes a few strands of auburn hair behind one ear and closes her eyes. Saint kicks a heel up onto his chair and wraps his arm around his knee, eyes focused on the stripper about to get busy for us. My fingers strangle the sides of the tumbler as it rises to my lips. This isn't my kind of music, but if it works for her audition, then fine. She looks like an angel on fire; I can definitely see why Saint selected this track.

The lyrics open up, and so does she, kind of. Her body twitches and jerks with spasmodic movements. Every tilt and roll of her head has that flaming mane whipping about, her limbs flailing along to a sensual beat that most definitely is not this song. When I look closer, I note her eyes are closed. Okay... at first and second glances, I'm tempted to check for groundwater and an arcing wire. She jolts as if she has a hand in a live socket.

"Does she require medical attention?" Feather asks in a low tone that has me curious. Cally continues with her spastic movements, arms circling above her head like a lasso? She spins on chunky shoes one size too small. Her toes stretch out over the end of the sandal as she twirls—at least I think it's a twirl. Holy shit, is this chick having a seizure? I spare a look to my left at Saint, who has a look of sheer horror plastered on his affable face. His head drops to his knees, and he turns his face to Feather first, before rolling it back in my direction.

"What the actual fuck?" he mumbles as the whir of pale limbs and scarlet tresses switches from the sprinkler, to smacking herself on the butt with alternating hands. Christ on a fucking cracker, this is where all erections go to die.

"How long is this song?" I query, my hand scrubbing over my face. Two of the earlier girls were not suitable for Kittens because their routines looked unpolished and cheap. There was no allure or elegance, no high-end sultry seduction. The Pistons are opening a strip club, sure, but not just any strip club. Alpha wanted it to be a destination for people willing to part with their cash, a sensual experience, not your run of the mill, sleazy, neon sign kind of titty bar.

"Three and a quarter minutes, over one minute left," Saint adds, exasperated.

"Fuck," I counter, blinking ahead but not wanting to focus too hard on the fiery tornado morphing from the bus stop into some kind of aerobics grapevine. Drunken wedding revelry at one a.m. looks better than this. Her arms snap spasmodically, legs stuck to the floor before bending and flexing with unnatural torsion and zero grace. A foal on unsteady legs. And meth.

"This routine would clear the place quicker than a fucking fire alarm," Feather quips, arms still folded across his massive chest. He's not wrong. I'd happily sign up for a colonoscopy rather than sit through this again. While we understand some girls are more nervous than others, no amount of directional lighting or routine-appropriate music can fix...

this. Whatever this is, it ain't sexy, it ain't sultry and it sure as shit ain't staying.

"Okay, honey, that's enough," I bellow at the same time as another voice behind our table booms. "What the fuck is going on here?"

The three of us turn in unison to see Alpha standing with another woman, this one with shorter copper hair, a lithe frame and a thunderous expression. She's in a nurse uniform. An actual nursing uniform, not the slutty, lacy stuff you might expect at Kittens in a couple of months.

Alpha strides forward, reaching our table in three steps. His huge bear paw claps down onto my shoulder with firm pressure. Feather and Saint look to the nurse, to the fire-haired freestyler who is the worst stripper ever, and back to our club president. Cally steers rogue locks of hair behind her ears and waves at the nurse. Waves. Her hand up and oscillating like a toddler would upon seeing a friend in the playground.

"Cally Rae, what the hell?" the nurse blurts out, face ashen as she too walks forward. With his free hand, Alpha slides the piece of paper out from under my now empty whiskey glass.

"Explain…" he roars, and the three of us straighten like naughty students outside the principal's office. Before any of us can get a word out, the nurse has the other woman in a fierce hug, talking in a low tone that none of us can quite make out.

"Why the fuck is she up here dancing?" he roars, his index finger pointing past the edge of the paper to the woman standing ten feet away. "What part of Cally Rae, Bar do you idiots not understand?"

"She wasn't dancing, think she was fitting?" Feather blurts out.

I jump to standing, pulling the scribbled paper from his thick fingers. Saint too is on his feet in an instant. Sure enough, instead of Call Rae and what we thought was a downwards arrow pointing to the word Bar, on further inspection it looks like the word Cally Rae, Bar. The 'y' is lower than the rest of her name. There was no Rae or Ray to call about a bar position; that's why there was no telephone number.

"That's a 'y'," Saint offers with a smirk, his finger pointing at the crumpled paper.

"I see that now, asshole," I fire back.

"Jo, I am so, so sorry. I don't know what happened here. I take it this is your lovely sister?" Alpha steps forward towards the women and holds out his hand.

"Yes," says the nurse. "This is my sister, Cally Rae. She came here for a job *behind the bar." Oh, fuck.*

Alpha whirls around at a speed that should be impossible for a man of his size. Feather has sunken into his chair, the tiny table doing nothing to obscure his bulk.

"Jo, I know you know Saint and Feather. The idiot in the middle is our new bar manager, Smoke. He's the one I gave your sister's information to while I stepped out for a while. Seems you can't find good help these days, hey," he adds, before turning his attention back to the women.

As the dainty, porcelain hand extends to meet his huge one, instead of grasping it and shaking it, he brings it to his lips and kisses the back of her hand with soft reverence. "It's a pleasure to meet you, Cally Rae. Please accept my humblest apologies."

The poor thing's face turns as red as her hair. The blush rises from the collar of her shirt, flaring up her neck and radiating across the apples of her cheeks. Alpha turns on his heel and marches back to our gathering, cuffing me on the back of the head for good measure. And I deserved it.

"If Cally is still amiable about working with you clowns, the job is hers. When can you start, sweetheart?" His voice floats towards the beaming woman.

"Anytime," she shrieks, bounding on those low, ill-fitting heels.

"Hope she pours beers better than she busts a move," Saint mumbles before he, too, is cuffed across the back of the head, hard.

"Your collective fuck-up, your collective fix," Alpha barks back to the three of us, before turning on his heel and marching back the way he had entered only moments ago.

"You thought my sister was a stripper, Saint?" Jo questions, head canted.

"Um, we…" he begins.

"Don't add me to your shit," I bark. "You're the one who sent her up there and asked for her music!"

"You thought Rae was a dude!" he counters, eyes flashing with fire. "And Feather was the one to send her back out here," he protests, finger thrust at the huge man still sinking down in the chair.

"Gentlemen," comes a measured female tone. Jo lifts her head and releases her sister. Yeah, I can see the resemblance now. Jo looks older, plainer. Still pretty in a classic way, but her younger sister is an absolute knockout, clamshell bra or not. "Save the arguments and finger-pointing for your clubhouse. All we want to know is," she continues, finger moving between her sister and herself, "that Cal has a job."

"Absolutely," Saint agrees, nodding emphatically. Damn kiss ass. The two women grin from ear to ear. Jo claps her sister on her back before pulling her into a tight hug.

"Sure you do," I add. "You can start tomorrow morning at ten. Please wear closed-toed shoes that fit properly, and as long as your handwriting is legible and not like this scrawl," I hold up the crumpled paper as reference, "then we should have no further problems."

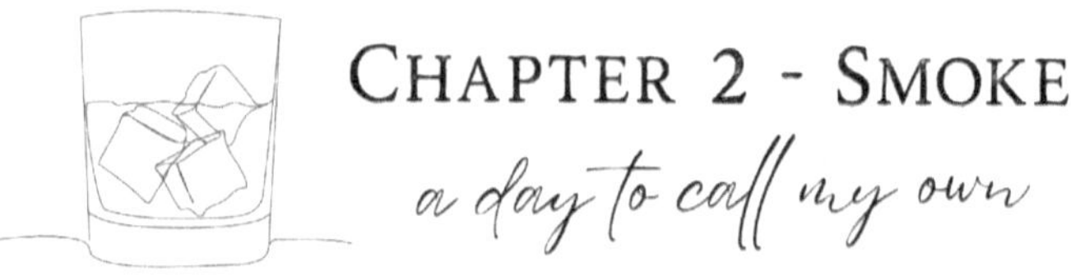

CHAPTER 2 - SMOKE
a day to call my own

TWO MONTHS EARLIER...

Yeah, I was born on April Fool's Day. Fucking hilarious, I get it. Only today, I am the fucking fool. Thirty-four years old; single, unemployed and homeless.

My home and job were in the military for over fifteen years. I was a Marine Sniper MOS 8541. Military Occupational Specialty, and my designation covered surveillance and target acquisition.

Spending the majority of your day looking through the scope of an ASR, in my case the Mk22 Mod 0 Advanced Sniper Rifle, you begin to view the world differently.

Circling back to unemployed and homeless, well, I had work after the Marine Corps. I tended bar at a hole-in-the-wall dive in a shitty part of Eugene, Oregon, calling the room upstairs home. The place is owned by a friend of a friend, and it suited me just fine. Regulars whose drinks I knew by their gait through our heavy door, or signature scents attached to their sweat-soaked skin. Grey Goose for Maria, the teacher's assistant, who started the school year bright and hopeful, but increased her order to "doubles, and keep 'em coming" after the snow melted and rain continued. Saul favored Evan Williams, neat, when his clients didn't make bond, which was more often than not.

As shitty as the place was, it was home, and work, until one stupid decision saw both vanish into the dwindling evening light as if they were never there in the first place. The only constant I had since returning stateside, and I couldn't shut my mouth or temper my anger. And I don't regret it one bit.

Lola, the daughter of the owner, worked a few shifts and her magic on me. Long, straight raven hair down to her pert ass and hips that you could hold on to good and proper when you fucked her, yeah, she was something else all right. She kept me company on some of the darkest nights, the nights where I'd have to sweep up the broken teeth at the end of the shift. Make a report of what got broken, how many stools needed replacing, and that kind of stuff. Only, her company was enjoyed by a long list of others. That wasn't what drove me to send one of her johns through the wall and tumbling down the stairwell though, no, that was because he was her father's business partner, and he was smacking the shit out of her every time he fucked her.

Chivalry isn't dead; it's just incredibly stupid. Did he deserve to have the shit beaten out of him? You betcha. Should I have done it somewhere I wasn't tied to? Yep. Hindsight is a wonderful thing; I should have removed myself from the situation, cooled off and thought about the best way to punish that handsy prick. Breaking every bone in his hands would have done the trick. Some of them might heal seamlessly and without incident, but not all of them, especially if displacement is involved with the fracture. Then we're talking extended healing time, extended pain, and a lifetime extended with swelling, deformity and agony. Only raw red rage flashed across my vision at the sight of her bloodied lip and bruised wrists. A red rag to a bull, and this bull charged full throttle.

I've mostly avoided my parents since I came home, unless you count the thinly veiled lecture about returning to Arizona and finding myself a nice girl to settle down with and procreate. It could be months before I see them again, so I'm tucking tail and heading back to my parents in Flagstaff, the visit disguised as concern for my mother, who is recovering from surgery for repetitive strain injury. She battled for years, most therapies helpful for a time, only for the inflammation to raise its angry head again. Adding to the chronic injury burden, is the fact that she's her own worst enemy with stopping if pain flares. Our nerves are a brilliant design, sending bolts of jolting pain to our receptors whenever we perform an action that may harm us. That warning jolt is beneficial only if the action is equal and opposite. If you touch a hot pan on a stove, you pull back the sizzling fingers and seek icy running water as treatment. My mother pushed through it all.

Dianne Weir and her aching hand, wrist and forearm? She just pushed through the warning jolts and swelling to the point of near paralysis, re-shelving books and entering library data as if it was the most important job in the world. To her, it was, along with raising three boys. Three, because other than Samuel and me, she referred to Dad as one of her kids, often remarking how he required the most supervision out of all of us.

"Yeah, Mom, I'll come look after you and kick Dad's ass if he's not fussing over you. I can stay as long as you'd like me to. No, I'm not in trouble, and no, I wouldn't lie to my mother. I just miss you, Mom. I'll be home in about a week. I have an ex-service reunion over the weekend in Portland, and I'll be leaving after that. Sure, I'll be careful, and I love you, too."

CHAPTER 3 - CALLY
a monochromatic rainbow

Pastor Rich tells us we can't be righteous without sacrifice, that modern-day conveniences were propaganda put in place by a government intent on indoctrination. That might make sense at some point, only the governments have changed during the modern-day conveniences he's adamant we need to relinquish in order to be righteous. Refrigerators, televisions, microwave ovens. Namely, most all electrical appliances. Items my father made an honest living selling out of a store, that paid for our home, our education and modest vacations. "He was being used as a vessel by the devil," Pastor Rich roars, casting knowing glances towards my dad, also facing us in a kneeling, subservient position by Pastor Rich's side.

Dad doesn't kneel before anyone, so seeing him deliberately contrite while this silly man continues to say awful things about him makes my heart ache for him. And us, because this is not just his salvational pilgrimage, we are sherpas of his new faith, brought along to share the cost of carrying his burden and aid his journey. He used to be a strict, but fair man, with a deep voice and kind smile. A smile not given freely, so when it was directed your way, you had won a prize greater than any lottery. As his smiles shone less and less, agitation grew into a beast of borderline savage cruelty; Mom, Jo and I spent more and more time at our local church and Bible study groups. Mom fought hard at first, a pained smile hiding the fact that the distance growing between her and her husband, the father to her daughters, was widening. Gaping like a fresh wound with the edges pulled apart and the internal gore visible and painful. Then, she too, lost her smile. Even the tight ones she used to offer my dad when he demanded she wash clothes using a bucket and soap bar, or cook his six p.m. dinners over an open flame in the yard.

Marriage unites loving souls for richer or poorer, in sickness and in health, forsaking all others as long as you both shall live. That's assuming you both entered the marriage with equal faith and loyalty, or faith in your loyalty. Divorce wasn't an option; we were all tethered to Dad and his increasing delusional episodes. Slowly but surely, he wore her down, eroding her sandstone exterior one pass at a time with rough grit sandpaper and attention to necessary detail.

If I could liken the drastic difference between young life in Texas and the oppressive hardship of cult existence in Utah, it would be as if a glorious rainbow of vibrant color was depicted in black and white or sepia tones. The bright pigments, formerly a shadow of their true identity, no longer arched and impressive, but sullied to a dull line I was expected to step up to and toe obediently, but never cross.

As a teenager with opinions and questions, observing insular leadership more prone to "doing as I say, and not as I do," I was always going to be an outcast. Only my willful disobedience, as Pastor Rich called it, spoke to a body already infiltrated with the government sin and refusal to repent. At first, my hair was dyed with dried powders of organic ingredients. Blueberries turned it a vile purple-brown, but only temporarily. Coffee grounds smelled as good as the berry powder and way better than the charcoal. All attempts to 'correct' my deep red hair were fruitless. Jo's hair, a lighter copper, took the coffee dye well. This resulted in a warmer brunette that the elders approved of. Her agreeable nature spared her the punishments I received. If it wasn't my hair's stubborn refusal to take on purer color, it was my bitter mouth and impure mind. Every barb they threw my way was another quill settling into my porcupine flesh. Soon, I would be covered in the amulets of protection they had set in place.

Wind back six hundred years, to the Counter-Reformation and the Thirty Years' War, and I, too, would have become my personal torch, decreed a witch and cast from society. If a burning at the stake were on offer right about now, I can't say for sure that I would turn it down. My spell-casting era hasn't developed yet, but please let it arrive forthwith! I'm done kowtowing to egregious men in self-imposed power who determine a woman's purity and purpose by the color of her fucking hair. Yeah, that's right. I say fuck. A lot. I never swore before we got to Pastor Rich's, and never around others. However, "gosh," "gee," and "golly darn" aren't always enough. "Fuck" was the only word I could think of that could be a noun, adjective, and adverb. And fuck me if fuck didn't fit this situation right about now. I was fucked.

CHAPTER 4 - SMOKE

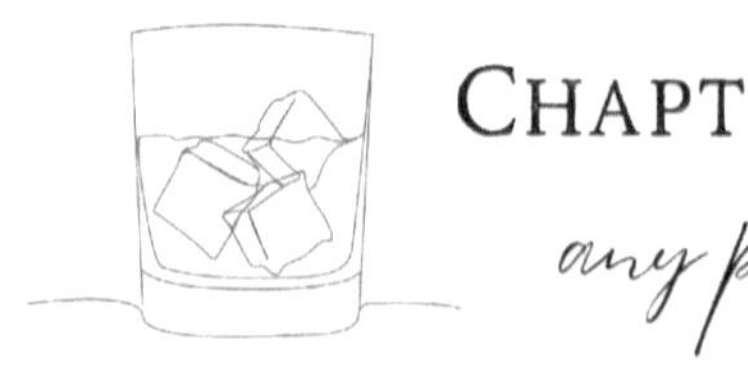

any port in a storm

"Hey, Smoke. Good to see ya, man. It's been too fucking long."

"That it has, my friend, that it has. You here with the Pistons?" I ask, leaning to shake the hand of the man I haven't seen in what, seven, maybe eight years? The man had both legs blown off in an IED blast. One below the knee, one above. I heard he was being fitted with a specialized prosthesis; yet today he's in his wheelchair, rolling his way through life.

"I am. I'm just gonna roll on over to the bar, grab a drink and I'll be right with ya."

Simon 'Scooter' Soderno was a 'two eight', indicating his MOS fell under Ground Electronics Maintenance. That was before he fell victim to the device that took his legs and the lives of two men in his unit. Remarkably, Scooter was still one of the nicest, most positive guys I knew. He'd lost his legs, sure, but at least his dick still worked. Fuck me, I don't know if I'd share the same happy-go-lucky, take each day as it comes outlook if I were rolling around. That just goes to show he's a better man than I'll ever be.

"Welcome, Portland. Good to see so many of you turn up to hear me talk shit for an hour," Alpha said, and that was the way the 'presentation' started. Alpha, so named because his first name was Anastasios and his surname even more complicated, was the President of the Ponderosa Pistons Motorcycle Club. A club his father had founded once he, too, returned from service in Vietnam and needed a new outlook. When men come home from foreign wars, they are changed people. Some recognize the change immediately, whereas others realize over months, or even years. Slipping seamlessly back into a normal life in regular society is harder than the brochures suggest. Alpha's old man bought up a chunk of land out of Bozeman, Montana, and built a club out of nothing but a few broken men and the dream they could still be so much more. A club dedicated to a simple life and the love of two wheels. Where expectations were few other than respect and loyalty.

"The reason we are invited to talk at these events is that we have been in the position you are right now. We know what burdens you carry, what visions you see once you close your eyes at night. Some of you will take up desk jobs and eke out a career plan with full benefits, and that's more than okay. For those of you sitting here right now thinking that isn't me, there are options."

His words hit me like a .300 Magnum round, the force struck my chest and reverberated through my torso, flesh, and limbs like sound waves. He's talking about guys like me. He's talking *to* me.

"We have a range of club-owned businesses that employ most of our guys, with more on the horizon too, depending on what skill sets new members bring to the table. You can live and work among like-minded brothers. Ride free among the mountains."

The group of us listen, transfixed by his words about what it's like to live amidst the mountains and the brotherhood. As ex-military, we were used to a life of ordered rules. Where you sleep, get up and move out, to the packaged, measured food you consume. Rules and order keep us safe. As safe as can be when you account for casualties and lifelong injuries. Scooter hates the term disabled, and if anyone dares take pity on him, he'll have them on their knees in a submissive hold in an instant.

"Don't pity me. Don't feel sorry for me. My life is full." Alrighty then.

Alpha continues with revelations about the Ponderosa Pistons, who they are and what they stand for. They are ex-marines, like me, with a SEAL or two in the mix. Each man worked in some capacity for the MC, and not in the field they had been trained for. Life has a way of showing you the direction you should go, even if you take your time to set your compass.

"If you're feeling a little lost, come find us," Alpha had said, before walking away from the microphone with a guy called Flint, who had been introduced earlier as a senior member who operated out of their metalworks. His wife and children had died in a multi-vehicle pileup on an unfamiliar stretch of road at twilight. In the blink of an eye, his entire world had gone up in flames like their Subaru. How do you emerge from a chrysalis after such heinous injustice?

"We make gates and fencing, although there is a market for garden art and sculptures that's really taking off," he'd added after his introduction. Do I see a future for myself welding butterflies for garden art? Fuck no, I do not.

There are almost a hundred guys hanging on his words like they are balm to shattered souls. Nectar dripping into the mouths of the hungry, the disillusioned and the derelict remains of the proud men who'd stood tall in polished shoes and crisp uniforms at parade inspections. Some, like Simon Soderno, would never sink feet into those high-shine shoes again.

"If you are relying on anything to help get you through the days, and the nights, have a think about where you may find yourself in a month, or a year from now. Joints, a line of blow, fine as long as you have it under control. If not, sort your shit out before those fingers dial up my number. We don't manufacture, push or sell drugs; we've seen it take too many good men who thought they were in control, or thought it was the answer to their nightmares. Don't suffer alone. We have jobs, we have rooms, and we have brothers at your back."

A brotherhood. The one thing I coveted. Once the presentation wound up, I waited for an opportunity to shoot the shit with the Pistons guys, taking a seat at the bar until the milling crowd dissolved. When all three men approached the bar, I adjusted my stool to the side for Scooter's chair, and conversation took off in earnest.

"Alpha, Flint, this here is Smoke, Ed Weir. Best goddam sniper we had," Scooter says, waiting while we shake hands and receive our poured drinks from the bartender.

"Smoke, hey. Tough job. Scooter told me earlier you were STANO. That true?"

"Yes, sir," I reply. He's not my superior, but my manners remain. STANO refers to Surveillance, Target Acquisition and Night Observation. *Tough job* didn't even touch the sides of what I did.

"Don't come across many of your caliber," Flint says, and the joke is corny as fuck, but we laugh anyway. Flint looks like he'd rather be anywhere other than this busy bar at a mid-tier Portland hotel. Some returned guys have issues with crowds and noise. I crave both.

"Mind if we chat further? We have something on the horizon that might be a good fit for you and the Pistons. Assuming you came here because you are more than just curious?" Alpha adds, and if I wasn't curious before, I am now.

"You smoke, man?" he asks, making a puffing gesture with his fingers and mouth.

"Doesn't everyone?" I counter, knocking back the last of my whiskey and following him outside to continue the conversation.

Alpha is a massive man with a head of dark unruly curls, deep olive skin, and a moustache to rival Hulk Hogan's. His skin is canvassed with inky stories of where he has been, what inspires him, and the names of what I assume are children on the underside of his bicep. His gravel voice, hoarse and guttural, comes from a place deep in his throat and calls to the thousands of cigarettes he must have puffed on, tobacco and otherwise.

"Can't say too much in there," he says, gesturing back over his shoulder, "but the Pistons were approached to formulate a kind of task force," he says, chewing out the last words.

"Okay," I manage, interest piqued.

"Here are our details," he adds, pulling a card from the inside pocket of his leather cut. "When it's the right time, call me up, or come by the club. You are always welcome."

"The right time," I say, spinning the card between my fingers once I put the filter paper to my lips and inhale, setting the cherry ablaze.

"Only you will know when that is," he says, setting fire to his own cherry. "Think about it, and let me know, yeah? Now, let's go get ourselves some pussy."

CHAPTER 5 - CALLY
Deliver me from evil

My sister is a role model, the perfect child and a first-class bitch. The moment she was old enough, she left to study nursing and now has a job at a hospital in Bozeman, Montana. Far enough away from the shitstorm that is life in the Jenkins house. Truth be told, she's not a bitch. Far from it. It's just that I can't help but feel a little envious and outraged that she'd leave me here with 'them' knowing their spiral into religious zealots was speeding up, and I'm the only one left in the vortex.

"Callista, is that you, dear? I've laid out an outfit on your bed for your date with Scotland. Please wear only the items I've laid out, nothing more and nothing less. Do not forget to cover that hair." Scotland Saleva. So fucking pretentious.

His "You may call me Scot" was only the faintest hint of his grandstanding. If he thought I would call him Scotland, he had another thing coming, which itself is grandstanding because I never came with him. Not once.

My mother's voice swirls with both faux warmth and depth from her upstairs bedroom. Like her scent of tuberose and violets, it is uniquely hers, and I hate it. She and Dad have found a 'lovely young fellow' from a neighboring church who is keen to meet a like-minded young lady for courtship. The fuck? This whole scenario is driven by my dad. The 'home schooling' and conservative clothing didn't work the way they intended. Now, they had garnered reinforcements. A blind date set up with a puppet of the doctrine. I can see it now—meet, marry, pop out a pewful of impressionable little ones to continue the broken messages I'd been reciting, and ignoring, for years.

That outfit seems to be from Mary Robinson's closet, complete with pearls. While Mary always looks regal and elegant, I will look like I'm playing dress-up in grandma's closet. Fuck my life. I'm twenty, not ninety! A plethora of high-necked, heavy tweed material flows down each arm to the wrists, and swishes to the ankles. Can't show off too much creamy skin to tempt the devil's thoughts. Then there are the shoes. Brown patent T-bar leather Mary Janes to complete the Mary Robinson look. A plain scarf awaits my fiery tresses; ready to encase them like a tomb, because we can't have anything red being broadcast to the world. No makeup, not even a light lipstick or sweep of powder. Fresh, dewy innocence in a tent of tweel and twill. Fucking fabulous.

Ah, my date. The wholesome Christian boy, handpicked for me by my parents. The boy I was expected to be seen with, without stealing the limelight like low-class trash. The boy I was supposed to converse with; nodding and agreeing with his opinions at the expense of my own, because that, too, was discouraged. There was no point in enrolling to be an esthetician because it catered to the vain and selfish, the pompous and prideful. Jo, as a nurse, scored her pass, as she was able to save sick souls. Squeezing zits and waxing pubic hair would not be viewed in the same light. It wouldn't be entertained, period.

"You don't need to work Callista, your role is to keep a tidy home, service your husband and his ambitions." My mother has lost her ever-loving mind. My dad thinks Lucifer himself is obtaining unlawful entry through the electric circuit, and Mom is a cooking, cleaning, husband-serving bobblehead doll in a starched floral apron and invisible gag. I'll pass on *all of it*. My aspirations are fueled by my impure soul and debaucherous thoughts.

Service and ambition. Yep, my parents want me to marry their chosen church pet, who has Senate aspirations. I would be his kept trophy wife and wholesome Suzy Homemaker. Mopping the floors and pressing his sensible slacks only after a batch of fresh cookies were baked, and the required children were schooled. That wasn't service; that was slavery. And it sure wasn't *my* ambition. Whether it was delivered through sermons in the front room of Pastor Rich's home, or via the chain of apron-wearing wives who opened their mouths for two things; their husband's dick, and to recount his opinions on everything.

When I open my mouth, my voice isn't a meek miaow. I long to roar like a mountain lion, tell everyone around me I don't believe their rules and rhetoric, nor do I plan on following them anymore. I had little money, no car, and any way out required at least a bus ticket or accommodation at my destination. I dreamed of a life free from judgement and tenure, where I could express my opinions and contribute to conversations and work in a proper job. Did I want to be a Senator's arm candy? Molded, mute and morose. Fuck no. I want more than the secretive, missionary vanilla sex we occasionally have with the lights off and low moaning. He couldn't find my fucking clit if he had GPS coordinates, Dora the Explorer's map and a fucking homing pigeon. The sex I crave is the 'bend you over the railing, pull my hair and fuck you into tomorrow' kind. 'Legs in the air on the hood of your truck in a public parking lot' kind. The kind I'll never take part in if I remain trapped here suffocating in their stale air.

Spying the delivery truck from my bedroom window, I take the stairs two at a time to accept the package before my mother can intercept it. Craft supplies, glitter stars to be exact, is what the item description states, and it's a gigantic lie. It's not like we can turn up at Hobby Lobby and pick up poster paints and scrapbooking items. Uh, ah, we don't shop at regular stores; there is too much temptation, too much unnecessary gaudy excess. We bedazzle bookmarks and sell them to church customers as part of the required fundraising activities. Pastor Rich takes all the money anyway. His circle lives like paupers in upcycled clothes while he has multiple cars and suits that fit him far too well to have been thrifted. The hymn books are falling to pieces, and the door in the bathroom has hung on one hinge since we moved here.

"Hey, Callista. Sign here," says the frazzled driver, not even looking at me while he thrusts his grimy phone in my direction. His pinked cheeks and thickset physique alluded to his poor state of fitness, and our steep driveway is challenging. Either that, or the cheeks radiate a smug awareness that the package has been x-rayed, and he's well aware of the contents. I scrawl some kind of curly looping C and J and make a mental note to sanitize my hands before, and after opening the box.

Greer Clarkson, a dear friend from Texas, has come to my emotional rescue again. Hidden among the tubes of glue and vials of glitter and sequins, is the ProMax Thruster 2000 in berry pink with a suction option. Fuck yeah. Greer gets me. Greer misses me, but not as much as I miss her. With the limited contact I'm allowed with the outside world, she is my lighthouse on a rocky outcrop as the storm rages around me. She's also the life buoy thrown in my direction when I'm drowning in the despair of doomsday indoctrination.

Greer is a part-time fetish model. She spends a few afternoons per week in a studio wearing rubber, latex, crotchless mesh and various handcuffs while touting a ball gag and sultry expression for catalogue still shots. How did she fall into that line of work? Who knows for sure? All I know is that she makes bank doing what she loves, and is not afraid to promote her body or the range of items coveted in the sex fetish industry.

"Callista, I'm heading over to Doris's house to help her hem those curtains she's been putting off for so long now. Idle hands are the devil's workshop, as you well know."

My mother takes great joy in the damnation of others. Only she could make herself look good and others look bad by turning up halfway through the afternoon to help a friend mend her fucking threadbare brown curtains. Doris isn't idle; she's no doubt been at it all day, just waiting for my mother to swing by and save the day with a stitch in time and some church gossip that 'shouldn't be shared,' but would be shared anyway.

"Many hands make light work," I offer while Mom tucks a curl of her formerly red hair behind her ear and smiles one of her hollow smiles. Any deeper and she'd risk more lines around her eyes, even though vanity is abhorred, she cuddles into its embrace secretly.

"If I am not back in time, have the most wonderful evening," she calls over her shoulder as she exits the house, waving at neighbors mowing lawns and an older couple out for a walk.

"I sure will," I say, choosing to leave the word "not" off the end of my statement because it will only mean another lecture on graciousness, humility and servitude. If I never hear those fucking words again, it will be a miracle.

I might just have time to introduce myself to Mr. ProMax 2000 before I have to pull on the revolting tweed ensemble. Tearing the package open in the crafting room, I line up the bottles of adhesive, jars of glitter, and shiny embellishments. Then, oh so carefully, I spring back to my bedroom and lock the door. Pulling the curtains closed, I hit play on the old CD player with Songs of Joy: Christian Classics. Electrics are allowed if they ship the lord's message only. Then, I remove Max from his box and see the handwritten note from Greer.

Babe, he's brand new and unused, but I charged him for you.
Can't leave this guy lying around all day connected to a socket.
Hope he rocks your world.

Love G.

New, unused, and fully fucking charged. Yeah, she did.

Slipping the earbuds into my ears, I hit play on my secret phone, and the delicious timbre hits my ears just as I put Max to work. He does *not* disappoint.

That night after dinner, Scot got down on one knee and presented me with the ugliest ring I have ever seen. It's uglier than my outfit, and I look fucking awful. He'd spent the better part of the last two hours sneering at the server when he placed the napkin in my lap, or ridiculing another when she couldn't remember all of today's specials, but would be back with a full list. He had snapped his fingers to summon more water at one point, the sound reverberating through the air like a stock-whip. Why people are such assholes to serving staff, I will never understand. They are to deliver your food safely, after all. If you rile them enough, who knows what they are doing between the kitchen pass and your table.

"You are radiance and all that is good. Please do me the honor of becoming my bride." I want to curl up into a ball. I don't want this ugly fucking dress, nor the ugly ring, nor to marry Scot. There is so much more out there to see, to do and to learn. Hemming curtains and teal twill might float some boats, but mine has sunk to the depths of the ocean, tiny fish darting amongst the cabin debris. With most of the patrons in the diner looking at me expectantly, I do what my parents, my partner, and even God himself wants me to do. I say yes.

Scot slides the revolting ring onto my finger to claps, cheers and congratulatory handshakes from other patrons, which he laps up like steady rainfall to a parched man. My face is stuck on the dial of vague pleasantness; a look practiced over many years. It's more than muscle memory for my jaw; it's a way of life. He held the car door open for me as we prepared for the brief journey home. At a traffic light, he leans over to sweep his thumb over my finger, playing with the ring while he smirks at me, eyes glazing. I feel sick.

"You know, if you're lucky, I might pull over somewhere quiet and let you suck me off."

At the next traffic light, I notice a crimson drip from his nostril. "Oh, Scot, you have a nosebleed," I mutter absentmindedly while reaching for the glove compartment for some tissues.

"C, stop, it's fine. Cally, stop," he says, his eyes darting from the road to focus on my movements. With every turn of his head, drops of blood fly through the air, settling on the console, heating vents, and his pale blue button-down.

After fumbling with the clasp on the glove compartment, the door hinges open and the contents reveal themselves. "It's okay, I'm getting some tissue for your—"

The blood-speckled fist cracks into my temple the moment the words hit my ears. "I said no! You wear my ring, you'll listen to what I tell you."

Chapter 6 - Smoke

remain vague and hopeful

My mom is fine, as I knew she would be. Her hand is encased in an ugly brace, but the surgeon's prognosis was positive. She'll need some therapy to keep the hand and wrist supple and pain free, so she'll be back to quilting, baking, and painting her nails in no time. Dad has been as helpful as Dad can be. Standing close, asking her if she wants anything, only to watch her get up and get it herself when he puts on his best "I don't know where that is" look. My brother Samuel came to visit around the time of the surgery. He's back home with his two loves now. His wife and his job. Missed him by two days. Fuck.

"Are you in any pain? What can I get you?" It's my way of letting her know I'm here, at least physically. When I was serving, I wasn't available emotionally or physically. While my folks were more than okay knowing that I couldn't elaborate on where I was, or what I was doing, the chasm of distance between us all grew greater. I can't blame the service; I blame myself. The Weirs are a tight-knit, extended family. I'm more of a loner; the guy you find on the back deck at parties, drink in hand, staring into the void of inky darkness. The one that well-meaning cousins try to steer their young children away from in case I have one of those "post-war flashbacks" they keep hearing about on the television.

"No pain, and even if I were, I'm more than capable of unscrewing the cap on the ibuprofen with my good hand. Will you boys stop your fussing?"

Mom is pragmatic. She's the nurturer, the healer, the fixer when we are broken. The role of a patient is unfamiliar to her, and I get the distinct sense that she despises being in a cast under medical directives. She is at her best bossin' her boys around, not beholden to them.

"If you want to make yourself useful, Ed, honey, you can help your father fix dinner."

"On it. I'm surprised you've survived this long on his barbecue dinners. Or is the freezer full of meals you made before you went into hospital?"

My mind creeps back to pouches of some unidentifiable protein, rumored to be chicken, and an additional pouch always containing some kind of cereal. Be it rice or pasta, these MREs from service kept active marines nourished in the field. The *meals* that were *ready* to *eat* were most often consumed cold because a fire was not always practical, or possible. My mother's meals were far better than those in the mess halls.

She doesn't need to answer that verbally; her face says it all. She will have cooked and frozen enough food to see them through her recovery, and then some. The plastic containers will be stacked into the deep freeze like Jenga blocks, one false move away from the frozen brick coming loose and striking the sensitive skin on the arch of your foot.

After dinner, once I'm lying in their guest bedroom that was my old room, I stare at the faded stars peppering the roof that used to glow so bright. Now, like my dreams and aspirations, they don't glow at all. Every single nebula burned out and claimed by the darkness.

ALPHA
Hey brother. Yeah, I remember.

I'm thinking about heading your way. You got room for one more?

ALPHA
Plenty of. Get your ass here.

"You don't want to stay longer? I'm reclaiming my position in the kitchen." Mum's eyes crinkle with a genuine smile. Even in my mid-thirties, I'm still her son, still one of her boys.

"I'd love to stay longer, but there's an opportunity up in Montana. I want to go check it out," I offer on an exhale. I'm not hiding anything, but if it doesn't work out, what do I say then?

"Oh, Montana. It's so pretty up there. You had a job offer?" Mom continues to collect vegetables from the drawer in the refrigerator, her head bobbing up to talk to me, and ducking low again before resurfacing with an armful of colorful ingredients.

"Yeah," I say, accepting the beer she offers me while still clutching at bell peppers and squash. This is the old man's beer. Weak shit he knows no one else will drink, so there's never a chance of running out unless he empties the case.

"That's great, honey. What's the job?" she asks, closing the refrigerator door with a hip bump.

"I don't know yet. It's a bunch of ex-military guys. I went to a returned service meeting up in Portland, and we just clicked." My thumbnail picks at the corner of the paper label. Maybe if I remove it, the beer might taste a little better if I can pretend I don't know what it is.

Mom slides a cutting board from its storage place between the toaster and coffee pot. She turns to run the peppers under running water, continuing her questions about work in Montana like the continuing stream of water over the jewel-skinned vegetables. If Dad follows the doctrine of feeding a man meat, Mom is the poster child for eating the rainbow. I can't provide the answers she's seeking; I don't know the information she wants. Better to remain vague and hopeful than hype it up, only for her to be disappointed later.

"They have some workshops and a bar, I think, and a foundry. Not sure what else they do."

"Be safe, honey, it's a long drive." She's always the worrier, and a warrior.

"I'm not driving, I'm gonna fly," I confess. My pile of crap car just made it to Flagstaff from Portland. There is no way in hell it's making it all that way back and then some, to outer Bozeman, MT.

Her placating hand settles on my forearm. "That makes me feel so much better, Edward. You know how jumpy I am about traffic. So many idiots on the road now."

She's not wrong. On the drive down here, I saw some crazy shit. At the end of the day, it doesn't matter how safe of a driver you are; it's the other vehicles you have to worry about. Vehicle safety ratings? All fine and good until you get rear-ended by a semi driver amped up on coke and amphetamines. All the stars in the world won't save you and your precious SUV when eighty tons are sliding on twenty-four wheels in your direction.

What she doesn't know is that I'll have my old Indian Springfield Dark Horse in storage in a friend's garage, sent up to Montana to meet me once

I know the lay of the land. A buddy I went to middle school with restores old bikes, and stores even more. All tucked up under tarpaulins ready to reunite with their owners, like a bear emerging from hibernation. As long as the storage fees are paid, the beasts are all tucked up cozy under their blankets, just ready and waiting to roar once more. I could drive it up there, but it's too risky on my own, especially staying in the motels I'm used to. Better for me and the bike that I fly up, get settled, and my Dark Horse be delivered once I summon her presence like an old whiskey coating the tongue, or the chewy, woodsy way a Cohiba's smoke lingers as it curls out of your mouth and dances with the surrounding air.

My love for Cohiba cigars was partly the reason the name "Smoke" stuck to me. The other was my job as a Marine sniper. My job was to smoke the target. I don't care which backstory is rolled out at catchups and conventions. As long as they don't call me fucking Edward, I'm happy.

> just finalizing some stuff here. I'm flying out on Wednesday.

> **ALPHA**
> Flying?

> Yeah. I'll fly up, get sorted, and the Indian will arrive later.

> **ALPHA**
> See you Wednesday. Pussy.

The hot blonde making eyes at me behind her magazine at the flight gate has not gone unnoticed. She looks up at me, only to break her gaze away the moment my eyes lock with hers. Only when her eyes rejoin the pages, she skims a little too fast for her to be reading and taking anything in. She's flustered all right. Nervous, darting eyes, tongue peeking out to lick her dry lips, the strand of hair she tucks behind her ear repeatedly, all while flashing the inside of her creamy wrist at me. Her ivory skin takes on a gentle luminescence under the airport grid lighting. If I placed two fingers on her pulse point right now, I'd know for certain her heart is pumping blood through her body like a fire hose sprays torrents of water at a burning building. Hard, fast, and strong.

When the boarding announcements begin, and the call for active service personnel to enjoy priority boarding crackles over the PA system, I feel pricks of nostalgia. One year ago, I was being thanked for my service while people made way for me to pass by, and dipped their heads in thanks. Now, a mother pushing a stroller with two small children ushered her little ones away from the empty seats next to me and towards the crowded section one aisle over. She would rather have them sit on the fucking floor than next to a washed-out vet with more ink than skin, one with a face that no doubt screams "breaking point" brighter than forthcoming Times Square Theater advertisements.

I take up my position in the line and wait because we're all boarding the same plane, right? Racing to the front of the queue makes no difference when the plane takes off and lands. Like those fucking iditols who spring to their feet as soon as the "fasten seatbelts" sign is disengaged, only to be stuck in the aisle of people searching overhead lockers and under the seat in front of them for wayward luggage. The same people who get bent out of shape if they are detained for even five minutes. The plane doors open when they open, pal, and your sighin' and hollerin' won't make the process any quicker. Don't even get me started on the applause when the plane lands either. Pilots do their job, part of which is to take off, keep the thing level during flight, and to land it in another city, or country. Part of their job. Do you receive a round of applause when you deliver a food order, tint your clients' hair or send an email? Didn't think so.

Now that I am in line behind the hot blonde, who has stowed her magazine in the front pocket of her fake designer bag, I just need to know if she's keen to join me in one of the plane's bathrooms on the flight. Four and a half hours up to Montana should be plenty of time for her and me to get acquainted. And to see if she breaks into spontaneous applause after I show her how I get the job done...

CHAPTER 7 - CALLY
You're done

There is only one thing uglier than the fucking gaudy ring on my left hand; the behavior towards me from my now fiancé. Before that infamous evening, he was a pretentious douchebag who liked to play golf with his father and his country club connections. Pressing the flesh with his wannabe Senate fundraisers in plaid pants and an argyle sweater was a fashion crime. Only now, when he "presses the flesh,'"it's not some oil tycoon's outstretched hand to shake; it's my cheekbone, ribs, or like yesterday, the corner of my mouth. This one will be harder to camouflage under the natural, organic pigments this fucking cult refers to as makeup. You will not find any Revlon, Maybelline, or Fenty beauty products in this community. Maybe the devil himself is hiding in the primer bottles or waiting to be wound onto curled lashes from the mascara wand. If Beelzebub is lurking on that brush, then he's welcome to my fair lashes. They can use all the extra help, and I'm not fussy when it comes to additional volume.

"Callista, baby, your mouth gets you into trouble. I don't mean to raise a hand to you, lamb, I do not. But like Pastor Rich always says, *the woman must* obey. Disobedience is as bad as the sin of sorcery and not without penalty. Repent Callista. Use that mouth for good. You will be delivered."

His beady, raven-like eyes stare back at me. Cool and calculated, cruel and callous. How I ever agreed to go on the first date with this fucking asshole, let alone multiple, has me thinking about inquiring with the senior ministers about a brain examination. I'm sure Pastor Rich would have a field day with the goings-on inside my head.

"Poor Callista Jenkins, she was a vessel for the impure and unrighteous. Look at all of that *uncovered* hair!"

I can see the spittle flying from the corners of his thin slash of a mouth as he works himself up to deliver that sermon. The man is all kinds of crazy, yet has the bald-faced audacity to cast aspersions on others. May the beaks of one thousand ravens peck your fucking soul out through your eye sockets. You sick, evil man.

"Don't touch me ever again," I spat back to my fiancé. The intense hue of reddish-purple creeping from his chest and along his throat let me know he's about to land more blows. Only this time, I welcome his swinging fists. Do your fucking worst, you pathetic piece of filth. His hands ball into fists, knuckles white with tension, his body trembling.

Scotland strides forward, grabbing a section of my hair in his meaty fist. He pulls it so hard, I'm wondering if he's pulled chunks of it out from the roots. My hands spring up, protecting my face, but they are no match for the balled fury careening my way. His curled mitt slams through my upturned palms and into the side of my nose, knocking my head to the side as long red hairs drift past the carnage and onto the floor, joining fat drops of pooling blood.

"Step away from her, asshole. You're done!" Jo screams, emerging from her hiding place under the stairs. Scotland whirls on her, and for the briefest of moments, I worry he will strike her too. Only when I look up through the unruly hair framing my face, do I notice she has a gun in her hands, pointed at Scotland Saleva. Oh fuck.

"Grab your shit, and get out," Jo spits, stepping forward and raising the pistol. Scot's hands fly up, palms forward in surrender. Not so fucking tough now, fucking asshole.

"Don't touch anything. Just leave and never, ever come back," Jo fumes, eyes drifting from his retreating form to me, and back again.

"My ring," he moans, and I can't get the heinous thing off my finger quick enough. Standing at full height in front of him, I fling it at him, hitting him square in the dick, before it crashes to the patterned hall runner below. Scot drops to his knees in a slow crouch, eyes surveying the detailed rug to find out where the hideous jewelry came to rest.

"You don't call her, you don't talk to her or talk about her. You don't even think about her. Do you understand me?"

My sister is reverberating with her own roiling anger. Scot locates his gaudy fucking ring and stands, tucking it into his pressed pants pocket. His other hand wipes away the remnants of white powder from his septum. What I now know to be cocaine, he depends on a scourge of pills, crack and vials of crap that might be GHB. Jo's the nurse, not me. Also, Jo is the badass gunslinging outlaw who rode into town and dealt with a pesky vermin problem like a fucking queen.

Once the pathetic human is through the front door and onto the second step, I surge forward and swipe the lock into place. Not that it will keep him out if he's on one of his crazy benders. I'm guessing you can't survive on no sleep and a cocktail of crap, only to lay hands on someone you are supposed to care about. Or when a particularly wealthy campaign partner pulls out upon hearing "disturbing rumors" about a drug problem. Not rumors anymore. My fingers tentatively touch the swelling skin at the side of my nose as my hair is tenderly pulled back behind one ear.

"He can't hurt you anymore, Cal. That's the last time, you got that? I love you big, girl."

Since we were young, Jo and I used the word big to describe everything important. I love you big, was our way of telling each other we adored them beyond the moon and back. Slipping back to the juvenile term meant she was under stress. I nod and instantly regret my actions. Mom will be furious when she sees the big red stains. The ruined carpet and the lost fiancé will be in her thoughts and prayers for the foreseeable future.

My nose? If I dare mention it, I'm proud and vain, so I don't even waste the breath. "I shouldn't have provoked him," will be the first words out of her tight mouth.

"Pack any shit you want to take with us. We're leaving," she adds, stabbing at the screen of her phone propped up on the mantle, the recording phone that captured the whole ordeal. "Don't worry too much about clothes. I've got stuff at home you can wear," she says. It's not like I'm attached to any of this conservative stuff, but I don't want to rewash the same outfit every night either. Jo flew down this morning, hired a car and arrived at the house only when she saw Dad's car leave. He and Mom are with Pastor Rich and his wife Pam, despite their shared eccentricities. She put herself in that position, so she can damn well stay there.

"I'm just going to get Max," I say, cupping my hands under my still-dripping nose. Once upstairs in the bathroom, I reach for the squares of toilet tissue and twist several sheets into a small wad that will fit into the affected nostril and hopefully plug the flow. Yes, you read that correctly, the "squares". We don't have toilet paper on a cardboard roll like most of the population. Once a week, it is my job to tear off squares of tissue and place them in neat piles for the household to use inside the bathroom.

"One square is permissible for liquid waste; two squares, with a maximum of three, are for solid waste," Dad proclaimed about a week after we arrived in Utah. This wasn't toilet paper hoarding like we saw when Covid hit. No, this is the full gamut of my dad's whack way of thinking, now that he is the mouthpiece for Pastor Rich and his kooky Moonyata bullshit. Speaking of bullshit, three squares don't go as far as you need them to when you've had a meal of lentils and rice with seasonal vegetables. Three fucking squares.

Grabbing Max in one hand, I don't even look for a box or bag. My berry pink prize and I thump down the stairs knowing I'll never set foot in this house again, never be rationed to squares of toilet paper again, and most of all, never be slapped stupid by a grimy little evil man who comes after three thrusts. Ambitions for the Senate? You are fucking welcome to him.

CHAPTER 8 - SMOKE
Reading the room

The Ponderosa Pistons clubhouse is not what I was expecting, but then again, I've learned that looks can be deceiving. Just flick through those cute as a button cartoon cover books in the airport gift shop and you'll know what I mean. Nothing cute or cartoon about some chick getting railed by three guys, six ways to Sunday. From the outside of the compound, it appears almost industrial against the rural landscape. A dichotomy of open grassland, rolling hills, and chirping crickets juxtaposed against boxy architecture, sleek straight lines, and Iron Maiden blaring from a speaker somewhere.

"Here we are, home sweet fucking home," Alpha says, pulling the blacked-out Suburban to a stop on the concrete parking lot in front of three high bay doors. Seated with me is a guy called Alex Jack, or Hammer as he is known more specifically. The guy has long, scruffy, dirty blond hair, and a face full of unkempt stubble. He could compete at Hawaii's Big Wave International at Waimea with a longboard tucked under one arm. He seems pretty easygoing, which is a plus. I like a chill, no-fuss attitude, as long as he is switched on when it matters and not some dope hound constantly chasing a high. Time will tell how well we get along. His old man lives just out of Spokane, and he arrived yesterday. He came out with Alpha to collect me because we are being introduced to the club at the same time. That, and he was bored as fuck until he starts work at the club-owned garage on Monday.

"Men," Alpha booms once inside the club and guys appear from everywhere dressed in identical black cuts with the Ponderosa Pistons logo on the back. Mountains and pine trees backdrop a skull and two crossed pistons, front and center.

"Mid-week service, right fucking now."

A flurry of boots echoes along the concrete floors towards a set of double doors. Each man stops at an inset bench where a drawer is open as pistol after pistol is retrieved from shoulder holsters, ankle straps, and the guys who carry concealed, empty their haul that has been tucked behind vest plackets or the waistbands of dark wash jeans. Each gun fits snugly into a grooved niche. Having come straight from the airport, I'm as clean as a whistle, but Alpha and Hammer both relinquish weapons into the drawer before it is closed and locked by one of the biggest humans I've ever seen. Now at just over six feet, I'm not a tall man. I'm about average, I guess. The wall of rock in cargo pants and a t-shirt stops me with a meaty paw on my chest as I attempt entry through the doors.

"Weapons?" he grunts, his large hand taking up so much real estate on my chest, his fingertips are at my Adam's apple.

"Feather, this is Smoke. He's the guy we picked up at the airport. He's clean." Feather? What in the actual fuck? Oh, I get it. The irony. Feather is a fucking fortress.

"No worries, man," he says, removing his hand and nodding in my direction. "Rules." I nod back, happy to have that huge paw away from me. Christ, that man could do some damage.

"Chief not back yet?" the massive man inquires. To this, Alpha simply shakes his head, his eyes rolling around in their sockets as if searching for the man might just make him materialize.

"Not yet," he whispers. "Sunday service."

Hammer and I take the empty seats indicated to us by a bald guy with a lip ring. Feather follows Alpha through the doors but only closes one. He doesn't seek a spare seat but stands sentry at the open doorway, arms crossed over his humongous chest.

"Brothers," Alpha begins, eyes darting across every member in the room and then to Feather in the doorway. "I'd like to make a formal introduction of our two newest members. Ed Weir is ex-Marines STANO and goes by Smoke, and to his left is Alex Jack, another SEAL and patched in as Hammer. Smoke will be managing the bar and the club we are opening next door. I know most of you savages will spend as many hours as possible ogling them naked titties, yet this guy here is being paid to do so. Lucky bastard." The room erupts with eager chuckles. "Hammer is going to work at the garage. Bike specialist, isn't that right, friend?"

"Yes, sir," Hammer nods, his shoulder-length sandy waves pulled back from his face with a black elastic band.

"Alpha or Pres works just fine, boy."

Hammer nods again, deeper this time. He's respectful, and I'm instantly taken with his manners and general demeanor.

"There is something else I wanted to bring you guys in for," Alpha says, two thick fingers working the sides of his handlebar mustache. "Something I haven't been very good at doing in the past, and I want that to change."

All eyes in the room focus on the man standing with heaviness on his shoulders. Throwing a hand back, he slaps the wall behind him. Underneath the Ponderosa Pistons logo are the words Honor, Unity, Respect, and Trust. The first letter of each word is painted a little differently, so the acronym is more obvious. HURT.

"We all hurt. Every single one of us," he trails off, vacant eyes fixated on an adjacent wall. After a long silence, he blinks rapidly before straightening. "But we don't do it alone. This brotherhood, this bond, we hurt together. Unity is just as important as every other word on this fucking wall, understand?"

I nod. Hammer nods, and the room fills with quiet affirmations.

"Some of you guys were here the last time Rodin was. Well, I have great news. He's on his way back. He's studied more of the headfuckery we all know and love. His return will coincide with an imminent announcement to further this club and every member. That's it, you can all fuck off now."

I'm shown to a room on the ground floor of the clubhouse. It's basic enough—bed, side table and closet. There is a bathroom on the opposite side of the closet that is also accessible from the room on the other side—Hammer's room. Guess they put the new guys together. Hammer walks right in, whistling a cheery, annoying as fuck tune the second my bag hits the bed.

"You don't knock?" I question, but he ignores my words, hands sinking into his pockets.

"I hear you have a classic Indian coming up," he asks, delight and anticipation spreading across his face. He's the bike whisperer, apparently. Makes sense that he's excited about classic bikes and exemplary workmanship.

"I do," I add, taking out the folded underwear and placing them inside the top drawer just so. You can take a guy out of the military, but you sure as shit cannot take the military out of the guy. I'm no neat freak, but the traits of readiness and order stuck with me. I cannot stand mess and disarray.

"Probably wise not to bring it up here on your own," he adds, nodding to himself and answering his own question.

There was no way I'd travel alone with that bike. Yes, I carry a gun, and yes, I am more than capable in hand-to-hand combat should shit go south and I get jumped, but it's more that I don't want some idiot changing lanes without looking to clip me and write it off. She's a classic, and an enigma. She is revered and deserves her reputation and recognition. Suddenly his eyes widen, and he clicks his fingers as if realizing something profound.

"You aren't sure whether you're gonna stay," he snaps, fingers moving from clicking to pointing in an instant. And he's right on the money.

"And you are?" I counter.

"Yeah, I am." His certainty is admirable. Either that or this is his last option. From what I heard out in Portland, some guys are a bee's dick away from drowning in a bottle or with a needle sticking out of the crook of their elbow. If they don't come here and sort their shit out, there is nowhere else other than a sliding drawer into a refrigerator and a toe tag.

"I left behind a part of me back home, a part of me that needs to be there, and I'm fine with that." Hammer's eyes flick up to mine as I make quick work of the socks and move onto the shirts and vests. "That was the past, this is my future, of that, I am one hundred percent sure."

His knuckles rap on the doorframe twice before he turns and disappears back through the bathroom door again. Just like that, Hammer time is over.

CHAPTER 9 - CALLY
Whelmed

Jo eyes me up and down, huffs, and eyes me up and down again. "Why were you dancing like a drunken fool in front of bikers at a job interview? I don't get it."

"You don't get it?" I all but shout back. "Put yourself in my shoes. Well, I know they are your shoes, but anyway."

"I work with Alpha's wife. She's the one who told me to come in and speak to him about a job for you. Only *you* could complicate something as simple as, Hi, I'm Cally Rae. I'm here about the bartending position Jo spoke to Alpha about."

"I did that," I wail. And I did, well, kind of. The huge guy at the door took one look at me when I mentioned a job and waved me out the back. I don't know why Jo is so bent out of shape about it; she wasn't the one dancing in front of bikers while sober in too-small shoes.

"I suppose we are lucky they didn't expect you to take off your clothes. A stripper? What the fuck, Callista?"

"Not my fault!" I protest again, but she's not listening. She's already scrolling through her phone as we walk back through the rest of the bar and out into the afternoon sunshine.

"And if that's how you dance," she says, looking up at me through her lashes, "you will be single for the rest of your life. I've seen dead bodies in emergency with more rhythm than you." Rude! And it's not like her dancing is any better! I mean, we had no practice. We grew up in a cult that rationed toilet paper and believed Satan was sending subliminal messages through power sockets. Dance lessons weren't a priority around Psalms, Revelations and Pastor Rich rhetoric.

"I thought it was some team-building thing. An icebreaker. That's why I didn't say anything," I add. How was I supposed to know they thought I was a stripper ready to audition for a job at their new establishment? Only one of them used the term audition. But it didn't click into place. I'm not the sharpest knife in the drawer, and we led a very sheltered existence.

"Look, I'm not yucking anything. If you want to strip, knock yourself out. Only that routine would knock out anyone sitting in the front row." She smirks. Again, rude! My arms cross instinctively, and I feel my bottom lip protrude and jaw set. I tried my best. That's all anyone can ask, right? Sensing I'm no longer moving along beside her, Jo slows and turns back before stopping altogether. "Cal, it's fine. You have a job. This is the best possible outcome. Today is a good day, babe."

Today is a good day. I am employed. At a bar run by bikers who mistakenly thought I was a stripper. By the end of the song, they looked like they'd pay me good money to keep my clothes on and stop moving. Jo's feather-light hand grazes my forearm. As a nurse, she is trained to provide comfort along with medical aid. I'm trained in nothing at all. I'm twenty-two years old, and it's polarizing.

"Cal, you know I'm joking, babe. I can't dance either. Thank the Moonyata for that," she says, rolling her eyes and shrugging her shoulders. "It's okay, you've got this. We have this."

Do we? She may have this, but I've got nothing other than a pity job and coworkers who appeared embarrassed by my sheer existence.

"What is it? Talk to me?" her eyes implore as her soft palm moves in a light sweep over my arm soothingly.

"I'm whelmed," I stagger out, lip wobbling and refusing to behave.

"You're what?" she asks, although I know she heard me.

"Whelmed," I manage again, louder this time.

"That's what I thought you said. But Cal, I don't think anyone can be whelmed. They are either overwhelmed or underwhelmed. Whelmed kind of feels like a no-man's-land of nothingness." Nailed it.

"Then I am whelmed. That's what I am feeling." Far from a state of flux where emotions are developing and changing, I am simply whelmed. The partially obscured rock cemented just off center in the stream as the water ripples around it and over it. Her hand moves to sweep away another rogue lock of hair. I should tie it back, but I adore the way it flows around me like a flaming protective cloak, ensuring my state of whelm.

"Maybe it's like Dakota?" she offers, brightening. Her words tumble from lips turned up in an optimistic grin. "There are North Dakota and South Dakota, but no actual Dakota, right?"

"That's right!" That's exactly how I am feeling right now. Feet planted on the painted line in the middle of the road, uncertain whether to step forward or double back. Whelmed, Dakota. I know I won't ever go back. Not to the Righteous Moonyata Circle, or the abusive ex who thought being high or stoned gave him the right to put his hands on me. If Jo hadn't freed me from that life, I'd still be there hemming curtains and covering bruises with natural pigments and high necklines.

"Don't you ever look back. Not ever, you hear me?" Her grip on my shoulders borders on punishing. She's not cruel in her actions, just focused and intent on letting me know she has me. I know she does, and in a roundabout way she always has done. If she didn't pay for my phone and have the bills sent to her little apartment, I wouldn't be standing on a Montana street right now.

"I'm grateful, Jo, I'm ever so grateful," I add, moving to wipe away a tear that wants to track down my powdered cheeks and drip off my chin. "If I earn enough money here, maybe I can save up and move back to Texas."

Her eyes widen momentarily before she schools her features. Nurses must need to do that with patients because it comes across as practiced.

"You want to move back to Texas?" She repeats, brow furrowing.

"Yeah. I do. Texas was the last place I was happy. I'm going to work as hard as I can, as much as I can, and when I have enough money, I'm moving back to Texas. To our friends and cousins and satanic microwaves and rolls of toilet paper, not just sheets."

"Hey," she all but barks, "I have rolls of toilet paper and a demonic hot box. You don't have to go back to Texas for that, babe. And here we have each other!"

"That we do, babe, that we do," I add ruefully. I don't want to upset her by leaving soon after I arrived, but she has her calling, her patients, and her apartment. I have a tote full of sex toys and a dream that I, too, will find my calling and move from my state of whelmed and out of Dakota.

Chapter 10 - Smoke

Addition and subtraction

"Have you worked in a bar before?"

"No, sir. I've never even been in one until my, um, interview."

"Coffee shop, restaurant? Any customer service experience at all?" I ask, hopeful.

"Not really. I sold bedazzled bookmarks at a church market stall. Does that count?"

Fuck my life. The hills really are alive. Given the three of us—well four, if you count Alpha and his scribbled, unreadable hieroglyphics—turned this poor woman's interview for the bar into some impromptu entertainment debacle, we are supposed to be on our best behavior and accommodating. I feel particularly bad because I'm the one appointed to oversee the whole shitshow, not slide into a spot on the Three Stooges ensemble. I don't even know what a bedazzled bookmark is.

"I'm a quick learner. I promise you won't be disappointed," she beams. This chick doesn't just smile with her mouth turned up; her entire face brightens. Eyes like smoked honey, set to burst with amber fireworks.

"As long as you pour drinks better than you dance, darlin', we'll be fine," I clap back. The last, absolute last thing I want is some starry-eyed, Bible-study homely type scaring away patrons at a biker bar. No one inside these walls wants verses from Malachi served up with their Maker's Mark. Nobody.

"Yes, sir," she repeats, and I'm stopping that shit right fucking now.

"It's Smoke, Ed, or Boss. I haven't been knighted, and that's highly unlikely, honey, so let's keep it as informal as possible, okay?"

She nods, all eager and anticipatory. At least she looks the part today. Cut-off denim shorts, a tight white top, and sneakers that are just as white as her smile.

"I'm going to start at the very beginning. You have a lot to learn, and you need to learn it quickly. Saint, Paul, and I will be here to help you. Any questions, just ask. The main thing is to be friendly and approachable, so any resting bitch face needs to be left at the door at the beginning of your shifts. You can pick it up again on your way out, got it?"

"Yes, si—"

The look I fire her way is pure poison. Does she not listen?

"Ed. Yes, Ed. Got it." Her head nods frantically.

Good girl. That's better. Look at you, learning and shit. True to her word, she did have it. By her second shift, she was pouring tap beers like a pro and had more than a handful of the locals wrapped around her finger like a strand of that magnificent mahogany hair. She is always early, smiling, and stunning. She listens, asks the right questions without being annoying, and is a sponge for knowledge and life in general. She has put the awkward first meeting well and truly in the past where it belongs, with no ill will detected. Cally Rae—yes, that is a 'y' and not a downwards arrow—is a great addition to the Wildcats staff.

The training bubble and pleasant introductions came to a crashing halt, just like the renovations next door, when the most unwelcome of text messages was sent to the entire club.

ALPHA
Service NOW. Chief. Semper Fidelis.

Fuck.

CHAPTER 11 - ALPHA
Semper Fidelis

As inevitable as death is, when it hits close, it hits harder. Chief Richter's death hit like a tsunami of anvils crashing into the MC with a ferocity never seen before. My vice president, one of my oldest friends and brothers, dead by his own hand, by all early accounts. Semper Fidelis is the Latin phrase meaning "Always Faithful". Callum "Chief" Richter was the embodiment of the words.

"Brothers," I begin once the room fills with club members and trusted close family. Rina, Scooter's old lady, cooks our meals and is as much a part of the club as anyone else. She's included in the cry of brotherhood, and isn't too proud, or too much of a feminist to insist I call her a sister either. "I regretfully inform you that Chief was found deceased this morning, single shot to the temple out by Hyalite reservoir."

The room full of rustling, breathing soldiers falls eerily still, as if the entire space is collectively holding its breath. No throat clearing, coughs, sighs or other "normal" crowd noises. Nothing. Time has stopped still, and we're all resisting that we must recognize what no one here wants to. One of our own has fallen.

"The police are still informing his family. As some of you know, Chief's brother, Wrench, is still deployed, and their folks are out east. I ask that you mourn together as a unit and not confirm anything outside of these walls until his family have been briefed."

Heads dip as slow, measured breathing resumes. We all hurt, fuck, the writing on the wall spells it out. This hurt is all-encompassing.

"I'm sure this will come as a shock to many," I add, when dozens of hollow eyes stare back at me blankly. "None more than me, trust that this sat me on my ass."

Eyes dart left and right, searching for answers where there are none. Flint and I already checked his room here. As soon as we are done with this, we'll be out at his cottage to check there. Chief put down a payment on a small craftsman about two miles from the club about a year ago. He and his on-again, off-again partner had been working on restoration, painting and building a deck out the back for cookouts and future family gatherings. There better be answers out there because there is nothing here. Nothing to indicate a man who was jovial and outgoing, employed and happy as far as we know, felt there was no way forward. As his best and closest friend, to say I am bereft is an understatement of canyon proportions. I am... gutted.

"What do we know so far?" Scooter asks, his arm around his sobbing wife.

"Not a lot," I answer honestly. "A couple hiking found his body near the trailhead. Called it in. By the time the police arrived, me and Flint were already in the parking lot next to his bike. Nothing looked amiss. I'm just—"

"What can we do?" Rina sobs. Darlin', I have no fucking idea. Anything we could have done should have been done long before this realization. We failed.

"Support each other. Unity is one quarter of our existence here, right?" The room echoes with murmurs and affirmations. "We are not losing anyone else. Do you fucking hear me? I don't care if it's three a.m. or you're three hundred miles away, you are not alone. Our psych came back this week; *talk* to him. Rodin, can you make yourself available for sessions as soon as possible? Let me know if you need to bring anyone else in to allow one-on-one sessions with the entire club. We didn't survive Syria, Afghanistan, and every other hellhole to shred ourselves at home. I'm not burying anyone else, you hear me?"

"Absolutely," Rodin confirms. "Men, this starts right now. I met Chief only once, on Thursday when I came back. I know you all loved and respected him, and his loss will be profound. Mourn him, yes, but also ask yourself some tough questions. That's my role here, and as Alpha just alluded, I can bring in others to get us through this trying time. No one should ever feel like that, ever."

Flint and I roar up the driveway of the little cottage, past marigolds and paper daisies, and stop before the porch stairs to gather ourselves. With utmost respect, his room at the club had been turned upside down in the search for answers. Chief wasn't a drug taker. He had no known mental struggles, although he arrived at the time we had no psych available. Maybe this is on me? But, fuck, the man was as solid as a granite boulder. There were times he kept to himself and might have disappeared into his own head, but doesn't everybody? This cottage was his way of attempting some kind of normal post-service life with perhaps a partner, a dog, and the whole nine yards. If the walls inside this cottage with the yellow door don't offer us anything, we are bereft and ignorant. Neither is a good place to be; couple them, and it compounds the grief and sense of loss.

My pounding knock is met by a woman with shoulder-length dark hair, red-rimmed eyes, and a wad of crumpled tissue in the hand not holding the door ajar. I never bother to learn the names of the side chicks until they are old ladies. At least by then you get the sense they are staying around for the medium haul, if not the long. A glance at Flint and a shoulder shrug tells me he does not know who this chick is either. She'd better have some answers, a whole fucking lot of them. Splaying a wide hand against the golden paint, I push with enough force to send her backwards, but not enough to send her into the wall. If she needs to be sent into a wall, that necessity will reveal itself in good time.

"Wait," she protests, "you can't just come in her—"

"Oh, yes we can, darlin'. We want answers, and we're not leaving until we get them."

Flint follows behind; he has my back if this little thing does something stupid like pull a weapon. She backs herself into a little hall table, but doesn't try to open the narrow drawer. Chief would never allow a weapon to be kept there, anyway. It's too obvious, and too accessible for people like us who gain entry without permission. My fingers wrap her delicate biceps, forcing her fingers to flex and drop the tissue. She stares at it cascading to the floor as if I've just severed her only lifeline, and the knowledge she is about to drown has her body quivering. That's right, sweetheart. You want to break a brother, you break the whole damn brotherhood. "Start fucking talking."

"I... I... I only found out about an hour ago." My fingers tighten the hold on her delicate limb. Her hands are splattered with paint all over them. She has scrubbed and scrubbed, but the pigments refuse to break the bond with her skin. In the end, she must have just given up and decided it was good enough. Did she do that with Chief, too?

"Chief is dead, and you're talking about information delivery?" I ask, incredulous. Flint stands off to the side, arms crossed, body filling the narrow hallway space. If she wants to escape, her only option is back out the daffodil door, and she's too freaked to grab hold of the handle. "What did you do?"

Her jaw slackens, breath rolling in and out of her open mouth like a soft summer breeze. Her eyelids blink spasmodically, and her pulse quickens. She knows something.

"Less than a week ago we were sitting around a firepit slugging bourbon. He was fine!" My words tear across her cheeks like physical slaps. My actual hand will follow up if she doesn't engage her fucking tongue and start talking. "Then he disappeared for most of the week, missed meetings and ignored comms, and now he's gone. So this is your last chance, honey, what did you do?"

"We had a fight," she stammers out after my fingers threaten to meet around her humerus bones. My jaw ticks as Flint adjusts his stance ever so slightly.

"Go on," I venture, and it's a double-edged sword. One she can flee from, or fall on.

"We had a fight, multiple fights actually." She wheezes through tear-filled sobs. "I said something horrendous. It wasn't true, but I said it anyway to hurt him."

My fingers relax, yet she makes no move to release herself from my hold. If I let her go, she's just as likely to fall to the hardwood floor below. As she stoops, her vertebrae are visible through the back of her shirt where the dark curls don't cover. This gaunt, sallow little thing is a mess. Good. Whatever she did, she can't fucking undo.

"It's all my fault. It's all my fault." Her wails permeate the silence, save for a large wooden clock in the sitting room off to our right. The hand sweeps around the dial, tick, tick, tick. My blood roars through each vein and artery with the same unrelenting surge. Tick, tick, tick. Before I lose my shit on this bitch, I lean her against the wall, pulling open that tiny drawer to check for a weapon just in case. Sure enough, nothing but small change, some decorative pebbles, and a sign that says "Home isn't a place, it's a feeling". Ugh. My fingers whipped to Flint, indicating he should take the sitting room, kitchen, and laundry. I've got the bedrooms. We search methodically anywhere a note or sign might be hiding. Sometimes they are in plain sight, or sometimes they are hidden amongst the pages of a favorite book, or in the pocket of a well-worn coat. Nothing. Flint joins me in the last bedroom, the one with splattered sheets covering the floor, and pots of paint scattered haphazardly around a bucket of murky brown water. Guess that's what you get when you amalgamate every color from the cans on the floor. I call it; devastation.

"Pack your shit, sweetheart, you're out." My boots thunder down the hall.

"Wait, what?" Her head jerks in my direction, eyes still fixed some place far away.

"You heard me. This was Chief's house. You said it was your fault, and we believe you. Get your shit, and get the fuck out."

She staggers to unsteady feet; tissue pressed to her palm again. That it's been on the floor and she wants it back makes me more nauseous than I'd like to be right now. If she puts it to her face, I really will be sick.

"Pack a bag," Flint orders. This time she complies, snapping out of whatever fucked-up fog her mind had drifted into. You reap what you sow, babe.

"Can you just give me a minute?"

"One," I bark back ferociously. "And time is a ticking." My head cants toward the wall clock, the hands still swapping continuously. Life and death. Tick, tick, tick. Just as the second hand drags over the four again, I pounce. "That's it, you're done. I never want to see you anywhere near here ever again. Do you understand me? That means this house, my club, the funeral, this whole fucking town. You leave, and you never, ever come back. You think good and hard about what you did, and I hope it fucking haunts your very existence."

Her lips quiver as she sucks in a fortifying breath, tears streaming over her puffy skin.

"If I, if any of us, see your filthy face again, we will shoot you where you stand. That, sweetheart, is a promise."

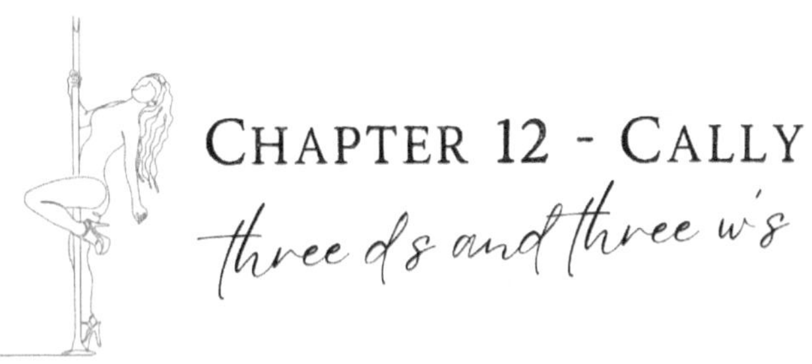

CHAPTER 12 - CALLY
three d's and three w's

The bar is quiet. Saint let me know that there had been a death with one of the bikers, and most of the town knew the guy. I can't remember whether he came in here to drink. Sometimes they introduce themselves; other times they get their drinks and say nothing other than thank you. I can't seem to shrug off my parents' words, that people who ride motorcycles are a breeding ground for drugs and debauchery. Danger, Cally Rae. Drugs, debauchery, and danger. Keep away from the three Ds. Only every member wearing the Ponderosa Pistons cut seems decent. If they don't engage in conversation, at least they are polite. And they've just lost someone they cared about a great deal.

Today I'm working my first double shift, into an evening. Smoke and Saint have taught me a whole new world of alcoholic drinks, bourbons and whiskeys, and the difference between an ale and a lager. When a keg needs to be changed out, make sure you prop the cellar door open because the handle is dodgy. Got it. There is a lady in the kitchen who is fabulous too, Sandra. She and her husband make the most delicious food. Thankfully, I take what I don't eat at work home in to-go containers because I can't cook and Jo is often working later shifts at the emergency room.

Paul and I are contemplating whether we should close early when the roar of what sounds like jet airplanes landing on the bar rings through our contemplative silence.

"Ah, no closing now. The Pistons have just rolled in. Looks like the wake is here instead of the club. Get pouring."

Get pouring. Okay, I can do that. It is my job, after all. Although I have another job lined up, just like these tumblers on the rich wooden bar top. My old friend Greer has come through with the goods again. The only downside is that this "job" is in Chicago, and only for a few hours. So, between learning about wine regions and the nuances of particular distilleries reflected in their final product, I've scoped out bus schedules to the windy city.

Dozens of leather-clad men pour through the double doors, and I almost drop the bottle clutched in my hands. At my audition, interview, disaster of a first impression, there were three guys at a table, until my sister appeared with a fourth. Streaming though past the chairs and tables to take up residence in the back near the pool tables, there must be nearly thirty. Drugs, debauchery, and danger, Callista. All I see is despair.

Smoke approaches the bar where Paul stands, and I fight the urge to feel offended. Does it matter from whom he orders the drinks? No, it does not, but a tiny part of me pangs with jealousy that he didn't wander up to me to place his order. It's 'cause I'm new. I get it. My gaze drifts to the wall of hulking black leather. There is no danger here, only intrigue. Some slap each other on the back; others lay a heavy hand on the shoulder of a comrade, gripping earnestly before letting go. A simple touch, a promise of unity. I feel so bad for them, losing someone important, but it's not like I can walk over there offering free hugs now, is it? They have sought the comfort of smoky char and honeyed oak, not healing hands of thoughts and prayers.

"Yo, Red, you good?" Smoke's question snaps me from my huggable offerings.

"Yes."

"I was just saying to Paul, it's easier to bring the bottles to the table. It's going to be a long night."

"Yes!"

"Give us the rest of that Pappy, the Gentleman Jack and the Johnnie Walker Blue."

"Yes, coming right up."

He eyes me suspiciously, his gaze dropping to my mouth before settling on my hands and roaming back up to my face achingly slowly. I should have said more than six words in that conversation, but my tongue feels thick in my mouth. This is the first time I've seen him, really seen him, in dark jeans, a black belt, and a black leather vest. His uniform of unity, and my gosh he looks delicious. The way his tattooed forearms pulse when his hands flex, his short, sandy hair framing a masculine jawline, and cool gray eyes nuanced with lavender that simper and smolder just for me.

Paul tucks the three bottles into his arms while I carry a tray of two dozen tumblers and a small bucket of ice and silver tongs. The chatter dissipates when we approach, and I'm conflicted about whether that's a good thing or not. Paul places a bottle at each end of the table, and another in the center, while I hover with the tray. A hand reaches up for the tray, and at the very last second before it topples, I realize it's Feather. The glasses slide and lurch across the black carbonite, before coming to rest as they were, steadied by the largest hand I've ever seen. This man would not find a baseball glove to fit him; his hand *is* the glove.

"Whoa there, church mouse," comes a voice I don't recognize, and the chuckles resonating around me are as insulting as the derisive words. Alpha holds up his hand, and the giggles cease. While not outwardly cruel, it was still unnecessary.

"Yo, Church, another bottle," someone slurs and I jump from wiping the same smear on the bar top towards the selection of spirits. I should fetch them the licorice one, the one that smells disgusting, and no doubt tastes just as bad, if not worse. Yo, church. Really? Whatever happened to not judging a book by its cover? Does he want me to reply with yes, drug pusher? No, he most certainly would not. Before I have the chance to clap back or select another bottle, Smoke and Saint leap to my defense of sorts. They tell whoever made the joke to pull his head in and pipe down, or words to that effect. I'm not church; it was a cult. And I want to put as much distance between that part of my life, and my plans, as possible. I work in a biker bar, for crying out loud, and my trip to Chicago? If that doesn't seal the deal, then nothing will!

As my reluctant feet carry me forward again towards the table of hulking humans, this time it's Alpha's words that cause me to stop mid stride.

"To Chief, to our brotherhood, and to not letting the three W's fuck us up any more than we already are. War, words, and women, boys. Watch out for all three, or you'll end up just like Chief."

"I just need two days off in a row is all."

"And again, Cally, why?"

My boss can be a dick. I can't lie to my boss, but I can't exactly tell him the truth either. Well, bud, a friend in Texas is a fetish model who makes a whole lot of money modeling latex and ball gags, and she's set up a meet and greet for me in Chicago with the same company she works for in Austin. And once I get this job, because I need the money, I'll save as much as I can until I can move back to Texas and away from here, the jabs about my clothes and past, and off my sister's uncomfortable couch.

"I need to head out of state for a day."

"Out of state. Where?"

Frozen frogsicles. Why all the questions? "Chicago."

He arches a sandy brow. See, this is why I can't lie to this man.

"Cal, remember when you started here. What did I say to you?"

What didn't he say to me. That my beer pulling had want to be better than my dance moves. That my clothes looked like I belonged on some hill in Austria. Hmmm, what else?

"Don't be late, don't be lazy, and don't lie." Ah yes. That.

"I'm not lying. I have an interview in Chicago. I have to go by bus because that's all I can afford right now."

He looks aghast. Does he not like Chicago? I've never been there.

"Interview? You've worked here for a week and a half. You have a job already."

Oh shoot. He's worried about me leaving. I have no intention of leaving; I love this job. I just crave another. An outlet for my sexual frustration after my true character and opinions were oppressed for so long. Give me ballgags over biblical passages any day. "It's for an additional income stream. Modeling. I have every intention of keeping this job, Ed. It's just that a friend set up a photoshoot for me in Chicago. I don't want to let her down, and I'm keen to explore where this takes me."

"Modeling?"

"Yes."

"In Chicago?"

"Yes!"

"And you're traveling to and from by bus?"

"Yes, Ed."

"Okay then. Lucky for you, your face is as honest as they come, darlin'. Just tell me when your shoot is booked, and you can take a day off either side of that. Would that work?"

If my face is honest, so too are my limbs. My arms are wrapped around him in a heartbeat, as my lips land on his cheek. "Thank you!" The man looks like I'm a skunk releasing directly into his mouth. He unwraps my arms and rubs at his cheek, attempting to dislodge any trace of the lipstick I may have left on his skin. I'm very pleased with the way it looks there. I'd be even more pleased if I could stain that sexy mouth with the same lipstick. Or somewhere else perhaps...

CHAPTER 13 - SMOKE
I missed you more

This was not the week I had envisaged. Move to Montana, they said. It will be calm and peaceful, they said. No drama, just bikes and brotherhood. That last part at least had some purchase, but the drama? Yeah, seems no matter where you live and work, drama has a way of seeping through your skin and settling deep into your bones like a winter chill. One you can't shake off no matter how many layers or blankets you pile on.

A funeral, a special service meeting at the club, and a disappearing redhead. All three have me on edge, and for vastly different reasons. Chief Richter was Wrench Richter's brother. I served with him, knowing only that he had an older brother, but not that his name was Callum, and that he found his way to the Ponderosa Pistons a few years before I did. Wrench has been briefed, and his intent to come here the moment he returns stateside has been relayed to the club. If he's looking for closure, he aint gonna find any. The quest for answers caused Alpha, Flint, and Rodin to upend the entire MC. And those answers? It seems they were lowered into the plot with Callum, never to resurface or offer any clarity. Rodin, the softly spoken psychologist with a Canadian intonation, addressed us, both individually and collectively. Reminding us that certain solutions may prove elusive, we must prepare ourselves. That Callum is at peace now, and no longer at odds with his mind or heart, is what we should focus on. God dammit.

The special service meeting was something I never expected. Even though Alpha had alluded to "something in the works" after his Portland presentation, I was not prepared for what those actual works were. I hate to speak for others as they have their own tongues to do so, but I'd put my Indian on the fact that the meeting floored more than just me.

A select group of eight of us sat around the table in the "war room"—seven Pistons members and a gentleman called Foley. On the speaker was another man called Akis. First names? Surnames? Call signs? I didn't ask, and it wasn't divulged. What was, was astounding.

"We set something similar up in Tennessee a few months back. With the Smoke Dogs. They, like you guys here at the Pistons, are ex-service, trained and trustworthy. We are looking for a mirrored contingent here up north," Foley said to Alpha, but it was intended for all of us.

"Based on our last conversation, we are lacking some arms that M .E.T.R.I.C.S focuses on," Alpha replied. I know I'm not the only one wondering what the actual fuck.

"We already have men in place for that. As you said, Rodin is back, and you have a STANO shooter already at the table." Foley gestures towards me. "We have a guy called RAM who we were going to place with the Smoke Dogs, but they have their own guy, Kode. So, RAM is on his way up here. He will liaise initially with Akis, but once your entire unit is set up and functional, you won't have to rely on Akis for missions. You can take on anything. Referrals from the Dogs, or from the tri-letter organizations."

What the actual fuck? We don't work for them. Foley glances around the room and notes more than one questioning expression. "Alpha, what exactly have you briefed?"

"Nothing yet," Alpha says. "Chief and I were the only ones who knew about this, and now that he's gone, I'm trying to be better. More inclusive and all that."

"By telling them... nothing?" Foley insinuates.

"Well, yeah." A wide palm scrubs down his thick mustache while he coughs. That wet cough is lingering like lint on a cheap suit. It's almost enough to make me give up smoking. Almost.

"May I?" Foley asks, and Alpha waves his hand in a gesture that opens the floor to him.

"Men. You can ask questions at the end, but know I can only answer select ones. Please bear that in mind. Several government agencies have banded together to fill a void they saw in domestic criminal activity requiring a *particular* brand of skill sets. The Tennessee Smoke Dogs are a similar operation to the Ponderosa Pistons down south. All ex-service. All are highly trained and remain in shape for ad hoc contract work. The missions fall under the acronym of M.E.T.R.I.C.S. Think Munition, Extraction, Target (Acquisition), Retrieval/Recovery, Intelligence, Combat, and Security.

My jaw hits the floor, internally of course. This sounds like your imaginary G.I. Joe shit. Sure, we are all trained and in shape. Do we want to continue these missions? Surely most of us would have remained enlisted if so. The voice from the speaker crackles to life.

"Jobs are lucrative, specialized and secret. All M.E.T.R.I.C.S. jobs are paid up front, with bonuses at the end for timely work or grateful clients. Think added income stream while using the skills you trained for, besides your more regular work for the club. The work is still dangerous, gentlemen, but the risk versus reward is enticing. You are paid well, and your efforts are appreciated. We have some suggestions on relaxation methods and interclub "enrichment" that works well in Tennessee. Put bluntly, a range of in-house service girls are kept for stress relief and are advantageous to the club. Saves you guys going out for any extracurric-ulars. Keeps everything nice and tidy in the house, so to speak."

"CIA?" Flint asks.

"I can't answer that."

"FBI, ICE, NSA?" Grave continues. Grave was introduced to me as ex-medical. Something horrific happened in the field, and he all but fell apart. He is one of the Pistons residing elsewhere, sharing residence with family.

"Again, I can't divulge much more."

"Doesn't matter. I like it," Alpha says, nodding. "A way to still make a difference. Clandestine and stealthy, with a juicy monetary incentive."

"Before you all get hung up on the money, know that there are some strict rules in place for this to work. Your tech guys will have incredible tools at their disposal. You will all have possession of automatic weapons as if you were still in service, because you are. Only the enemy is domestic. But," he pauses, glancing at the speaker before continuing, "You are still accountable. You can't end anyone because they took your parking spot. You are more than guns for hire; you are the trained elite. Should anything go wrong, there will be investigations involving some pretty heavy firepower. Do not get trigger-happy and do not go rogue. Every target must be cleared with Akis first. He will monitor every website, every piece of code. If you think Kode and RAM are good, this guy is better. You will be subject to blood tests every three months to ascertain physical health and any illicit substances. We find any, you're out. A whole lot of money is tied to this. Don't fuck it up."

Extracurricular in-house *stress relief*. Now, that is something I can get on board with! I've been here a few weeks already and only wet my dick once with some skanky thing at the back of the bar. It wasn't planned, that's for sure, but I'm not complaining. She was bent over one of the pool tables in the shortest of short tight skirts. Of course, it looked more like a belt than a skirt, and when she leaned over to take her shot, her full lips, pink and plump, were just begging for attention. Who am I to turn that kind of opportunity down? I had her bent over the corner pocket and was deep inside her before anyone had potted the black. Her friend fingered herself while watching the whole thing. Classy? No. Necessary? Well, it was at that point in time. It was all I could do to take my mind off a mane of mahogany hair belonging to an angel with alabaster skin and horrendous dance moves. One I have no business thinking about, but the mind is its own master.

Hot damn! If our red-haired little church mouse was channeling the Austrian hills before her "photo shoot", she's now embraced her inner Nicki Minaj. Cally Rae has just turned up for her first shift back at Wilds in thigh-high boots, a silver body-con dress, and what has she done with her hair? The color may have subtly changed; deeper, maybe with more highlights? Whatever happened, she's had the sexiest fucking glow-up I've ever witnessed firsthand, and my dick is her number one fan. The chorus of wolf whistles and growls of appreciation alerts me that she has plenty of fans in the bar, and her new look has been noticed and appreciated.

"Thank you for letting me have time off," she purrs, and fuck me, her voice had a glow-up too. Sweet and simple has left the building. She's all smoky and seductive. My dick loves the way she sounds too, all the blood rushing south while my brain attempts to reconcile this new version of Cally.

"Anytime," I croak back, and it's borderline embarrassing. With a little makeup and some pleaser boots, I'm a hormone-riddled teen again.

"Are you okay?" she questions, hand splayed across my chest, nails dripping in the same deep red as her hair, all of it screaming sex siren and hold on to something. What I want to hold on to is granite hard and all but bursting through my zipper.

"Fine," I say, although fine is a stretch. "How was your modeling shoot? Did it go well?"

"Well," she says, tapping a blood-red talon to her equally blood-red lips. Couple all the deep red and sexy seduction and I'm gonna be cleaning up a mess in my jeans in under a minute. "It was ah-mazing!"

Her face explodes with joy. She's not happy; she's over the moon ecstatic. I get it; she's a gorgeous woman with a classic, natural beauty. One of those women whose features are enhanced by makeup when applied with a talented hand. She's not hiding under a thick layer of it, or trying to be someone she's not.

"It was phenomenal! I signed a contract, and I have more work booked over the coming weeks and months. I hope that's all right. I'll need more time off, but it might be easier for me to fly there and back next time. It will save me from missing too much work here."

Whoa, whoa there. Calm it all the fuck down. First things first, she's signed some kind of contract. Probably not the wisest without having legal representation look over it first, but she's not my problem; she's just an employee. Second, how much did she make that she already had enough to fly in and out, rather than ride the bus? And last, I'm the first to admit I know nothing about women and their maintenance requirements, although I can hazard a guess that her outfit wasn't cheap, and that hair transformation wouldn't have been either.

"That's great news, Cally," I offer with genuine happiness. Today is the first time she has looked at ease and comfortable. It's a far cry from when she was hoofing around the floor like one of those bucking rodeo broncs desperate to dislodge the rider. Or a tranquilized giraffe, swaying and loping before the dart takes full effect. That's a memory locked in the annals of my brain—that's for sure. Although this Jessica Rabbit image is burning itself into my retinas, thankfully.

"What's the matter, did you miss me?" she drawls in the faintest southern twang, and my cock is now three from three. Jesus Christ.

"Did I miss you? You are hard to miss," I say, deadpan. She is pure fire.

"Awwwww, thanks boss," she retorts, her pink tongue settling on her bottom lip for just a fraction of a second longer than required. She knows what she's doing to me, right?

"Anytime, sweetheart," I say and mean every word. "Just come to the office before your shift. We need to do a quick toxicology test, and then you can get back to it."

Seven minutes later, she passed with flying colors. I even ran a second test to be sure. She passed that too. She's not drug-affected. Not even a faint reading. She's high on life with a newfound confidence and some cash in her pocket, no doubt. What she also is, is a damn mystery. One I very much look forward to unraveling soon.

Chapter 14 - Cally
too many hats

"What do you mean, special project?" When I was in Utah, they gave me a special project too. Upon discovering I had no affinity with animals, my primary job was to be up before dawn, to measure out the grain from the store to prepare for the bread making. A storage unit riddled with dozens of darting mice. To this day, I can still feel the phantom itch at the back of my neck when I think about that place. Silos make me all kinds of nervous.

Ed summoned me to work thirty minutes earlier than my start time to discuss something with me. In the back of my mind, I thought I was about to be fired, but Jo pointed out that I'm working every day at Wilds, and with my additional work out of Chicago, I'll have enough cash to find my own place. She refuses to talk about my wanting to return to Austin. Every time I bring it up, she shuts it down just as quickly.

"You know this back space; the old restaurant is being turned into a strip club. Well, the guys thought you would be the best person to design the aesthetics. You know, all the colors that go together. The club wants an upmarket feel without being too prissy or pretentious. We are trying to avoid sleazy, and well, that's kind of all we know." He has the grace to look embarrassed. "Neon lights and stripper thighs."

Is he serious? "I'm no designer."

"I don't think you have to be. Not really. You just have more of an eye for what works, and what doesn't."

"I've never even been near a strip club. What makes you think that I would kno—"

"How hard can it be?"

"Very! It's a strip club." He doesn't laugh. His face doesn't even move. Not one muscle.

"We'll pay you extra to pick out furnishing and fixtures. Other than the bar going along the adjoining wall to make it easier for restocking, where is the best place to put the stages? The restrooms? What type of furniture would provide an upmarket feel yet still be comfortable enough for patrons staying here for hours?"

"You had me at 'pay you extra,' but how deep do I have to go? I mean, I know nothing about Feng Shui."

"What the fuck is that?"

"It's Chinese, I think. It has something to do with placing furniture and objects in a room for positive flow and energy. If you do it wrong, all the energy gets trapped in a corner, or it flows out the door. Feng Shui is important, apparently. For success, and all that."

The man stares at me. Cool gray eyes fix on my mouth, and I draw my lips between my teeth self-consciously. Feng Shui *is* a big deal. I'd hate to see all this stripper energy being trapped in a corner and the tips flowing out the door and onto the street. Right?

"Cally, this used to be a Chinese restaurant. I'm sure if their fang sway was any good, they'd still be in business. I don't know about energy flow, and I don't give a crap about it. All I know is that we are too busy to look at lighting and flooring and bathroom tile samples. If you don't want to do it, we can get someone else to help us."

"I'll do it!"

"Wonderful."

"Do you want me to run it past the new guy?"

"What new guy?"

"I think he had RAM on his vest thingy. I can't remember, to be honest. Maybe he might be a good place to start." This time, muscles move. He's laughing... at me. Bloody hell, it was only a suggestion.

"*On his cut*. RAM is a cybersecurity expert. He spends all day in server rooms staring at screens, honey, not strippers. And I'm pretty sure he's gay and half Japanese, not Chinese."

"Oh."

"Yeah. OH."

Feng Shui is hard work. I just know they won't have any plants in their sexy stripper bar, but I still want to do this well, as it's a job I've been given and doing it to the best of my ability will reflect on me. Positively, just like good Feng Shui. As there aren't any strip clubs nearby for me to compare it to, as usual, Greer is my go-to. I mean, I could look it up on Jo's laptop, but I don't know how thrilled she'd be to see a host of strip bars in her search history.

Greer, bless her little cotton socks or mesh tights, has been amazing. Not only did she set up my interview in Chicago, for a job that I was hired for on the spot, she's a fountain of knowledge for all things sultry, seductive and sleazy. I just need to remember to leave that last part out when I report back to the Pistons.

How did you go with the club fit-out homework I gave you?

GREER
Fantastic. I understand the assignment. Here are

some pictures from a BDSM night at one of the local clubs. Same, same, but different.

Amazing. Wow, you look great!

GREER
Thanks, babe. I mean, décor-wise, is this the kind of thing they want? Ignore the suspended cages and St Andrews cross and such, the stages, poles and lighting?

Yep. That's what I need.

GREER
Oh, I bet you do. Tell me all about Chicago!

Too much to type. I'll call you instead.

It sometimes takes me a while to remember I'm out of the Moonyata clutches and have a fully functioning cell phone. One that sends and receives explicit images at sex clubs, and of Greer and myself in all manner of latex, rubber wear and fetish items. We spent the next twenty minutes talking about plugs and whips, cosplay and beads, gags and clamps. This whole new world has lit my soul on fire, literally. I want to know it all, and I want to experience all of it. I feel like I've been wandering the desert for months and have just been dropped into an enormous swimming pool of fresh water. I can float, I can swim, and I crave to drink it all down. The initial shoot was so much fun. I thought I'd be shitting myself, but I woke up from my introvert coma. Now, I'll never close my eyes again. And holy shit, how turned on I was. All I could think about was Ed's cool, gray eyes staring back at me when I posed for the camera. All I could think about when I played with a range of plugs and clamps was his thick fingers using them on every inch of me. The man is my kryptonite. When he's around me at work, I'm a puddle, and it's not all drool either. What the fuck do I do? Watch me Feng Shui that, too.

"Cally, these are great. This is exactly what we are looking for. Has Smoke seen these?"

Saint and I are eating lunch at the back table while Paul runs the bar. It's quiet on a Tuesday, so we can sit together for a few minutes at least, without disruption.

"Not yet. I wanted to run them past you first. Let me know if I'm on track or not." And I'm not even kidding. I've redone the interior of this club four times now, realizing partway through each draft what won't work, and why. I've tried to maximize viewing angles for all the tables and the raised booths. This way, there can be multiple girls performing simultaneously, as well as easy access for wait staff to roam about. The last thing a strip club wants is bored patrons. If we keep the action coming, it's more likely the patrons will too. And if they stay, so does their money."

Smoke sinks into the chair next to me, and the scent of his cologne is mesmerizing. Either that, or it's his deodorant. I don't care what it is; I just want my tongue to run all over his skin. Oh, holy hell, is it hot in here?

"What's that?"

I crane my head to see where his finger is on the drawings. "That's the Pistons MC booth." I put it there so members could slip in and out, avoiding any lines at the door and swelling numbers if security was overwhelmed or staff needed a show of support. Who is going to misbehave in a club run by a biker gang and mess with a guy called Feather, who is Ohio, literally?

"That's a great idea," Smoke says, genuinely impressed. His knuckles tap the table, and I instantly want them somewhere else. All those years of sexual repression and frustration have caught up with me, and I want to throw myself at this man. My boss. I wonder what the energy flow would be in that scenario?

"Although we are a motorcycle club, not a gang," Saint adds. I should have known that. Fuck.

"Are these the colors?" A thick finger slaps at the swatches of paint slapped on the side of the plans at the last minute. I'm a visual learner. Maybe these guys are too.

"Yeah. For the walls, I chose a deep, dark purple. Not black—that's too much of a goth vibe, but the purple is sexy and sophisticated. Combined with the red chairs down here." I lean in and regret it instantly. My left breast is on his forearm. That's got to be bad energy flow in front of a third party.

"I like it," Smoke says and pulls his hands from the plans, severing any contact with my anatomy. I instantly miss the warmth radiating off him. I'm a lake freezing over, the chill starting at the shallow water lapping the shoreline before the crystals move towards the center to solidity. The cold and snow can fuck right off. I'm desperate for a hint of his molten touch, those calloused, powerful hands to hold me as reverently as he did the document.

Jumping to his feet, he rolls up the plans, and my hopes in an instant, securing the scroll with one of my elastic hair ties sitting on the table. Um, okay then. Help yourself, I guess.

"Great work. I'll show these to Alpha at Sunday service. You've done a fantastic job; be proud of yourself. Let's see this vision come to life, hey!"

"What do you mean your boob was resting on his arm? You're not even a C cup; you don't have enough boob to rest *anywhere*, let alone your boss's arm. Please explain it to me again."

For someone who is supposed to have a grasp of anatomy, Jo Jenkins sure is dense sometimes. "Here, say you are him. I was sitting here, I leaned over like this, and my boob is on your arm. That's what it was like. Do you need a picture too?"

"That's not even that bad. The way you first described it, I thought your whole tit was out there hanging! That's like a graze. A kiss. A kiss of tit."

My groan isn't quiet or ladylike. Tits don't kiss anything. Other things kiss tits, and suck, and bite and, *ugh*.

"You say he got up straight after, yeah? Was he embarrassed? Or perhaps he had to go? If someone else was sitting with you, it's kind of awkward, babe. Not going to lie. Unless you are all on the same page, like I was a few weeks back with the guy from radiology and the sports injury clinic clerk." Oh my god, stop!

"There might be a policy about getting involved with staff. Do you remember reading anything when you took the job? They may be bikers, but there is still a chain of command, right?"

Yes, Jo, there is still a chain of command. I'm the only female member of staff other than Sandra in the kitchen, and she's like eighty and married. No other examples of workplace associations at Wildcats Bar.

"Pretend it never happened. Let's be honest. In a few weeks, the other building will crawl with naked chicks. Do you reckon the club guys will road test them all? Break 'em in, so to speak?"

"Ewww." I don't know. Naked chicks, yes. That's par for the course with strip bars; even I know that. Do I want my boss inside one of the strippers? Or more than one? No, I do not. "I can't help staring at him, Johanna. I'm becoming obsessed. It's borderline stalker ish."

My sister gives me one of her knowing looks. The kind that tells me she's about to drop a news bomb I won't care for. Like when we moved to Utah from Texas, or when she moved out to go to nursing school before she left me altogether. I can already tell I don't like her words, and they're not even out of her mouth. Don't say it, don't say it, don't say it.

"Callista Rae."

Yep, full name. This is bad. So bad.

"All I'm saying is, he's a biker. He runs a bar and is about to manage a strip club too. If you are making eyes at him and you guys end up with his pole in a hole, just know you won't be the only one, okay. I don't want you to get your hopes up and heart broken, is all. There are a lot of guys in the club who are sexy, sure. But an MC and monogamy don't go together, babe. If you want something more, find someone else, okay?"

I nod in agreement, because she is right about all of it. Except the pole and hole analogy 'cause that's just crude and limiting. Pole in a hole? Just the one? I'm not crude, I'm a goddamn superstar who deserves the world.

Her tit was on my arm. Just lying there as if it had no care in the world, no other place to be or time to be there by. Me? I all but jumped from the chair, scooped up the plans and evacuated that room quicker than reactive bowels after spicy Indian food. Nope, not going there. She's an employee, smoking hot and way too young for me. She's also so meek and trusting, yet curious, like she has something hiding among those whiskey eyes just waiting for an invitation to play. Play? Sure we could, I guess. Unless she's one of those chaste chicks saving her virtue for her wedding night to her prince. I'm no prince, and my thoughts of her are far from virtuous.

"Is there anything preventing employees from forming attachments at Wilds?"

Alpha's brow twitches. "Cally Rae? Who's she fucking? Feather?"

"Fuck. I don't know. I just thought I'd ask?"

"Nothing is off limits. Fuck, we all have urges. I couldn't give a shit if she's blowing you while Feather fucks her. I don't care. As long as the bar makes money and everyone is happy. We're all adults, right?"

"Right," I murmur. I don't want her fucking Feather. The man would split her in two.

"But, as Foley and Akis mentioned, stress release on site is the best option for everyone. The guys won't have to worry about chicks getting pregnant, or some husband coming home early to his wife being railed. You get me?"

"Yeah."

"Chin up, champion. This is a good thing. Just like a forty-eight. Nothing nicer than a couple of days off, a curvy woman or two and one helluva good time."

A forty-eight refers to two full days off in the Marine Corps. A ninety-six was even better. Alpha is a simple man. Or incredibly complex, depending on your point of view. He had an old lady and a toddler. His second marriage, after his first, went to complete shit the moment he returned. The legacy of the Pistons as a haven for veterans seeking either refuge or direction is his primary concern.

"Regarding her plans for the fit-out, what do you reckon?"

Alpha's fingers pick up the curling paper once more, his eyes surveying the décor items, paint samples and furniture placement. On the side in a sort of key elements tab, she's outlined reasons for her selections and table placement, to maximize viewing areas and sales. With the way his handlebar mustache moves, he likes what he sees.

"She knows her shit," is all he says before the scroll is thrust back at my chest and the man disappears back down the hall to his room.

The bones of Kittens Strip Club are solid, and the little kitty cat is ready for her glow-up. Per Cally's plans, a bank of raised booths is framed out, as are the main stage and side support stages. This makes sense to me. The substance under the surface, underneath all the silken and shiny, that is just for show.

Feather and Grave have left for the night. With only a handful of patrons remaining, I can handle any security situation that may arise, and Saint is behind the bar for backup if needed. The fiery whirlwind that is Cally had just completed a last sweep of the place for empty glasses, unloading them into the glass washer before turning it on. As the machine rumbles to life, one of the beer taps froths and spits like a cornered asp.

"I'll change it," she offers over her retreating shoulder.

Swapping out beer kegs is part of bar life. It's fairly simple, uncoupling the empty one and rolling it away so a full one can be rolled in and coupled to the line. Back at the bar, a few test beers are poured to remove any air from the line and ensure the new beer flows through. As she disappears down the stairs to the cellar, I spy Saint locking the front double doors behind the last patrons who lingered right until closing time.

"Go home, bud," I say, closing out the registers and preparing the stocktake for Cally's return.

"You sure?" he asks, clearly wanting to leave, but also checking that everything is as done as it can be before we open in the morning.

"Positive. Get out of here," I say in a terrible Bronx accent. Saint flicks up a hand as he departs, spurred on by the suggestion or terrible dialect. Long moments pass, and the lithe little fireball hasn't returned from the kegs. Once the cash and credit card statements are in the office safe, I trudge down the rustic staircase to investigate. The stairs are fine, crumbly in parts and a tad creaky in others, but as long as they pass an inspection, they don't need to be pretty. It's a cellar for keg storage, not one of those fancy ranch-type glass door setups with fake barrels and shelves full of overpriced wine curated by rich homeowners.

"Hello darkness, my old friend," I whisper into the dim room, my hand pushing the door.

"Fuck!" comes her harsh reply, and I leap forward, taking the stairs two at a time as the door swings closed.

Cally is on her hands and knees, battling with the coupler. Instead of sliding the closest one forward, she, for some inane reason, went to the other end of the stack and hefted it further than necessary. Ruddy and out of breath, her fingers aren't behaving themselves and the line won't affix properly.

"Here, let me help," I say, finessing the line and affixing it to the fresh keg. Now all we need to do is go back upstairs and pull a few glasses through the line, and all is good. Except when I stare up at the door, it's closed. Oh shit.

"Thank you," she beams, pushing to her feet. She's in a tiny pair of denim shorts, a Kings of Leon cropped concert tee, and combat boots. "I think maybe I fucked up with the keg situation, then I got frustrated with myself because I couldn't move it. I didn't want to ask for help, and then my fingers were so sore." Her babble is cute. Except it won't be cute in around thirty seconds.

"Once the line is okay upstairs, could you take me back to Jo's? That couch has my name on it tonight for sure. I ache everywhere."

Hold up, she sleeps on a couch? She's on the third step when she realizes what I'm staring at. Racing up the last few, her hand wraps around the doorknob to turn the handle. When it comes off in her hand and almost tips her backwards, our precarious situation just got a whole lot worse.

"Oh, shit, sorry. Saint, SAINT!" The hand not holding the doorknob frantically hammers on the door I swear I will rip off the hinges and fucking burn.

"Stop Cal. I sent him home already." Her pale face turns towards mine.

"So you and I are the only people here?" she asks. Her head bounces, already knowing the answer to her question. Yeah, babe, we're kind of fucked right now.

"Can you open the door somehow?"

"I can try. I mean, the only thing down here other than you and me is a keg coupler. I'm not MacGyver, but I'll try, sure."

"You were a Marine! Isn't that the same thing?" Not really.

The door is painted steel and no doubt heavy as fuck. If I had my pocketknife, I could undo the screws and take the hinges out. But my knife sits in the top drawer of my desk in the office. With my phone and keys. Her phone is in her bag in the cubbyhole next to the office.

"If you threw a keg at it hard enough, would it punch a hole through the door?" She compared Marines with MacGyver, so now she thinks I'm the Hulk?

"That won't work. First, the door is solid. Second, it opens inwards, meaning even if the door was damaged, it wouldn't fall into the hallway. Third, if I hurled a keg at that door, it would most likely bounce back and take both of us out like bowling pins.

"So, what do we do?"

"Darlin', we wait."

Cally Rae Jenkins was born in a nowhere little town between the triangle of Austin, San Antonio, and Houston. Her dad sold appliances while his wife and the girls' mom stayed at home. Devoutly religious, the tight-knit family spent their days devoted to church and faith, community and family. Until one day Mr. Jenkins uprooted them halfway across the country to a commune in Utah. Only Cally calls it a cult.

"They thought appliances and electricity spread the devil's message?" I repeat, thinking I've missed a chapter or two somewhere.

"Yup."

"And you had to cover your hair because red was Satan's color and tempted lust?" She nods again. "And you couldn't consume red food or drink for the same reason." Her head movements continue. What the hell did these poor girls endure?

"Nothing red—it fired the loins of impurity." Oh, fuck this. Now I've heard it all. My favorite color is red, especially her brand of red.

"Then I was forcibly engaged to a douche. Another cult member who used to beat me when he was high. He wanted a subservient wife, and I wanted nothing to do with any of it. One day after he split my lip and almost broke my nose, my sister, luckily, had recorded it all. She got me out and drove me up here."

My blood seems to simmer in my veins, the volume somehow increasing to thrum through my system. I despise violence towards women. Her fiancé used to beat her. I'm making a mental note to take some Pistons down to Cult-town, Utah, when she speaks again.

"Smoke?"

"Yes, darlin', what's up?"

"I'm getting cold, can you cuddle me?"

The issue with this cellar is that it remained cool. Her tiny top and shorts provide no comfort. Without hesitation, I whip my shirt over my head and step forward to hand it to her. "Let's sit down and conserve our body heat," I say, noticing she's beginning to tremble. I sink to the floor onto a piece of cardboard and stretch my legs out, patting my thighs for her to take a seat.

"Come here," I add, arms outstretched to welcome her to me. Almost reluctantly, she sinks down, her own thighs straddling mine, tucking her knees close to my hips. Pulling my shirt over her head, it dwarfs her lithe frame and hangs like a dress down to mid-thigh.

"It looks so much better on you," I offer, adjusting the fabric around her shoulders.

"But now you'll be cold," she adds, indicating my bare chest. The tip of a manicured finger traces the base of my throat just under my Adam's apple, down the valley between my pecs and settles on one of my many inked designs, an eagle.

"I won't be cold, I have you," I counter, arms pulling her to my chest. The soft material of my t-shirt paired with her soft breasts pushing into me has my once furious blood rushing south to its favorite place, my dick. The crisp apple smell of her shampoo tickles my nose as much as the tips of her strands on the hair of my chest. She fits so well clutched to me, my arms settling on the small of her back as she presses into me. This is going to be a long night.

"Tell me more about you," she breathes into my neck, and the vibration of her warm breath fanning over my skin is erotic. We are employer and employee, locked in a cellar, clutching each other for warmth, nothing more, nothing less.

"What do you want to know?"

"Everything." Her enthusiasm makes me smile. I might even chuckle as she jostles in my lap and her denim shorts are moving right over the top of my zipper.

"Born and raised in Arizona, I have a brother. My parents are not religious freaks; no one in our family is. I mean, we *believe in something*, I guess, but we eat red meat and smother ketchup over most things. Red food and drink are on the menu, although Mom does daily yoga and wants us to eat more foods without a barcode. You know, health nut." Every time she moves, her hips drag over mine and the friction is as dangerous as the woman herself. My hands settle on her waist to stifle her constant wiggling.

"Favorite band and color?"

Ah yes, the quintessential chick questions. "I like Kings of Leon and Wolfmother, The Black Keys and The Foo Fighters, but I'll listen to pretty much anything that isn't backed by a techno beat or made by a machine. But, a secret between you and me," she leans in closer, her tits pressed up against my chest, "I love steel drums. The tinny sound is mesmerizing."

She nods, chewing on her bottom lip. Is she familiar with steel drums?

"Your sister seems nice. I'd met her a couple of times before you turned up. You sleeping on her couch can't be the best option though?"

Her head lifts from my shoulder. "My sister saved my life, then my sanity. You know she's a nurse, right?"

I nod, because sometimes she drops into the bar in uniform. And I'd since found out that Alpha's wife—ex-wife, whoever she is—works at the same hospital.

"She has a tiny one-bedroom apartment. And we can't share the same bed anymore; we're not kids. I mean, I sleep in the bed some nights when she's working late, but don't tell her that. I feel bad enough that I took over her tiny lounge room. Then there's the issue of me not having a driver's license or a car, so she feels obliged to help me out there too."

"How do you not have a driver's license? You're in your twenties!" As soon as the words escape my mouth, I want to claw them back. She was dragged up in a cult, dickhead, of course she wouldn't have access to driving lessons or a car. When my rock-hard dick becomes too much for either of us to politely ignore, she sucks her bottom lip between her teeth and looks at me through hooded eyelids.

"Ah ha, ignore him," I tease. "What is he supposed to do with a gorgeous woman writhing all over him?"

"What if I don't want to ignore him?" she teases, and he twitches at her invitation, causing her to wiggle even more. Forget the circle of life from the Lion King, this is the circle of strife. She says shit like that to send him insane; he obliges, and she wiggles. Rinse, repeat.

"Not sure what you have in mind, sugar. Thought you were cold? Losing the small amount of clothing you have on won't do your body temperature any favors, sweets."

"Intense physical activity is also good for maintaining core body temperatu—"

I seize her mouth. My hand weaves through the hair at her scalp as my tongue breaches her lips. My other hand cups her ass, dragging her down and over my shaft again and again and again.

"Take these off," I growl into her open mouth, tugging at the tiny shorts. "Now."

Her fingers fly to her button and zipper, undoing each fastening and leaning up onto her knees, pulling them down before flipping positions. Seated on her butt, she wiggles each ankle free, as I help her by grasping the denim and flinging them aside.

"Now, you," she says in a raspy, salacious tone. Her eyes trace my own fingers at my button. I work to free myself and hinge my hips so they clear my ass and pool around my knees. Stooping, she wrenches them off until they join hers after she relieves me of my boots. She moves to straddle me again, my fingers cupping her ass and finding a tiny black G-string still in place. A firm tug at each side has the tiny slip of lace free, and her dripping pussy bared to me.

"Hey, they were expensive!"

"I'll buy you another pair."

Cally resettles herself over my lap again, and this time, her wiggling has been replaced by intentional grinding. "Oh, that's it, baby. Grind that dripping pussy all over me."

Her delicate hand frees my engorged and straining cock from the confines of my boxer briefs until it springs free. Her hand trails up and down my length with slow, practiced movements until her thumb collects the bead of pre-cum bursting at the tip of my slit. I watch in awe as she brings it to her mouth before sucking it seductively, hollowing her cheeks as she moans. Fuck! She leans forward to lock her mouth to mine again, and I capture her bottom lip between my teeth before sucking her in. Our tongues tangle while she continues to grind her arousal into me, smearing the wetness and soaking my briefs.

My hand finds her core, slick and ready. I move my thumb up to her swollen bud, pressing and circling as my tongue continues its dance with her own. "How do you want this to work, darlin'?"

"Fuck me," she pleads, and I am more than ready to oblige. Only she's not quite ready to take me. Yet.

"You need to come on my fingers before I let you have my cock, sweetheart," I growl. Her palms vice my cheeks while she rises, allowing me room to work. Her breathy little moans are cute as hell, but I want the moan that says she's right fucking there.

"Oh, OH!"

"That's it, baby," I praise, as she works her hips to meet my circling thumb. I slide a finger into her drenched pussy, then add another. She's so wet. My fingers lazily pump in and out while I alternate circling and pinching her clit. Both actions have her muttering unintelligible gibberish. "Come on, darlin', you're right there. Come on, let go, baby." And she does.

Her body spasms and jerks in the sexiest way. Head thrown back, the curtain of hair tickles my thighs as she continues to writhe. Once she's joined me back on Earth, I grasp her chin and stare into those honey eyes. "Are you sure you want this?"

"Positive," she pants. And that's all the invitation I need.

I can't lay her out on the filthy floor and fuck her like an animal. If she rides me, I can prevent most of her from coming into contact with the floor. I prefer to be in charge, but an exception can be made in these circumstances. Plus, I can set the pace from below. I raise her up so she clears the weeping head of my cock before asking silently one more time. The tiny nod just before she sinks down will be something

I remember for a long time. She lifts and lowers her hips, rising and sinking, swallowing more and more of me every time. The sight of my cock disappearing into her sweet cunt is the vision I never knew I needed. Never thought I'd be this lucky today. Aiding her up by her hips, my hands span her tiny waist, one thumb dropping lower, lower to where she needs me most. Man, I should have checked she wasn't a virgin before we got this far, but the way she's riding me right now, she's done this before.

"Oh, my god, Smoke!"

Her breathy moans are increasing in both duration and frequency. I got you, honey. The hand not busy with her clit snakes up under the billowing fabric to pinch her nipple, hard. Expecting her to cry out or flinch, she rides me harder. Her ferocity is impressive. Cally Rae is fire, and we burn deliciously. Thrusting up into her wet heat has me seeing stars, the familiar tingle building from the base of my spine. Our wet slapping echoes in this darkened room that exists only for us. Right now, her climax, followed by my own, is all I'm focused on.

"Faster, harder. More, mor—"

With firm upwards thrusts and the pressure of my circling thumb, her body unfurls pent-up need and electricity as she comes apart all over my saturated cock. Her mane of flames riots about her shoulders and torso, swaying in time with her choppy breaths. Feeling the pressure of her inner walls vice around my cock has me following right after her. White heat exploded from my groin and radiated along every limb, every fiber. The back of my head contacts the wall harder than it probably should, and I couldn't give less of a shit. Holy crap, that was intense.

"You okay there, babe?" I inquire about her wellbeing because I am an asshole, but not that much of an asshole that I don't inquire about the woman who just rode me like a rodeo bull.

"Perfect," she slurs in that cutesy, dick-drunk way you hear about but never seem to witness firsthand. This is new.

"That's wonderful, doll, because you're leaking all over me, and in a couple of hours there will be people arriving, wondering what the hell we got up to down here."

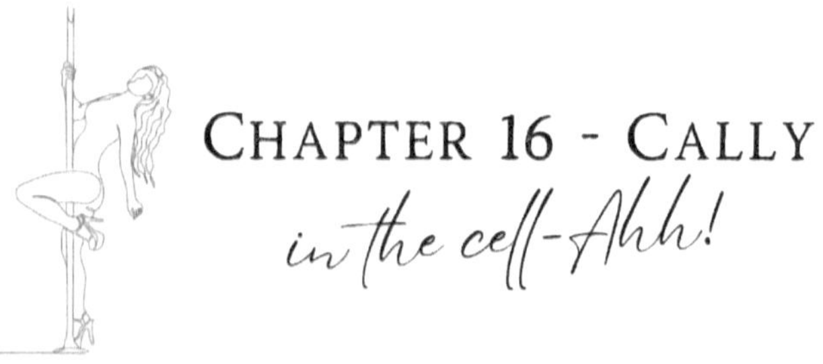

Chapter 16 - Cally
in the cell-Ahh!

I understand now! All those porn star moans I thought were over-the-top fake, and the romance books citing weak knees and a shortness of breath. The way they describe how a body moves, trembling with climax. Here I was thinking it was all horseshit. It's not! I mean, I got myself off hundreds of times because no one else had before. My trusty battery-operated boyfriend, Max, is a very generous silicone soul indeed. Now another human handled my pleasure, and he took to the job as armed guards protecting royalty. Holy hell.

We were released from the cellar, or should I say cell-Ahhh! By the morning cleaning crew around nine a.m. Our bodies slick and sore, trudged up the stairs once Smoke told them to get Flint on site to work with the handle from the other side, setting us free. We must have looked a sight. Me in a shirt that fell to mid-thigh and hid my shorts entirely, Smoke shirtless and sexy as all hell in just his jeans and boots. No one asked us what we did down there for nearly eight hours. Nor did we volunteer any information. Our little sexy secret, except we both looked well fucked and smelled like sex.

Only reality has crashed my dick-drunk delirium back to earth with a thud. I had to endure complete mortification of limping like a bow-legged cowboy into the pharmacy for Plan B emergency contraception because he didn't use a condom. Just us, the kegs and the cardboard. Then, I am on hand as part of the "panel" overseeing a slew of gorgeous women dance, thrust and slide around the back area of Wilds, awaiting the installation of the floor-to-ceiling poles next door. The tradespeople have cracked on with the work, hanging drywall, and plumbing in glass washers and ice machines. A club member named Volt has been through with a team of electricians, asking me about spotlighting and track lighting. Now, people are asking me about my opinion of potential strippers. I am the first to confess my ignorance.

"Her tits are fake, and she looks like she's addicted to something," Saint said after a pretty blonde finished a routine. Her tits are fake. How can he tell?

"Fake tits are fine as long as they're sober and able to work reliably," Feather adds, and again I want to ask how he can tell.

"Cally, number of confirmations, plus how many potentials?" Smoke asks. He's been distant after leading me from the cellar. Not that I was expecting anything from our time down there, our interaction has gone from boss and employee, to insane fucking, and back to boss and employee quicker than a three-finger pour of Pappy.

"Three, and two," I answer, looking up from my notes. The club opens in a week, and high-end exotic talent seems to be scarce in Montana. Alpha has made inquiries as far away as California, although tempting them up to the wilderness with a heap of snow hasn't been as easy as he thought.

"Bar staff?"

"I just thought Saint, you, and I would do it," I answer, confused.

"Guys coming in here want to see it dripping with females," Feather adds. "No one wants guys serving drinks or collecting glasses. Chicks everywhere, that's why you have us." He gestures from himself, towards Grave and Smoke. I guess it all makes sense.

The next *audition* is an older woman with ebony waves and a chest to rival Feathers. It too is obviously fake, as Saint confirms, but not so fake as to not be sexy. Her build is curvy, and she's tall even out of her stripper heels, so her proportions don't look unbalanced even when she leans forward and looks in danger of tipping into the tumblers of whiskey.

"Nice, nice," Smoke coos as she hinges at the hips, facing away from us. She drags a coffin-tipped black nail up from her calf to the crease where her round ass meets her thigh, and the guys around me gulp audibly. She's okay, I guess. I prefer the blonde from earlier. Younger, perkier. This chick must be at least thirty-something. She has extensive experience in the art of seduction.

"Holy shit, tell me she's a definite," Saint adds while Feather nods. I look to my boss for confirmation, but his eyes are fixed on the crystal encrusted bra falling to the floor. Okay then. Guess I'll wait until her song–*Dark Horse* by Katy Perry–ends. Looks like the perfect storm just roared into town and swept up all the smoke in its wake.

The thunderous boom snaps my head up and turns my blood to ice. The echoed scattering of broken glass and car parts while vapors sat thick on the air is something I won't forget for a long, long time. Smoke is already through the double doors and outside, sprinting to the wreck of what must have once been a white car. It's now upside down and split almost in two. Carefully stepping through the scene, he tells me to halt before I can set foot onto the road and follow his lead. Pieces of deployed airbags flap in the breeze; the residue from the charges required to set each bag off mixes with the metallic waft of blood and … gasoline. Oh shit.

"Cally, three injured. Looks like maybe a mom and her two kids. Get my knife from the desk drawer and as many cloths as you can carry. Hurry."

I watch Smoke use brute force to peel back the twisted metal of what was once a car door, poking at splinters of glass with his fist wrapped in his shirt. I hadn't even realized he'd taken it off. "Cally, MOVE!"

By the time I return, there is a woman cradling a small child, both covered in blood, leaning against the wall of the bar.

"Cally!"

"Huh?"

"The knife. NOW!"

Racing to where he is crouching amidst the strewn wreckage, I hand him the multi-tool and watch his trembling fingers flick out a series of instruments before a blade slides out with a swish. Next to his shoulder, an infant is trapped in a capsule carrier, wailing its little head off.

"Get back. Use the cloths to help the others." His gray eyes implore me while he saws at the little harness tethering the baby to the capsule. The orange button to release the straps is deformed and unusable. The baby's mother is crying and begging for help, her hands clasped together as tears streak down her face, diluting the blood. Crunching my way back to the curb, I'm relieved to see more people arrive, shop owners still in aprons, and a dry cleaner holding a bottle of clear fluid. Did he even comprehend it remained in his grasp during the rush to assist?

"Back! Everybody back!"

The sawing action continues as the stench of gasoline drifts from somewhere. I don't know which part was the fuel tank. I spot the fire licking under the caved-in hood and, holy fuck, my adrenaline spikes. Orange flames lick red and blue as the growing blaze searches for more fuel.

"There's a fire!"

"Well aware," he deadpans, still sawing at the straps. The baby's tiny pink fists flail as he or she voices his or her extreme displeasure at the entire situation. One strap is severed, and Smoke tries, and fails, to pull the bub free, but the other strap is too tight.

"And I think gas is dripping from something."

"Again, well aware."

The dry cleaner makes his way to the other passengers, commencing first aid using the towels I dumped when I made my way over with the pocketknife. The mother lies on the sidewalk while a small crowd barks into cell phones, and one looks like he's kissing her? Here, in the middle of all this?

The remaining strap hangs precariously. "Come on, come on," Smoke chants as he saws back and forth, being careful to clear those tiny fists. Sirens wail in the distance, lights strobing down the street as people are torn whether to step forward and help, or stay back and continue recording on cell phones.

"Move!" he barks again as the last fibers give way and the baby is tugged from the mangled capsule. Urging me forward with him, we crunch across the crumbled glass and reach the mother and other child when the second boom, and a third, sends a cloud of orange-black smoke into the air as the fire department pulls up. Uniformed men leap into action, one cordoning off the area with some kind of tape, while others pull equipment from the back and sides of the truck. It's a riot of noise, smells and chaos, flailing fists and crunching glass. Smoke hands the baby to paramedics, who must have arrived around the same time as the fire department and police cruisers. People are directed back into businesses if they are far enough away from the burning wreckage in the middle of the street, parts now covered in a white foam.

Smoke's dirty, bleeding fingertips brush back the hair from my face. "Are you okay?"

I blink up at him, shirtless and filthy. "How did you do that?"

"Once a Marine, always a Marine, darlin'."

Right! This was a war zone of sorts. The car must've struck a pole or something and then rolled before landing on its side. Smoke didn't just free the mother and older child from the burning wreck; he cut the infant from the capsule moments before the whole thing exploded. Like real-life hero shit.

> **JO**
> Going to be big late. Vehicle explosion victims just brought in.

> I know.

> **JO**
> Are you psychic now? How tf do you know?

> it happened outside Wilds. Smoke is the one who pulled them out.

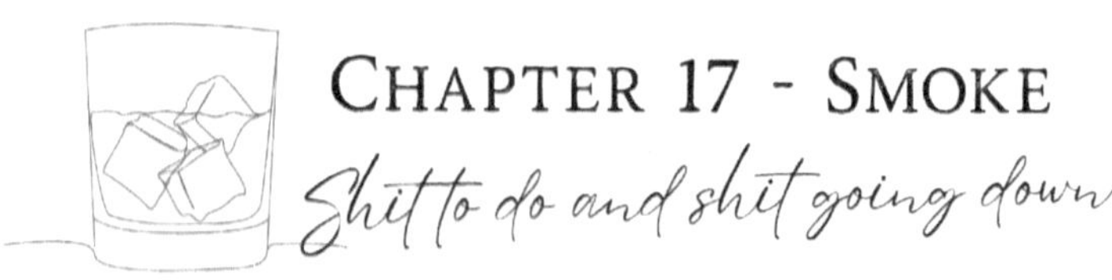

CHAPTER 17 - SMOKE
Shit to do and shit going down

"Mr. Weir, Mr. Weir! Ed!"

The incessant shouting of my name burns a hole through me more than that vehicle fire ever would. Paramedics asking questions. Granted, they needed to know who may have been conscious after the accident and who wasn't. Then there were all the police questions. Did you witness the collision, sir? No, I did not. Just heard the boom and raced outside. Would it pose an issue to visit the station promptly to offer an account? Sure.

Media vans line each side of the street, with more around the corner emblazoned with names of networks I don't recognize. Immaculately groomed reporters chat to crew toting huge lights and fuzzy boom microphones. Apart from the fact that they are taking over the parking lot for the Pistons' bikes, they are unrelenting and fucking annoying.

"Just do one or two more," Alpha drawls, leaning against the Wildcats wall, one knee bent and booted sole kissing the bricks. "Then you're done. We have shit to do."

Always more with this guy. I feel like what I offer is never enough. Scrubbing my hand through my short hair, I wince. One or two more, and we're done? I'm done already. I'm no hero. Anyone who saw the carnage unfold would have done the same thing. The exact same. That I was the first person on site means nothing.

"Over here, Mr. Weir. Ed, this way." Fuck.

"Is he too washed out for the camera? Should we pop some makeup on him first, warm up that sallowness a touch?"

An assistant of sorts is gesturing to me while talking to a reporter and a guy messing with cords and microphones. Audio dude.

"Sure, I guess. I mean, some warmth will really make those eyes pop." Ok, that's enough.

"If anyone comes near me with a brush or sponge, I'll snap the arm that holds it. I'm tired. I have work to do. I just want to get this done and go. Got it?"

"It has to be the adrenaline drop," the assistant whispers, and I give him a look that shows I understood his murmurs. I've been trained to understand how sound behaves, asshole.

"Alright, Mr. Weir. That is more than fine. Ed, can we call you Ed, or Edward? Your look will resonate more with the viewers, anyway. Raw, rugged hero, straight out of the action."

Fuck my life. "Smoke. You can call me Smoke."

"Alright then," the anchor chirps. Fixing her hair, she blinks rapidly and nods several times, her mouth rolling in strange directions before it opens fully and then closes back into a neutral expression. An overhead light is directed, and the audio guy in headphones nods, holding up five fingers before closing each one into his palm. Five, four, three, two, finger-gun.

"We are live on the scene with Edward Weir, the former Marine who risked his own life to pull the Hereres family from the burning wreckage. Edward, do you consider yourself a hero?"

"No, I'm no hero. I just did what anyone else would have done when faced with the aftermath of a wreck like that."

"So brave and so humble. We found out off-camera that you have done this before. When you were a teenager in Arizona, you pulled a lady from her wreck too! Do you just go around saving women from car accidents?" The hand not holding the oscillating microphone touches my bicep. Is she for real right now?

"The woman in Phoenix hit the gas pedal instead of the brake. In her panic, she couldn't open her door. All I did was open it, and she climbed out by herself. My name was only in the paper because she bought me baseball tickets as a thank you, which again, was unnecessary."

"Again, so humble, Edward. They are incredibly fortunate that you were standing by. You manage the bar behind us, yes? Wildcats. Have you heard any updates about the family you so heroically saved?"

"No, because I was talking with paramedics, then the police and now a slew of reporters."

"Heroic, brave, and busy! Mr. Weir, you are indeed a guardian angel for that family."

Thumbing over my shoulder, I fire, "Are we done, cause I've got shi—"

"Edward Smoke Weir, ladies and gentlemen. Bozeman car inferno hero."

The next Sunday service is brutal. Guys giving me shit for not getting the reporter's number or at least providing her with my microphone to work with. Hard pass. The media was a piranha pack circling for a tasty morsel, irrespective of what facts they reported and what was wholly embellished. The police had not even come close to determining the cause of the crash before the media speculated the driver may have been drunk or drug affected. The seed required no planting. Enough viewers will feed and water it, determining the driver to be at fault before the next commercial break. Christ.

"Listen up, fellas," Alpha booms before the shenanigans get too out of hand. "Foley and Akis have completed their initial reports regarding a M.E.T.R.I.C.S. operations base being run out of the Pistons. They're awaiting the last of the medicals we did last week. Psych reports and so on."

My psych eval and blood tests had been the morning of the car wreck. To say that day is but a blur of questions and assurances is an understatement. Not one club member has pushed back on the opportunity to serve again, even if it is for cause and not country.

"The stress relief they suggested will arrive later today and tomorrow. I trust you will make them more than welcome." The room erupts in howls and whistles. Alpha calms the chaos with a raised, meaty paw.

"If Chief's death taught me anything, it's that relationships are complex and dangerous. Some of you may swing something, but some chicks are fucking mental. They break your spirit and leave you feeling a shell of yourself. We are brothers, first and foremost. If you want to get your dick wet, do it here with one of them. No expectations, no complications. Stay the fuck away from outside women who want and want and want. They deplete everything through continual taking. Choose wisely, gentlemen."

He drums thick fingers on the tabletop, brow furrowing. Whatever he is about to say weighs heavily on him, no doubt. Rodin, the returned psych peers at the president through dark-rimmed glasses, offering support and encouragement with his facial expression alone.

"One last thing before we go," Alpha says, focus regained and purposeful. "Wrench Richter is on his way here. Chief's little brother."

Air squeezes from my chest like a fat kid working an accordion. Wrench and I served together. He mentioned a brother, one that he looked up to and adored. Only time serving and distance seemed to separate them even further. I never made a connection until now. Chief, the guy who took his own life weeks ago. Richter, of course. Can't be a common surname, although possibly not at that rate either. Chief and Wrench Richter. Fuck.

Kittens is popping off. There is a line to gain entry, with Feather manning the ropes. Inside the club, heavy bass music pumps. Not the techno shit that plays in clubs and college frats, just special mixes of familiar songs with enough bump and grind for the girls to add their own bump and grind.

Cally has outdone herself with the interior. Walls are dark purple, almost black, providing a rich contrast to the textured, plush red chairs and leather booths. Bankers lamps provide ambient light and an opulent feel at the low tables around the pole stages. The bar is a symphony of style and elegance. Blackstone countertops and high-shine silver metal meet around the Kittens sign, a nod to industrial glamor and garage chic. I'm surprised she nailed the assignment, given she's not long left an insular cult.

The first shift was a spectacular success. Every MC member was in attendance during the first week; even the married and relationship guys came for some window shopping. The look but don't touch policy wavers and flexes to the point of snapping, depending on who is waving the cash and where Feather, Grave and Saint are. Our town dentist seems enamored with the ebony-haired temptress with the enormous chest. Her stage name is Delta. During the day she works at a local salon, waxing and primping paying customers before coming to work here for a different clientele. I can also attest that she went to work on me after her last shift in the office. She came in to double-check some paperwork before she bent over the desk and had me fondling those double D's while I thrust into her from behind. They're too goddamn big for my hands! My only problem now is she won't leave me alone. Stopping by the office when she knows I'm in there doing paperwork or placing stock orders. She'll make a point of touching me in the club if I walk in while they are practicing. No wonder Alpha talked about women wanting and taking. This chick wants more, and it's taking everything I have not to tell her to back the fuck off or find another job. If she didn't bring in so many eager, cashed-up cowboys, she'd be gone already.

Wrench flew back home to Boston before grabbing his bike and making his way out west to the Ponderosa Pistons. From our last conversation somewhere near Kabul, I vaguely remember him saying his family wasn't close. I can't relate. Mine are like the hug from your grandmas in matching Christmas sweaters, static cling and all. He rocks his bike backwards into the second space outside the Wildcats bar. This brother requires a beverage before anything else.

"Smoke, my man." He smiles. We grasp hands before pulling each other in for a bro hug. That's the extent of affection towards one another in the MC. If you don't have a gun pointed at you or a pool cue smashed over your head, you're on good terms. In all fairness, that rogue element was moved on once Foley and Akis received the psych evaluations and the medical results. The same batch of testing provided a spotlight on who was full of fentanyl and methamphetamine. Opioids are fine post-surgery for chronic pain, but mixed into a cocktail with stimulants, alcohol, guns and explosives. Yeah, nah. Out you go. Sort your shit out. The same battery of testing also provided Alpha with requests for further testing. Seems something showed up that shouldn't have, and he was at the doctor's office seeking answers, at his wife's insistence of course.

"Wrench Richter, as I live and breathe."

"It's been too long, brother." His mouth morphs from thin line to grimace.

"That it has."

We're about to slip inside the double doors for that long overdue drink when a fury of light sandy hair and a whole lot of sassy attitude comes storming down the street. This little thing would make Wednesday from the Addams family appear positively joyful.

"Are you Edward Weir?" Her voice is small but mighty. Who pissed in your lucky charms this morning, sweetheart? Wrench and I share a look. This kid, a teenager all storming and stomping up the street, demanded to know if I'm Ed Weir.

"Who wants to know?" I counter, and her face morphs from annoyed to downright thunderous. It must be all those teenage girl hormones we learned about in sex ed. Christ, it's been a long time since teen hormones and I were situated so close. The vibrating pillar of furious anger, fists clenched and knuckles white, is in one helluva mood. Did we deny her a job at Kittens? If so, we were within our rights because this girl must be thirteen or fourteen. There is no way, even with makeup and suggestive clothing, she could pass for twenty-one. None whatsoever.

Her brows pinch with an intensity that scares me. I want to warn her about anger, like the kind Wrench and I are witnessing. Both of us are trained to diffuse hostile situations, although two Marines versus a teen girl are outrageous odds. Still, her chin remains in the air, defiant.

"Again, honey, who wants to know?" This time, my tone isn't playful or questioning. It's clear, concise and fucking cutthroat. I'm in no mood for this shit today.

"His fucking daughter," she spits back, all fury and ferocity.

For the first time in my life, I am fucking speechless.

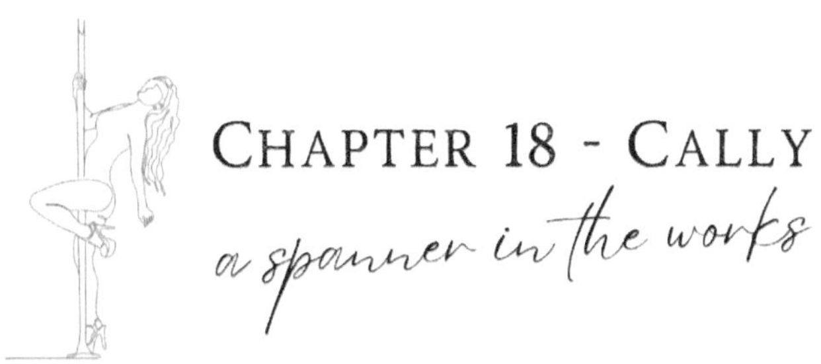

CHAPTER 18 - CALLY
a spanner in the works

Tequila, tits and tassels. That's my life at the moment. I work every shift I can at Wilds and Kittens, begging for more if Smoke is overwhelmed or short staffed. I've been back to Chicago once since I was hired. This shoot was more in depth, intimate and the paycheck was almost double the first one. If this continues, I'll be able to fly there and back rather than take the bus. While it's cheaper, obviously, it's also crazy long, and every second seat has someone talking to themselves, talking to me, or smelling of urine. There is a reason so many songwriters sing about journeys on Greyhound buses. No two are ever the same, and while I'm here for diversity, please shake your dick more than once at the urinal, bud, before you tuck yourself back in.

I'm booked in again in three weeks time. Greer says the sporadic bookings are normal at first. They need to see how well you photograph and whether fetishists like your look. How could they not love me trussed up like a Thanksgiving turkey in studded black leather, clamps and a studded collar? That is my favorite so far. Greer sent about fifty heart-eye, fire and jalapeno emojis when she saw that picture.

"Cally, this here is Wrench. He's our newest MC member but comes with a senior rank, darlin', so make sure he's looked after extra special."

Smoke doesn't have to treat me like I'm vapid. I treat every MC member to the same high level Cally Rae service. I smile a little broader and swing my hips a little more for the MC guys. The rest of the bar, and that creepy fucking dentist get the standard issue Cally Rae spit and polish. Nothing more.

Wrench is tall, like taller than Smoke by roughly three inches. Where Smoke is fair, with cool gray eyes and a permanently furrowed brow, Wrench is dark with eyes like icicles. The furrowed brow is the same though; must be standard, military issue.

"Hey." I smile. "What can I get ya? If you're unsure what you want, I can choose something for you?" The glare he fires back makes me want to give him that disgusting licorice stuff. The clear alcohol that looks like purity and smells like fucking death in a trash can.

"I know what I want." Okay then. Care to elaborate, you moody bastard? I pull a hair tie off my wrist and start pulling my hair into a ponytail.

"It's okay, Cal, I've got him." Smoke moves behind the bar and begins pouring a drink for the grumpy, tall, dark and handsome. Come to think of it, they were both in a mood when they came stomping through the doors. Must be some club business gone wrong. Anyway, don't let your inner turmoil be your outer self, Jo always tells me. If you have a cyclone going on in your gut, or your mind, you still need to turn up for work, and work to the best of your ability. Maybe these military guys need to get *that* memo.

The two of them continue in hushed whispers, deciding to move to the MC booth before being joined by Alpha, Rodin, Grave, and RAM. When I bring over a tray of fresh drinks, and move to clear away the empty glasses, the conversation continues.

"She's at the Bison. We have a couple of guys stationed outside. She's not going anywhere until we get some answers. Grave, how long did you say the tests will take?"

"Depends on the lab. A week usually. Might rush it if we know the lab or throw some money at them. The sooner the better, right?"

"Absolutely. Can you just see all the crazies coming out of the woodwork now our poster boy here has been on national news as a hero? This could well be the tip of the iceberg, buddy."

When I accidentally clink two glasses together, Smoke snaps. "Cally, just fucking go, will ya? Now."

Silence descends over the group as I clutch at the tray with trembling fingers. I don't even think either of the glasses broke, let alone cracked. My cheeks burn the same shade as my hair. Ducking my head with embarrassment, I scurry back to the safety of the bar. The rhythmic whir of the glass washer spraying soap over the upturned glasses in the rack is both satisfying and comforting. I could watch the action through that door like a television. I'd rather be irrelevant than ridiculed. To be stuck in a no-man's-land of apathy rather than wear Smoke's disapproval dripping over me like the sweep of suds from the glass washer.

Feather appears at the end of the bar, arms crossed and sullen. Before I've even said hello and checked if he's here for business or pleasure, and would he like a drink or not, he tells me that Smoke wants me to go home. Just like that. Ordered out of sight, now wanted out of mind. Couldn't even come over here and tell me himself. He sent a minion, even if this minion is a mountain, over here to do it for him. I throw the black hair elastic in frustration, wishing I could strangle that man's fucking dick with it.

"Sit down and don't go anywhere. Cally, if she needs to go to the bathroom, you will accompany her. Understood?" Um, I guess? There is a teenage girl looking scarier than a Texas tornado blowing through at Cat 5 after flattening everything from Georgia westward. This girl, who I was introduced to as Kiara, is stabbing ice in her soda glass with her straw as if it's personally wronged her. Or someone has.

"Hey, Kiara, is it? What brings you here all by yourself? Are your parents around?"

"Fuck off, fireball. I'm not interested." Um, rude! But I know this girl wasn't placed at this back table with me without a particular plan put in place by the Pistons. Several in full leathers are drinking at stools by the main bar, and not at this table, which is odd in itself.

"You don't sound like you are from around here?" I venture again.

"What part of fuck all the way off do you not understand? And they say blondes are stupid. Talk about a skewed stereotype." This time her paper straw is thrust into a cube with so much force, it concertinas under the force. Soda sloshes over the rim of the glass and onto the table. Her derisive snort and sour expression show she's as pissed off with the paper straw's lack of integrity as she is with something else.

Smoke and Wrench appear from the office while Grave approaches from the bar's double doors. The members on stools swivel to face us. I feel like a pinned butterfly in an entomologist's display case. Kiara raises her chin and glowers.

"Grab your shit, princess. We're going to get tested."

The surly teen picks up her backpack and heaves it over her slight shoulders. She raises double middle fingers to the men approaching the table.

"Whoa, whoa. Is everything alright?" I query as the men move closer. I haven't seen the Pistons do anything untoward in the time since I've been here. They provided me with this job, after all, but I draw the line at the clandestine involvement of a teenage girl.

"We will know soon enough," Smoke snarls. "Seems Suzie fucking sunshine here thinks we are related." My jaw slackens. Related? As in a long-lost cousin or something? Noticing my slack-jawed expression, he clarifies. "Kiara blew into town with the absurd idea that I'm her father. Isn't that right, peaches?" His mocking tone is callous and unnecessary. She's so young and vulnerable if she's here on her own. I mean, where is the mother?

"Yes, Daddy," she coos back, all syrupy. And I want to crawl back into those suds all over again.

Chapter 19 - Smoke

Alpha is an influential man and perfect in the role as Pistons President. Right about now, staring at my phone screen, I more than understand his words about women being dangerous and encouraging a union of fornication only, and foregoing any *feelings*.

I am a father to a foul-mouthed almost fifteen-year-old who called me every name under the sun, and then some. Spying the Kitten's sign over the doorway next to Wilds, her brain decided not only was I a deadbeat dad in dereliction of every parenting role, but I was also an abhorrent predator. That my blood made up half of hers was a fact she hated more than what I did for work, my biker "gang" and everything else wrong with the universe. I was chewed out and stepped on, raked over her years of pent-up rage, believing I'd deserted her mother when she needed me most. The truth could not be more polarized.

I vaguely remember a bar in Phoenix in between deployments. I couldn't tell you the name of the bar, let alone the name of the woman. I wrapped it up; I always do. Condoms are what, ninety-eight percent effective, right? And if she was on the pill and we were careful, then that should knock on the door of one hundred percent. Only I don't remember if she was on the pill and definitely not how careful we were. Fuck! And now a living, ranting, raging teenager was born from that union, knowing only my name and that I was a Marine from Arizona too, but little else. Color everyone fucking shocked when the story broke about my heroics in the wilds of Montana rescuing a family from a burning car wreck. The broadcast reached Flagstaff at the minimum because my mom was in touch that same night asking about how many traffic signals Montana had and was I getting enough sleep because I looked *tired*. Gee, Mom, hacking into a baby harness to release a trapped infant might do that to a guy.

Kiara stated her last name was Finlayson at the lab we used for a rush DNA result. Right after that, she bolted. RAM, the tech wiz, has been hacking into bus and train station manifests, but until he receives unfettered access as part of the M.E.T.R.I.C.S. setup from Akis, his reach is limited.

"Take the night off. That's not a request, that's an order," Alpha says. I don't want to hang around the clubhouse in this melancholy. I'd rather busy myself with menial bar tasks. It's better if I don't defy a direct order.

"Yes, sir." The reply is one of rote. Muscle memory and madness. I fathered a baby I had no knowledge of until two days ago. Ignoring her fucked-up diatribe and vehement anger, I want to tell her I had no idea, and I am more than ready to step up in whatever capacity they need me now. Only she's vanished, and so has my opportunity for redemption.

My fingers race across the phone screen before my breathing evens. It's still choppy, unstructured. Kind of like my life right now. I want to talk to the one person who won't judge, won't offer platitudes and sure as shit won't shut up. I don't want to spiral in silence. I need to hear something, anything, from that sweet mouth with full lips as perfect as a peach. And because I control her roster, she isn't working tonight, and that's all I need.

I swing my leg over the bike and proceed to the ground-floor apartment address I know by heart, having stared at it for way too long after her first shift. The walk along the path is long enough for a calming cigarette, the cherry glowing with each inhale. The front doors are clustered together, so this place is more broom closet than studios for rent. How do two adult women with all the usual shit women accumulate, cohabitate in this tiny space? The answer lies within the question itself. These women are unusual. Cally Rae is bereft of the usual accumulated shit because she's been free from her cult upbringing for months only.

"Hey, you," she exclaims when she sees my bulk filling her doorframe. Her sister is working triage and won't be home for hours.

"Mind if I come in?" The space smells like she's frying something delicious.

"I'm not sure you'll fit," she groans, fitting her body flush with the wall so I can move past the entryway. I'm not as tall nor as broad as some of the MC guys. That suited my sniper role, anyway. Now that I leave a tiny space for Cally in the entry, I wish I were smaller again.

"Sorry," she mouths, hastily moving a pillow and blanket off of the tiny sofa she's been sleeping on. Holy shit, how does she fit on this? In the opposite corner sits a tub chair. It looks all kinds of uncomfortable, but I can't fall into her bed now, can I?

"Don't move anything aside on my account, sweetheart. I'm the one intruding on your space." Her bright-eyed smile tells me she's more than fine having her space intruded upon. Well, that's one female who doesn't hate me today.

"I take it the test results were not what you were expecting?" Ain't that an understatement.

"Not in the slightest. I mean, I wrapped it up. I always wrap it up." As soon as the words escape, I realize it's a millisecond until this woman hates me too. I know what she's thinking. I didn't wrap it with her, so my paternity status shouldn't be so shocking, right?

"My wording was poor," I say, just as she speaks, "You needn't apolo—"

Damn straight I do. I never even asked about her welfare after the cellar. What she did to ensure no pregnancy, and what burden of cost she bore alone. Could I be any more of an asshole?

"I do owe you an apology, though. Christ, I owe you more than that!"

She ducks her chin to her chest, and I want to leap forward and raise it to the room. She has no right to feel embarrassed. I'm the idiot here, not her. "I don't want you to think that I am careless when I fuck someone. Because I'm not usually. Careless, that is." Ugh, I'm making this worse. Those eyes of dripping honey stare back at me, unfazed. She's busy trying to pile blankets and strewn clothes together to make the tiny space look less cluttered and chaotic. All I see is her, and another one of those black hair elastics around her wrist, before she tugs it off and sweeps her hair up into a hasty ponytail. Now, all I can think about is tugging on that ponytail while I rut into her. Wrapped up, of course.

"Can I get you anything? I know we don't have any whiskey or bourbon here. There might be a beer or two in the fridge, though I don't remember. I can check though."

She's so earnest, so ready to serve and play gracious hostess when I've been anything but gracious towards her. My head sinks into my hands, and instead of agreeing with my self-loathing and questioning my sanity, she uncurls herself from the tiny sofa and slinks over to me. Not quite kneeling at my feet, she places a cool palm on my knee, next to where my elbow rests, and squeezes. It's not overtly sexual or suggestive. It's a touch of comfort. I'm here, and I'm here for you. Even when you've treated me like trash, I'm above your shit and here for you, anyway. I'm screwed.

"Cally, I—" It comes out on a choked sob. "I'm fucked up. My daughter knows it. Called me out on it before she skipped town because she couldn't stand the sight of me."

"Smoke, shhh. That's not true," she coos. Oh, honey, it is. "She came up to seek you out because she saw you on the news, and she wanted answers. I don't think she's disappointed."

"She called me a lowlife, pervert cunt because I manage a strip club full of naked bitches but can't spare time for my daughter. The kid I never even knew existed, mind you. Christ, Cal. The hatred tumbled from her lips. She was so angry."

"Maybe she was confused and scared." Her fingers flex across my thigh, and her touch speaks to me differently now. The comfort remains, but something else flares every time those pink-tipped nails dance along the denim.

"I'm confused and scared," I admit to the one person I don't think has an ounce of judgment in her body. Well, none that I've witnessed, anyway. Then again, we barely know each other apart from the hours we spent clutched to each other in the cellar. The time I spent inside her only for it to dissipate like bike exhaust once we were released and went back to being boss and employee. Only I want inside her again. To forget the week and this crazy long day and not sleeping since the car wreck and... smoke? I may be a smoker, but my sense of smell is still acute. An acrid haze wafts from the kitchen, and because this place is so tiny, right over the top of the tub chair, and Cally perched on the floor. Her eyes bug out when I fly out of the chair and in three strides face a burning pot on the stove, which has ignited lace curtains over a window. Flames lick the walls and overhead cabinets. Lace ignites with a whoof and drifts to the sink below, tatters of black and orange settling over the pile of dishes. There is no fire blanket and no smoke alarm. Moving back into the main room, I tug at a blanket, hoping it's more wool than synthetic, and cover the flaming pot. The curtains should burn themselves out, but containing the fire before the cabinets alight and threaten the apartment upstairs is my focus. I'm searching for another blanket when I spy Cally with a container of water from the bathroom.

"NNNOOOOOOO!" I snap. "Never water for a fat fire! It spreads it further." Only my words take too long, and the panicked woman flings the water, container and all, towards the flames and steps backwards. And fuck.

"What the heck, Cal?" Jo doesn't look irate as such. More confused. The fire department arrived and contained the blaze to the kitchen and the wall that separates the bathroom and Jo's bedroom. The entire room is blackened and acrid. Small wisps of charred lace rise from the sink debris only to drift down again. They can't stay here. *She* can't stay here.

> That cottage your brother owned. It's empty, yeah?

> **WRENCH**
> It is. Why?

> Because Cally almost burned her sister's apartment down.

> **WRENCH**
> The fuck? You want an arsonist to move into Chief's cottage?

> Yeah. Jo and Cally. Under strict supervision, of course.

WRENCH
Of course. Keep her out of the kitchen.

> Oh, I plan on it.

Some club guys helped Jo and Cally pack their crap into Jo's tiny car and headed to the cottage. What is it with girls and tiny stuff? Until you get to those ridiculous hoop earrings, handbags big enough to camp in and water bottles that look more like scuba tanks. Chief's place is furnished. With a bed in the primary bedroom, they'll have to share until Wrench goes over with his truck to pick up Jo's frame. Everything else in that place smells like burned plastic. I thought, before dismissing it, that Cally could share my bed at the MC. Alpha would be fine with that, right? It was a crisis. She'd literally set the place on fire. Only I recall Alpha's speech and block the idea entirely. We're not dating. We fucked once, and shit, I still owe her for morning-after contraception. And I owe her a lot more than that, too.

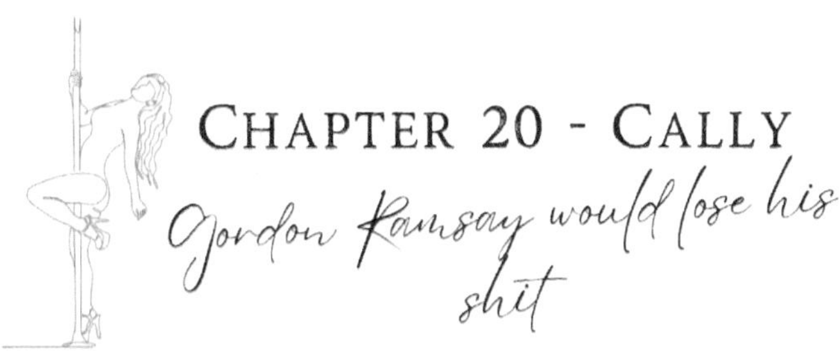

CHAPTER 20 - CALLY

Gordon Ramsay would lose his shit

It looked fine. It looked more than fine. It was crispy and golden brown, just like the photos. How was I supposed to know it wasn't cooked all the way through? Steak is still pink when it's done, and a heap of videos have a ton of thumbs up reactions and comments about how succulent and mouthwatering it looks. I haven't cooked a whole chicken before. In fact, I've hardly cooked anything before because my father enslaved our mother into the role of food provider, and I was always being sent away and out of the room, including the kitchen.

Smoke is lying on a gurney in the very hospital my sister works triage at. It was she who first suggested food poisoning, and I was too confused to be offended until she pointed out that chicken bleeding and pink inside is most definitely not cooked and can pose a threat of all kinds of poisoning. I wanted to say thank you for helping to put out the apartment fire and for organizing our stay in a gorgeous little cottage that used to belong to Wrench's brother. Wrench had the final say, of course, but that man is so moody and tight-lipped, getting any conversation out of him is like prying open a frozen car door. Too much effort.

"The doctor will be in to rule out other causes, like appendicitis." Jo fusses with a setting on the IV bag one of her fellow nurses administered not long after Smoke was admitted. She offers the stricken man a pitying glance before huffing out a breath. Perhaps she's weighing up whether we'll be evicted from the cottage for poisoning one of the Pistons. I mean, I did her a favor if she thinks about it. That apartment was too small for two adults, so I was sleeping on her couch! She didn't get her bond back, and I'm sorry for that, but we have this gorgeous place now with hardwood floors, crown molding, and she even has this cute bird mural in her bedroom. I took the master because Smoke organized the cottage when he found out I was homeless. And she had had the *only* bedroom. It's *only fair* that I get the pick of the bedrooms now. So, I took the master, which is average size, but the closet is smaller than a hummingbird's wing. There is a third bedroom though, and Smoke didn't see a problem with me converting it into a wardrobe space. He didn't see a problem coming at him like raw chicken. So now we wait in triage.

"Ed, is it?" says an older Asian gentleman in scrubs and glasses. Smoke can't do much but grunt, lying on his side with his knees to his chest. He looks pale, but perspiration beads on his forehead, so he's probably quite cozy lying there. Perhaps this is the rest he needed after all the drama with the car wreck and finding out he had a teenage daughter, who then chewed him out for being a deadbeat dad. Silver lining. The man needs his rest.

"Ma'am, I'm going to ask you to leave. I need to perform an internal examination." He wheels his little stool over to a wall with boxes of latex gloves affixed in ascending sizes. As he pulls two gloves from the medium box, I note Ed's hands gripping his knees, all white-knuckled and strained. He has huge hands. He would need gloves from the large or extra-large box.

"Ma'am," the doctor says again.

"I need to leave?"

"You're the only ma'am here, Cally. So go." His voice wheezes out with effort. Strained and struggling. Small bubbles of saliva foam near the corners of his mouth, joining the perspiration beading a sheen on his pale skin.

Smoke sure is snappy. "I'm going!" Jesus.

The latex slides along my thighs, coming to a stop under the crease where my butt cheeks meet my legs. This is where I feel most alive. I'm not made to cover my hair; quite the opposite, in fact. It flows around me like fire, and I'm the one who lit the flames. I'm also not sequestered away or told my opinions are irrelevant. Sando, the photographer, confers with me often about how he thinks a shot should look, or whether I have any input on something new. I have input, opinions, and wants and needs. I need all of it. All the dopamine highs that posing like a lust bomb kink goddess brings. The kind of sinning that speaks to my shattered soul; anointing it with lubricants and latex. Greer may have escorted me into this world, but my cum-fuck-me boot heels are dug in tight and I will never, ever leave. Nipple clamps, spreader bars, hoods, masks, gags, heels, hose, corsets and collars. The wearables are insane. Then there are the toys. Sucking vibrators, clit stimulators, strap-on dildos and dongs. It's debauched decadence, and I'm addicted to it all.

My male model colleague is kitted out in peekaboo rubber shorts, a studded shock collar and matching heavy chain leash and motorcycle boots. Does he ride a motorcycle? Or is he usually a tax accountant called Gerard who drives a Tesla? I don't know, and I don't fucking care! What he gets out of this is his own journey, and those boots are for him to travel in. Just like mine are for me. I do this for money, obviously. But even if I didn't earn a cent for dressing up in ribbed rubber, accessorized with a jeweled butt plug, riding crop and raised rib choker. I can't say for sure whether I would care. I would do this for nothing, because nothing can provide the same non-chemical high I get from this dressed-up version of someone else. I crave the kink. The "tie me to the bedhead and rail me till I'm raw" kind of crazy sex that leaves the best kind of bruises on my creamy skin.

I'm sick. Absolutely, I'm sick. And slick! And I never want to heal. Pastor Rich and the rest of the Righteous Moonyata Circle would spit out their dandelion tea if they knew I was tethered to a submissive by a collar and lead. Only I was the one who was tethered and submissive. To their wacky shit and ridiculous ramblings.

The plug moves deeper as I straddle my sub, who defers in a tabletop position for my pleasure. I thought this was called hands and knees, but the position is so much more than that. His cock is thick and rigid. Pre-cum glosses the angry tip, pooling deliciously before dripping onto the floor below. Every vein pulses under this pink light while Sando continues to stalk around us, pointing and flashing away.

"That's it, Cally, more, more."

Oh, I hear you, more, MORE! As Mikael, not Gerard, my sub, drops his head, I rub the riding crop between my trussed breasts before sinking it lower, lower until it's clamped between my other lips. Each swipe has my overstimulated clit wanting more, more, more! Of course, this is role play. I'm no more a dominant than I am a debutante, yet pour the girl into garters and gags and watch her brilliance bloom.

Keep your skydiving and ice bath plunge pools. I feel alive when a camera points at me, dolled up and decadent in my costume of choice. This is the dopamine high that counselors warn you about. The hit you crave and then require increasing amounts of to quench your satiation. Lips so slick with gloss, they stick together, and another set so glossed with slick, they fall open. I'm your urban fantasy, your smuttiest secret and your ultimate undoing. Here you can look to your heart's content, and dream and desire as much as your consciousness and web browser allow.

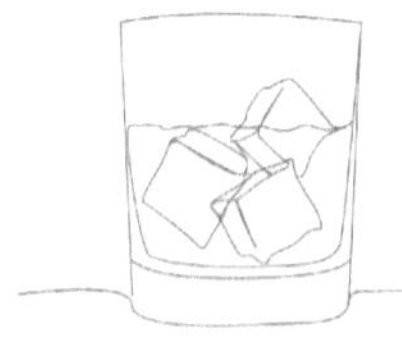

CHAPTER 21 - SMOKE
something in my ass

If the saying is accurate, and there is no rest for the wicked, I must be downright devilish. Laid out for almost seventy-two hours with a bout of food poisoning didn't help, but the doctor's diagnosis method has raised more questions than answers. One: it was Cally's undercooked chicken that had me bent over in agony and not a near-ruptured appendix and two: I am not averse to the feeling of something in my ass. Not averse at all.

This week we are busy with planning two missions. One is for the newly developed elite team that is M.E.T.R.I.C.S., and the other is an annual toy and book drive for the kids in surrounding counties. Maybe one will balance out the other? Doesn't matter. Once we were sent the information about a pedophile teacher at a school out west with ties to a West Coast MC chapter, his fate was all but sealed. RAM has mirrored his database and uploaded sickening footage for evidence, should we ever need a defense. If we are clean, we never will. The West Coast MC erupted once news came to light about the rogue teacher, but nothing about this hit can have its grimy hand anywhere near them. They know it; we know it. So Akis gave it to us knowing we were located closer than the Smoke Dogs. Game fucking on.

The other mission has one of the MC garages piled high with fluffy toys, electronics, books and sporting equipment, remote control drones, cars, bikes and boats, and even the old school board games that started every family argument on Thanksgiving and Christmas. The Weir family wasn't immune to Samuel Weir's Monopoly theft. I remember everything. The drive is a benefit for disadvantaged children and young people, but it's more than that. It's a chance for us to connect with the community and show them an MC doesn't have to be all meth dens and *Sons of Anarchy*. That was one of Kiara's parting barbs that hurt the most. Your biker gang. We're not some outlaw south of the border cartel. Jesus fucking Christ, we're an organized club, sharing common goals and an exemplary work ethic. We serve, we work, we vote and we pay our taxes.

"More than happy to meet with you, Smoke. Is it Chief's passing, or Wrench's arrival that has you uncertain?" Rodin, the psych, has been balls to the wall busy since Chief Richter took his own life. The poor guy had only arrived back here from Canada three days beforehand, and he took the news hard. As hard as any of us. Losing a brother is profound. The loss of a beloved brother by his own hand has guys second-guessing everything. No one was immune to the fallout, the accusations and relentless questions. Then Wrench came back, and any pain dampened and dulled down has risen like a pus-filled boil threatening to inflame a tenuous situation.

"No, it's not about Chief," I say. Because it's not. "It's something I'm questioning, and I don't know who to talk to about it, or how to move on."

"That's okay. No topic is off the table," he beams. "Why don't you start by sharing what's on your mind?"

Here we go. Just rip the band-aid off. Don't stuff around lifting taped corners and going slow. Grip and rip. "I had a rectal exam when the hospital thought I might have appendicitis. Even writhing in pain, I..."

His gaze is considered. Thoughtful without reproach. "It's okay, Smoke."

Is it? I let out a long breath through my teeth. I grip and rip. "I enjoyed it. A lot."

"Okay then."

"Am I gay?" The words pour from me like parachuting troopers out of a C-47 Chinook.

"Do you sense an attraction to other men?"

"Fuck no." Tension grips each limb and twists. I am surrounded by men and have been for some time. Never once have I thought about another man. Even now, in a club full of guys, sitting across from one, nothing. Hammer showed me his pierced cock, for fuck's sake. It wasn't sexual, nor pretty. That he voluntarily had holes put through his shaft for decorative metal made me question his sanity rather than my sexuality. But, still...

"Alright then." His eyes shine with a gentle, neutral gaze. Even behind his glasses, they seem to dance with care. Like no news is good news, everything has a silver lining somehow. "The anus has a set of very sensitive nerve endings. Coupled with the prostate gland, many men become aroused with anal stimulation. Whether that's a medical probe detecting inflammation, or more sexual kinds of stimulation."

"But you're gay, right? Can you tell me how you discovered you were?"

"Ed, this isn't about me. It's about your awakening to stimulation you may not have felt before. If you aren't attracted to males, it's the sensation of those nerves being stimulated that turned you on. A gloved finger differs from an erect penis."

"Fuck. I get it! I'm..."

"Confused?"

"Yes. I spent over a third of my life in the military, surrounded by thousands of men. Women too, but mostly men. I showered with them, slept in barracks on cots a handful of feet away from the next cot, and I never once entertained the idea of another guy. I still don't see men like that. I've seen plenty of cocks and hairy sacks and not once did I consider dropping to my knees and licking them. But I've had nothing up my ass before either. So I was wondering if the two might be connected somehow. And whether this was part of some awakening that people talk about. If I'm not pure gay, so to speak, am I bi?"

His nods grow more robust. "It was an awakening of sorts. But not to homosexual urges, and I'm hesitant to add in bisexual either. As you've stated yourself, you are not attracted to men in any capacity. You enjoyed anal stimulation as a heterosexual man. That's it. There is plenty more that can be explored safely with the use of—"

I shake my head. "No, I'm good. I wanted your considered opinion on whether my awakening was... I dunno."

"Gay?"

"Yeah."

"Not from what you've shared, Smoke. However, I'm open to discussing anything further with you after we get back from the op if you'd like?"

"Nah, I think I'm good."

If she hadn't been twenty minutes late for the start of her shift, I wouldn't even have noticed she was absent. Since the night of her infamous chicken sashimi, Cally has become a master of blending into the background. When she started here, she looked like a quiet choir girl with wide eyes and big dreams. Then she sort of morphed into a wannabe seductress, but the clothes looked alien on her girl-next-door persona. She was playing dress up alright. Turning up to work in skimpy leather bras and tiny shorts with stockings you wanted to tear off with your teeth, not remove delicately from her alabaster legs like a gentleman. She was as much a draw card behind the Kitten's bar as any of the pole-riding strippers. And everyone knew it but her.

So, color me fucking surprised when she comes racing along the hall, all out of breath, heels clacking as her feet try to eat up the ground towards the cubby for her to place her things. In her haste, she hasn't seen me perched behind the desk, half hidden by the computer screen as I recheck the roster for the ninth time, confirming that yes, Cally Rae Jenkins is rostered on to work tonight. Taking another deep inhale, I marvel as the fiery end burns up the waiting paper, burning it all shades of black before it dissolves into the myriad of grays. The club is never that busy in the first hour of opening, only my annoyance that the ethos of "don't be late, don't be lazy, and don't lie" seems to have been snubbed at point one.

"Hey, Red," Feather greets her on his way back to the entrance of the club. He throws a meaty hand over his shoulder with a non-verbal greeting because he, too, is late to his post.

"Fuck," she squeals, hand flying to her throat as the contents of her stupidly oversized tote go flying in all directions. Unaware of the spectacle, Feather disappears deeper into the darkened club and out of view.

"Gave me a fucking heart attack," she whispers, almost to herself, because she still hasn't peered into the office and noticed me sitting here, watching her like a creep. I'm tempted to call out to her, to alert her she's pushing the line of almost thirty minutes late now, and the ensuing discipline that offence carries. But when I look at the items that were once contained in that stupid bag, now strewn about the corridor, I freeze. There are dildos and vibrators, and some silicone thing. I have no concept of what it is, only that it's pink, shaped like some kind of flower and lying on the floor just inside the threshold of my office. One strap of the stupid bag hangs limply from her shoulder while she turns in a circle, causing a heap more stuff to spill out.

"I got you," I state, rising from the chair and emerging from behind the screen to cross the office. Cally swings around again, hand flying back to the same spot she clutched mere moments ago. A new litany of goods cascades from the open bag. She's a struck pinata of adult sex toys, and every movement, every nuanced turn, has more shit landing on the floor between us.

"Fuck," she gasps for the second time. "What is it with you Pistons scaring the shit outta people?" She's not scared. Her pupils, blown wide and pulsing orbs of pure ebony, may relay anxiety and panic, sure. But to me, she looks turned on.

"Lemme help you with your things, honey. The more you move, the more this looks like a Hansel and Gretel breadcrumb trail. And not one that leads back home."

Picking up the flower, I hope like hell it's new, or cleaned. But then again, if it's been sucking on her clit, I could almost lick it myself. My cock jumps in my pants at the thought of it.

"Fuck," she wails again, once she's seen the trail of items that escaped confinement of her bag. As I bend to scoop up item after item, she joins me in a mirrored crouch, not the slightest bit embarrassed. Where is the choir girl, and who is this sex siren? Does she use these items on herself? Or does she have a side job selling sex toys, along with the modeling gig she has in Chicago? Between the two of us, the bag is filled once again and thrust into her cubby space. She whips off the wrap sundress she arrived at work in and stuffs that into the cubby too. I watch her pull a hair elastic from her wrist and scoop up her gorgeous mane into a high ponytail, wrists and fingers moving as one to encase the glossy hair in multiple wraps and twists of the elastic. Just as I'm about to ask her to stop, say hello properly and ask her if she's okay, Delta fucking double Ds come sashaying down the hallway in her own click-clack heels. She's almost entirely naked, a skimpy black lace thong covering just the crease of her pussy lips, and black glitter heart pasties adorn each nipple, just.

"Hey, Cally," I plead, wanting more contact time with the firebrand whirlwind of sex toys and secrets. Only Delta opens her mouth at the same time.

"Ready for round two? Happy for another fuck, or do you just want me to suck your cock?"

CHAPTER 22 - SMOKE

Torture me some more darlin'

The butter-yellow door doesn't even have a peephole. I guess Chief didn't think it was an issue. I mean, whoever came knocking at the door of the Ponderosa Pistons Vice President was friendly, incredibly brave, or inherently stupid. The thought of Cally and Jo not knowing who was on the other side of the door makes my skin itch. Then again, not my house. Not my circus, not my monkeys. The cigarette I've all but finished is discarded onto the cement below and crushed under my heavy boot before I kick it into the shrubbery framing the walkway.

The unmistakable sound of a deadbolt releasing has my nerves calming. Cally's tired, makeup-free face peers back at me through the gap between the door and the frame. She's in a Foo Fighters band t-shirt that falls mid-thigh, her porcelain skin peeking out from below the hemline and to her pink painted toenails.

"I thought I told you to wait for me in my office," I bark, my hand fanning over the golden paint.

"You did," she agrees. "I thought better of it, so I ignored you. I took an Uber."

I can't say for sure whether it's her blatant disregard of my direct order, or the way her inky lashes fan her doe eyes, but my blood instantly heats. Warm and thick, too viscous to be pumped, and not a thing I can do about it until she hears me out. Leaning my bodyweight onto the barrier between us, it springs wide enough for me to enter, and enter I do. Not even stopping to take off my boots, I'm past her gaping mouth and through the entrance foyer before she can protest.

"Don't mind me," she slurs with enough sarcasm to sink a frigate. "Come right in."

Oh, honey, don't threaten me with a good time. With more force than necessary, she hurls the door towards the frame. It clatters home with a thud. She makes no move to fasten the deadbolt. Clearly she'd rather have any danger outside ready to come rescue her from the danger inside; me.

"You want to tell me why you've got your panties all in a bunch then?"

"You fucked Delta? She's old. And like, ewww."

"She's younger than me." Not the right option to fire back.

"That's 'cause you're ancient."

"Once. It meant nothing. We fucked once. That's it." The moment the words are free, I want to claw them back in. Cally and I fucked once too. Her rounded, battle-ready shoulders soften and deflate, just like that. My words have done more damage than a fifteen-millimeter round. And I can't unfire, can't pull it back and chamber that round. "Darlin', that's not what I meant."

"You need to go," she says. "If this was your welfare check because I was brought home by someone other than you, well, as you can see I'm safe and sound. So you can turn around, through that door and onto your bike, to fall back into your stripper. Unless you'd prefer her to just suck your cock?"

Her words bite. She's throwing back Delta's words from the corridor. She wants me to know that if my "we fucked once and it means nothing" statement is gospel, then she intends to worship far, far away from me.

"I get it," she shrieks, arms thrown wide. The hem of that shirt rides higher, higher.

"I don't think you do," I retort, eyes still focused on that rising hemline.

"You're all the same." It's a muttered whisper. She's talking to herself, and I'm the voyeur in the hallway. "Look," she concedes. "It's late, I'm tired and I'm going to bed. Lock the door on your way out, thanks."

"I didn't come here to fight with you. I want to talk to you." The lie rolls off my tongue. Empty promises and raw want all dripping in beads of bourbon. Sinking into the closest chair that, thankfully, isn't that tiny fucking tub thing from the apartment, my shoulders relax for what feels like the first time in weeks. Cally takes up a similar position in the adjacent chair. I want to reach over and pull her into my lap, but while her claws are still extended, I opt for safety first and remain separate from the fired up, fed up female currently glaring at me.

"We don't owe each other anything," she begins. I nod because she's right. "We fucked once too. I'm naïve in a lot of ways, Ed, but I'm not that dense."

Her self-deprecation and use of my actual name make my already overheated blood boil to additional levels. It takes all of my military training to restore my resting pulse rate. This battle is unlike any other I've faced before.

"True," I agree, noticing her posture soften further. If she believes this is the end of the discussion, she is sadly mistaken. "What we can offer each other is more on my mind, honey." My arm snaps out to secure her by the waist and hoist her onto my spread thighs. Her audible, breathy gasp has my cock stirring more than the expanse of creamy thighs lying across my denim-clad legs.

"Discipline," I bark, arranging her body over mine to my exacting standards. If she wants to be a brat, she'll suffer the consequences. "What did I tell you when you got the job, sweetheart?"

My breath ghosts the shell of her ear. She's fierce and furious, wanting to buck and writhe like my own damn rodeo bull. *You're not in control here, honey. This is my scene.*

"You told me a lot of things," she rasps, and my dick has signed the contract and is already recapping the pen. The way she grinds her hip down lets me know she feels it too. Yeah, baby. Just like that. But I set the rules, and the pace. You defer to *me*. "What specifically..."

"Don't be late, don't be lazy, and don't lie." Her words are spoken to the hardwood floor below. The one covered with a woven, geometric-patterned rug to absorb her words, tears, and breathy moans.

"That's right," I croon, my elbow securing the middle of her back and forcing her to comply. Trailing a finger from the back of one knee, up her alabaster skin, elicits a bloom of gooseflesh. Her heart is almost breaking free from her ribcage, the heightened rhythm evident behind her chest mashed against my legs. She looks beautiful like this, and her scent? The heady perfume of her arousal has my nose twitching and tongue coated in saliva, desperate for more. A touch, a taste. More, more, MORE!

"Now, we both know you are *not* lazy, Cally Rae, but you were late to work today. You defied a direct order for you to wait for me. So—" My finger teases the hem of the shirt, sliding it up and over the swell of her firm ass. The ass clad in pale pink cotton panties. If I don't swallow that pooling saliva, I'm gonna drown. "All I'm asking is for you to tell me the truth about why you were late. Only that, baby, the truth. Don't lie to me. *Not ever.*"

The way she wants to squirm and writhe, to escape my hold and our closeness, would be cute but ultimately futile. I could subdue her with one hand. This isn't about her feeling scared; she has all the power here, if she'd only realize.

"Why were you almost twenty minutes late for your shift?" I edge up the hem of her underwear on one cheek, and the other. The material collects in her ass crack, flossing her supple cheeks and allowing me the perfect, palm-sized access to each swell.

"I... I wa—" With her head to the side, she's trying to tell me only what she thinks I want to hear. Oh sweetheart, that simply won't do.

"No, no. I wasn't finished with my line of questioning. You will learn to be patient, and answer only when appropriate. Do you understand?" When I'm met with long moments of silence, my hand is forced in more ways than one. *Crack!* My open palm smacks her ass, hard.

"Oh, fuck!" she wails.

I soothe her pinkened flesh by rubbing soft circles. This is punishment, yes, but it's not supposed to be a house of pain. I want pleasure coursing through her, like it vibrates within me.

"Let me begin again, hmm?" I rearrange the delicate cotton of her underwear, offering almost unfettered access to the swells of her cheeks should she dare defy me again. "Now, question one is why were you late? And question two: why were you carrying around enough sex toys to host a bachelorette party? Before you answer me, you will address me as Smoke, or Sir. Understand?"

"Yes," she nods. *CRACK!* "Yes, s -sir." Her pulse fires like a whirling jet engine.

My hovering hand pauses. She is learning. "Good girl. Now, answers."

Cally Rae turns her head towards the window and away from my direct line of sight. This won't do. Hauling her up to a sitting position, I drag her back to my front, banding an arm around her waist, and the other vicing her jaw with tender authority. Yeah, I'm the poster boy for dichotomy. Leaning forward, I plant a kiss on her jaw, her earlobe. Her breath seizes before resuming in choppy bursts. If she wants immunity from further spankings by sitting in my lap, she's kidding herself. "I'm waiting."

"I was... I was late to work because I came straight from another photo shoot. It ran over, and I was late getting back."

"Yet you didn't call me or text. Why is that?"

"Um, because I didn't think you'd notice. Or care. Take it out of my pay. Or I can make up the time."

"Oh, you'll be making up the time, but not at Wilds, or Kittens. You'll make it up to me in about ten minutes. And my second question, please."

That jet engine roaring in her neck is set for takeoff. Auburn lashes flutter over alabaster cheeks before her plump pink lips separate once more.

"The modeling I do is very specific," she begins, and I release her jaw so I can concentrate further on what she's about to announce.

"Meaning what exactly?" The arm banding her waist loosens enough so I can skim her shirt fabric up her thighs again. When I draw a finger over her crease through her dampened panties, I know she's as aroused by this little scene as I am. More, even. If I inch under the elastic seam and into her...

"I'm a fetish model. All the stuff in my bag is what I'm photographed with. They give it to the models because they don't want those items back. I mean, who wants a job cleaning rubber underwear or ball gags worn by fetish models?"

Um, okay. So, that's not typically something I've thought about before. Hold up. Little Miss Church Mouse, Hills Are Alive models ball gags, rubber wear and dildos? She's shitting me? She's going to burst into giggles and say the joke's on me. Any second now. Only, she's stock still, blinking those auburn lashes over those whiskey eyes that I want to dive into and swim laps in.

"Are you being exploited?" She looks like your typical door-to-door God botherer. Yet some sick fuck takes pictures of her in what exactly? Is she naked? Like porn?

"Before your mind goes somewhere it probably shouldn't. Let me just say that we're all over twenty-one and this is consensual. I have a contract."

Yeah, so did Brad Marchand. Boston still traded their captain. I spin her body to face mine. This conversation cannot be had with her in profile.

"And you're okay with this, this fetish modeling?" I sound like a concerned parent. Well, I am concerned, and I am a parent. Just not her parent. And for that, I'm fucking thankful because my thoughts are impure and unholy.

"I am," she coos. "I love it. I feel..." Her head cants from side to side, assessing my reaction and searching for the perfect word to describe how it makes her feel. "Empowered," she finally adds, nodding to herself, a sly grin beginning at one corner of her mouth before spreading across her beautiful face.

Well, blow me down with an actual fucking feather, and not our head of security.

"Tell me the difference between a kink and a fetish," I ask, genuinely curious. I have some ideas, sure, but if she's in the industry, she might know more than I do, and that thought stiffens my dick further.

"A kink relates more to something outside the scope of what is considered "normal" sexual behavior," she clarifies, making air quotes around the word normal. "While fetish, on the other hand, is a specific type of kink and sexual arousal around a body part not used in the act of sex." Her delivery is measured and assured. She knows her shit, which means my dick wants to explore just what else she has in her little tote bag.

"Some people have foot fetishes, so I'd get a pedicure and wear specific heels or maybe a toe ring while I rub pudding all over my feet. So far I've done custard, maple syrup, and pudding. Then there are the cum requests, but we use melted coconut sorbet or liquid soap depending on the lighting for those shots."

She hums, looking pleased with herself. I realize that this gushing interpretation of her *other work* is something she is at ease discussing with me, and she's proud to share her knowledge about the subjects. I'll be more than an eager student under her tutelage, early for classes and drinking in every drop of her knowledge.

"The armpit fetish stuff is harder, but harnesses work well for most torso fetish work, either hands cuffed to the back, or with a front binding."

I nod, transfixed and so painfully hard. If I readjust my straining erection, will she think I'm some creep getting off to an in-person phone sex chat line? "Is there any crossover where kink and fetish coexist?"

"Sure is!" she exclaims. "Kink can cover a wide range of desirable and pleasure-inducing activities, like BDSM, and that is the connection to harnesses, restraints and other wearables. The only stuff I'm not okay with is the ABDL stuff and the more extreme options. That's where they use other models, like this one Russian woman who has zero issues ticked on her job cards. Like, anything goes."

"ABDL?"

"Adult baby diaper lovers. Sometimes there is a crossover from pleasure and acceptance into mental health, and that's not something I'm equipped to deal with after Moonyata," she adds solemnly. "That's more for the experts. I'll do the splash sheets and blankets though, but that's it."

Knowing Cally has defined limits settles me. The thought of her in leather and rubber wear with a ball gag and butt plug is doing wonderful things for my aching cock, but her in an adult diaper kind of weirds me out. Rivulets of sweat run between my shoulder blades, sinking towards my waistband. It's so hot in here. Is she warm too, or just me? "Splash blanket?" I croak, loosening the collar of my shirt that is nowhere near my throat, nor restrictive.

"For the liquid play."

Fucking Jesus and his joystick! Pressure builds from my balls along the length of my pinned erection.

"Do you want to see some photos?"

Do I? My dick is already flipping the pages of her fetish album, planning on burrowing inside her tight heat once that cover is breached.

"Sure. I'm hard as fuck already, but why not? Torture me some more, darlin'."

Chapter 23 - Cally

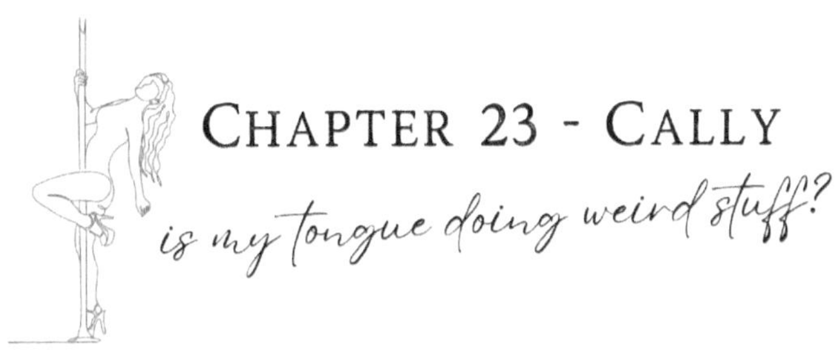

Fetish modeling was purely for me; an outlet of self-expression to release all those years of pent-up, closed-off repression. It was supposed to be my dirty little secret, only I don't think of it as dirty; I consider it long overdue *liberation*. Consenting adults are free to indulge in whatever makes their cup full and runeth over, and if that's bondage instead of baseball, hoods instead of hockey, and collars over charcuterie, so be it. I fucking hate sports. Perhaps it's because I don't understand most of what is going on, and because it dominates the screens at Wilds; rowdy middle-aged men all whooping and hollering over other men chasing some rubber disc or pigskin. I don't understand the allure. Male athletes in their physical prime, sure. I'm on board with that freight train. But talk of pucks and punts, points and assists; plus, minus, and yeah, you've totally lost me.

Only my liberating little secret is no longer clandestine. I blurted it out to—of all people —my boss. The fact he spanked me for disobeying him kind of had my mind fogged for a second, because I loved that, too. If the Righteous Moonyatas think sinners will be denied access to paradise and refused supreme happiness and beatific visions because of their impurity, the big man himself will be deadbolting his entry door if I ever ascend on one of those promised clouds. And it will have nothing to do with sneaking more toilet paper than was acceptable, either.

Removing myself from Smoke's lap and praying to anything that might listen to me, I don't drip all over him, I moved to stand. I had planned on grabbing my phone from where it was charging beside the bed and bringing it out to him. But no, he couldn't stay seated, could he? No! The man followed me right into my bedroom and around the bed to access the phone, effectively caging me into the space between the window, bedframe, nightstand, and his wall of hard-packed muscle. *Talk about impatient!* Keying in my passcode, which I can tell he's memorizing, I bring up the album titled "other work" and hand it to him. And I wait.

"Fuck, sugar. These are insane." He studies each image before thumbing to the next, his tongue sweeping out to coat his bottom lip, before he drags it between his teeth. He sinks onto the mattress, knees wide. "Has anyone else seen these?"

My head moves from side to side. I want to grab the phone, only he holds it away from me, unwilling to part with his prize. His enormous erection is evident, and he wants to play? Sure thing, let's play.

"Looks like those pictures made someone all hot and bothered," I tease, sinking back onto the mattress in my best alluring position. I'm still a novice at the art of seduction and might look more like a walrus lounging on sun-warmed rocks than a sexy siren. Sando often gets frustrated with my poses, urging me to relax more and go with it. Go with what exactly? I was raised in a cult, dude, what do you want me to go with, and how?

"One more question," he teases, reluctantly handing the phone back to me.

"Yes, sir," I say, plugging the phone back in and giving him my undivided attention. The serene smile that lights his face lets me know I've pleased him. Surprised, absolutely, but pleased.

"Your fetish modelling, the way you dress up and pose with items," his hand sweeps past me to the charging cell, "is impressive. But you must have your own wants. What do you need?"

"I've had sex before, as you know. But pleasure is new to me." My reply is shy and borderline embarrassing. Heat suffuses my cheeks, and he licks his lips once more.

"Have you ever come with a guy before?"

My head shakes vehemently. "Not until you in the cellar. I get myself off, but never with anyone until you. And now that I've experienced it, I want more of it."

"I can imagine," he says, chuckling.

"But it's not just climaxing with a partner," I add. "I want something else..."

"Such as?" One brow arches.

I can almost sense the cogs in his mind turning with each passing second I don't commit to an answer. Here goes nothing. "I want *rough sex*. I want to be railed raw, a thousand ways to Sunday. I want bed-breaking sex you read about, the no-holds-barred sex you can hear throughout the entire house. I want to serve and submit. I want to beg before I blow. I want it all. *All the time.*"

Smoke looks pensive. Rubbing a hand over his chin, he's deep in thought, and I fear he's about to tell me not to report for work anymore, but to go join a travelling circus because I'm a freak. I know I'm a freak. A freak who wants to get freaky. I want to burn down the bedroom until we're nothing but ash, knowing we coaxed every ounce of arousal and depraved pleasure from each other before collapsing into wrecked ruin. Finally, a salacious smile appears on his handsome face. The face I want to ride until he damn near drowns.

"Cally Rae," he all but growls, his hand reaching out to cup my cheek. The reverence of his touch, his calloused fingers on my tender skin, is a flame to my ready wick. "I believe we can offer each other something quite unusual, but profound. Is that something you are interested in?"

My body leans into the heat pouring off his body in waves. He's a tidal motion, a course set by the moon, and I'm the expanse of shore waiting for each future wave to lap. "Yes, sir!"

In a flash, his eyes hooded before widening to twin full silvery moons with blown onyx pupils. The cool lavender blue-gray is almost erased entirely, replaced by liquid alloy.

"Cally, I swear we need to talk about this a lot more, but right now, babe, I need to be inside you." His dexterous fingers have my makeshift nightwear on the floor in the corner before he sets his sights on my underwear. Torn between whether to aid the removal of the only item I'm wearing, or set to work on his clothing. I'm freed from my decision making when he barks his next command.

"Get on your knees in front of me."

I comply. See, I can follow orders. Maybe it's his military background, or that he's so goddamn sexy, but my willpower, like my clothing, melts away when Smoke Weir is at hand.

"Undo my belt. Mmmm, yeah, just like that. Now pull it through the belt loops and present it to me coiled in your palms."

Fuck. The concentration required is insane. Please don't let my tongue fall out the side of my mouth. Clamping my lips shut, just to be sure, I feed the pliable leather through each loop, giving the buckle a firm tug to assist my ministrations. Once his belt is freed, I wrap it in a tight circle with the buckle to the outside and lay it on my upturned palms for his approval. Smoke waits a moment, eyeing me with pure fire and unbridled lust. His fingers creep forward to accept the wound leather and silver, turning the coil over and over in his large palm, before placing it next to his thigh.

"Undo my jeans. Take them off. Briefs, too."

Once his button is undone and zipper lowered, Smoke hinges his hips so I can pull the heavy material off his frame, inch by torturous inch. All the while his gaze never falters from me as I concentrate on the task at hand. Getting this man naked should be an extreme sport, and I'd broadcast it on every television. Sliding each leg out of the denim, more inked skin is revealed. He has swirling designs on his arms and chest, but in the cellar's dim light, I couldn't make out particular objects and words, only that they had prominent real estate on his skin. Here in the warmer light of my bedroom, his calves and shins are revealed to host a series of geometric images, all jostling for space with a buck, a bear and a python.

Smoke sits on the edge of my bed, hands on his spread knees in only his work shirt, like a revered king. I kneel before him, in only a pair of cotton panties, his wanton slave. And if I could bottle this sensation and sell it at markets, I'd make a fucking fortune.

"On your feet," he barks, only his roughened timbre releases it more like a croak, the words thick on his tongue. "You are perfection, Cally Rae. Do you know that?"

His eyes drink me in like nectar flowing from a vessel, nourishing his soul. I could bottle this feeling too. Maybe sell them as a duo packaged deal. I stand tall between his bent knees; his presence makes my body reverberate with want. His hands grip my hips before skimming up my torso to settle at my ribcage, thumbs resting just under my breasts. My pebbled nipples begging for his touch or tongue. He offers neither. Smoke pulls me forward; his mouth collides with my belly, peppering a series of hot, quick kisses around my navel, before his mouth moves lower, his hands rising simultaneously. Just as he palms each breast with benevolent worship, his mouth covers the dampened area on my underwear while he *inhales*.

"Your fucking smell," he praises, "unlike anything else, so uniquely you. It's enough to start wars and end them all at once. Perfection."

Back in Utah, odor was something I was constantly worried about. Our clothes, whilst clean, were never dry, and the unmistakable waft of moldy fabric clung to us like cloaks we couldn't shrug. I used crushed flower petals and spices to mask the smell, with varying success. That awful fucking rot is by far the strongest reminder of that dangerous lifestyle. Now I beeline to store perfume counters like I'm being chased by bears, covering myself in anything from pretty bottles just as long as I *don't* smell bad. Smoke has his nose an inch from my pussy, and he's breathing me in as if I should be bottled on those counters.

My jaw slackens, head desperate to fall backwards and observe his dedication. I'm in so much trouble with this man. Without preamble, his hands lower, taking the dampened cotton with them before gravity takes over and they sink to the floor. As he stands, he tugs the shirt free from his body by grasping a section behind his neck and tugging. I've always found it particularly sexy. Today, I have no descriptors for his habitual action that has my pulse quickening.

"Normally, I'd like to cover every inch of your body with my tongue. Take my time savoring you. Learn what your body likes, and what has you coming like a train. But right now, darlin', I have no patience."

He grabs the base of his dick, squeezing it hard before running his hand down the entire length from root to tip, then repeating the action. I'm drooling like a melting popsicle. "But you've just admitted you want to be railed into next week, and I'm here, and lucky enough to oblige that wish, sweetheart. All I need you to do is get on the bed, on your knees, and hold on tight to that headboard for me. There's a good girl."

I'm no longer dripping; I'm gushing. A geyser of arousal at his filthy words and dirty promises. And I'm his eager student. "Yes, sir," I reply, fashioning myself into his directed position. Smoke falls into place behind me, adjusting my knees wider apart and further down the bed so I am in a kind of tabletop, submissive position. His hold is heated and tender, at odds with his barked orders and sharp thwacks on my backside if I disobey or take too long to comply. Every slap of his palm on my skin has arousal dripping onto the comforter, and I'm beyond caring how lewd this is; I just want his cock. The anticipation, I realize, is all part of the theatrics. His dominance over his submissive. His need to control while he fulfills my every fantasy. Smoke drags two fingers through my sodden slit, groaning when they come away coated in glossy release. I want to crane my head to see if the tip of his dick is leaking as much as I am. My subtle change in position sees another sharp sting, this time alternating on each cheek. Just when I think I can't take his torment for a moment longer, his cock is at my entrance, sliding, probing. He jerks his hips forward, only to drag them back again. I'm about to combust. When I think he'll repeat the motion for a third time, he changes the angle and enters me fully in one thrust.

"Oh my God," I squeal, shocked at his size. From the cellar, I remember him being long and thick with prominent traversing veins and the slightest curve near the end of his shaft. He is way longer and thicker than Scotland, and every guy I sucked off as a freshman before I was imprisoned into homeschooling. This position allows for deeper penetration, and Smoke knows how to move. Rocking his hips as his body curls over mine like the most delicious blanket. Rather than let my back absorb his entire weight, his hands bracket mine on the headboard, a battered pair of tattooed, masculine parentheses. With every thrust, my body surges forward, my head mere inches from the headboard as he powers into me again and again.

"It's Sir, or Smoke," he chastises as another *thwack* resounds on my tender ass. "You may feel like I am your god, but such accolades are premature given you've only had a glimpse of how I can satisfy you."

Lost in the moment, all I can do is nod, which earns me another, this time on the other cheek.

"Yes, sir," I say with gusto as his body straightens, his hands moving to my breasts to pinch and knead. Oh my, I don't have words for this!

"You are my every fucking fantasy," he groans, rutting into me while my hips press back into his groin, meeting every forward thrust with an opposite one of my own.

"Yes, sir," I say again, keen to avoid further spankings. While it's delicious, my ass is smarting, and I'm pretty sure I'll have enough trouble walking tomorrow. I'd like to sit without strategic cushion placement. He's so deep in this position, I swear I can feel him in my throat.

"Drop your hands, head down, ass up," he demands, and I'm more than ready to comply. My arms ache from having to hold that unnatural position. I'm more than ready for his next order. There is no next order, or positional change, because once I'm in a pose I think is referred to as child's pose in yoga, his pace quickens, as does his simultaneous attention to my clit. His thick fingers circling and pressing as my palms push further into the mattress. My inner walls are pulsing before I even remember to breathe. It all comes out in a flurry. My release, his release, and a slew of incoherent gibberish. He fucks his cum into me while I continue to flutter, body trembling and mouth so devoid of anything meaningful to say.

"That's right, breathe through it, baby. Just like that."

Smoke bends his knees like a frog, mirroring my position as he continues lazy thrusts in and out, while my body, languid from climax, welcomes his slower pace. "Was that what you had in mind for your first fetish session?" His nose nuzzles through my hair, seeking the shell of my ear. "Kink would have to be my second favorite four-letter word that ends in k," he says, nipping at my ear.

"I love dick, and cock, and lick and suck," I add, breathless.

"Woman," he groans.

"That's five letters, and doesn't end in k." His final *thwack* on my ass is the last thing I hear before collapsing into exhausted, satiated sleep.

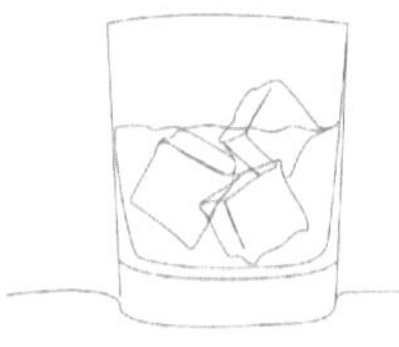

Chapter 24 - Smoke
The driving force

"Um, Smoke. Why did you stop here?" Her cute little button nose scrunches adorably.

"Because darlin', I'm going to teach you how to drive. Then you can get your license."

She looks across at me like I've asked her to donate a kidney, pulling that plump lip between her teeth before huffing out a long breath. I thought she'd be over the moon to learn how to drive. For a young lady so keen on her independence, being mobile must rank high on any list.

Unbuckling my seatbelt, I open the driver's door and make my way around the front of the car. Opening the passenger door, she still hadn't moved. "What's wrong?"

"What if I crash?"

"Then, you crash. Which I'm not expecting because I'm confident I'll be as good a teacher as you are a student."

She unbuckles her belt and, ever so slowly, collects herself and gets out of the car. I'm still leaning on the door like I have no actual place to be—a little enthusiasm would not go astray.

"Out!" I coax, frowning at her tardiness. She rounds the grill and places herself in the driver's seat, fastening the belt before realizing her feet don't reach the pedals, nor her hands to the wheel.

"Press the button to the side of the chair and it will bring you forward." She fusses with the buttons, first laying the seat almost horizontal, before slowly rising again. A siren to a sailor, a real-life Ariel emerging from the salty brine below. Then the headrest does something I wasn't aware it was capable of until she's in position to tap the pedals and steer the vehicle.

"Can you see out of the mirrors?" I ask, noting how different her driving position is from mine.

"Yes!" she barks back. Settle down sweetheart, I was only asking.

"Fantastic. Now, the numbers here tell you what gear you're in. That little one is for first gear, all the way up to five for fifth gear, and R is for reverse." She nods, taking everything in. "That's fantastic. This here is the parking brake, and if you peer down at your feet, you'll see in order the clutch, brake and accelerator, or gas pedal. Any questions?"

She shakes her head, the red wisps floating around her face like a flaming halo. She's a meld of devilish angel, and she's hanging on every word.

"Okay darlin', now we're going to put a foot each on the clutch and brake pedal. That's great. Now move the foot from the brake to the gas pedal nice and easy. Good, good girl. That's right. Now, when it's clear to go, I want you to slide the gear shift into one, and ease up off the clutch while simultaneously pressing down slowly on the gas. Then it's a matter of repeating the process to go through the gears to second, and then third."

She nods enthusiastically, the tiny freckles on her nose catching in the setting sun, looking so much lighter in the golden hue of early evening. "Here are the indicators, that's left, and yes, flip it the other way, that's turning right. Flip it down again to show that we're going to rejoin the traffic, and once it's clear, you can go."

Hindsight is a wonderful thing. What isn't as wonderful, is the clusterfuck of a disaster that is Cally Rae behind the wheel of an automobile. She lurches forward just as I look over my shoulder to a line of approaching vehicles. A jeep is followed by a motorcycle, and cresting the hill around half a mile further back is a semi-trailer. Without a single fuck to give, she steers us into the path of the jeep with a hiccuppy-hop at the pace of a sloth, before dismissing first gear altogether and opting to go straight into third. We're going to die. With one palm flat on the glove compartment, the other grips the plush padding at the shoulder of the passenger seat while I survey the surrounding scene further. How bad can it be?

"Watch out!" I yell as the jeep sounds its horn and the bike steers around the chaos and onto the other side of the road toward oncoming traffic, which thankfully there isn't any... yet. The semi is fast approaching, the *chhhhhhh* of the air brakes and squealing tires a noise I'll forever hear in my nightmares. Unperturbed, she begs the gas pedal for more power, and we shoot forward, following the bike onto the other side of the road before she over-corrects her error.

Perspiration shoots from every pore on my forehead, a machine gun peppering salty fluid. Throat dry and pulse hammering, I manage a panicked, "Um, Cally, maybe turn at the next road and we can reassess, yeah?" My mind pictures a visual of me hooked up to an ECG, the line cresting and dipping off the paper in violent directional changes.

With one hand on the oh-shit handle, I pivot in my seat trying to assess the biggest threat. Is it the semi barreling down on top of us, the approaching traffic, or the redhead humming, *fucking humming*, along to the Four Non-Blondes song on the radio? What's going on? We're about to die, that's what. Do not pass go, do not collect two hundred dollars, just await every critical decision to flash before your eyes. Almost four decades of memories blurring and fizzing across my vision like kombucha. This was how I was going to expire? No hardened battle hero succumbing to a sniper kill shot, or insidious disease as an octogenarian.

"Aw, we found what was left of his arm clutched around that hand grip there," a trauma response officer would dictate into a recording device before depositing plastic numbers throughout the macabre scene. "The rest of him was shredded through the windshield, as far as we can tell."

"Turn, Cally, turn! Brake first, indicate, no, the other way! Oh fuck, oh FUCK!" We somehow lurch around the corner, cheered on by the windscreen wipers now sliding in arcs across the dry glass. The echoed screech of the rubber blades, the diminishing sound of the air brakes and my percussion heartbeat—timpani of doom. The car comes to a complete stop at an angle near a driveway. She didn't pull it to a stop; it stalled. Unfazed, she smiled, pulled on the handbrake and looked expectantly at me, and the corners of her mouth turned up. I'm clutching the oh-shit bar with both hands, half hanging from the fucking thing and out of my seat. Holy mother of fuck, how are we both still breathing?

"Was that... okay?" she questions in between hums, pulling her hair into a ponytail with the elastic from her wrist. It's a move so practiced, unlike driving.

Was that okay? How we're not both jammed into the glove compartment is anyone's guess. Time for a lotto ticket, because the real Christmas miracle just occurred.

"How do you think you went?" I rasp after the ability of speech returns to my person.

"Pretty good," she beams, fingers tapping the wheel along to the beat. My heart is not working to that rhythm, all jammed up in my larynx. Holy shit. Breathe in two, three, four. Out two, three, four.

After a long moment passes, I turn to my student. "Cal, when you said you could see out of your mirrors, *what* were you looking at?"

She angles her body. "Well, that one shows the sunroof and the roof lining thingy, and the other one has some part of the car. I think it's part of the door handle; I don't know. I didn't bother with that one."

"And the other one?" I query, gob smacked. When I asked her if she could see out of the mirrors, I should have clarified exactly *what* she had vision of. And that's on me.

"Aww, that's my favorite one." She smiles, her shoulders rising and falling. "I can see you in that one, and you looked like you were having as much fun as me! When can we do this again?"

CHAPTER 25 - SMOKE

You have hairy tuckles

The pain in my shoulder is next level. I feel like I've done fourteen rounds with Joe Frazier. I'm surprised to find a swathe of fire draped over my arm, as well as radiating from the muscles and joints inside it. Cally is curled into me, the small spoon to my big one, my morning wood pressing dangerously close to the seam at the base of her back. While I absolutely will go there, the morning after while her sister sings Katy Perry songs in the kitchen isn't the time, nor the place.

Stretching theatrically, I dislodge her head of flames onto a pillow and extricate my way out from the tangle of bedding. I awoke in the early hours of the morning drenched in sweat, needing to kick my socks off for relief. Guess I forgot them in last night's order directive, and my body temperature let me know all about it around 3 a.m. Sharing a bed with another soft, warm body added to the incineration. It's been a long, long time since I've slept *a deux.*

"Good morning," she murmurs, wiggling backwards and finding no resistance. Her face pinches into a tight frown; her head swivels to seek me out.

"Morning, princess. I need a shower, then I'll be out of your way." Thumbing over my shoulder, I back towards the bathroom door, disappearing inside as her head falls back to the pillow and further slumber.

Her bathroom looks like the cabin of an ocean liner that spent hours in rough seas with a broken stabilizer. Bottles of lotion and tubes of cream fight for the space on the countertop. What hasn't claimed any real estate has slipped into the sink or fallen to the floor. Do I pick them up? If I do, where do I put them? The shower cubicle fares no better. Bottles of shampoo, conditioner, hair masks, conditioning treatments, and hair miracle. I stopped reading the rest. Sure, her hair is her literal crowning glory, but fuck me. Why so much shit? In the Marines we had one solid bar for hair and body cleansing. This chick is not high maintenance; she's in the atmosphere with Elon's rockets.

I grab a towel and wrap it around my hips, stepping free of the clutter and chaos of the bathroom, and into the chaos of Cally Rae, who is now alert, dressed and waiting for me.

"Did you find everything you needed?" Her tone is optimistic. Maybe she has to rifle through treatments to find the exact balance of volume and hydration her tresses require, but I'm just fine with a bar of soap, thank you very much.

"I did, thank you." Sitting down next to her on the bed, all I can think about is if Jo left some of whatever she made herself for breakfast on the kitchen counter. If not, I'll get something from Rina at the club. Pivoting to collect my discarded clothing, I straighten to find a look of horror on her delicate face.

"What?"

Her mouth contorts as her brows pinch together. "What the fuck is that?" I follow her gaze towards the floor and scan the timber and rug beneath the bed. A spider? Something tells me if there was an eight-legged intruder, she would be more screamy, and less accusatory.

"The fuck is what? What am I missing?"

"That!" she bellows, index finger extended towards my feet. "All that hair!"

Looking down, I follow the path her finger alludes to. Sure, I'm a guy with a few mid-digital hairs on my primary toes. Her reaction is more suggestive of an alien invasion.

"Your toes look like troll doll hair. Holy shit. You have hairy tuckles."

"Hairy what?"

"Tuckles," she says, oozing a clarity that isn't in the room with us.

"Cally, the knuckles of your fingers are just that; knuckles. They're not fuckles, so your toes don't have tuckles." She pulls her bottom lip between her teeth. I know now that that is one of her tells when she's deep in thought or pulling words into the English language that have no right to be there. "And troll doll hair? Come on."

Her resounding nod is cute, but really? I'm not *that* hairy. Not that I've compared my hairy tuckles —wait—*mid-digital toe hair* to anyone else's.

"Enough to tie up with one of the million fucking hair elastics you have lying around the place?" My question comes out exasperated, and I don't mean it to. She's a live wire in more ways than one. A refreshing innocence that is paired with a kind of smoky sultriness when she lets loose. Like she did last night, with me.

As I dress, pulling on my socks, briefs and jeans, I stay shirtless for as long as possible, reveling in her lustful stare and furtive glances. Sure, I stay in shape, and for a mid-thirties guy, I'm doing okay. Only now do I question the amount of body hair on my lower digits. "I need to eat, and then we need to talk. Set down some mutually beneficial ground rules." She's grabbing one of those elastics and tying her hair back as she moves past me to exit the bedroom. She pulls her long hair into one of those sexy as fuck messy bun things, while my shirt slides back over my torso.

"Oh, hey," Jo greets us as we make our way to the kitchen at the back of the cottage. "Thought that was your bike out front. Next time, let me know, and I'll make space in the garage." Next time? What is she planning for our future dates and the space between the requisite children?

"Sure," I mumble, slipping into the closest chair. Cally does not try to help her sister with anything on the other side of the island. She drums her nails on the table and peers towards the cooktop.

"We're kind of hungry," she says, looking longingly at the pan of sausage and eggs.

"Oh, I'll bet you are. The two of you worked up quite an appetite last night. I'm betting you didn't even hear me come home."

She's right, of course. Jo was at work when I arrived and came home sometime during the night. The idea of her walking into our symphony of wails and grunts doesn't disturb me anywhere near as much as it should. Then again, I have troll doll hair on my tuckles.

"There's sausage and eggs over here, Smoke. Make yourself some toast if you'd like because between you and me," she waves a spatula in our direction, "I wouldn't even trust her to make that. Also, coffee is from the machine just over here." She taps the capsule machine with the tip of the spatula. "Cally doesn't drink it, so don't let her make it. Coffee is a religious experience for me. And we were raised in a cult, so that says a lot."

I like Jo. She's a take no shit, pull all the punches kind of chick. A nurse who could hold your hand and soothe your aches away, or ram in a needle before ripping it out again kind of Nurse Ratchett if you did her dirty. All while smiling either way. I'm glad that at least Cally had her big sister growing up, even if she fled the home to start her own career as far away as she could manage from those crazy Bible freaks.

"I'm heading out in about half an hour to go shopping at Goodwill," she says over her shoulder. "Although *now I know* why you've given up shopping there, and everything you bring home now is silicone, leather, mesh or a combination of all of it." If Cally is embarrassed, it doesn't show outwardly in her body language. She helps herself to juice from the fridge, watching while I put two pods in the machine to make my one coffee. I like it strong and with as much caffeine as possible, regardless of the time of day. If you could stand a spoon in it, then I'm good. Coffee like river sludge and cigarettes gets me through the day until it's acceptable to get into the whiskey. Before nine might be frowned upon.

Wolfing down three eggs, three sausages and three pieces of toast, I watch her smear an unhealthy amount of raspberry jelly onto her toast. When she licks the rest from the knife, my cock twitches in my briefs again.

"Oh, sorry," she says, not the least bit sorry. "Remember we couldn't eat or drink anything that was red? Well, I'm kind of obsessed with strawberries and raspberries. Even with their icky little hairs, I still eat them. Oh, today is quite the hairy theme, hey!"

Her eyes shine with a childlike fascination. She must have had quite a shitty childhood to be marveling at icky little hairs on raspberries. What else has been repressed? Perhaps the fetish modeling and curiosity about dominance and BDSM are the tip of the proverbial iceberg.

"When your tongue is finished licking that knife, I understand we need to set some ground rules and talk about our expectations in the future. That will help ensure we are on the same page, and this exploration is beneficial and enjoyable for both of us. Agreed?"

She nods enthusiastically, her mouth clamping around a thick corner of toast before biting down hard and swallowing. My swallow sticks in my throat as I down the last of my coffee.

"Do I need to get a pen and paper, or do I just take notes on my cell?" I hadn't really thought that far ahead. With anyone else, a verbal contract would be more than fine. But with Cal, she is still so young and inexperienced. She knows what she wants, sure, but this exploration might open up other doors to areas she's interested in. Better to be thorough than to have it all turn to shit somehow.

We pull our respective cellphones from pockets and place them on the table. Fuck, I need a smoke. I'll need a drink too after we thrash this out.

"Rules," I begin, forgoing the cigarette in favor of sorting this out and leaving. Grip and rip, just like I did with the shrink. "You and I will enter into a mutually beneficial exploration of kink, the parameters of which are fluid and flexible. We will stipulate what we are keen to explore, what we might try, and what is a no-go zone. Is that fair?"

"Absolutely," she says, fingers poised over her phone screen.

"You've expressed a desire to be dominated. Railed raw; a thousand ways to Sunday, I recall your words were?"

"Yes," she says succinctly.

"Rough sex?"

"Yup."

"Sex while restrained?"

"Please."

"Anal?"

"Of course!"

Holy shit, this woman may damn near kill me. If she's not every fucking fantasy I've ever dreamed about, all wrapped up in a bright red bow, just for me.

"Spanking and discipline."

"Always."

"With paddles, belts, floggers and implements other than my hands?"

"Yes. I have a riding crop in the wardrobe. It's with the shock collar." Jesus fucking Christ.

"Any degradation?"

Her nose twitches as she chews on her bottom lip. "Some, sure. But I don't want you to urinate on me or make me walk the streets in a dog collar or eat from a bowl on the floor. Anything like that is in the freaky shit window. I'm not there yet."

"The fact that you recognize limits is a good thing. I would never urinate on you because, frankly, that's disgusting. Or treat you like an animal. That will never happen, so don't worry."

She nods, satisfied. "I'm happy to swallow cum though. Give me everything."

"Noted," I say, adjusting my erection for the second time this morning. "Is there anything else you request of me? If nothing comes to mind right now, that's okay; we can talk about it more if an idea floats into your brain."

She nods, but again, remains quiet. At least she is taking this seriously. Either of us could get hurt if we don't set down some parameters and limits now. Her eyes widen as if an idea has just lit the Edison bulb hovering above her pretty head, like in a cartoon. "I want to be tied up and restrained. I understand that's part of being submissive. I've done role-play photography as a dominant, and while it was empowering and all kinds of fun, I think I would prefer to be at your mercy."

She has thought about this. If she only realized she's giving me the greatest gift. "Is that where the shock collar came from?" Again, she nods, twirling a lock of hair that's escaped from her bun between her fingers. I want to be the one twirling that hair.

"Alright, then. Please know I will take the utmost care with you whether I am in a submissive or dominant role. While it's not normal for a sub to act as caregiver, I think we both need to agree that the wellbeing and safety of both of us is paramount, as is our mutual pleasure."

"Absolutely. I mean, if you choke me to the point I pass out, and can't work, well then you will need to find a replacement for me at work, right? And we both know I am impossible to replace."

A broad smile illuminates her delicate features. She's spot on about being irreplaceable.

"You may well be," I say, humoring her words. Everyone is replaceable, including me.

"Your turn to spill your wish list," she exclaims, continuing to grin like I've reached up and lassoed her the damn moon. This is her chance to hear me out and decide I'm not worth her time.

"Okay. I'd like to explore anal," I breathe out, eyeing her across the table. She doesn't flinch, fingers poised above her screen. When she says nothing, I continue. "As the recipient."

"Oh," she says. Tapping away, I'm desperate to see what she's inputting. This guy with the hairy toes is a freak. Do not pass go, do not collect two hundred dollars. Just fucking run. "Sure thing. We photograph a variety of strap-on cocks. If you give me an indication of what size you feel will work best, I can grab it the next time I'm in Chicago."

Just like that. Pick the dick you want, and I'll feed it to you, inch by glorious inch. She truly is a gift. Sent not from heaven, because neither of us is destined for salvation, but not the mires of hell either. "Okay. I hadn't thought about it."

"Maybe I get the closest to your dick. So you understand what you dish out, you'll also be taking. Isn't that the easiest way?"

The easiest way. Nothing about this is easy, per se. But it's necessary, hopefully all kinds of pleasurable fun, and educational for both of us.

"Sure. Do that."

"Any other requests? Other than your subbing for me occasionally. Are you okay with being tied up, degraded? What about breath, spit play, primal play? Hot wax, piercing, choking?"

"All of it is fine. And if it's not, we can address it at the particular time."

"Noted." Okay. Should we shake on it like a business deal? "Your safe word? Mine is raspberry."

"Hmmm, you've put more thought into this than I have." Chuckling, I add, "Chocolate."

"Any further expectations?" she asks before we both say, "Orgasms."

Researching fetish, kink and as many forms of bondage and discipline as I dare before the rabbit hole becomes one I want to crawl out of, was less fun and arousing, and more educational. It turns out that safety precautions and protocols are in place as much for the dom as they are for the submissive. Lost in heady pleasure can fog a mind and mute speech. Sometimes in particular scenes, a sub may not have full use of vocals, a mouth gagged or stuffed with cock. Safe words and signals aren't only for the movies; they're a requirement.

The relationship between the two, or more, depending on which particular rabbit hole you venture down, pun intended, transcends physicality. The mutual understanding of how the scene will play out, the trust required by all parties, makes the entire scene one of important parameters and opt-out clauses for everyone. The aim is pleasure, after all. No one should feel coerced or uncomfortable, and inflicting pain is more on the sadism route, and one I'm keen to avoid other than spanking. The way her cheeks pinked up so beautifully. The contrast between the fiery reddened handprints and the ice of her creamy roundness. Although the act was disciplinary, Cally was more aroused than I was during that scene, and I was granite-hard.

There is information on knot tying for purpose, the Japanese practice of bondage as an art form, of shibari. The way it is used can be aesthetic, sexual, or to aid healing from physical or emotional pain. It is both complicated and beautiful, and well outside of my patience levels even if Cally Rae were naked in front of me. Would I put it on the to-do list to explore down the track? Absolutely. Are there other forms of bondage and discipline and kink that provide a ... more *timely* gratification? Why yes, yes there are. And these forms of expression will form part of our mutual homework for the foreseeable future. Right now, though, let's just keep it simple. No knots, no ties, no props, no cries; just lots and lots of sex.

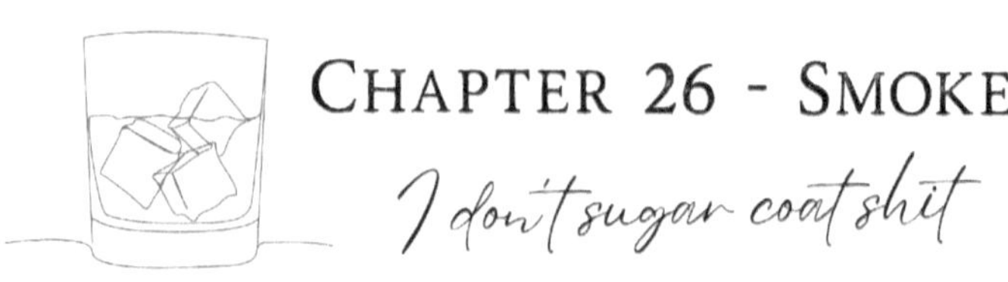

CHAPTER 26 - SMOKE

I don't sugar coat shit

"As most of you know, my initial bloodwork required for M.E.T.R.I. C.S came back with *anomalies*," Alpha says around the end of a dangling cigarette. "In the months since those first few tests, it seems the cunt that is cancer has joined me on life's journey." Ashing his smoke in the heavy blown-glass ashtray that always seems to be full, the room waits amid the thick air for the rest of his speech. While it should come as no surprise that an almost pack a day smoker for decades has been diagnosed with cancer, the realization is still a sobering one. I smoke way too much too, and I have a daughter to think about. A daughter that vanished just as rapidly as she appeared, and nothing our tech guy can do is providing anything solid.

The name and date of birth she provided on her laboratory sample seem legit, but we can't tie any social security or health insurance to that name or date. Christ, her mother could have remarried or changed at least her name and location after Kiara was conceived, let alone born. Part of what we do is locating people, so a teenage girl with a dumpster load of angst and rage should be a piece of cake. Should be. As the days turn into weeks, and then to months, I'm not as hopeful as I once was. Now my focus is pulled in equal and different directions.

Cally was promoted to the role of assistant manager by Alpha himself. He opted to pass over both Saint and Paul, the decision a strategic one. Elevating a woman to a senior position is not only great for optics in a progressive environment, he's set her a challenge to manage the male and female staff working under and alongside her. Not just another pretty face ruled over by men in positions of power.

The promotion makes sense now, alongside my new role as all venues manager because Alpha wanted to step away for a time. Step away my hairy fucking toes! He's been secretly dealing with a cancer diagnosis. One that he is now sharing for reasons I didn't absorb because I was busy thinking about Cally Rae on her knees before me. Focus!

"You know I don't sugarcoat shit. Life's too fucking short to play games. Yes, I have lung cancer. No, I'm not dying right fucking now, so if anyone treats me like I am, I'll shoot you myself." Hammer and one of the new explosives guys, Boomer, I think his name is, chuckle. I'm not sure they know he is serious.

"This is the first opportunity I've had to get the cabinet sorted, if you like. As you all know, we value time served here as much as we honor rank and title from your military days. Because we don't concern ourselves with biker gang petty squabbles, no need for enforcers. We all share that load, right, boys?"

Alpha stands to a chorus of "hear, hear," or "fuck yeah." Tapping the motto under the pistons logo, he turns to face the room again. "I need chemo. Probably radiation too. I'm gonna lose my hair, but not this club. With that being said, the decision I made is strategic, and one I think is best for the club while I am *otherwise indisposed, fighting this bitch*." His fingers raise to air quote his statement. All assembled members brace for what's coming. His preamble has done enough to raise the hairs on more than one neck. Hell, maybe my toes are joining the party.

"Wrench Richter, Chief's brother, is my new VP." The air thickens further. Wrench hasn't been at the club for all that long, and this announcement has the potential to ruffle a few feathers.

"In rank, we have a good core of seniors for decision-making protocols. Flint and Grave, plus Smoke and Rodin. Adding junior Richter straight into a senior role came with careful consideration. He outranks pretty much all of us. I don't think I'm talking out of turn to add that one of the few reasons he sits with us today is the passing of Chief. You definitely had another tour in you, son. At least." Wrench dips his chin. That's the extent of his involvement.

"Second, he's a prettier face than most of you assholes. We know about the town hall meeting next week. If anyone has to get up and speak on behalf of the club, best it be someone who looks okay on the evening news, right? Don't want your picture in the paper, Feather. That's a face that scares children."

Feather gasps in mock horror, his hand at the base of his throat. He's not the prettiest thing going around, no one other than Alpha would say so to his face though, for risk of having their own sent to the back of their skull.

"For some unknown fucking reason, the club has drawn the attention of Tanner Fulton, the trucker and logistics guy out towards Billings. The fucker tried to stop the compound being built almost a decade back. Before that, most of us just stayed out here in RVs. Anyway, once the plans were approved and construction of this clubhouse began, the guy has been pissing and whining like a bratty toddler. So, we turn up to the meeting in force, on our best fucking behavior, yeah, and we let Wrench do any talking. Any questions?"

Before anyone opens their mouths, a curt "We're done, everyone fuck off," sounds from the end of the room, the orator now facing the wall with his forehead pressed into the words we exist by. Honor, Unity, Respect, Trust.

"Listen, Wrench. All I'm saying is, if we go with her and take the bikes, she is less tempted to pack more shit. And if we go to that closing-down sale she keeps banging on about, same thing. The less she buys on the company dime, the easier it is to transport home."

Wrench flashes me a disapproving look. The one that tells me I'm full of shit, and he knows. And he knows that I know that he knows. Glacial blue icy rivers delivered deep into your very soul. Wrench shrugs a shoulder; it's easy to see he's finished discussing the matter. He wants a break from his—er, *girlfriend* is probably a stretch, but hookup seems a little too shallow, even for him. I don't get what Rochelle is exactly, other than an annoying pain in the ass, but to Wrench, she has the potential to be something. Only our trip away has been chaotically crashed by one Cally Rae Jenkins. All set to fly to and from Chicago for her latest photo shoot, only I opened my big mouth and told her that Wrench and I would join her this time. And because bikers bike, she has excitedly agreed to come with us, rather than the two of us riding there and meeting up with her.

I want a set of eyes on the company she signed a contract with, and some muscle handy if anything untoward is uncovered. She may be a demure, naïve young woman sometimes, but the people she works for need to know that if they fuck with her, they fuck with us. Nothing like former Marines kicking your door down to alert you to a problem. Only after I agreed to borrow Rina's helmet for Cally, and set up a bitch bar on the Indian to make the ride more comfortable, did I see the size of the bag she planned on taking. Um, hello! Bikes don't have trunks, sweetheart. Where do you suppose I strap your case to? My dick?

"Less is more," I huff out again. Frustrated, I offer her one of the small packs we used to stow our essentials for the trip. Granted, we wear the same thing pretty much every day. Riding leathers and boots. A hotel cake of soap doubles as shampoo, and we carry a toothbrush and change of underwear. This chick has packed enough shit for a month-long vacay for a family of seven. "Essentials only."

"They are my essentials," she pouts. Fuck me, why did I open my fucking mouth.

"I'm done watching you two fuck around. Come get me when, and if, you are ready to go." Wrench strides from the garage, shouldering out of his jacket. What is the common-sense solution here? Compromise—there has to be one.

"Cally, pack a change of clothes and toothbrush only, and your photo shoot makeup if you have to, in this bag only. If you need more crap in Chicago, or you end up buying stuff at the sale, then you can fly home. How does that sound?"

It must have sounded like a gospel choir because her eyes shone brilliantly. Flying to Chicago and back is logical and the best use of her time. But not her budget. She can't drive, doesn't even hold a license. Seems her kooky fucking cult family didn't see the need for subservient women to be independent. She complained that the bus smelled like old piss and was full of addicts, so the ride seemed sensible in my brain. Wrench's too, until he discovered I would be toting a *passenger*. Then his brows furrowed with enough force to crack glass. Except Cally Rae is the reason we are going to Chicago in the first place!

"Wrench, we're good. Time to go, buddy."

I watch him step into the garage just as Cally stuffs the last of her crap into the backpack. I, in turn, stuff it in the sparse storage bags on either side of the rear guard. This is probably the last big trip we can do before the weather turns truly savage. Twenty hours there, twenty hours back. More than fine for a couple of old Marine Corps buddies who love nothing better than to shoot the shit and marvel at the amalgamation of evolving scenery. The way the mountains kiss the fields and bow to the lakes beyond. How rural properties stretch for miles; bisected by the faded ebony snake, now a dull, silvery gray, before it's hemmed by lush pastures and state forests.

The first comments were welcome and, dare I say it, refreshing. Usually, the comms in my ear are barked from a masculine voice of command, not a soft feminine timbre of soft sweetness. Then my ears started bleeding, and I was an inch away from severing the comms connection between our helmets entirely. But there was still the issue of her arms snaked tight around my middle, patting or pinching me if I took too long to answer a question, or ignored her entirely. At the last stop for gas, Wrench gave me the look I knew was coming for about the last two hundred miles. The "it may have followed you home, and I let you keep it, but you clean up any of its puddles" look.

Her ass was sore, then it was numb, then it was sore again. Could she put her legs anywhere else? Um, no, not really. Could she swap seats with me for a while? Fuck no. Did she want us both to die? She said cow every time we saw a cow, and we saw a lot of damn cows. Then it was horse, and then I wanted to play Jolene on repeat for the next seventeen years, or until my ears gave up. The last straw, the final fiber of me holding everything together for the sake of this fucking road trip, was coming back from using the urinal at a diner to find one of her fucking hair ties dangling from the handlebars, and another on the gear selector. What the fuck? My ride has decorative ebony calamari. This is an Indian Springfield Dark Horse, and I am a man losing every ounce of damn patience with the woman who lights my fire but might damn well ruin me while it burns.

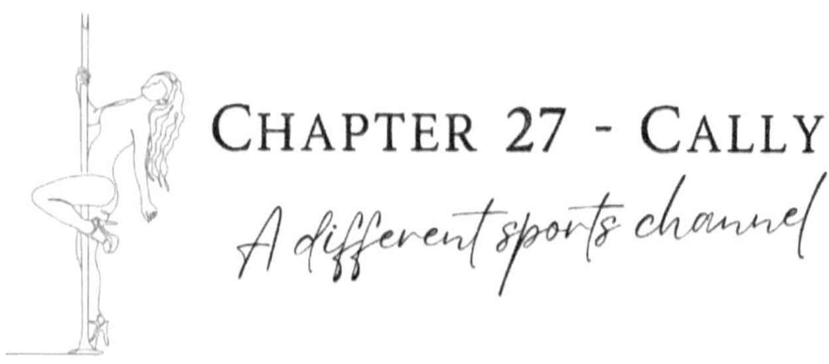

CHAPTER 27 - CALLY
A different sports channel

This sale is top-tier. I mean, I'm sad for the business that is going bust and all, but no one in their right mind would pay the original prices on some of these items. There is a bustier-type bra thingy with enormous cups covered in a tiny strawberry print for four dollars! Four fucking dollars. The ticketed price was eighty-five! It's well made, with a deep red satin ribbon tie to match the strawberries, but no way would I pay the original price. I have a feeling I know why they are closing down now, and I'm no business expert. Anyway, their pain is my gain, and I have two broody bodyguards with long arms ready to hold everything I manage to snap up. Manage, because this place is full of thirsty bitches ready to fight to the death over tube tops. I need to roll my eyes and glance over my shoulder for any argument over that metallic, ribbed bodysuit to be stomped out. Any tug of war dies an instant death once they spot Wrench and Smoke behind me. I don't even need to pry their bony fingers and unfilled acrylic tips from the item; they let go and back away. Ha, see ya! Don't you start your shit with me!

Now that we're back in the hotel room, and everything is laid out on the bed, I offer to show Smoke and Wrench the haul. I mean, this is *exceptional!* The Kittens staff will have enough costume changes for an entire year. Except for that fucking bitch Delta. She wouldn't squeeze her inflated assets into any of this, and that's something I was mindful of. Bitch can buy her own shit. Smoke knows my feelings on the subject, but I understood his, too. Kittens is a business for the club, and all our livelihoods depend on it doing well. As much as Delta is a desperate skank, she brings in a lot of middle-aged, overweight, balding men with big mouths and even bigger wallets. I don't like it, but I understand his principles. I just want her to stay far, far away from me, and him, even though he's not mine to claim. The thought of him being inside her makes me want to vomit.

Now that the successful shopping spree is over and another photo shoot is in the can, I can let my hair down and use some accessories on Smoke later tonight. Last night was a no-sex rule, because I need to stay fresh and tight for photos, not swollen and sore. The agency stipulated a forty-eight-hour moratorium on sex prior to shoots. How enforceable that is might be anyone's guess, but I need the work and am trying to behave myself.

Smoke enjoyed his blowjob though. Eyes rolling back into his head as his hands held my hair, pulling me on and off his rigid length until he came. The power you can wield having a man's dick deep down your throat is a heady elixir. With a pass of your tongue along a veined ridge, you can bring him incredible pleasure. Unsheathe your teeth and swap out those licks for bites, and yeah, it's a whole different sports channel. Smoke, I only ever want to see groaning in ecstasy, and the practice is proving positive for both giver *and* receiver.

Having him sit in on the shoot was *interesting*. Sando tried to dissuade him from watching, citing that some talent can be self-conscious or inhibited with someone they know looking on. When everyone on set realized that this wall of leather wasn't moving, they continued to set up the lighting and lenses, and I got my fetish on with a flourish. Some of my best work, even if I say so. Sando was impressed, even if he was less vocal with his usual directions, opting to whisper in hushed tones rather than his exuberant "Yas!" Wrench chose not to stay, not that the shoot was explained to him in much detail. When Smoke said modeling, I think he incorrectly assumed I was flogging shoes or mascara, rather than naked except for the leather hood, sub with nipple clamps and prince piercings.

I think he went off to some museum or art gallery thing, which is weird enough, but hey, I'll never pretend to understand the guy.

Once we had enough shots for magazine and retail clients, we wrapped. As is standard with every time I'm here, everything inserted somewhere inside some part of me is mine to keep. Stowing everything inside a plastic bag, I stroll over to where Smoke is waiting. He sat quietly on a box prop, legs wide in the manspreading way guys do when they relax. Just how relaxed he was is anyone's guess, and yeah, I noticed him adjusting himself more than once while we worked. We saved any discussion about the shoot and my bag of t*hings* for a time when Wrench isn't around. Smoke suggested it might raise too many awkward questions, and whatever. It's not like I'm trying to hide what I do, and I am one hundred percent not ashamed of what I do for work in either job. People are going to judge you with or without explanation, so I'll save my breath.

"These walls look pretty thin, so let's save some of the other stuff for when we're back home. Deal?"

Ugh. Fine. I mean, I'm keen to try anything and everything straight away, but Smoke has a kind of cool patience I can only aspire to. I'm all red rag, hey bull! And he's all methodical Marines stuff. We could not be more different, yet so very much the same with other traits. I'm sure poets and scholars have all kinds of fancy words for the predicament we find ourselves in. Whatever it is, whatever we are, it *works*.

"What toys can we use then? If you don't want any of the powered or vibrating stuff?"

"Keep your voice down, woman. If you talk that loudly about vibrators, it defeats the purpose of staying quiet."

"What if I don't want to stay quiet, or can't stay quiet?"

"You won't be once my hand strikes that ass, woman. Come here!"

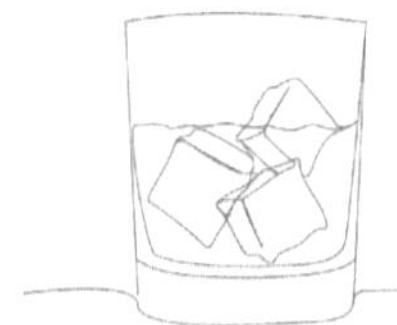

CHAPTER 28 - SMOKE
Gone with the wax

One eyelid cracks open, scanning the room for clues. Marines basic training: Evaluate, react, respond. No light penetrates the pulled blinds, meaning it's still nighttime. The bedside clock radio blinks 3:12 in a neon green, seven-segment display. Only then do I realize I'm the only occupant of the bed, and something smells like it's burning. I bolt upright. The warm tingle in my feet has my mind racing, and my heart rate irregular. "Cally?"

"Here," she beams, her cheery face coming into view next to the bed. She's waving at me with a popsicle stick covered in some purple dripping goop in one hand, and the flashlight from her phone in the other. She should appear demonic in the synthetic glow from her screen; instead, she looks *satisfied*. Either I drank way too much last night, and this is some crazy-ass dream for the ages, or real life just got all kinds of interesting. I ate her out and made her cum drip down my chin and neck before using it to lube up her ass, which I fucked deep, deliberately, and deliciously. We kept the kink to a minimum while Wrench occupies the room next door, so this isn't part of some scene I fell asleep in. But that smell! Do dreams smell? What is that, and if she's cooking, I ain't eating.

Without warning, pain slices across the top of my toe, through my foot and reverberates off every nerve ending up my calf and thigh towards my chest. What the actual fuck? Am I on fire? Cut? Burned? Bleeding? "Cally, watch out!" I scream, panicked.

"There, there," she soothes as I extract myself from the tangle of bedding and her hand on my ankle, almost kicking her in the face in the process. If there's a snake in the room, she needs to get off that damn floor now!

I stand, bare ass naked in the middle of our hotel room while she kneels next to the bed. Even in the dim light, I can tell her attention is on a small container of purple crap plugged into a socket near the baseboard. She rests the popsicle stick on the side of the pot. She jumps to her feet, feeling for the bedside lamp. Once she switches it on, the full horror of what is unfolding is evident, and I've never wished more for something to be a dream than I do right now.

"Is that... wax?" My head drops to stare at my feet, each toe dripping with varying degrees of liquid or semi-solid purple—wait, what is that?

"Yup," she beams. "I thought I'd get them all done before you woke up, but that was the first toe. Ta Da!" She holds up a raft of purple, twisting it to show the tufts of sandy fibers clinging to the goo like a carpet. Fuck my life. At 3:12 a.m., Cally Rae decided it would be a splendid idea to wax my toes.

"That hurt like a motherfucker!" I yell back. "Wash the rest off. Now!"

"No can do, I'm afraid." She smiles, and I almost feel nauseous.

"Fine," I bark, moving around her into the tiny bathroom. Turning on the water, I wait for it to warm before grabbing a washcloth from the side of the sink.

"Smoke, wait. No can do because you *can't* just wash it off. It doesn't work like that. You need to pull it off. That's how the hair comes out. They go with the wax."

"I'm familiar with the process of waxing, woman. I never signed up for it, is all." She lets out a frustrated huff, as if I'm the illogical, annoying one. "It's fine for you. You're on a flight home at nine a.m. Honey, I have a twenty-hour ride I need to be rested for!"

"The sooner you let me rip them off, the sooner you can go back to sleep and rest," she says like she's stating the obvious. Where did the wax come from anyway? If she packed it as part of my "essentials only" stipulation, I'm gonna be more pissed. If that is at all possible.

"Is there another way you can get it off?"

Her throaty laugh is scary. "No, silly. You rip it off. Be a big boy and you'll be as good as new, and silky smooth, in no time."

"That shit hurt. I can't do nine more." I shudder at the memory of the sting.

"I think you can. And right now, you've got no choice." She leads me out of the bathroom and towards the bed. If this has to be done, then I want a minor distraction in the form of her wet pussy.

"Get naked and grab your ankles, darlin'." If she thinks I will sit there and let her rip molten wax off my skin without something to keep my mind occupied and my dick busy, she's more deluded than I thought. And my mind is racing with what goes on inside that head of hers. If I'm balls deep inside her wet cunt, at least my mind will be on the *woman* and not the *wax*. Or that I was an unwilling victim in this *dehairing*. It's fucking toe hair, who cares? Cally Rae does.

"You're going to have to stand up and take me from behind. As long as I can reach your feet, we're good."

She doesn't have to tell me twice. Cally braces her hands in the tangled bedding, gripping the sheets in both fists as I enter her. The purple blobs taunt me as I thrust into her, establishing a steady pace. Reaching around, I pinch her nipple as she drops her hands and gets back to work.

"Fuck, fuck. Owwww!"

"Sorry," she exclaims. "I need to pick at the edge first with my nail so I can get a better grip." Her ass slams back into me every time I pull back before surging forward again. I'll give her a better fucking grip!

"Okay," I pant as I try to block out the pain of having tiny hairs ripped out by the root on such a sensitive patch of skin. How do women wax their pussies bare? Repeatedly. "Fuuuuuck," I roar as another wad of purple comes away. Attached is another forest of short, sandy hairs, which she discards, before bending again, ready for the next one.

My hands vice her hips in a punishing hold, but it's got nothing on her picking solidified wax off my toes. I've never wanted to punish anybody more in my life!

"Oh, that's it," she mewls, "right there. Right fucking..."

"There!" I finish for her as another marriage of tufted hair and shiny purple comes away. That better be the last fucking one. I want to look down and confirm, but the thought makes me momentarily dizzy.

"More, more," she wails. "All of it!" Her pussy walls contract around my dick like a wet fist.

"How many more?" I demand because I'm too scared to look down.

"I could hear you assholes. All night! More, more, and ow, OW! What the fuck were you doing to each other? Fucking root canal?" His tone is far from amused.

Wrench isn't known for his joviality. His cool look of focused fury fired right at me. "Um, the opposite end of the body, but just as painful." We've left a still-snoozing Cally Rae so we can get a start on the ride back. All she has to do is wrestle her bag in and out of an Uber to the airport for her flight.

"Get on," he barks. "Let's get as many miles as possible behind us before we need to stop for a rest. And you're paying for the coffee, asshole."

Flexing my toes in the cotton blend socks, I revel in the new feeling of... softness. The way the fibers slide over and caress my bare skin, uninhibited. It's the Bruce Willis moment from *Die Hard* when he flexes his toes on the carpet. River water coursing over submerged smooth stones without a hint of resistance. When I plant my boots on the dampened concrete, every step is... raw purity. The corners of my mouth tip up. Well, damn!

"Are you good? Or did your IQ slip out the tip of your dick along with your load last night? You're out here walking around the parking lot like Neil Armstrong on the fucking moon. Are. You. Good?" Wrench stands, arms crossed, studying me. Like he's not sure whether to confront me or have me committed. Or a little of both.

Man, I'm better than good. I'm silky smooth and supple, with no nicks, no cuts. Just baby-smooth skin for weeks. Damn, I sound like a commercial. Wrench cradles his helmet, flipping the longer strands from his face and smoothing them down. Before he situates his helmet and drops his visor, I ask the one question that's been playing on my mind for weeks now. Something for him to contemplate on the ride home.

"Hey, Wrench. Are your toes hairy?"

CHAPTER 29 - CALLY
Welcome to Toad Hall

The air is thick and stale inside this musty old building. It doesn't help that hundreds of people are crammed into a room that holds around half that amount. The rows of interconnected fold-out seats stopped long ago, so I mill about at the back of the room with the rest of the Ponderosa Pistons crew. A notice about this town hall meeting has been up at Wildcats for weeks now. Every effort has been made to ensure a powerful presence in favor of the Pistons and their collective businesses. Most of the people here work for them in some capacity. If they get run out-of-town like the mayor and his business executive mates are angling for, then a heap of these people will be out of work, including me.

From what I overheard at Wilds and Kittens, plus the limited stuff Smoke has volunteered, there is some crazy rumor circulating that the MC is running a drug operation out of their compound. They manufacture and distribute a range of illegal drugs as part of a crime cartel ready to bring down not just Bozeman, but the greater area and the state. When I was at my regular hair salon only last week, some ladies in nearby chairs were gossiping non-stop about the Pistons being an outlaw crime gang. Well, that was until I told them to shut their overfilled lips before I grabbed the closest pair of scissors and cut chunks of their fucking hair off. It took my colorist and his assistant marching me off to the wash basins to separate us all, and by the time I was marched back to my chair, the women were gone.

The sea of black-patched leather moves as one while members angle to get a better look at the setup of the space, and who is present at the speaker's table. I couldn't give a shit who is sitting up there or not. I'd much rather be enriching my educational experience with Smoke or binge-watching *Supernatural* with the packet of sour Skittles I hid from Jo. She arrived straight after her shift and snagged one of the last remaining chairs next to a colleague. I don't begrudge either of them that comfort, as trauma nurses they spend so many long hours on their feet.

"Ladies and gentlemen," booms a raspy voice into the microphone, the sound echoing around the wood-paneled room. "Thank you all so much for your presence here tonight for this very important meeting. Hopefully, we can allay any of y'alls concerns about who lives on the periphery of our great town, and what steps we can take to remedy this." A loud boo is heard, along with a few snickers, but the speaker presses on. When Volt ducks out of my way, I see it's the fat guy in a blue suit who reminds me of Boss Hogg. Come to think of it, every last one of the men sitting behind that table is fat, old, and skeevy-looking. Because I recognize all of them from Kittens. Demanding assholes who don't tip, but like to blurt outlandish requests to the serving staff while getting way too handsy to boot. Yep, this is a real-life *Toad Hall*.

"I'm handing the microphone over to a born and raised local and proud business owner. He's a respected member of the community, one that you all know. Fulton Industries and Fulton Transport are the reason so many of y'alls ranches and farms are thriving. I hope you keep Tanner Fulton and the entire Fulton family in your thanks and prayers at night. Tanner, why don't you step up here and speak to these kind folks about your concerns."

The mayor steps back to a short, polite round of applause, red face grimacing as he slaps his esteemed colleague on the back like toads do. I hate all of it. The boys' club, the backslapping and corruption leeching from business to business, infecting us all. Tanner Fulton is a carbon copy of our Boss Hogg Mayer, only he's in jeans and a red plaid button-down. It's difficult to tell where the collar stops and his flushed neck fat starts.

"Good evening, everyone. Most of you folks know me as Tanner, Mr. Fulton, or just Big T," he begins, before a voice says "Big Turd" and is chastised. The Pistons dissolve into raucous laughter, raising the ire of the bulbous man.

"Now, I will not sugarcoat anything. I want our town safe from crime, safe from gangs," he growls into the microphone, drenching it with spittle. *Why the fuck am I here instead of with Jensen Ackles?*

"Those bikers are no good. We don't want them on our land, infecting our businesses with their dirty corruption and poisoning our good folk here with their lawless lifestyle. I say we turn them all out and burn that clubhouse to the ground. All in favor?" His crow-like eyes survey the scene in front of him. *Oh, what a view he must have!* Church and bake sale ladies occupy the first two rows along with similar slimy, robotic business owners. *The back of a balding head with a horrendous comb-over belongs to the dentist, of that I am certain. I've seen it enough at Tanner's table at Kittens. Of course, if the Pistons were sent packing by locals with pitchforks, I'm tipping Tanner and his toad friends would have no issue taking ownership by force of the strip club. How convenient.* There are a few "hear, hears", but not nearly enough to satisfy the sweaty man in a crowd like this. *He'd want demonstrative declarations of war. And the crickets are chirping. LOL.*

"What are you basing your bullshit on, Tanner?" comes a female voice with a heavy Irish lilt from the middle of the seated rows. Only the lady in question is now standing, in a similar button-down, silvery hair swept up in a bun at the crown of her head. *She's been to Wilds a few times to eat and drink. She always ends up chatting to Sandra from the kitchen at one of the back tables, or when Sandra smokes in the alley.*

"Ms. Rand, sit down this instant," the mayor leans in and barks into the microphone dangling in Tanner's sausage fingers.

"Make me," the defiant woman retorts, and the room erupts into chuckles again. "Answer the question. Based on *what, exactly*?" Her voice all but sings to the rafters.

"Ms. Rand. You are speaking out of turn."

"Is she?" Wrench cuts in from the rear of the room. In his boots, he stands taller than everyone else except for Feather, and maybe Alpha, who leans by the back wall, knee bent up under him.

"And you are?" Tanner says, his hand flat at his eyebrows to see past the mass of bodies.

"Wrench Richter. Most of you non-club folks might know me as Jayson at the PMC garage, although non-club opinions don't matter much to me. Except for the lady who asked the question. Ms. Rand is a neighbor of the clubhouse, you see. If anything untoward was going on, as you alluded to earlier, don't you think she would be one of the first to know?"

The fat man coughs into his hand. "Well, you see—"

"No, I don't see. And I wasn't finished. If our closest neighbor has no idea what you're talking about, she has every right to ask her question, and we as a collective crowd here at your assembled meeting, demand an answer. So, *Big T*, what is your bullshit based on?"

The meeting descends into explosive chaos; the mayor is back on his feet shouting, while Ms. Rand is shouting right back. The crowd resembles one at a tennis match, necks swiveling first to one opponent, and then the other as a volley of verbal shots ensue. One has a microphone; the other has a fierce passion and an iron will. And Wrench, striding purposefully down the aisle towards Iss Rand. His impressive gait, powered by long strides, is almost regal. It's no wonder he is a commander of battalions, companies, fuck whatever they call it in the Corp. He and I have a kind of understanding. We tolerate each other's presence, realizing the role the other plays for the people we care about. He and Smoke are close, and Wrench knows I have the club's back not only out of loyalty to my employer, but out of a kinship with the mélange of burly bikers who come to drink, play pool and ogle naked women.

"We're going to take a supper break now. Won't you please partake of the refreshments on offer while we rectify this disturbance and remove those who have outstayed their welcome."

The person speaking is the third man. Younger than the other two, he has none of the sun-weathered lines that display a lifetime spent working outdoors. Oh no, this man has soft, almost manicured hands. He's a pen pusher if ever there was one; only the beady eyes are reminiscent of ol' fat man Fulton. Ah, this is his other son, Teddy, or Theodore. Hard to be impartial, Mr. Mayor, when your pockets are filled by the fucking Fulton family.

The front-row ladies dripping in pearls and gaudy floral prints are in the zone now. Lined up behind white-clothed trestle tables, they move with a choreographed precision, serving pieces of cake and tiny sand-wiches with stupid silver tongs. They move like the Righteous Moonyata Circle used to, when optics were important for winning over any possible new lemmings to Pastor Rich's rhetoric. Fuck their fancy sandwiches, I'd rather pick the hairs off every raspberry and just eat them.

"You, Tanner Fulton, are the issue here, not the motorcycle club, nor anyone else that stands against you. So shut your damn maw and sit your fat toad ass down, cause no one gives a damn about anything you have to say."

Iss Rand's words echo around the room. Junior Fulton snatches the microphone from her hand and retreats, not deigning the irate woman a need for explanation or apology. What a bastard. Not one of the Pistons moves to eat or drink either. They can shove their fancy food and uptight fake smiles that are all teeth and no principle. Jo and her colleague make their way over to me. Guess that's one perk of fire-engine red hair down my back. I stand out in a crowd.

"Never a dull moment, hey, Cally Rae. Sis, this is Jennifer. Jen, this is my sister, Cally Rae." I shake the older woman's hand and offer her a genuine smile. She has tanned skin and the tightest ebony curls I've ever seen. I want to stretch one out and watch it snap back to the mass of others on her head. But I hate people touching my hair without permission, and Jen might be the same. Alpha joins our circle, nodding to each nurse before bringing his palm down on my shoulder. Tonight must be hard for him. The man is battling a cancer diagnosis, and now this good ol' boy alumni wants to oust him and the club from the state. Yeah, good luck with that, only I do not know how powerful the Fultons are, and they have the backing of the mayor. How many others are under the umbrella of that filthy name?

The meeting came to an abrupt and early end after everyone assembled realized that the Pistons weren't despised as Tanner alluded. They were respected, revered even. Jen, Jo's nurse colleague, spoke of how supportive they were of the hospital. Always on hand for fundraisers and offering sick kids a ride on the back of a bike when their days comprised painful treatments that made them sicker than the diseases they were fighting against. A representative of the fire department talked about how many members volunteer their skills in the fire season, using small explosives as part of the fire containment system to protect thousands of hectares of at-risk forest. Speaker after speaker spoke of positive connections established, and questioned what right the mayor and the Fultons even had to try and run these guys out-of-town like it was the 1800s turning on alleged witches. The answer was none. Nothing illegal, save for a couple of speeding fines, all of which were paid on time. Wrench and Alpha were refused the microphone, and Iss Rand had been escorted out along with workers at her ranch. Not that it mattered though. Their voices may have been temporarily muted, but the voices of so many others spoke in their place. And their words were beautiful.

CHAPTER 30 - SMOKE
the things I wanna do to you

The town hall meeting was a distraction that postponed my plans by a day. That day was spent planning, perfecting and practicing. Now, all the patience I had has dissolved into the pavement like a popsicle in July. We're at my favorite part, actioning the plan.

"Fuck darlin'. Look at you. Cuffed to a pole, all tied up pretty for me. That tight ass in the air, high and proud, those heels slipping and sliding in the pools of cum soaking that hot cunt and dripping down your milky thighs. If I were a patient man, I'd take my time with you. Inhale your dirty scents, lick every inch of exposed skin until it pebbles in anticipation of the next sweep of my tongue. Then I'd fuck every hole until the stage was slick with a coating of cum that the cleaning crew would take hours to rectify. But honey, I am many things, and patient ain't one of them. Not anymore, and not with you..."

My muse stands, her skin slick with sweat. The chain securing each nipple clamp hangs loosely between her breasts. Her full lips are coated in a deep red color that matches her hair and the rings around my cock. Today's task was punishment behind locked doors and dim lights. No one has access to Kittens other than my master key, and I bolted every entrance point once Cally Rae marched inside in her crazy transparent heels and little else. The slip of a dress was torn from her body in seconds, strips of the filmy fabric sinking to the floor like discarded feathers. I hope she brought a change of clothing, although the armloads of stuff we bought on our Chicago run are in one of the storerooms, with select pieces also stored in my office.

We've fucked, she's sucked me off, we've fucked some more. Double penetration with me and a thrusting vibrator, and now she's cuffed to the very pole we walk past multiple times a day while managing the venue. I've dreamed of her lithe, silken body attached to it, at my mercy. Detailed visions of me smacking her ass while she deep-throated my dick, only to spin her around and fuck her some more before collapsing over her, spent and exhausted. Reality has been an eager, responsive mirror.

"Tell me again, the consequences for leaving your hair ties on a very expensive, very rare and important piece of engineering, Callista. Do I want your hair ties on my Indian?"

"No, sir," she purrs in a tone that suggests she's not remorseful at all. This will never do. My hand strikes her ass with precision. She yelps before pushing herself back into me, an effort to soothe the sting. Oh no you don't. Stepping back, I admire the blooming hand shape on her cheek. The contrast with the creamy flesh is delightful.

"Where do hair ties belong, Cally Rae?"

"In my hair," she grits out. Hmmm, that slap must really sting, huh?

"That's right, sweetheart. And when they are not in your hair, where do you put them?"

"On, or in something that isn't yours," she recites. Good girl, you *do* listen.

"That's right," I praise, and she smiles that honest, brilliant smile. The one that makes me think I am enough. What I have to offer, while meagre, is enough for someone to smile like that. Then, that dream dissolves alongside the popsicle drips, and the mirrored reality is a cruel bitch. This is an agreement, nothing more. We are here to explore each other's desires and passions. To see our needs are met and not fall into some starry-eyed fucking emoji about feelings. Restored to military settings, like always.

"Hands and knees, sugar. I'm going to fuck you one more time. To ensure you understand who sets the rules, and how I expect them to be followed." I lean forward, my index finger working its way through the slick mess to write three letters in the glossy pool.

"But there's cum on the floor. And it's kind of icky—"

"What does that say?" I point to the letters staring up at her from below.

"Now," she replies, eyes glistening with raw desire.

"At this point, darlin', you're lucky I don't make you lick it up. I would if I could vouch for the cleanliness of the floor, but I can't. So you are off that hook, but only that one."

"Gee, thanks. So generous." Her sass is spectacular.

"You should have thought about that before you defiled my machine. We haven't even covered the toe waxing yet."

"You loved it. Admit it. You even walk differently now. Your toes are free." Is she for real?

"You keep sassing me back, honey, I'm gonna shove something thick and hard between those pretty lips. Is that what you want?"

"You fucking know I do. Stop threatening me with a good time, sir."

"Such a fucking brat," I reply. She's the fucking tease, and I'm here for all of it; only the curt instruction dragged through the arousal hints at my intent.

She sinks into the glossy mess of our combined releases, the chain connecting her clamps clinking against the pole as she slides her cuffed hands lower. If I fuck into her from behind, I'm going to have to kneel in the mess too, and I will because it's proof that we recognize how to make each other hit the limits of our sexual pleasure, and tear through them.

"Fuck, I love it when you kneel for me. Smudged lipstick and thighs covered in cum. Don't think I've seen anything prettier," I state, admiring the beauty at my mercy, as part of our *agreement*. Shoving the thought aside, I part her thighs wider, opening her up to provide the most delicious vision of her well-fucked and swollen pussy lips clenching around nothing, just begging for my cock once more. I reach a hand around to increase the tension on her chain. Cally throws back her head in a euphoric moan. All this and I'm not even inside her yet. So responsive, so fucking eager for me. Lining my aching dick up with her entrance again, I thrust forward until her shoulder stops just shy of the pole. This is domination and punishment, granted, but I don't want to cause her an injury. Plus, I have shoulder issues from my time in service. I don't want to inflict that kind of pain on her while so young. There is a difference between being eager to submit and serve, and putting yourself, or someone else, at risk.

"Take my cock, mmmm yes just like that. You like it hard and deep, right?"

"I do, you know I do."

"You love it when I fuck you like this?" My hips pulse forward with each deep thrust. Given all the cum we're kneeling in on the floor, I'm surprised she's still so fucking wet. When I pull back, leaving just my tip inside her, my pubic hair is coated in a sheen of her slickness.

"I love it when you fuck me any way," she replies, her chain still clinking against the metal pole with each thrust. The metallic sound joins her breathy moans every time the tip of my dick contacts her womb.

"Good girls get fucked. And what do bad girls get?" I grunt, finding a deeper angle that has us both uttering a series of gasped profanities.

"Fucked harder," she confirms between her salacious moans, right as her cunt starts clenching around my thrusting dick. That's it, baby, strangle me. Her spasming inner walls grip me so exquisitely, I see stars.

I empty inside her again as white spots dance in and out of focus, a mesh of snowy fireworks and euphoric hallucinogens.

"Are you gonna behave for me then?"

"FUCK NO!"

Back at the cottage, I assist a bone-weary and half-asleep firebrand into a soothing shower, holding her up between the shower wall and my frame. Aftercare is as integral as the sex itself. The tender cleansing, the ointment applied with a soft touch to any wounds or forming bruises. Drinking adequate water and eating a hearty meal is also high on the list, especially considering how much fluid we both lost, either through perspiration or cum. Cally should resemble a crumbling fall leaf right now, bereft of moisture, parched, arid. Instead, she leans her head on my shoulder as my hands smooth a heavenly-smelling shampoo into her long locks, avoiding her eyes and sensitive skin on her face. Coconuts and vanilla and frangipanis, perhaps? The kind of alluring tropical scent you want to drive into, and swim laps in. Like her.

My fingertips massage around her temples, the crown of her head, and through to the shorter hairs at her nape, all the while she burrows into me, humming softly. That's it, darlin', let me take care of you now. Just relax, I've got you. Angling the shower head so that the flow meets her hair without it running down the front of her face, the hand not holding her up smooths back the curtain of white sudsy foam. It runs off her deep scarlet strands and whirls into the drain below, the rich scent lingering between us.

I use a loofah and a generous squeeze of equally heavenly body wash, this time a deep pink color, and gently swirl over her flesh. Achy muscles seem to sink at the gentle pressure, soft and warm under the stream of water and my gentle ministrations. Cally continues to *ooh* and *aah*, and this is one of the most perfect moments I've been involved in. This is dedication and devotion. An act of care towards another person. An act that swells my chest and turns up the corners of my permanent frown. This feeling of post-coital contentment and care lights me up from the inside out, knowing I'm responsible for someone else's pure happiness.

After she's tucked up in bed, with the comforter pulled high to her shoulders, we devour bowls of soup and crusty bread. I don't want to dismember our bliss bubble by allowing her anywhere near a kitchen appliance, for both her safety, and mine. Scooping the bowls into a nest, she places them on the nightstand and turns, tucking an arm under the pillow she rests on.

"Who would play you and me in the Netflix series about us?"

"Huh?"

"Hypothetically," she adds, readjusting the pillow to fluff it more to her satisfaction.

"I don't know. Brad Pitt, maybe?" We're both sandy blondes.

"He's so fucking old," she exclaims. "Wait—so are you!"

"Very funny," I add, pinching her nipple through her tank top.

"I think I'd want Emma Stone or Jennifer Lawrence to play me. And for you..." She drifts, tapping her chin with an index finger.

"Is Brad Pitt suddenly unavailable?" I venture. "As long as it wasn't Ryan Gosling. That dude has the most pinchable face. Anyone but him."

She's pensive some more. "Hmmmn, how about Charlie Hunnam?"

"Oh, I get it. He played a biker already, so you think he'll just slide into my shoes."

"Eww, no! You don't wear other people's shoes. That's gross. Plus, your hairy tuckles have been in there, just lurking..."

She makes a sour face, but it's the cutest. I have the softest, smoothest tuckles in the country. "Ever heard of socks, woman? A fabulous little invention. A tube of material sealed at one end that slides over your foot as a barrier between your feet and your shoes."

"And your hairy tuckles," she says, mouth disappearing under the blankets.

"I heard that."

"You were supposed to. What about Alexander Ludwig? He's pretty hot."

"Are you saying I'm hot?"

"For an old guy with hairy tuckles, you'll do."

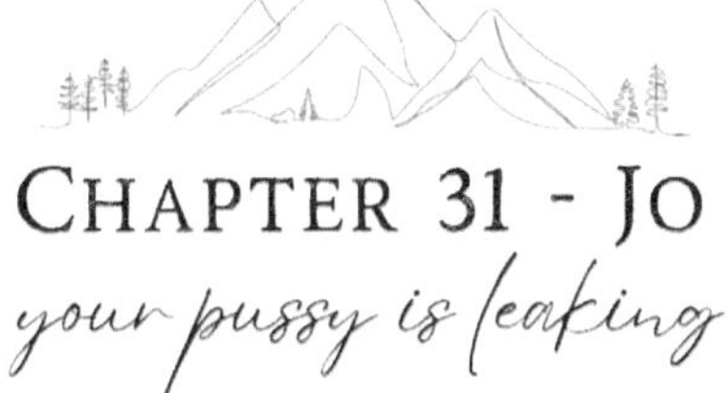

CHAPTER 31 - JO
your pussy is leaking

A nurse coming home at almost four a.m. is not unusual. A nurse coming home at four a.m. to her slob of a sister stress-cleaning is *highly* unusual. Slob is too harsh of a word. She tries her best in the common areas, but her bedroom and bathroom are a whole different war zone. To see her on her hands and knees, singing along to Sleep Token in a pair of pink rubber gloves I didn't know we owned—well now I'm more than a little concerned.

"Cally." I announce my arrival in case she hasn't heard me over Vessel's vocals, and I don't want to startle her. Whatever put her in this frame of mind has the makings of something emotional.

"What," she huffs out, looking up at me through red-rimmed eyes. Now, that could either be from crying, which I swear I've only ever seen her do twice, or the fumes from the ammonia.

"Lose the gloves, grab a drink, and talk to me about it. The spot you're scrubbing is a knot in the wood. All the effort in the world won't get that out."

Frustrated, she moves to stand, peeling each bubblegum pink finger off her own, before tossing them into the sink. I sidle past her, grabbing the half-full bottle of vodka from the freezer and two glasses. Toeing off my shoes, I sink onto one end of the sofa, gesturing for Cal to take the other.

"Spill woman."

"Uh," she groans, blowing out a long breath, whipping her hair over one shoulder.

After I left to study nursing, I was aware she suffered more than anyone should. I wanted so badly for her to come with me, but she was a minor, and I would be arrested for child endangerment or kidnapping. Potentially both if Pastor Rich was on one of his crazy rants. I will forever regret not helping her sooner. Before her fiancé laid hands on her, before the batshit crazy religious rhetoric turned into emotional *and* physical assault.

"Weren't you going to the MC tonight? I remember something about Alpha's birthday?"

"I did. And it was," she says, picking at her chipped nail polish.

"Right. So why the attack on the kitchen floor? What happened, babe?"

"I don't know. Everything was fine, until it wasn't."

"Okay, so everything was fine. Why don't you start from the start and fill me in as the events happened in chronological order? Then we can work out when things were no longer fine."

"I can tell you when they were no longer fine. When some asshole let the whores out," she spits.

Alright, looks like the band-aid was ripped off. No good story ever began with whores being let out. Pouring enough vodka into each glass to get her to open up further, I pass over her tumbler and settle back into the cushions for the rundown. Cally has a particular way of reciting stories. She'll get sidetracked five times, circle back twice, start a whole new story, introduce new characters and stop repeatedly. Only her furrowed brow tells me she is affected by whatever happened, or should have but didn't. Her behaving this way is most definitely not okay.

"A few of us were in the big room out back. There is a bar there, as well as pool tables and a dartboard. Your typical guy stuff." Yep, I can picture it all. 'And?"

"Smoke and I were sitting on one couch, waiting for our turn at pool. We were supposed to play the winner of Wrench and Hammer, or Rodin and RAM. These skanky bitches come sauntering in. They draped themselves over every guy there. Every guy there, Jo." She says the last part into the last of her vodka. Hurt is radiating off her like a furnace. She is burning.

"Did something happen to you? Did one of them—"

"No, no. Well, kind of. One came over and sat herself on Smoke's lap. She had only these tiny shorts on and was smashing her tits into his face and chest until he kind of pushed her to the side."

"Okay, well that's good, right? That shows everyone that he respected you enough to move her on."

"Yep."

That's way too curt to be convincing. "Something still upset you, though. Talk to me, girl."

"Another one came over the back of the couch and asked if he wanted *another round*. Like he and Wrench had previously. She was holding the hand of the topless chick, who was licking her lips like some thirsty slag."

"Whoa, whoa. Wind it back a second there. So, Smoke and Wrench sleep with the club whores. And you're not okay with that? Cally, it's a *motorcycle club*. Not sure what you think goes on there, but I'm pretty sure a whole lot of sex features prominently."

"I am aware of what goes on there, Jo, it goes on at Kittens, and in his office too."

"Okay. But something else is going on. You're bent out of shape about something. Want to tell me what? And let me preface that question by saying I know you and Smoke are also fucking because I hear you most nights. I mean, I'm sure the whole damn street can hear you two."

Her face sours, and she downs the rest of her drink and lays the empty glass on the edge of the table. Cal crosses her arms, her bottom lip jutting out like a petulant toddler.

"Wait," I exclaim, almost tipping over my glass in my exuberance to sit up. "You want more than a hookup with him. I'm right, aren't I?"

"No!" Her adamancy is hollow at best. She so does.

"And he doesn't realize because you didn't tell him."

"Oh my god, stop talking!" Her eyes roll to the back of her skull. Still not convincing.

"No. You need to listen. If he thinks it's a hookup, and you were fine with it being just a hookup, and now you're not fine because you want more, you must tell him your feelings evolved."

"I'm not saying that!"

"Changed. Say your feelings changed. Evolved makes it sound a little too Charles Darwin."

"Jo..."

"Cal..."

"Listen to me for a second. How do you think Smoke feels about the state of your bathroom?"

"What the fuck, Jo?"

"Humor me. Is he okay with the crazy fucking mess? I mean, Chris Hemsworth could be lying unconscious on your bathmat, and no one would know because you have so much crap everywhere."

"I'm sure he's fine with some stuff lying around."

"Ah, see!"

"See what? You want to go hunting for Chris Hemsworth?"

"No, silly. See my point now? You don't know how he feels about the revolting state of that room because he has said nothing, and you're just assuming he's fine with it. And you haven't asked him. That's what I'm getting at with your feelings for him. Do you see now?"

"You want me to say something. To him." She glares at me through narrowed eyes, incredulous.

"Yeah, Cal. I think you have to. Otherwise, one or both of you might end up getting hurt here. Fuck his brains out. Hell, honey, fuck the whole MC if you want to. But you all have to be on the same page, babe. I'd hate to see this go pear-shaped, and you scrubbing at spots on the floor that have every right to be there. You get me?"

"Yeah, I get you."

"Wonderful, cause I had a super shitty night. I was vomited on, yelled at and had to clean up two shits from a bedpan. One was so soft it was hanging over the sides."

"Stop. STOP!" She holds up both palms facing me, her mouth drawn in a tight line.

"Okay, I'll stop. But honey, talk to him. Please. And if you're hell-bent on cleaning anything, clean your damn bathroom."

Laughing, she turns to me. "Fine. And Jo Jo, thank you. I'll send Daddy Thor in to you when he regains consciousness."

Clutching the cardboard box to my chest, I offer hushed reassurances and carry the hope that I haven't just done something idiotic enough to get us all evicted. When Smoke and Alpha assured us that Wrench was fine with us moving into his brother's cottage, the subject of pets never came up. And if it wasn't mentioned as a priority, then it must be fine. My plan is to introduce the two rescue kittens as ours; one for me and one for Cal. Only Cally knows nothing about my plan and will torpedo this ship before it can even sail.

There are a handful of club members lounging around watching television, which might make this more difficult than I'd hoped. I mean, they have their own clubhouse for fuck's sake, can't they watch TV there? Then I could sneak these little cuties in, feed them and offer them some water and act like it's no big deal.

"Hey, Jo Jo," Smoke says, looking up from whatever movie they're watching. Cally is between him and Hammer on one couch, while Boomer and Wrench occupy the chairs. Nothing like having the actual homeowner here to witness my insubordination. A member I don't know lies on the floor, head propped up on his hands. Pushing himself onto his knees, he offers me a wave and a "Hi, I'm Volt."

"Hello. " I nod, not risking a wave because the load displacement inside the box is far from even. Both babies must be huddled in one corner. Awwww.

"What's in the box?" Cally asks, wiping the residual sugar from her fingers. She is addicted to candy, and her teeth will rot out of her head if she's not careful about oral hygiene.

"Um, well."

If I'd hoped to ease into the situation, all hopes were dashed when one kitten crashed into the side of the cardboard with enough force to dent it. All heads turn to face me, and the box, which I set down onto the floor at the edge of the rug.

"Wrench, I hope you don't mind. It's just that they were abandoned, and I felt bad, because I am a nurse, which means I am empathetic by nature. So I don't want to see anyone or anything suffering, so I—"

"The box, Jo." Oh, shit. Now I know why everyone fears this man.

"Kittens. Two of them. I'm sorry, I know I should have asked first, but they're all on their own. They need somebody. We can't have a dog because Cal is petrified of them, so I thought this might be a compromise, you know." He either doesn't know or doesn't care. Wrench blinks at me while I reach into the box to pull out the two tiny balls of fur.

One sinks its tiny claws into the rug, frozen in place, while the other walks underneath the table and across to Volt, who has sunk himself back down onto the floor, and is talking to the tiny bundle in the cutest baby voice.

"You don't mind, do you? I didn't think you'd mind. I should have asked you first, but I don't have your number, Wrench. Not that I want your phone number; it's just that if I had it, I could have sought permission first, rather than forgiveness and understanding now, which is what I'm doing now. Is it working?" Projectile word vomit is an ugly thing.

"Fuck, you talk more than your sister does," Wrench says, raising one shoulder. Is that a good shoulder raise, or an annoyed shoulder raise? Do I ask him to elaborate, or do I shut up right now and await the fate of these little babies? If he's mad enough to throw us out, I'm going to find alternative accommodation that allows pets, and fast.

"You won't even know they're here. I swear." I offer my best cheery smile and pray I don't look constipated. Having been raised the way we were, we know we're socially awkward. Trying to undo all the damage is a constant work in progress. Smiling in a mirror only helps so much.

Volt is cradling the mewing baby while the other extracts her claws from the rug tentatively before inserting them again. She repeats the process, tiny paws clawing at the rug, and releasing, her little backside wiggling from side to side. Aww, she's so cute! She's making herself at home here.

"Yosemite and Yellowstone. So cute, right? They can stay, can't they?"

Wrench waves his hand in a dismissive motion. He's not concerned about the politics of two tiny kittens.

Hammer straightens, laughing. "Um, Jo, your pussy is leaking." Sure enough, the closest kitten, the one making herself at home on the rug, is urinating all over it. The stream runs off the edge of the rug and begins pooling onto the floor. Oh, fuck.

"Ewwww," Cally shrieks, pulling her feet up under her. The kitten shakes off her hind paws and continues further under the table, all sets of eyes following her path.

"Welcome to the Pussy Palace," Boomer grins, doubling over with laughter at his own joke, while I fetch paper towels and cleaning supplies from the laundry.

CHAPTER 32 - SMOKE

"Mark in sight," I confirm into our shoulder comms. Our mark, or target, is the reason we're out in this weather. Tick Tock, fuckers, until we're home, and my fiery redhead and I act out our next scene.

"Copy that," Wrench confirms. "Teams two and three, move out." Our latest M.E.T.R.I.C.S. op was sent to us in a roundabout way by Akis and the FBI, is my guess. A prominent senator's daughter kidnapped with no ransom demands as yet. How this plays out on the news, if it even makes the news, is anybody's guess. What they won't divulge is the Senator's campaign funded by dirty money. Money paid for by some offshore mafioso contingent who now want their very generous donation refunded. You don't mess with the Bratva. When the senator's office shut down that scenario, the donors took a different tack. Now, Miss Kenya Klein is bound at her arms and feet, and if the widened whites of her eyes tell me anything, it's that she's fucking petrified.

Teams two and three are our explosives and munitions guys, plus Hammer, a former seal and Volt, who was a signals intelligence and ground electronic warfare specialist. RAM has a view from inside the warehouse, as well as the remote cameras around the factories where she is being held. Some Russians have been identified, and anyone left alive is to be collected by a team also under Akis' umbrella, which screams FBI and possibly CIA to me. My role is to keep my scope trained on the filth holding the teenager, with Flint watching my six, and Freezer watching his. Through the comms, I hear mumbled words in Russian before a gurgling sound, indicating Hammer has slit the guard's throat.

"How many?" Wrench barks.

"Three, maybe five, maximum," Tunnel affirms, once he's past the slain guards and has eyes inside.

"Copy," Wrench agrees, and the sound of muffled gunfire drifts through the chill of the early morning stillness. Kenya Klein won't step foot inside that building; she'll be liberated and bundled into our waiting vehicles inside the next sixty seconds.

"Clear," Boomer says, and the "Go, go, go" streams through the comms. All teams other than team four, my team, are mobile. Kenya is pulled to the side as the last guard's neck is snapped. The screechy, drawn-out *crack* sounding over the comms confirms he's done and dusted.

Team one takes possession of the mark, still screaming and crying, with panicked eyes and a stumbling gait. She's loaded into a waiting blacked out SUV with two of our medical team before it speeds away. Racing to the scene from the opposite direction is a series of more SUVs. This will be the cleanup crew. Akis, and whoever is overseeing this op, wants all bodies, deceased and otherwise. Those clinging to life will wish otherwise once the interrogation tactics amp up. In situations like this, the "who are you working for" is of little consequence. The key players are always known. It's the side dwellers, the parasites that use people and politics like pawns in the greater game of life and death, that need to be brought to justice. The whispers on the wind, the apparitions that no one knows of; who evade all drones and surveillance, that are dangerous.

Group four is the last to disengage. I provide cover fire for any teams or individuals who may find themselves with unexpected push back, sometimes it's a guard unaccounted for, other times it's some wayward, cowboy-type good Samaritan who thinks carrying their 9mm pistols concealed gives them license to get involved in shit they know nothing about. Thankfully, none of them get too close to be a threat, although that scenario is always expected, and trained for. Once we receive the all clear, I dismantle the rifle and scope, edging away from the lip of the rooftop. We sprint down the stairs, our boots thudding with metronomic precision as we move out. The final SUV waits for us to pile in, and we too, speed off after the rest of the convoy to deliver the mark and debrief the mission. Then we'll chopper home, shower, fuck and sleep like the dead for days.

The comfort my mattress provides is disturbingly absent. Perhaps that's because I've spent limited nights in my bed, opting to stay the night with Cally Rae. Her place, or Chief's old cottage, works better for our *agreement*, especially with Jo on night shift; we have free rein to do whatever we want and be as loud as we dare. Scenes aren't limited to her bedroom; no, we've had some outrageous sex in the lounge room and the kitchen. A kitchen I'm pretty sure she's banned from entering, unless I'm the one entering her in there.

So, I toss and turn and toss some more. I rubbed one out in the shower, desperate to ease the ache in my throbbing dick. The club girls were more than happy to see the Op guys return, and I thought about sinking into one of them, but stopped at the last second, passing her off towards Feather, who was more than happy to dive right in. My mind drifted towards her every day we were away. No matter how hard I fought to focus on the gathered intel and mission requirements, my focus was foggy at best. She's with me even when she's not. Then, I pulled a long, red hair out of my ass crack the morning before our final briefing, and it was a sign. A sign that even hundreds of miles away, that fine scarlet hair had me tethered to her more than any cuffs or ropes could. Heat fires across my skin, itching and burning as the contact of the sheets turns toxic. I want her. Even if we were not intimate, I'd be content to hear her laugh or glimpse one of those special smiles. Listen to her talk about her day or last shift. She has a habit of guessing what the occupations of some of the Kitten's clients are. I overheard her telling Grave one night that two out of towners in expensive suits could be mafia but might have another *cover occupation* to *confuse* us common people and keep the ruse alive. One she suggested could be a taxidermist because he had a funny smell about him and his stained hands looked like they were used to finessing skins and pelts. What the actual fuck? Where does she come up with this shit?

"And the other guy?" Grave asked, bemused, arms crossed in the typical security stance.

"Him?" she said, topping off glasses of spirits with cola from the soda gun. "He's a paper towel sniffer." A fucking what? Only you, Cally Rae! Only you.

My cock strains against the limits of these jeans; it feels like my entire blood volume rests between my legs. Tonight, we explore pegging for the first time. Cally has assumed a dominant role, and as much as I am her willing submissive, we have taken the scene further using restraints. She began by telling me to remove my boots, socks and shirt. Then she fastened thick leather cuffs around each wrist with the metal buckles located in such a way that the wearer cannot access them. Given time,

I could release myself, but right now, the only release I crave is out the end of my aching cock.

Guiding me forward towards the wall, she lifts my cuffed hands towards the hook where her bathrobe hangs. It's affixed to the drywall just above my head. Clever girl. The hook pierces the middle link of the chain connecting the bucked leather.

"Are you comfortable?" she asks.

"Yes, ma'am," I answer before her palm cracks into the arched flesh at my side. Heat blooms on the side of my ribs where a pinked palm print will be visible. She's not entirely comfortable in the Dom role. She's happy to be photographed as a dominant, but in real life, she is ill at ease as a succubus. Her desire to please and give pleasure overrides any intent to demand the same from me. I take her cues, her needy moans and increase in arousal, as confirmation that I'm bringing her the heady pleasure she craves, along with a side dose of depravity and domination. For her to wear a strap-on and fuck me, she will naturally be the dominant partner for that portion of the scene. We opted to lean into it and created a fantasy to satisfy both of us.

"Yes, Cally Rae," I correct. She remains unaffected by title. Depending on who you talk to, she is a fantastic dominant, or a terrible one, based on her ambivalence toward power. In any mutual exchange, both dominant and submissive carry power, the balance of which swings back and forth like a metronome. If she only knew how much power she had over me, clothed and cuffed to her bed, or otherwise.

Reaching around me, she slides manicured nails between my pecs and into the hair that starts again under my navel. A firm tug on a cluster of hair has my dick twitching again. Dropping my head between my flexed shoulders, the sight of her cherry fingertips so close to where I need them to be, but oh so far away, is pure torture.

"Hands flat on the wall," she commands, and I comply instantly. Nimble fingertips delve towards the button on my jeans before grasping the zipper with painstaking slowness. Once the zip releases the teeth, she introduces hers, nipping at the side of my ribs where her palm landed mere moments ago. Her hands grasp the denim, lifting it out and over my straining erection and down each leg to the floor below. A finger taps one calf, an instruction for me to step free, and then the other. Naked and restrained, I watch as a pearl of pre-cum beads at the tip of my crown. This anticipation, the buildup of flooding chemicals into a bloodstream heading straight to my groin, has me enraptured.

Her hands finesse each foot into position until I'm spread shoulder width apart and semi-reclined towards the wall, holding my hooked hands. Gloriously vulnerable in this position, my back arches when her fingernails skate back up my legs, now covered in gooseflesh underneath the layer of leg hair I won't let her anywhere near with hot wax. The delicate trail along the inside of each thigh has pre-cum dripping from my tip and onto the floor below. Holy Christ, she can tease. The popping noise alerts me that the lube cap is open, before the cool liquid drips from the base of my back and into my seam, where it's worked with one finger, then another.

"Breathe for me, baby. Do you trust me to make you feel good? To meet all of your needs?"

"Yes," I roar, panting. The way her fingers pump the cool liquid in and out has my cock weeping for joy, jerking in response to her ministrations as she prolongs the suspense, as awed at the pooling cum on the floor as much as I am.

"Holy shit. Cally. Stop fucking around and just fuck me already." My head lolls, shoulders flexing under the torsion from the binding leather. I hear more clicks, and hope like fuck it's the fasteners on the strap-on belt she brought home, the one that offers a selection of dildos that attach at the front of the wearable, all different shapes and sizes. We're not new to ass play, having incorporated it into almost every session together, especially when she's on her period. The first time I fucked her ass in the shower as she pulsed around me had the water running pink down the drain. We both agreed that it was a scene to be repeated. Only this time, it's my ass being fucked. Sure, she's worked dildos and vibes in and out to stretch the hole, but she allows me time to adjust to the sensations and offer up any suggestions on how the experience could be heightened. My only answer was her thrusting into me, just like I do to her delectable ass.

The puddle of cum on the floor threatens to spread to my splayed feet. If she doesn't enter me soon, I'll combust. Every touch, every hint of contact has my reddened tip releasing more and more of the pearlescent liquid. With teeth gritted, abdominal muscles pulsing. God dammit, woman.

"That's quite the picture you're painting down there," she deadpans, as one palm presses to the space between my shoulder blades. My toes, still silky smooth, flex in place as I concentrate on slowing my breathing to a relaxed rhythm. The way a sniper breathes when he's lying in position at a readied scope.

I detect a sensation at the taut ring of muscle; she's right there. Right fucking there.

"Do you want to use your safe word?"

"Fuck no!"

"Then I'm going to fuck you."

With her other hand resting on my hip, she enters me slowly at first, allowing me to get used to the size and circumference of the intrusion. To a guy, a dildo is a dildo. I've enjoyed most of the toys we've used on each other, save for the torpedo-shaped vibrators that are rigid and artificial. These cock-shaped attachments are firm while retaining flexibility and are realistic as fuck, right down to the veins and curves. This right here is why chicks get the better deal with sex toys. I can't imagine any silicone snatch mimics the real thing. I'd rather use my left hand than penetrate one of those ghastly things. Only I don't need either; I have the most incredible woman on my team. Ready, willing, and always horny.

"You okay there?" Her check-in is welcome, and necessary. A good dom defers to his or her sub constantly.

"Yes, Cally Rae," I moan, as she pushes deeper. She stills when she's fully seated, talking me through how much is inside me and how good I look with an ass full of cock. My brain is exploding with flooded dopamine, my cock openly dripping at a steady rate, rigid, thick, and the most aroused it's ever been when not inside a wet pussy itself.

"Keep breathing for me, baby. I have a little surprise for you." The hands at my hips lift, and I mourn their loss instantly. Only then does she reach around, stroking the length of my rigid cock with one hand. From root to tip, she strokes as her hips punch forward. The sensation is wholly immersive, and rapturous. As she completes her next stroke, she pulls a hair tie from her wrist before lifting my cock up, and fastening the elastic around my sack, ensuring it's as high as it can go. A pinch, a pull, but not painful. Holy fuck—we didn't talk about this, and I'm glad she kept this little nugget of information private.

"On, or in what's mine, was your stipulation," she purrs, while pulling down firmly on my sack before rolling it between her fingers. The sensation, along with the silicone cock rubbing along the nerve endings, is otherworldly.

That's it. I'm done. What usually begins with a tightness in the base of my spine explodes like a detonated nuclear bomb with her thrusts. White slashes my vision before everything fades to a glorious swirling black. Palms splayed on the wall, feet flexing, it's all I can do not to bite my lip as I growl, "I'm coming. Fuck, Cally, I'm... ughhh—"

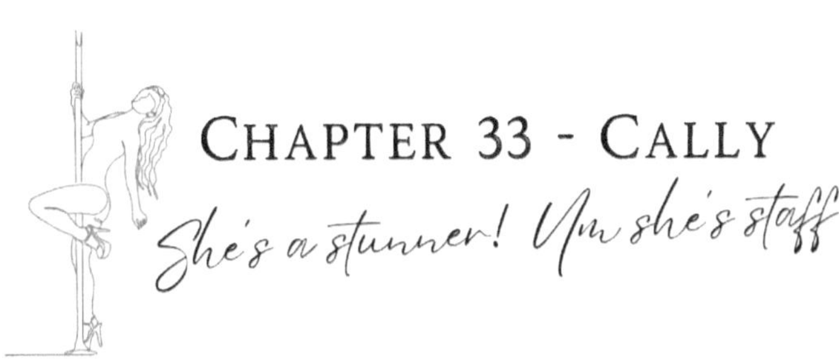

Chapter 33 - Cally

"Why the fuck am I not rostered on both nights? I always work both nights?" Delta is pissed, running her hands through her black locks, ready to pull them out. Well, that's unfortunate.

"We have a new girl, and we're mixing things up a little," I say with a practiced smile that hurts my jaw.

"Hell no. Where the fuck is Smoke? I'm not taking this crap from you, little mermaid." She stomps around, stabbing at the screen of her cell phone angrily. If he hasn't answered me, honey, he sure as shit won't be answering you.

"As assistant manager, I do the rosters. It's up to me to—"

"I don't give a fuck. No one here is interested in what you do or say. I need to work both nights!"

"You're not rostered on Saturday night. Only Friday."

"You stupid fucking bitch. I get why you hate me. You're jealous. We've all heard about how you dance! Bet you'd love to be up there with everyone drooling over you, only you can't because you're a pasty hoe with no coordination. I almost feel sorry for you! You know Saturday night is better for tips, right?"

Yes, Delta, why yes, I do. That's partly the reason why we're bringing in new talent on our busiest night. She's come from a club in Vegas. I'm pretty sure she can take care of your balding regulars while you stay at home and do whatever it is you do there. The thought of the girls hearing about my *audition* from the club guys sits in my stomach like a raft of sour milk.

"You know he'll take my side. You know that, don't you? That's why you're pissed and petty. I don't take orders from you, Strawbs. The minute he sees my message, he'll reinstate my shift."

"Maybe he will, and maybe he won't. He's busy with something for the club, which means *I'm in charge*. So, Coal, I suggest you attend to the sprouting chin hair that is so fucking long, we could rope off our VIP section with it. And get the fuck out of *my* office."

The stricken woman's eyes bug out, fingers desperately pinching at her chin. I note when she finds the hair, eyes bulging more than her mouth drops open. Yeah, that shit is nasty. For someone who works in a salon, you'd think she'd take more care of her own hirsutism before accepting clients. Who's the dumb bitch now, hey?

"That's Smoke's parents." Wrench gestures to an older couple who just walked into Wilds. "Anything they want is on the house, obviously. Blake and Dianne Weir. Be nice, CR."

"Absolutely," I say, holding two thumbs in the air, but he's already turned his back to greet the older Weirs. Kinda rude, Wrench. He's the annoying type of pseudo-older brother. The one that comes into your room, farts, and leaves. I keep hearing about how much he's been through and that he's a genuine guy once you get to know him. Only the club guys were a little worried when he flipped his lid after finding out his girlfriend was riding more than just his dick. Alpha arrived back at the club early after a chemo treatment, opting to relax in his room at the club rather than at his ex-wife's house. When Rochelle was spotted exiting a member's bedroom, rather than deny it, she propositioned Alpha instead. *Classy.* Rumors had been swirling for a while that she was getting around. Like any rumor, it was best ignored until proven right or wrong. I'd always thought her questionable breath was because of bad dental habits. Seems more likely it stemmed from the plethora of cock she was sucking. Good riddance to foul trash, I say.

Smoke emerges from his office in a charcoal henley over his dark jeans. Looking every part the sexy bar manager who had me on my knees again this morning. Wrench breaks free from the couple after sharing a handshake and brief conversation, slapping the man on the back before disappearing out the front doors. As the couple make their way through the pre-dinner patrons and regular drinkers and diners, Smoke leans over the bar, tilting his head for me to come over.

"That's my parents," he says. I nod, beaming my brightest smile. He'd told me this morning that his parents were popping in to say hello. His mother wanted to visit the MC and see how her son was living up in the wilds of Montana. And his father did what made his wife happy, so he tagged along for the reunion with his son. Part of me had hoped he'd elaborate further about his family, but post-orgasm, hurrying into the bathroom was not the ideal time or place. He hadn't even commented on the fact that I'd cleaned and tidied in there, culling empty product bottles and clearing the counter enough for him to add a toothbrush and deodorant. Not one word about it. And no Daddy Thor on the bathmat either...

"Son," the older man says while his wife shrieks, "Edward!" These guys are so cute. His mother is dressed in dark leggings and boots with a pastel sweater and matching scarf under a puffer coat. Senior Weir has an argyle sweater, suede jacket and blue jeans on, the same sandy hair with more salt dotting the crown and temple, he is the vision of Smoke in twenty-five, maybe thirty years. Same cool gray eyes, same honest face.

"Hey Dad," Smoke says, moving further along the bar to return his mom's embrace and loud kiss. She holds her son at arm's length, checking him over from hair to heels, as if to find out he's eating properly and getting enough sleep. He has given up cigarettes, though I hope he's communicated that to his parents. If anything good came out of Alpha's diagnosis, it's that Smoke quit cold turkey and several others, except for Sandra, have cut down on their nicotine usage.

"Have we got time for a drink?" his dad asks.

"Always, we're in a bar, Pop. The usual?"

His father grins and claps his son on the shoulder. "We've been worried about you, glad to see the wilderness agrees with you. And this frigid weather. At least your young bones can cope with these temperatures. Wait until you're our age, and you'll be back in Arizona whip-quick."

Smoke chuckles, raising a finger for my attention, and his father to cease his weather versus old bones analysis. "Cal, two Macallans and a Riesling. Please."

His mother points a finger, raising it up and down in quick succession. "Oh, I remember you. I recognize your stunning hair from the news story." She eyes her husband, impatient for his recognition. "Ed, who is this lovely young lady, please?"

Placing the scotch and white wine down on the bar, I hope my hair is tamed into a reasonable array of craziness, and wipe my damp hands on a cloth. Please like me, please like me. Please be open to welcoming me, to hug me like you hug your son, because we're pretty close, he and I.

"Cally, my parents. Mom, Dad, this is Cally." Wow, thanks, Smoke. Great job. I mentally slap him for his casualness.

I thrust a hand across the counter. "Your parents. Of course they are! Your good looks are a blend of both of them." Dianne shakes my hand, while Blake pumps it up and down in his meaty fist. He looks like he'd be the kind of dad to help swap out tires on your car, and have an arsenal of appalling dad jokes.

"She's a stunner. Classically beautiful. I can see why you're the face of these bars, Cally. You're way prettier than these ugly mugs in all that leather. Right, son?" Oh, Mr. Weir, you sly dog, you. But keep the compliments coming. Let's hope your son is taking notes.

"Right," Smoke almost mumbles. Tell him. Tell them. Claim me.

"Always nice to work with a view, right?" Oh, Dianne. Please continue! If only your son were so ready with the compliments, and weren't shifting from foot to foot, looking embarrassed. Where was all this nervousness when I was deep-throating his cock while thumbing his taint? Where? Where!

"Such a pretty little thing, and no ring. Blake! She's not wearing a ring. Are you single, honey?"

"I, uh—"

Blake adds, "No ring. I like it. Let's let them all think they have a chance, hey." Gulping down his scotch, his eyes twinkle towards his wife. Smoke looks like I've waxed his toes again. No one has a chance. There is only one man. The man shifting uncomfortably next to you.

"Is there a special someone?" Dianne gulps down a generous sip of wine.

"Um. Well, you see there—" My words are cut short by Smoke's statement.

"We'd better get going if we're going to make that dinner reservation."

"Oh yes. Right. Sorry, Cally, sweetheart. We're off for dinner now, we fly out tomorrow. That's the crazy life of retirement. Always so much to do when you thought you'd rest!"

"Mrs. Weir, please don't apologize." Tell them Smoke. Tell them about me. Please!

"Perks of being the boss, I guess. That's the best part of being a manager, right Ed? Knowing you surround yourselves with skilled staff. You look like great staff, Cally."

"Maybe you could join us once your shift ends. I'd love to hear more about what it's like living up here among the snowcapped mountains and the bison. Oooh, and the bears. Ed doesn't offer much, and even then it's after we've pushed with twenty questions. Bet you already know that, right?" I do know that. That's about all I know right now, lady.

"No. She has to work, right, Cal? Dad, you're corrupting my staff. "The older man baulks. "Right. Sorry, son."

Sliding his empty tumbler back across the bar, I scoop it up and almost crush it in my fierce hold. Yes, we work together. But we're so much more than that. We are, I'm certain. Leave out the juicy details but tell them *something*.

"The bar is in very capable hands," Smoke says, his arm around his mother as he guides the group towards the double doors and out into the night.

A trillion fire ants burn and blister my skin. I want to claw it off. Staff. I'm staff. He introduced me to his parents as staff! Bile burns my throat before I force it back down. Humiliation and I are old acquaintances. Nothing new here. Only this deeper level cuts through flesh and settles bone deep. A cavity overflowing with inadequacies. Another quill for my porcupine.

Shut up, Cally Rae, you've used your quota of words for the day.

Go away and cover that offensive hair, Callista!

No one is interested in anything you have to say.

It doesn't matter what you want; your opinion is irrelevant.

Your place is as a mute, obedient wife. That's all.

You're hidden away because no one wants to see you, or hear you. Ever.

The remembered, hateful words cleave through my sternum with hurricane force. A roll call of why I'm the one sequestered away. The one you don't properly introduce to your parents because I mean nothing other than three warm wet holes and a pretty smile. Daddy Thor may not be hiding in my bathroom, but I sure as hell want to.

CHAPTER 34 - CALLY

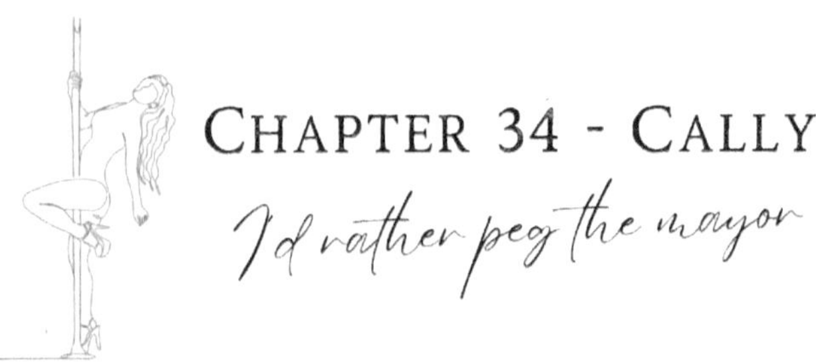

"All I'm saying is, you don't look sick, you don't sound sick, and your temperature is perfect. I don't know what could be wrong. Maybe you're..." Her brow furrows.

"Sick! Jesus! A great nurse you are."

"Hey. I am an exceptional nurse. You take that back before I empty the litter tray in your food."

"You probably do that, anyway. Is that why I'm sick?"

Today is the first official sick day I've ever taken. Even back with the Moonyatas, a day off was forbidden. The grain still had to be collected for the bread, and sitting idle was the devil's beckoning. And Jo is one hundred percent correct. I'm not sick. Well, I'm not ill, I'm just sick of everyone's shit. My attitude is at the top of that list, but I can't shake myself out of it. If Jo is right and I should've told him how I felt, and still feel, could all this have been avoided? Would I converse with the Weir parents, laughing at Blake's corny jokes and complimenting Dianne on her knitwear?

> **SMOKE**
> Hey you. Sick? Want me to come over and kiss something better?

Um, no thanks. *Right about now, I'd rather peg the mayor.*

SMOKE
The offer remains. I'll swing by on my way home tonight. Reach out if you want anything.

Pass. Anything I want, I can get myself. Or Jo can bring home. The only thing I want from you is the one thing you will never give.

The repetition of frustrated knocking just after midnight does nothing to ease an ache that isn't muscular, or some fractured bone or torn ligament. I lay awake and unmoving in this enormous bed, staring up at a ceiling I only focus on when under him, and count every time his knuckles meet the yellow door, then the siding, before moving to my bedroom window.

Saint's cheery smile and waves are a comfort as I take up my position at the other end of the bar. I took three days off in total, thwarting all attempts at contact. When Smoke sought Jo out, she shrugged and said it was probably a virus. That's what medical people do when they need to say something. Hmmm, it sounds like a virus. Drink plenty of fluids and get plenty of rest. Come back in a week or two if symptoms persist. I am unsure what is wrong with you, but if you disappear for a while, hopefully you'll repair on your own. How many people go back after that week or two is up?

Smoke and Alpha are both seated at the back table when I walk in, both offering me vague waves from a distance. That's not suspicious. When Alpha beckons me over, I think I'll throw up for real, virus or not.

Alpha stands from the table, kicking his chair back underneath with his boot.

"Just remember what I said, yeah?"

Smoke nods twice, blinking as the president departs with a dip of his chin at me.

"Glad you're back, Cally Rae. I'm going to take my leave because I've been told to be cautious around illness. I hope you understand."

Oh shit. The last thing I want to do is make him feel uncomfortable, like his immune system has enough shit to deal with, without adding my bogus virus on top of everything.

"Alpha, I'm so sorry. I came over because you waved me here. But I'm feeling much better." The lie tastes bitter on my tongue. The man is battling cancer.

His hand pats at the air, silencing my ramble. "I need to go. Smoke has something to discuss with you." Before I react, he's down the corridor towards the back of the building.

"Hey, you," Smoke begins. His usual placid face looks taut and pained. The lavender flecks present in his gray irises are absent. The party has gone, and the prison remains.

"Hey." The word slips out with little effort, or excitement.

"Feeling better?" he asks, optimistic.

"I was. Maybe not now. You're freaking me out a little. Smoke, are you firing me?"

"Firing you?" His eyes pop and lips part before he schools his features. "No. You think we'd fire you for taking a few sick days?"

Smoke, I do not know how your brain works, so, yeah, the thought crossed my mind.

"We are not firing you. This place would be lost without you." *This place* would be lost, not *I* would be lost.

"I need to tell you something. It's important and can't wait." His hands flatten on the table, fingers caterpillaring forward and back while he chooses his next words. "I have to stop our agreement." My head swivels in his direction. You what?

"Okay," I offer, numb to his statement. He could have done less damage with a long sword.

"Something came up, and I'm not in a position to continue. I hope you understand."

Staring down at the wood grain, I nod. "Absolutely. We'd run our course anyway."

He looks shattered. Like I took the same long sword to him. "Sure," he all but whispers.

Hiking a thumb over my shoulder, I motion to the bar. The very quiet bar that Saint has under control. "I better get back to work."

"Cally. I can't tell you why. I just didn't want to do it over text."

"I don't want to know why," I add, standing so fast the chair tips over. I don't even bother to fix it before I stalk back to the bar, my jaw-crushing smile set across my face. Horror rises from my gut as an oily sheen, gelatinous and repugnant. It coats the walls of my chest and settles at the back of my throat. I know that being punched in the mouth would be less painful.

CHAPTER 35 - SMOKE

you dirty fucker

One week earlier.

Feather and I wait by the door to the building, weapons drawn and ready. We've been shooting the shit and telling each other dirty jokes about what we've done to each other's mothers. This smaller op was supposed to be a get in, get it done, and get out mission to take possession of a prosecution witness with cold feet who thought skipping the state would keep himself and his brother safe from both the law, and the cartel he was testifying against. Only this dipshit didn't factor the Pistons into the equation. Cut and bleach your hair all you like; your fingerprints don't change as readily. RAM could match two partial prints on a door and a discarded soda can, so we came to pick up this shitbag and send him packing back to the DPP or hell, even the cartel can have him right now. That's because this shitbag flew out of the door we're guarding, spraying bloodied vomit around like a fucking fire hose. Dirty fucker.

Alpha and RAM saw it all from the vehicle, as did Wrench and Hammer, holding each brother by their cuffed hands. We know both are junkies, using way too much of the supply they're supposed to test, sure, not live rent free on. Wrench adds a little punishment to the procurement; rotating the asshole's shoulder in such a way that it dislocates. The squelchy, rolling *pop* as the glenohumeral joint, also known as a ball-and-socket joint, separates is a satisfying sound as long as the parting joint doesn't belong to you. The filth screams in agony while being frog-marched towards the waiting vehicles. Feather and I strip out of our gear, being careful to avoid further contact with this fucker's fluids. I freeze when I notice a glob of it on an exposed area behind my wrist, the area I cut open while making my way through a fence onto the site. The cut is tiny—the size of a grain of rice and not life-threatening—except it's an open wound in contact with bodily fluids from a known drug user and high-risk infection site. Fuck.

Boomer and Grave assist our gear removal, Grave washing us down with bottled water from his canteen and once we're at the SUV, saline from the supply kit. Feather is in the shit as deep as me, having picked at a zit or ingrown hair or something on his chin, where vomit also landed before it was wiped off. If I had to pick, I'd rather wrist than face any day of the week.

"Stand down, both of you. You'll need blood drawn once we confirm what that piece of shit has floating around in his veins along with the heroin," Alpha says, brows pinched taut.

"The risk of infection is minimal, but not zero. As you both know, not every disease has a vaccine. We do everything we can to mitigate the risks, but that dirty bastard rolling around like that while spewing, Christ it went everywhere." Grave shakes his head. Once we're buckled in, we head to the closest medical facility assigned by Akis to get a start on our blood tests.

The massive man sitting opposite me on another gurney is terrifying. The ugliest creature I've ever seen is tattooed across his ample chest and down his torso, the talons of which hang either side of his groin. The wings crest his shoulders and across each bicep.

"It's a Himalayan griffon vulture," he clarifies, noticing me studying his detailed ink.

"It's fucking ugly."

"So are you, but I'd rather have this on my skin than your ugly face."

He tells me that the bird is the second-largest Old World vulture and true raptor, with a wingspan of between eight and ten feet. The head is featherless, and its neck ruff causes an optical illusion of fake eyes, serving as a defense mechanism to make the bird appear larger and more intimidating to potential predators. More intimidating? It's fucking terrifying.

"Is that where the name came from? Feather?" The big man shrugs one richly tattooed shoulder, and the side of his mouth turns up in the slightest smirk.

Forty minutes later, Feather and I both had vials of blood drawn, some treatment called post-exposure prophylaxis, which comprised an injection of hepatitis B immunoglobulin and the hepatitis B vaccine. Plus, another briefing as to the risks of cross-infection. Fine in theory, only Feather wasn't in a face shield because they fog up in this weather, and my tiny, open cut was on a square inch of exposed skin where my glove stopped, but sleeve didn't cover as I moved.

As part of the debrief, Alpha makes a point of using today as an example of how it's not just an enemy with a knife or loaded gun, explosive device or physical attack. No, the risk of biological or chemical injury and death is just as lethal. Thanks for the pep talk, boss.

"Going by the lab results here, you both had decent hepatitis immunity according to your last blood tests, except for you with hep B, Smoke. You were flagged for a booster, and I'm thinking from your face that you didn't get to it yet?"

No, I didn't get around to it yet. The results stated a low-normal level of immunity, not that I needed another fucking shot. If it were that urgent, bold the font or make it red or some shit. Fuck. First Feather's ugly bird, and now this.

As the rest of the operatives disperse, Alpha, Grave, Rodin, Feather, Wrench and I remain in the situation room to discuss further scenarios. Pamphlets of information on HIV and hepatitis are strewn across the table. I can't bring myself to open either of them. Feather is pissed, muttering curses and vibrating with a furious energy. Guess he'll never pick spots on his face again. At his age, he should already know better. Me? Well, there's a reason I'm the guy lying under camouflage clothing on distant rooftops. A tiny nick from a piece of galvanized wire made a cut smaller than a peanut. It bled for less than thirty seconds. It was so fresh, with very little coagulation, that's why I'm in trouble. Again, fuck!

"Both of you need to lie low until the last of the results come back, which, as you know from the lab earlier, can be up to nine weeks. In that time, your bodily fluids are as much of a risk to other people as that fucker was to you two," Alpha says, monotone. "No unprotected sex for either of you. Ideally no sex at all because condoms are only 98% effective."

"Your semen is a risk factor for partners, as is saliva," Grave adds. "Until we can confirm no infection."

"No fucking, no kissing, yee-fucking-har," Feather erupts. "For two months. Fuck me."

"We can't, you're an infection risk," Wrench counters. Is that supposed to be humor, asshole?

"Feather, you can't work active security either," Grave says and the big man explodes.

"What the fuck do you expect me to do for two months then?" his sonorous voice booms.

"If you bleed on anyone you are removing from the bar, we're in a heap of it. You too, Smoke. Although you don't do a lot of work as it is," Grave adds.

I flip him my middle finger and reassess my next two months. Fucking hell, Cally Rae. I can't put her at risk, so I won't.

"Both of you are on full club pay, so don't panic," Alpha confirms. It's not the money; it's the principle. "And keep this between us, at least until we have anything to confirm, yeah?"

You don't need to tell me twice. Being vomited on by a hepatitis-ridden junkie dog isn't something I want to highlight on a billboard. Both Feather and I were careless, and we need to wait for the negative results.

"You can always come into the shop, me and Ham can find stuff for either of you to do," Wrench suggests. I know little about Feather's background, but I don't know the first thing about engines or transmissions. If something fails on the Indian, I send it to the shop to be fixed. I love it enough to stay away from working on it.

"Pass," I say, knowing he won't be offended in the slightest.

"Fuck that," Feather agrees. "I'm going to go stay with my sister in Ohio for a while and drink myself into a happier fucking mood."

"Great idea," Grave counters. "Get the most out of that working liver while you still can."

Asshole.

"Hey, Smoke. Thank you for coming to this scheduled session," Rodin says, pushing his glasses further up the bridge of his nose with his index finger.

"I didn't think I had a choice."

"You mean you wouldn't have attended if it were optional?" Good question, Doc. Would I attend a meeting with a club psych about my feelings regarding being deliberately sprayed with blood and vomit by some crazy junkie? I'd rather eat Cally Rae's cooking again, to be honest.

"I'm not a *talk about your feelings* kind of guy, no offence."

"None taken."

"You look offended."

"Do I?" He smiles warmly, uncrossing and recrossing his ankles. "Tell me how offense looks."

Nice move, Rodin. I'd never play chess or any competitive sport against this guy. I've seen too many brothers complain about always losing to him at snooker, only to declare they were too drunk, or he had the better cue. It's never the alcohol, nor the cue. The guy calculates risk more than anyone else, including me. And I was trained to calculate wind direction and velocity, trajectory and a multitude of other factors when setting up a kill shot.

"It's acceptable to be angry."

"I'm not angry," I bark back angrily. "I'm just frustrated."

"Again, perfectly acceptable."

Nodding, I counter, "Is Feather angry?"

"Smoke, you know I can't discuss other patients with you." He sits forward, resting his clasped hands on his knees. How the fuck does RAM put up with this? The body language, the mannerisms—it's all part of the same chess game. One I won't win.

"He sat on this same couch twenty minutes ago. I could have stood in the hallway and listened to the entire conversation," I add, more frustrated with the psych's line of questioning than the whole deliberate contagion. Well, almost.

"Ah," he says, smiling. "That would be unethical of you."

"Like some HIV and hepatitis-ridden asshole blowing chunks all over us? Unethical like that, you mean?"

"I can't speak for the person taken into custody, Smoke. But I agree his actions were inappropriate."

Inappropriate? That's buying a Phillips-head screwdriver when you need a flathead one. Not covering people in your own bloody vomit on purpose. When the silence drags on, he changes tack. In military terms, abandoning a frontal surge assault and opting to move around the back in a pincer movement. Only you need the other side of the claw for a pincer attack to be effective.

"Is there anything else you'd like to talk about? How is your sexual exploration going?"

"Well, Doc, it isn't. It dived over the same fucking cliff as pussy sex did when that prick vomited on us. So, I'm guessing all roads lead to Rome."

"I apologize if I was insensitive, Edward. All I meant was, you can continue to explore this awakening in other ways, without penetration." That soft smile ghosts his lips once more.

"You know what is insensitive, you calling me fucking Edward. Are we done yet?" I fume.

"Sure, thank you for your time, Smoke. See you next week."

Ugh.

CHAPTER 36 - JO
You using the word lubricants...

"Out with it."

Cally has been cleaning the cottage as if she's being paid by the hour. The floors, baseboards, power sockets, lights, lamps. She's vacuumed, dusted, polished. I'm pretty sure she emptied the litter box without being asked to. Not in my food either. She gets up, eats, cleans until she has to work, works, comes home, cleans some more and collapses into bed to do it all again. I'd be ecstatic about her homemaker skills except I'm certain there is more hiding under her baseball hat and rubber gloves.

"Jo, come on. I'm tired."

"I'm not surprised. You dusted the fucking ceiling roses in a house with fourteen-foot ceilings." Her exhausted body slumps into the nearest chair before Yosemite sneaks around the side of the leg and grabs hold of her socked feet for dear life. Her foot is held hostage by the tiny paws as the kitten bites down on her big toe.

"Fuck, fluff. Fuck off." With a subtle shake, she dislodges the wee beastie and tucks her feet up under her butt for safekeeping. Annoyed, the kitten pulls a stray hair tie off the low table and flings it into the air.

"If you have the stamina to clean, you can converse, woman. Spill."

Cally eyes me, half frustrated, half—is that relief? She doesn't have a whole lot of female friends up here and couldn't stand any of the circle from Utah. That leaves her old friends back in Texas, me, and a couple of strippers and the cook from the club? If she has something to say, she's limited for options if I'm at work. Now though, she's my entire focus, and we are not moving until I work out what the hell is going on.

"I'm fine."

"You're not though. So try again." I read people's body language for a living.

Blowing out a breath, she pulls the cap from her head and tosses it to the floor for Yellowstone to explore. "I'm whelmed again. I don't know what to do."

"What happened?"

"I don't know. Ugh, Smoke's parents came to the bar, and he introduced me as staff."

"Right," I encourage, because when the rubber hits the road, she *is* staff.

"What were you hoping to be introduced as?" My hand claps over my mouth. "Wait, you never told him how you felt! Cally Rae, what the hell?"

"Shush!" she growls, as if Smoke can hear us from the MC. "I was going to. I never got the opportunity to."

"You liar!" I chide. "That was weeks ago. What is wrong with you?"

She stiffens, shoulders rounding. "A lot, apparently."

"No, no, babe. Don't you beat yourself up over this. At least he introduced you to his parents, that's a start, right?"

"Yeah, *as staff*!" Her face is aghast, mouth puckered and brow pinched.

"Okay, so his delivery needs work. That's okay." I clasp my hands, hopeful.

"No, it's not. If that was all it was, then I'd be okay because we could work up to something more."

"What are you guys?"

"Oh," she says under a bitter laugh. "Nothing. We're nothing *now*."

"But you were something, right? You guys used to scare the cats with your slapping, thumping, gagging, and moaning. My God, the poor things were terrified." I scoop up Yosemite and bop her tiny nose.

"We had a kind of mutual agreement."

"Is that what you kids are calling hookups these days?" I'm interested in the answer to this. I'm not old, and we were both dragged into, and out of, a cult.

"Hookups sounds so *middle school*, Jo. We were helping each other with sexual exploration."

I almost choked on my saliva; pools of it collected, threatening my ability to speak. "You were what? He's a mid-thirties army guy who is part of a biker MC. I'm pretty sure he explores all kinds of sex, honey." The number of times I swallow must look odd.

"Not like that." Her arm waves at me dismissively. "He knows I like it rough, and we tried all kinds of kinky shit to work out where my limits were. Turns out I have none!"

She looks way too proud for me to interrupt, so I stare at her, hands clasped so I don't fidget. If she's talking, I'm listening.

"And I stuck a whole heap of sex toys up his ass to work out what he liked most. And it ended up being me pegging him in a strap-on while his balls were bound with a hair tie. Probably that one."

She gestures at the circle of elastic being chewed by my kitten, flicked up into the air before she rolls to her back and attacks it with all four paws. When I say that I'm not freaked out by much, I mean every goddamn word. The vivid imagery playing inside my head right now is well and truly freaking me out.

So, I call on my best triage nurse persona. "Do you understand how dangerous objects in the anus can be? We see hundreds of patients in the ER each year with action figures and kitchen implements shoved where—"

"All perfectly safe, clean and brand spanking new silicone dildos and vibes, Jo. It's not like Buzz Lightyear was shoved up there searching for infinity and beyond. How irresponsible do you think we are?"

When I'm silent a beat too long, she sighs and rolls her eyes. "Don't answer that."

"I don't think you guys are irresponsible at all! If you're using proper lubricants and clean silicone toys, then that shows a high level of maturity." I nod, continuing to squeeze my hands tightly.

"OMG, stop! You using the word *lubricants* like that makes me think of sex-ed class."

Yeah, noted. This is all kinds of weird now. I'd stress-clean too if my fuck-buddy had my hair tie wrapped around his balls. "Did something else happen?"

"Yeah, it did. He called me over to the MC table before my work shift about a week ago. Alpha called me over. He and Smoke had been talking, then Alpha beckoned me over and left. Not before he told me Smoke wanted to talk to me. And Smoke ended the agreement. Just like that." Her lip trembles as she speaks the last words.

"Oh, Cally. This is what I was worried about. Someone getting hurt."

"I know," she sobs. "And I tell you what, I worked that shift like a damn boss. But the minute I came home, I fell apart. Because it was an agreement, and we both knew that, and that it would have an expiration date, but it still stings like a hundred pissed off hornets."

"I'll bet. Did he say why?"

She blinks up at the freshly dusted ceiling, seeking solace, answers, anything. "No, other than something came up, and he's not in a position to continue. He also couldn't tell me why—that he was sworn to secrecy. Once he had *further clarity*, maybe we could circle back."

"Bastard," I spit out. Such a coward's way out, being all vague. Women want detail. If you're going to break our hearts, at least have the decency to do so with detail so our own morbid thoughts don't race down some crazy speedway of him having someone else or knocking up a side piece. A trickle of icy dread pours down my neck and across my shoulders. "Unless..."

"Unless what?" she asks, picking at a hangnail.

"Rochelle came into the hospital the other day. She's pregnant. Won't say who the father is, other than it isn't Wrench. Seems there are a couple of candidates from the MC, but she is refusing any paternity tests until after the baby is born, because of the bleeding scare she's had. The doctors tried to allay any fears, telling her the testing wouldn't hurt the baby, but she flat out refused."

Cally freezes, looking up at me in alarm. Her usual pale creamy complexion is so wan, I'm tempted to rush over and check for a pulse.

"You said his words were *something came up*, right?"

She nods, lips sucked between her teeth. "And that he couldn't continue but wouldn't say why."

She nods again, a lone tear slipping out of the corner of her eye. Her balled fists unfurl, wiping both eyes with furious energy.

"I'm not important enough to be introduced to his parents as *anything other than staff*. Meanwhile, he's out there fucking his buddy's skanky seconds. Probably in some fucked up tag-team scenario. He's *not in a position to continue* because he's too busy creating baby cockroaches with that filth."

CHAPTER 37 - SMOKE
with a score of...

We received an early call that last night's insane storm had ripped a section of roof off next door's barn. The property next door to the MC is a well-known horse ranch, owned and operated by the same couple who set it up almost sixty years prior. Only the husband passed away, leaving his widow and her ranch hands to continue the bustling business. I care little for horses. They always looked at me as if the moment I sat in the saddle would be the moment they tipped me out of it. Not even a rodeo bronc either, just your regular horseback riding horse. Not that I'm particularly heavy, horses just don't like me, and the feeling is mutual.

Notwithstanding that fact, a roof off a building is an emergency, and the boys are busy calming the horses and providing their own running repairs on the various stables and other outbuildings. It's a good thing the MC is a fortress. Sure, the winds lashed against the windows and walls, the driving rain doing its best to pierce holes in the glass. It was designed to halt bullets, so some fierce squally wind and rain should be no match for the engineering. An almost sixty-year-old barn though? The damage could be catastrophic.

The symphony of awakened engines spurs the hairs on the back of my neck and the ones on my hands. Yes, we are on adjoining properties, but the trek from the clubhouse to the damaged barn would take hours on foot. Plus, we have no way of knowing what tools will be on hand, especially if Dusty, Dev and the others are busy with their own tasks. Feather and Volt have their own trade tools, and with the eight or so bikes roaring down the dirt road, we have the workforce covered. All I want to do when I arrive at the T-intersection is turn right and head towards a little cottage and distinct yellow door. Instead, my Dark Horse follows the convoy of leather-clad muscle, each rider avoiding the potholes large enough to trap bears. Yeah, the mayor isn't fixing any of these soon, what with Iss Rand being ejected from the Town Hall meeting and Wrench doing his level best to receive the same fate.

As the bikes roar along the uneven road, the widespread destruction becomes clearer. There are sections of fence torn clean off; others are lying in splintered fractures, the red tannins of the interior wood bleeding out metaphorically. If a similar type of fencing is used further up the property in the horse paddocks, it is no wonder the ranch hands are run off their feet and called in reinforcements. Alpha slows his Harley to a gentle roll before a complete stop just shy of the main house steps. Waiting on the porch, watching the cavalry arrive, is Isobel Rand, proprietor. She's dressed similarly to the night of the infamous meeting, all work sensible in faded jeans and a flannel shirt, silver hair pulled up in a no-nonsense bun. She smiles as Alpha dismounts, walking over to the waving woman and wrapping her up in a hug that lifts her off her feet. Her ensuing blush is almost as red as her shirt, before she playfully swats at his forearms and makes a show of recovering her footing. She comes into Wilds to drink and eat every other week. Her sharp tongue and quick wit were a favorite with Saint and Paul, who tended bar, although she took well to Cally Rae, dubbing her an *honorary Irish lass* with a head of flames like that.

Alpha crooks an elbow for Iss to weave hers through, and the two of them set off to survey the damage. If it were under different circumstances, it would be a wholesome sight. Two long-time neighbors, old friends and a united front against the tyrannical abuse of power coming from the civic municipality towards the businesses that abut each other. The ranch has been operational longer than most of those men have been alive, but they still like to flex their testosterone-fueled misogyny towards any lone woman deemed weak by their ilk. Iss Rand would chew them up and spit them out; all of them, one at a time, into neat rows.

Sheets of discarded corrugated iron lay where they fell, whipped up and off in a maelstrom of fury. None of what I can see is salvageable; most are warped, or split, or have holes the size of my fist peppering the wavy metal. Hammer and Boomer fall into step as we search around the site for any other pieces in danger of hurting any passing person or animals. Flint and Volt are unloading the trucks with extra crowbars, hammers, ladders and spools of wiring. Both of them will need to inspect the structure further before allowing any of us near it. The rest of us do what we can to clean up, donning safety gloves and collecting fallen debris before dumping it all in a heap near the water tanks, which suffered no damage, because they were full and more resilient to the brutal forces.

By mid-morning, Iss has settled herself into an Adirondack chair, nursing a steaming mug of tea on one generous arm, and her reading glasses are perched on the other. She's taking the opportunity for her own rest period, having served us tea, coffee, cake and cookies first, because we needed nourishment to continue with the task.

"Can't have any of you boys feeling lightheaded and slipping off that damn beam now, can I?" No, ma'am. She's a funny old thing. I can only wish I held an ounce of the humor she possesses at her age.

As members cleaned up in the makeshift washroom before morning tea, I noticed Iss and Hammer in cahoots about something, giggling amongst themselves like schoolgirls. Making my way over to the table set with teapots, cups, saucers and sweet treats, I heard a distinctly feminine voice say, "Eight."

Looking up, I see Hammer's brows rise, a tight smirk licking at his mouth. "Not bad, not bad. I'm still winning, right?" Winning what? What's in the tea he's drinking, and where can I get a cup? There are some upturned crates for chairs set to the side near Iss and Hammer. I make my way over, balancing coffee and what I hope is vanilla cake.

"Yes, Ham, you're still winning," she beams back at him, and he puffs up proud as a peacock.

"She's rating the MC boys. Alpha was a seven point five, Vegas was a nine, damn pretty boy. But I told her he's a dog handler and prefers canines to people. She said it didn't matter; it's just her rating on looks. She's not gonna marry the guy, just stare at his working muscles."

"If Vegas was a nine, what were you?" I ask him, sipping at my scalding coffee. These little teacups are impractical for men with large fingers. I can't fit any of my fingers through the gap in the handle, so I opt to cradle the hot cup. Motherfucker.

"Eight point five, but I added on an extra point for my winning personality," he jokes.

At least I think he's joking. He's a decent-looking guy, sure, but the women go nuts over Vegas and his chiseled jaw, blindingly white teeth and spiky blond hair, always styled to perfection. Of all the members to share a bathroom with, he would be my absolute last choice. Hammer takes his sweet ass time getting ready to go somewhere, but Vegas takes business days.

"Nine point five," she shrieks. "Oh my god, those eyes. I love his eyes. Ten, he's a ten."

We all look up to see Wrench strolling over with his own coffee and cookie. He bypassed all the floral-print china and went straight to the mugs, holding the handle with ease as he sank onto a crate beside mine. Ten is a stretch. Perfect? Wrench? The ladies seem to fall at his feet too, fuck knows why he took on someone like Rochelle. As if being summoned like a specter, Wrench bats his eyelids at Iss while sipping his drink. The poor woman almost has a medical episode. She pulls a tissue from the cuff of her flannel and wipes at her face.

"Two?" Hammer roars with laughter. "Tunnel, you're last."

Tunnel and Flint are the last to take up the available crates. Volt worked through our break, deciding fewer bodies in the barn was easier for him to run any replacement wiring because we were *in the way*. Whatever.

"She scored you a two out of ten. You're last."

"That wasn't two," he protests. "She was sneezing, asshole. Achoo! Not two, get fucked."

Iss morphs from laughing into full-blown wheezing. Wrench, the sullen, stoic type, even manages a grin.

"You have allergies, right, Iss? That was a sneeze, right?" Tunnel implores.

The older woman covers her face with her hands, body continuing to ripple with laughter. Only Tunnel would take this shit so fucking seriously.

"I do, son. Terrible. But I take my antihistamine every day. Can't get too blocked up with the COPD. My doctor says another acute infection might do me in."

"Oh, we can't have that now, can we?" Wrench soothes, and she damn near bursts, a rosy hue creeping up her neck and spreading across her weathered cheeks.

"Only if you all turn up sans shirts to deliver me my soup and fluff my pillows," she fires back, with a wink.

"All except for you, Tunnel. Cause you were a two," Hammer says again, causing Tunnel to stand and stare his brother down. "What? I heard two," Hammer continues, and Tunnel fires a look at him that promises retribution.

"Same," Vegas choruses, if only these assholes knew what they were doing. Even Boomer is laughing his head off at his fellow munitions expert. The old saying of not poking the bear has been ignored, torn up and shredded. This bear is pissed.

"Don't be surprised if you fuckers wake up with sticks of Semtex up your ass," Tunnel declares, before miming an explosion with his hands flying off his hips. Whether it's his little visual of promised revenge, his salty mood, or Hammer and Boomer continuing to laugh like hyenas, the rest of us dissolve into hysterics as we eat our fill of cake, cookies, and Iss Rand's views on the MC men and life in general.

"Rodin," I greet our MC psych with a warm smile. "I'm here voluntarily, without anger and ready to share with the group."

He eyes me, no doubt knowing I'm full of shit. To his credit, his expression doesn't waver.

"Smoke, I am pleased with your positive outlook." He gestures to the couch, and I sink down on it knowing I don't need his invitation to do so. What I also comprehend is that none of this is his fault, and he has a job to do. Namely, the head health of every MC member, including me.

"How are you managing at work? Are you finding any limitations to be a hindrance?" As manager of Wildcats and Kittens, I could spend most of my time locked away in my office, delegating all manual tasks to my second in command. But if I did that, I'd never get to mingle in her proximity, the waft of soft florals and sweet spices mingling with her own feminine scent. Since halting our agreement, she has limited our contact time to the bare necessity. Timesheets and staff rosters are emailed, with detailed notes rather than the in-person discussion we used to have with her across my lap, or bent over my desk.

"I'm still managing, if that is a direct question. But if you're hinting at any difficulties, then yes, there are some," I add. He's a psychologist here for my benefit. If he can't help me, who can? The only other person I want contact time with declared we had *run our course* and wants nothing to do with me.

"What difficulties. And how can the club best support you to get through?"

That's just it, Doc. There is nothing you can do, nor the club, to help me through this. Feather is in his own prison cell; I'm in mine.

"The awakening you mentioned last week, the one that came to a grinding halt," I venture, and he nods, eyes warm and welcoming.

"Go ahead," he gestures.

"The person I was exploring this with has been inadvertently hurt by my actions. Because I couldn't say anything other than I had to stop. I fear the damage has been done, and I won't be able to fix this once the results are clear, *if* the results are clear."

"Smoke, it's important to remain positive until we know for certain your immunity and infection status has changed. There is no point in draining your battery over something that may not even manifest. Keep up your fitness routine. Keep your life as normal as possible, and the stress hormones as low as possible."

"Easier said than done." My hands cup my spread knees.

"Sure," he agrees. "In relation to your exploration. Would you like me to talk to your lover and try to allay any fears they may have about the situation? Of course, anything specifically pertaining to you and your health, I will not discuss. However, I am here to help."

Nodding, I lean back, extending my arms along the back of the couch. The MC has been incredibly supportive, as have Akis and the Smoke Dogs in Tennessee. The incident was used as a learning experience, and stricter protocols were put in place. The perpetrator was delivered back to the M.E.T.R.I.C.S. client with his shoulder still hanging loose. A fitting punishment for his crime? Maybe. Don't skip out on testifying and don't spray your filthy fluids on others trying to do their job. With that in mind, I thank Rodin for his generous time again and decline his offer of assistance through a discussion with my lover. Once the last tests are clear, we will have our own conversation, and words will be the last thing on my mind.

CHAPTER 38 - CALLY
Home girl

My stay here was always meant to be temporary. It's not like I came up here voluntarily, to all this snow and mountains, and bears and bison, and shit. I came up here when my sister literally saved me, and I had no place else. I'd find a job, earn some money and head back home to Texas. To family, cousins and aunts and uncles who were disowned by Dad and his imprinted outlook on a righteous life of sacrifice.

So why do I feel so ill thinking about my next move? I mean, it's logical, and it was the planned next step. I should pack my shit into the Rav 4 and turn towards the gulf, back through Wyoming, Colorado and a blink in New Mexico before I revert to childhood hopes and happiness. To church on Sundays voluntarily, chicken fried steaks followed by pecan pie and afternoons chatting on the wrap-around porch while younger cousins play amongst the grape-scented purple flowers of the Mountain laurels. Even though Jo and I are in a cottage now with all the room we need. I'm sure she'd be okay with her cats. Plus, the gentleman callers who grunt like wild boars when I arrive home from work. She'll be... fine. I'll be fine. Everything will work out just as it should.

Picking my cell phone up from where it is charging on the nightstand, I text Greer. My friend, and fixer.

> Hey G. You mentioned work back in TX last time we talked.

> **GREER**
> You coming home, girl?

> I am. But I need a job.

> **GREER**
> A friend started a production company. They need girls for xxx videos. Shoots start next month. Cannot wait to see you. I'll see him tomorrow and give him your details. Big love.

> Thank you. Big love to you. Always.

Bile rises at the words production company and xxx videos. Porn? She's found me a job in porn? While I'm more than comfortable doing a fetish photo shoot, part of that is because it's a static fantasy, a moment in time. Sando is amazing, and every other model I've worked with, bar one or two idiots, has been great. We discuss the desired outcome of each look first before we get close to any of the wearables or toys. This process is coveted desire—not pornography. Yes, there is a difference, a fucking huge one. I can't disassociate physical sex and intimacy for work with the sex I have with a partner. And that's rule one of porn. I also don't want my groans and moans available to guys like Scotland, who one thousand percent watches porn.

Do I take the risk and drive down, anyway? I mean, I'll sleep in the car in their driveway if I have to, or work in a diner. If the options are slinging pizza and living like a homeless person in Texas, or watching Smoke raise a baby with that *thing*, then it's option one every damn day. The fallout from the drama with Kiara is still warm. Would he throw himself into daddy mode, diapers and debt for them? Absolutely he would, because that's just the man he is. I saw how haunted he was when he talked about Kiara growing up and him not even knowing she existed. It cruelled him. He won't lose that opportunity again, of that I am certain.

"She's divine, isn't she?"

My head cants towards our newest stripper, Cedar Woods, sliding suggestively down the pole from an impressive batwing. Her core strength would put the MC guys to shame, and of the torsos I've seen, eight packs are standard military issue.

"She is. We're lucky to have her." Whatever, or whoever, makes Delta's presence here less frequent, is fine with me. I'd put Ursula the sea witch up there if it were my decision.

I busy myself with filling drink orders, washing glasses, polishing the dry glasses, and avoiding Smoke as best I can. We share only polite, limited work conversations. I don't ask him about his day, like I used to, and depart before he asks me anything. If I have a question, I seek Saint, who is more than happy to assist, but no doubt catching on to my avoidance of the boss. I could say he's busy, so I found another avenue to a solution, only he's busy watching me. When I lift my head from the register, or slink out into the client space with a drink-laden tray, I feel his cool steel-lavender gaze sweep over me like a paintbrush. Whisper soft bristles to daub me in a color of his choosing. Then, the bitter reality slashes across the canvas with hurried, almost violent strokes of obsidian energy. *He impregnated someone else,* so I have to let him go. *Let us go.*

The MC booth is packed with members. Typical Saturday night revelry with free booze and naked, writhing bodies. Flint has had to step in for Feather while he's on vacation. Prior to his stepping into the security role—with Grave and Saint switching between monitoring the crowd or slipping behind the bar as needed—I'd only met Flint twice. He's around the same height and build as Saint, and could even be the same age, perhaps. The notable difference is that both men—well, all men when you think about it—are smaller than Feather. That is not an insult; it's pure fact. Feather is a wall of hard-packed muscle, towering above everyone else. He oozes dominance and protectiveness. His biceps would crack walnuts with one flex.

Because of his absence, the crowds have been getting a little bolder. Rogue hands sliding up bare thighs without invitation, and more than one tray of drinks has been upended when a server has been slapped on the behind or pulled into a lap. It's gross behavior, and Alpha looks set to implode. He'd be the better choice for security if his diagnosis and treatment weren't affecting his energy levels. Still sharp as a whip, still smoking way too many cigarettes, still scary as fuck to anyone he's unfamiliar with. He's quite the puppy dog once you warm up to him. Luckily for me, I know him pretty well. So when he slides into the MC booth between Wrench and Hammer, I deliver his bourbon of choice the moment his backside hits the leather.

"Cally Rae, do you know how much I love you, darlin'?"

Smiling, I collect the empty glasses, making a mental note of who had what, and how many refills I need to return with. "I bet you say that to all the girls."

His big body hums as he chuckles. "Absolutely not. Only you."

"Well, that's a good thing then. Because I don't want you to hate me when I tell you this next thing."

His sparse eyebrows rise. "And that is?"

"That I quit. I'm... leaving."

CHAPTER 39 - ALPHA
Mr. Fix It.

I'll never pretend to understand things I don't. Women are prominent on that list, if not at the fucking top. Two failed marriages will attest to that. Some lessons I've learned along the way steer certain decision making. Like the things I fucked up with as a younger man, I learned to remedy with maturity and experience. From what I can tell, women want... fuck, sometimes I don't even think they know what they want. Either that, or it's a developing fluidity of emotional fulfillment. To be honored and protected, sure. To be ravaged and defiled, sometimes. Then there are those who demand freedom like a protest march banner, only to seek solace when their hard-fought freedom no longer appeals or didn't pan out to their exacting standards.

Then there is Cally Rae Jenkins. The flame-haired firebrand of spontaneity and unpredictability. Spent a good portion of her life in some fucked up cult, living off light colored purees and food that didn't require microwaves, or hell, anything with electricity. Jo had several in-depth conversations with my old lady. About how toilet paper was rationed and some self-appointed crackpot guru was at war with anything electrical, brightly colored—namely red—and anything foreign to their little *circle*. That was pretty much everything. Both sisters had it tough, but none more than the younger Jenkins girl, who suffered longer because she didn't have an out. Trapped in the turgid teachings of an imbecile with great sway over his brethren flock.

Cally is more than a worker at Wildcats and Kittens. She is integral to the woven fabric of the business. She designed the fit-out of the club we're in, for fuck's sake. Along with all this Feng Shui stuff about energy flow to promote prosperity. I dismissed it at the time, but she was right after all. The club is thriving; Wilds is pumping, and none of it has shit to do with table placement or living plants to absorb and redirect any wayward fucking chi. Uh-uh, no. We thrive because of her presence. She's a beacon when you walk through the double doors, all creamy skin and flame of hair. A smile that could rival power grids and a youthful exuberance and buoyancy that infects everyone differently. Once she burrows under your skin like a splinter, you don't want to remove her pink sting of pain. That's Cally Rae. The same Cally Rae that quit earlier tonight. Sure, she clarified later when I pulled her aside that she felt like she needed a new environment and was exploring other avenues and other work. Fine, as is her right, but fuck me. This isn't good.

Sucking in all the noxious chemicals that I know have already diseased my lungs, my head turns at the sound of the rear door being creaked open. Wrench and Hammer tense beside me as I exhale a whorl of carcinogens into the night air, relaxing once they see Smoke's hand steady the door as his head comes into view around it.

"You wanted to see me?" he inquires, and I nod, striding over to him in four long steps.

The end of the cigarette sizzles against the back of his hand where I've intentionally stubbed it out before discarding it to the snow-dusted cobblestones below. A whip of pungent, acrid flesh licks at the still air before dissipating.

"Ow, what the fuck?" he seethes, attempting to pull his hand free and inspect the injury.

"Great fucking question, asshole. Want to tell us why Cally Rae quit tonight?"

Stone overtakes his softening features. He wasn't aware. Those two have been joined at the fucking hip. Unless he's the reason she's leaving, in which case, stubbing out a cancer stick on the back of his hand will be the least of his fucking problems.

"What did you do?" I spit each word with intent.

"I, er. I—"

"What. Did. You—"

"Exactly what you fucking told me to," he says, scooping up a fistful of snow to soothe the reddening flesh.

"Meaning?" I demand, lighting the next cigarette that will mark his body unless he provides some damn answers. The flame flickers bright orange, morphing to a light blue as it meets the end of the paper. Wrench shifts beside me as Hammer pulls his jacket collar around his sandy hair.

"While we wait for the bloodwork, I put us on hold. Like you said." He blows out a long breath, particles dancing in the frigid stillness.

"And what reason did you give her for stopping things so suddenly?"

He blinks, balking. "None! You said not to say anything until the tests came back."

"Are you basic?" My patience is wearing wafer-thin, and I'm not an overly patient man to begin with. I know he and Feather got the shit end of the stick with this hepatitis bullshit, but that doesn't excuse his current brain fade. "Say something. Fucking lie to her if you have to."

"I'm not fucking lying to her. No way."

"Then you're dumber than you look."

"Fuck you," he spits back, enraged. "Does the R and T on our wall only mean something to you when it's shit you're dealing with?"

My back stiffens. "What did you just say to me?"

"Whoa, fellas," Wrench interjects, with an outstretched arm towards each of us. "Brothers, remember?"

"That's fucking hard when this bastard seems to forget respect and trust when it suits him. I wouldn't lie to any of you, and I'm not fucking lying to Cally Rae. I get that this is all my fault, and maybe I am basic for thinking I could fix this." His head drops, eyes narrowing to slits.

"I don't expect any of you assholes to understand, but she and I have a mutual understanding. I respect the hell out of her, and until recently, I'm guessing she did the same with me. If I've hurt her by not elaborating on why I had to pull the plug with us, then that's also on me. One thing I won't do is fucking lie."

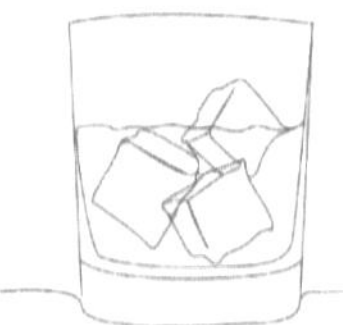

Chapter 40 - Smoke
Primal prison

Back inside the venue, I scour the place for the crimson flash. There is none. I check the cubby where she keeps her bag and note it's empty. Fuck! It's been no secret that she's been avoiding me, but leaving when I was busy is damn infuriating. Pulling out my phone, I tap out a text and wait. And wait and wait.

> You resigned to Alpha? Ignoring me? Wtf Cally.

CR ⊠
Alpha was the one who technically hired me. My resignation goes to him.

> He won't accept it.

CR ⊠
He didn't.

> So you're still working then?

CR ⊠
No, I'm still resigning. I don't need his permission to start a new job.

> Christ, Cally. This is crazy.

CR ▧
I don't need yours either.

Dammit! If we weren't at an impasse, I'd flip her onto my desk and redden that ass so magnificently, she'd be unable to sit for a week. I love her fucking spirit and newfound sass, but why, oh why does it always seem to be aimed towards me?

Another day, another trip to the florist shop to have a bouquet of flowers sent to the cottage with the yellow door. No card, no contact details, even though she may have guessed they were from me. That, or someone else has the audacity to send her flowers? No, I push that unwelcome thought from my head, intent on ordering another bunch of happiness and hope. Cost, that's irrelevant too. I need some conduit to the way I'm feeling to reconcile with how my omission has crowbarred a void between my Carolina Reaper chaos and myself. She's saved in my phone as CR with a jalapeno emoji. She herself is saved under my ribcage in a compartment I never knew existed. Until her. Wrapped up tight with those little fucking hair ties for reinforcement. She can't leave, not now! Not when I am so fucking close to finding out if I need to push her away, or draw her to me.

Finding out from Alpha that she had quit hurt more than the burn on the back of my hand. Asshole. Technically, he's still the big boss of all our businesses, so it makes sense that she'd hand her notice in to him. He also—if we're getting down to the nuts and bolts of her hiring—was the guy to offer her the job after Feather, Saint and I did our level best to fuck it all to hell and back. From day one, it's been a shitshow, until the two of us made a mutual agreement to assist each other's explorations, fulfill their needs along with our own. When it's just the two of us, everything is rainbows and fucking sunshine. Or butterfly harnesses and cum stains. When others get all up in our shit, we fall apart like a wet paper bag in a hailstorm.

"These are so pretty. And no card. You are most definitely a secret admirer." I pay the florist, ensuring they will be delivered like the others before them. To the cottage with no other information provided should she pester the delivery person. Not that they'd have much to provide. Pays in cash, no name, no card, nothing to tie my identity to the barrage of deliveries landing on her doorstep. Of course, I only hear about her reactions secondhand, sometimes third. We've gone from wholesale fucking each other into oblivion, to strangers in a line at the bank. Gotye wrote a song about it: *Somebody that I used to know.*

Nothing has shifted my opinion of her, or where we are. If anything, I respect her more. When this all began, she was the fresh-faced redhead who walked into a bar about a job. I almost fucked it up. Then she became my employee. A bartender so green and ignorant, her training went on over many weeks, rather than a couple of shifts like usual. *Usual,* that's a word you cannot use with Cally Rae Jenkins. She is a mythical unicorn creature of Norse prophecies. A maiden so pure, of fire and ice, strong of heart and fierce of will. I have to thank all the gods that her lateness and exploding tote bag of silicone dicks set us on a path we might never have ventured on our own. A fetish model with the most insane requests to satiate her sexual beast. Request might be too mild here, she demanded, and when she did, she was *perfection.* The rule-following, suppressed child of a cult, emerged from her chrysalis a butterfly of incredible opinions and the foreign ability to put herself and her own needs first, for the first time in her life. Then I fucked all that up too, by being careless with a wire fence on an op. Careless, because I was no doubt thinking about how long it would be before I could sink deep inside her again.

Sleep continues to elude me. There is a saying that if you can't sleep, you are awake in someone else's dreams. Nice metaphor, but just that, a fantasy created by some dreamer with insomnia to make themselves feel better. There are no dreams, only fucking nightmares. Hammer is noisily plowing into Whitney, I believe, judging by the other moans. Moans I was familiar with before Cally and I became intimate. Well, that's not true either. We had sex for the first time in the cellar, and the club girls still kept me company. I stopped when our agreement was sealed. Hello again, nightmare. Yes, I'm a fucking tenant now.

"Harder, faster! Oh my god I love your cock so much," comes drifting through the walls, and I wince. I don't begrudge my brother any of it. The guy works long hours at the auto shop with Wrench as his boss. He's entitled to hammer anything he wants in order to wind down for the night. But her outlandish squeals can stop right fucking now. He may have barbells in his dick, the newest one he proudly showed off only three days after the hepatitis event. Why any guy wants to erect a scaffolding platform around their cock is beyond me, but again, each to their own. At least his cock is getting pussy action. Mine is married to my palm again.

Alpha strides into our Sunday service looking like a sleek king. He's shaved his head now, and the impressive mustache is gone. He looks more imposing, if that is possible, and the cigarette dangling from two fingers makes me glance at the silvering scar centered on the back of my hand.

"Brothers," he booms, sinking into his throne at the end of the table. Theatrics are par for the course with him; he's all dramatic pauses and glaring stares. Maybe it's time to fine-tune a plan or finesse alternatives should something go south. Either way, his silences put more than just me on edge. Rodin and RAM look up from their laptops while Alpha stubs out his cigarette, thankfully in an ashtray this time, and continues.

"The preliminary blood work for Smoke and Feather is good. We can't say for sure that they're 100 percent out of the woods, but it's encouraging, right, Doc?"

Grave nods. "The lab said the parameters are great. Chances of infection were low to begin with. But going by the latest tests, it would be probable they escaped any cross-infection. The last tests in a couple of weeks will say for sure."

"That's great." Hammer nods. Sitting next to RAM, he's the most positive in the room. Happy-go-lucky, glass is half-full Hammer is the beacon of light we need on some of the darker days. Most of us are morose and grim reapers of tightly held emotions. Not him. He's the clown, the playful kid, and his rugged good looks have the ladies sinking to their knees to please him. He never has a curt word or quarrel with anybody. His hopeful smile makes me think that maybe, just maybe, everything might be okay in the end.

"Another M.E.T. op is on the cards. RAM, you are awaiting confirmation of details for that, yes?"

RAM nods, elegant fingers moving away from the keyboard to fold in his lap.

"Timeframe?"

"None yet. We're still in the reconnaissance phase."

"Noted," Alpha nods, removing his packet of cigarettes and withdrawing another one, before sliding it back with the tip of his index finger. A man at war with addiction. Join the fucking club. Letting out a long breath, he recovers and turns in his chair. These meetings would be over in half the time if he simply stated what he came here to say and saved the sighs and dramatics. He's a relic of an old Greek tragedy, clad in a toga, citing the ruination of man. All we need are the laurel leaves and the draped sheet.

"Some other news came to light over the past couple of weeks. This is a developing story, literally."

Alpha's salty glare lifts to Wrench, who returns it with a glacial one of his own. Whatever this is, it can't be good.

"Most of you folks will remember Rochelle, the er, ex-partner of Wrench."

"Not just his partner either," comes a muffled voice from the rear of the room.

Wrench's head swivels at a whiplike pace. He knew she was sleeping around. Hell, we all did. But again, that was his situation to rectify, and he did so by kicking her out. That was months ago, why the hell would he bring up her name now?

"Agreed. And Wrench, I mean this with the utmost respect for you as our brother, but that chick was bad fucking news. The day the door hit her ass on the way out was indeed a beautiful one. Only, a development has made me worried. And today provides an opportunity to get it sorted, and plan for the future." His almost onyx eyes settle on me, and my lip twitches. More theatrics.

"Rochelle is pregnant. Was brought into the hospital a little while back with complications." All eyes are fixed on Wrench, who, to his credit, doesn't flinch. Not a single muscle moves. "No father was listed on the admitting paperwork. In fact, the next of kin was her sister."

"Does that mean she's moving into the MC? Because, not gonna lie, she's kind of disruptive," Boomer says, half apologetic towards Wrench's stoic state.

"Fuck no," Alpha snaps. "There was a reason Wrench didn't move her in here. She didn't indicate any father on the paperwork because she probably doesn't know who he is. That bitch bounced on more dicks than a roulette ball did around the wheel. No offence, Wrench."

"None taken. It's not my kid. I was one thousand percent wrapped."

Alpha nods, and the rest of the club murmurs in consolidated support. Thank fuck, and he dodged a bullet there. He sure did. I pity the poor bastard who's now tied to that bitch for the next eighteen years.

"Does anyone here want to take any accountability? Own up to the fact that they are on the hook for this until a paternity test can prove otherwise?"

"Fuck," Tunnel groans. "Me, fucking me, okay. One time. Maybe two. I'm sorry, Wrench, she wandered into my room, naked and ready to go. I'm sorry, man."

"You will be, if it's yours," Wrench says, as smooth as aged whiskey.

"Anyone else?" Alpha questions. Freezer uncrosses his arms and lifts a hand. "Me, once."

"I see," Alpha drawls, fingers drumming on the table. "Both of you idiots will need to provide a sample for paternity testing. See Grave and Rodin about what is involved there."

The two men begin their own reconciliation with what could unfold. Tunnel, running his hands through his close-cropped hair, mouth pulled tight. Explosives guys are a little on the crazy side. Dealing with shit that explodes daily should better prepare them for news like this. I guess C4 and an unexpected pregnancy are different volatile scenarios.

"Anything to add, Smoke?" Alpha blurts, and I blink, confused. Does he want me to tell the room that Cally Rae quit and is seeking other opportunities?

"About?"

"This situation with Rochelle." Those eyes, those penetrating fucking eyes. Centers of coal and malevolent, accusatory hate.

"No, sir. While Wrench is one of my best baddies, I'm happy to hear that there is little to indicate that baby is his. Best news, if we're being honest."

"Interesting," Alpha drawls again, his eyes alighting with some kind of mischievous glee. Fucking Shakespearian theater. Seriously. "Because the word I'm hearing—the word coming out of the hospital actually… is that the baby is *yours*."

My pulse quickens in direct contrast to my blood volume feeling like wet cement.

"What?" My throat constricts, an inwards unrelenting pressure powered by my thundering pulse. I know the techniques to quiet it. Only, I can't retrieve any facts from my brain.

"It's yours. That's what I was told."

"You were told wrong. I never, *ever* had sex with her."

"Really?" His forehead wrinkles. If he had brows, they'd arch like a rainbow.

"Really," I state, standing from my seat. Leaning on flattened palms, I announce to the table, including our thespian president. "Never, ever. Respect, that fucking word up there. Hell, I embody the whole thing. I respect one of my oldest friends not to touch his wallet, his whiskey, or his woman. You assholes down the end need to take a good long look at what's important. I found out I was a dad a while ago, and it changes your life. That was long before Rochelle was in the picture, and no disrespect to Wrench, but she was filthy. I was in a relationship with only one person. I haven't touched a club whore for months either. So, to sit here while I'm awaiting test results and to have this untrue allegation of infidelity thrown at me when I have enough to deal with is pretty fucking low."

Alpha throws up a palm, but it's too late. "No, you threw that line out, let the anchor sit heavy on your chest. You may be my president, but you are a fucking asshole."

Kicking the chair behind me, I flee the situation room and make for my own. If this intel came from the hospital, that's where Cally's sister works. It's only a matter of time before grubby gossip like this reaches her delicate ears. Fuck, fuck, FUCK!

CHAPTER 41 - CALLY
making a statement

Shut up, Cally Rae, you've used your quota of words for the day.
Go away and cover that offensive hair, Callista!
No one is interested in anything you have to say.
It doesn't matter what you want; your opinion is irrelevant.
Your place is as a mute, obedient wife. That's all.
You're hidden away because no one wants to see you, or hear you. Ever.

The phone nestles between my shoulder and ear. Part of my brain is begging for her to pick up and talk to me, the other hoping it will ring out and no further conversation will be had today. No one will prioritize my mental health like I do, and calling my mother to say hey isn't putting my health first at all. Only I feel so much time has elapsed now, even she may be amiable to a conversation about my welfare, what Jo is up to, and the state of the increasing humidity, if we get stuck for topics. I don't care about Pastor Rich or the rest of the circle; even my father's welfare is ambiguous now. He is, after all, the reason we made the pilgrimage to Utah in the fucking first place.

"Hello, Jenkins residence. We invite our Lord and Savior into our lives. Please join us."

Fuck, I'd forgotten about that little nugget. Only the Lord and Savior for the Moonyatas was Rich, not Jesus. Most callers hung up when they heard that little spiel.

"Hey, Mom. It's Cally."

Her sharp intake of breath and hum of annoyance crawl down the phone line and through my speaker, reaching out with the face slap I know she'd let me have if I were standing in front of her. She exhales through her nose, the slight whistling telling me that her lips are pursed shut, and I can picture her thunderous face and furious demeanor.

"Ah," she says. "The one who needs saving the most. Glad you've remedied the error of your ways."

"No, no. I'm not calling to be saved, Mother. I was already saved. By Jo, and the Pistons."

"The who?" she asks, shocked. Her voice rises at least an octave.

"A motorcycle club called the Ponderosa Pistons. They gave me a job working in their bar, and a cottage to live in with a bright door! Jo and I have two cats now. We'r–"

"Enough," she spits. "Living under the rule of a biker gang. You are *beyond* redemption."

"I'm not though. In fact, I don't give a fuck about what you, or anyone else, thinks, Mom, because I'm happy. For the first time in my life, I have dreams and aspirations. I am independent."

Her bitter cackle sends my skin into hyperreactivity. "You speak about independence as if it's a good thing, something to hope for."

"Because it is!"

"Fool," she snaps back. "The most any woman can hope for is the attention and care of a holy man who keeps to a routine. One who returns home for supper at the same time every night not smelling of perfume or liquor, who rules with a firm hand. I can't even see that for you."

"That's the last thing I want in a man. I may adore submission, but you can keep your subservience. That shit is for lemmings who don't have a spark of an idea to call their own."

"Such vulgar profanity. You were raised better than that."

"Was I though? The only positive about the way I was raised is that it no longer affects my life because I refuse to let it. Keep your skewed rhetoric and rationed toilet tissue. Slurp your beige food while you repair clothes you wash by hand. That's your life, Mom, not mine. I don't covet it, nor do I tolerate it. Not anymore."

My finger snaps at the end call button before she can fire another barb in my direction.

"Of course, of course. We will do it all," Dominic, my colorist, croons. I'd stalked into the salon demanding attention, even without an appointment. They had nothing available, but I wasn't deterred.

"Fit me in around your other clients. I don't care if I'm sitting in that chair all damn day, I'm not leaving. Here," I say, slapping a wad of hundred-dollar bills down at the front desk.

True to his word, he did it all. It didn't help that I sat there with a desperate look in my eyes that demanded I be given what I wanted. It looked foreign on me, sure, but this newfound determination flowed through my veins like a drug. Dom moved some clients on to other stylists and offered me a gloss treatment once foils and highlighting had developed. This helped tie my freshly processed hair in with his availability to tone and work further magic. So I sat there, or reclined at the basin, beholden to his technical abilities, and liquid, soothing voice. We gossiped about celebrity rumors, absent staff, and whether Chick-fil-A or Popeye's had the best chicken sandwich. Not that Dominic looked like he consumed much of either. His tanned skin and thick, wavy hair were the cherry on top of his lean but fit frame. He had smoky eyes that lit with interest, sparks bolting in all directions when the conversation centered on Justin Bieber or Henry Cavill because, of course, Dom was gay. Dom was gay and fabulous.

"Speechless, SPEECHLESS!" Dom's hands fly across his heart when my chair was turned for the last time. "OMG, Calista, I can't. I simply cannot!"

Can't what, Dom? Cope? My hair was always red. Even with the coffee, charcoal, or blueberry powders, it was red hair hosting a temporary powdered color until the red weaved its ruby hues once more. Now, I look like a goddess. Shades of red are still present, sure, only they mingle with scarlets and clarets, and some deep burgundy more at home in a wine glass. One of those fancy bordeauxes that Smoke used to grumble about ordering because it was so expensive and out of reach of most of the bar. Now, I was his liquid nemesis, expensive and out of reach of most of the bar. Take that, you dick!

My sparse, stubbly lashes were now thick and long, and a warm chocolate, thanks to additions at the rear of the salon while dyes were developing on my crown. Doing it all meant doing it all. My brows also wore a rich tint, now plucked, pinched and brushed into a natural, modern shape to frame my face. If feeling prideful and vain are deplorable sins, then I look like a fucking snack, and punishments can come at me.

The bill was more than the slapped-down notes, of course it was. And it was worth every cent. I paid the counter clerk, tipping generously because miserly tippers have their own seat waiting in hell, and made my way to my next appointment that I hadn't made, hoping that they, too, would simply let me in and work their magic.

"Cally, what's going on, doll? You look... feisty."

Picasso is the manager of Inkubus, the MC-owned-and-run tattoo parlor about a minute walk from Wilds and Kittens. The walk I'd never take again, seeing as I'd quit and was leaving the city. Better late than never, though. This succubus needs some inkubus.

"Feisty, hey," I laugh, smiling up at the tattooed, pierced man with kind eyes and a gap-toothed smile. "So feisty in fact that you'll take me on now, even though I don't have a booking?"

"Never too busy for a beautiful lady like you, Cally Rae." Ah, flattery will get you everywhere, it seems. Only I'm not tending bar to him and his MC friends. Picasso could tell me to piss off and come back when he's free, only he does no such thing. He gestures for me to walk through the curtained doorway and into the back of the studio. Pages and pages of intricate artwork caress the walls with an inky sheen. This chapel too has its Michelangelo, only his road name is Picasso.

"Holy shit, P. Did you do these?"

"Most of," he says, almost sheepishly. "Onyx did that specter, and some of the fantasy stuff. She likes realms and other-world art." Whoever Onyx is, she too has incredible talent. While Picasso's work is clean and sharp, hers is more whimsical and soft; elfin faces taking on an almost real profile in a world I'd do anything to be transported to.

"Do people ever come back here not knowing what they're after, and just pick something from the walls and ceiling?"

"More than you'd think," he says, chuckling. "What were you after today, CR?"

I describe in detail what I want inked onto my virgin skin. Picasso weighs in at times with suggestions to lift the piece or move it to a less sensitive area. He explains the process, paying particular attention to preparation and aftercare, and slides his stool across the floor to a low desk with paper and colored markers to begin the design. My mind stiffens at the mention of *preparation* and *aftercare;* both words integral to scene planning with Smoke. Only those scenes, like me staying mute and compliant, or covering my hair, would never happen again.

My newfound self-love and independence, however? They were now as much a part of me as the blood in my veins, the pale, newly inked skin clinging to my muscles and bones, and the voluminous eyelashes that carpeted my eyelids. CR 2.0—don't fuck with me.

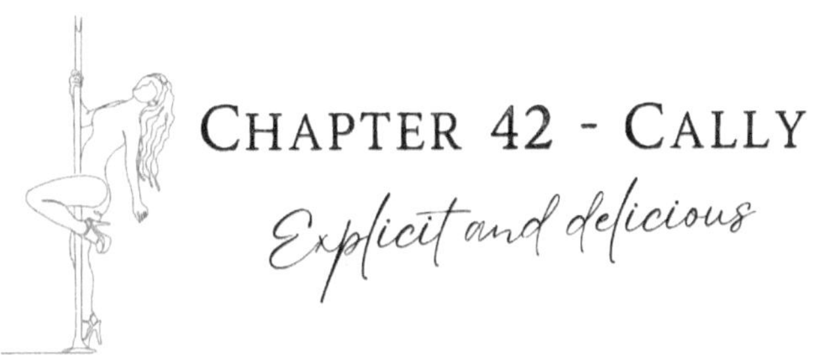

CHAPTER 42 - CALLY

Explicit and delicious

I'm freer. Or am I still whelmed? I can't quite put my finger on the exact emotion, only I don't feel as if my insides were shredded over a cheese grater anymore. And insides being vital organs, not my vagina. Because I haven't had sex with a living, thrusting cock in a long, long time. My battery-operated boyfriends, though? They're so overworked, they're putting in demands about vacation time. And they deserve a break. Only I freeze when faced with the real thing. There is nothing I'd like more than to get back on the proverbial horse and ride 'em ragged. When I think about any other horses, none of them have that light, sandy-colored hair, or the cool gray eyes rimmed in lavender.

I washed his masculine scent from the bedding, and rounded up all the underwear he'd left here, and trashed everything. I'm not trying to be *vindictive;* I like to think it's more *assertive.* If he can be a dick, then I'll be an ass. Part of me wants to wish him and his new baby momma all the best with the rest of the pregnancy and birth. All the moments he never got to witness the first time around; he now has a front-row seat for. The scan appointments, the shopping for baby goods, and even the diaper changes. Then I find myself inexplicably angry and wish her ankles would swell like buckets, and for Smoke's first diaper change to be filled with explosive diarrhea. These aren't Christian thoughts. Hell, they aren't even logical, sane thoughts. But that is my way of thinking. I considered if I was being punished. To have something so magical dropped in my lap, only to be snatched away again? Yeah, that's definitely all the raspberries and tomatoes I've eaten since Moonyata. The hand giveth, and the hand taketh away, Callista. Well, that hand can go fist it's own ass. I'm staying mad.

A resounding, thumping knock sounds at the front door. Not a tentative check for occupants at home, this is a demand for attention, like the person making all that damn noise will kick the door in if it isn't answered in the next second.

"I'll get it," Jo calls, as her voice trails off down the hall. She has the bedroom at the rear of the house, so the trek to the front door takes longer than if I walked the five paces from the primary bedroom at the front of the house. Once I leave, she can claim the front bedroom, so it's only fair she gets her exercise now. It's probably the thickset European guy from the other night. The one with the mono brow that cries with a high-pitched wail after sex, and whose name I can't for the life of me remember. I didn't think she was planning on inviting him back when he said he didn't like cats. Maybe his D was worth it?

"Hey, Smoke," I hear my sister exclaim, and I freeze. What the fuck is he doing here? Isn't it bad enough that I have to see him every shift at work? The weekly meetings to discuss profits and staffing and whatever else he brings up to make the meeting last twice as long as it should. "What are your thoughts about this, Cally?" Or "I'd like to discuss that further with you, in private perhaps?" No thanks.

"Cally, Smoke's here," she says brightly. Captain fucking obvious. If the crazy thumping at the door wasn't the first clue, she greeted him by his name. Do I change clothes? Pour myself into something figure-hugging and slinky? Something that a pregnant woman wouldn't be comfortable in, so he knows what he's missing out on? Or do I go with aloof? Walk out there in sweatpants and this old hoodie because I'm comfortable in it. I choose option B because I'm a badass who doesn't need to change for any man, and because most of my clothes are already packed away in anticipation of my imminent move.

Rounding the corner, I almost run smack-bang into Smoke, standing awkwardly in the hallway holding a bouquet of roses so dark, blood red, they're almost black at the inner petals.

"Hey," he says nervously, thrusting the flowers in my direction. "I said no to lilies again because they are toxic to cats, and I didn't think."

Said no to lilies. Again. Toxic to cats. Someone has been sending me flowers every few days. I thought it was maybe someone like Alpha feeling sorry for me. Or perhaps discards from the hospital when a patient dies? That would be something Jo would do. She'd swoop in and grab them, thinking a grieving family would only receive more, right?

"You've been sending the flowers?" I ask, an almost accusatory tone to my shaky voice. When he doesn't answer, opting instead to dip his head, I have my answer. But why? Jo sweeps into the hall, grabs hold of the roses and makes her way back to the kitchen in search of a vase. We don't have one large enough. Only because a bunch from last week had to go in her water bottle after I removed the lid. The stupid thing looks like a vase anyway. Who the fuck drinks that much water? She's no damn camel.

"Why?"

"Because I fucked this all up. And I wish I could go back and change things back to the way they were. Before," his voice trails off when he notices Jo unapologetically leaning in to hear better, "before I lost you."

"You didn't lose me," I lied. "We were never each other's to begin with."

Smoke stretches out a hand towards me, and as much as I want to melt into his touch, I step back. It takes all the willpower I have, but this is for the best. If I have any shred of self-respect left, it's that I'll be no one's second choice.

"Cally, please. I have to talk to you. Please just hear me out."

For such an imposing man, military trained and lethal, his words have a pleading, childlike quality. It's as if he's asking for one more bedtime story, or another candy before dinner. Is he... vulnerable? Before I can dwell on his fragile state, Jo strolls back into the sitting room with the vase of beautiful flowers. The dining table and kitchen countertop still hold the most recent deliveries.

"These are my favorite so far," Jo beams, talking to Smoke as if he hand-delivered flowers to her. Ask monobrow, cry-boy to bring you flowers, Johanna Maree.

Because the bedroom still looks like a disaster zone after packing began, and we're not just alluding to hiding Chris Hemsworth; the whole family could be taking cover in there for real. I move to the sofa and sink down without the *ugh* I want to release. "What's up?" *What's up, what's up?* That's the very best I could come up with after weeks of practicing what I'd say and do if this very scenario played out. This was so much better in my mind.

"I got some test results back this morning. Well, I've received a few test results back of late, but today's result is the most important." He looks almost pleased with himself. I feel more nauseated than his baby mama ever could. How the hell can he sit there with a self-satisfied smirk on his face right now? Jo slinks into the chair opposite with her fist under her chin. I bet she wishes she had popcorn ready.

"Good news? Or bad news?" Jo asks, and I want to kick her. But that would mean uncurling from the tiny ball I'm tucked in, hoping a cushion will explode its feather filling all over the room, so I can slink away and never return.

"Great news, actually," Smoke says, eyes bright and face hopeful. I'd kick him too if I could reach him. May several of the cascading feathers lodge in his throat and choke the fucker.

"Do tell," Jo encourages. "I'm sure Cally would like some closure before she leaves."

Smoke's throat moves on a swallow. "You're leaving?"

"Yeah." It's nowhere near as nonchalant as I practiced either.

"Alpha said you quit. He mentioned nothing about you leaving."

"Well, he's not *my* president, so I don't need to clear anything with him." I don't mean to be a bitch, but he can take his *great news*, and shove it so far up his ass that Buzz Lightyear never locates it.

"True," he adds with a rueful smile. "I hope you're not going too far. Chicago is a twenty-hour ride, right? It's been done before." He smiles again, this time with a hint of grit and conviction. I never said anything about Chicago.

"Florida is a little longer than twenty hours," I reply, inspecting my nails for chips, as if it is the most crucial task on the planet.

"Florida. Fuck, no, that's quite a lot longer."

Yeah, asshole. I may be a Hicksville cult princess, but I know enough geography. Florida might be enough distance between him and me. If not, I could save like crazy and venture overseas to somewhere exotic, like New Zealand.

"I landed a job at a club down there. In Fort Lauderdale. It's called *Explicious*. It's a cross between explicit and delicious. It's a brand-new kink club, owned by the same throuple that run the one out of New York. I'm done with fucking snow, so the Florida club will be perfect. Plus, I will be way closer to my Texas family, so it's a win-win."

His head moves, slow and deliberate. Every movement looks borderline painful. Jo rearranges her legs under her, chin still resting on her fist as she waits like an expectant father for news. Oh wait, we already have one of those.

"So, when is she due?" I blurt out, as frustrated as Jo.

"Excuse me?" His brows pinch, confusion bleeding over his features.

"Rochelle. When is she due?" I say with a calmness I never knew I possessed.

"How the fuck should I know?" he roars, a thick vein in his neck pulsing.

"Um, because *you're* the father?" My chin juts forward so far it's borderline painful.

His callous laugh borders on bitter. "I am *not* the father. The only person I impregnated was fifteen years ago. I wouldn't fuck Rochelle with another guy's cock. She's putrid."

Anger simmers off him like a foul stench. His body language is calm and still, but his forehead is pinched, brows so low, they are almost on his lids. Well now, we can all agree on that fact. What Wrench ever saw in her is beyond me. Bleached blonde hair with dark roots, and lips so inflated with filler she wouldn't just suck cock, she'd suck your damn soul out through the hole in your dick. Just *eww* in every way.

"I only found out she was pregnant when the rest of the club did. Seems there are a couple of potential fathers at the club. Plus, the rest we don't know about. It isn't Wrench's, and it one million percent isn't mine. I never fucked her. How do you girls know about this, and what made you think I was responsible?" Veins throb at his temples. He's not mad, he's furious. Where he sits behind his desk with languid muscles, here he sits taut with coiled tension, like a raptor ready to spring forth and claim prey.

Jo picks this exact moment to decide she's overstaying her welcome and bounces up to leave the room. "Oh no you don't," I say, holding her arm. "Sit your butt back down."

"If that isn't your great news, then what is?" Jo asks, exasperated.

"There was an incident on one of our operations a couple of months back. I nicked my wrist passing through a hole in the fence. Feather had an open sore on his face from something. Anyway, we were covered in bloody vomit from a junkie. Both of us had to have treatment and prevention of hepatitis infection. The final tests came back this morning; we're both negative."

Jo's jaw drops open before snapping shut again with a pop. "That's why you couldn't continue with your sex agreement. You were waiting on HIV and hep test results?"

"Yeah," Smoke confirms after a beat. "And it wasn't a sex agreement."

"It kind of was," I assert, causing both heads to snap to mine. "After you shut it down, I kind of poured it all out to Jo." I indicate towards my sister with a raise of my chin.

To his credit, Smoke doesn't look the least bit embarrassed. Jo looks like the nausea might have settled itself in her gut. "I think this might be my fault."

Smoke's head whips in her direction. "How so?"

"Well, Cally mentioned you couldn't continue your agreement at the time because something had come up, and you couldn't say what." She wrings her hands in earnest. "Only a couple of days before, Rochelle had presented at the hospital with pregnancy complications. She didn't list a father on the paperwork, and..."

"And you assumed it was me?" he roars, incredulous.

"I didn't know about the hep test. All I thought was perhaps you were involved with Rochelle and shut things down with Cally when Rochelle became pregnant."

"We use a private lab for club testing! No one wants that stuff to be part of the nursing gossip mill! Fuck!"

Now Smoke looks like he's going to be sick too. "You mean to tell me that for the past eight or so weeks, I've been fucking dying inside, and it was all some fucking hoax based on assumptions and whispers?"

My heart fills my throat. I want to kick my sister. Hard. "This was around the time your parents came to visit. You introduced me as—as staff. I was hurt by that, Smoke. Then, not long after, you pulled the pin, and Jo mentioned Rochelle was in the hospital."

"Fuck, fuck, FUCK!" Smoke threads his fingers through his hair, almost pulling it out in clumps. "I wasn't sure how to introduce you to my parents." His body rocks forward and back silently, subtly.

"Well, you could have come up with something better than staff," I say, exasperated.

"Like what? Oh, hey, Pop, this here is Cally. She pegs me with a ten-inch veined, blue jelly dong, *and I fucking love it*. We're both into some kinky shit, though. Shall we head to dinner? Do you want the chicken or the steak?"

His face resembles a rolling thundercloud, all dark and irritable. His words cement the tempest brewing inside him, the complex derision roiling from his body. Why didn't he say the baby wasn't his? That's because he probably thought any sane person would never connect him to Roach. She was Wrench's girlfriend after all, plus the slew of other men she bounced off of.

Jo rises from the chair almost silently. "I'm just going to go empty the litter box." She'd left the room for mere seconds when Smoke slid along the couch and all but pulled me into his lap. "What the fuck, Callista?"

"I'm sorry. I didn't know! You didn't say anything," I offer. It's a feeble protest, but it's all I have. Now that he's sitting next to me, face aghast, I should have realized how stupid this entire story was. Only I didn't think it was so stupid. When you're already low, your mind has a way of sinking the boot in. That little voice on your shoulder whispers a little louder when doubt creeps into your marrow and sets up camp.

"I couldn't. I can't divulge any details about any active operative. You know that. I wanted to tell you so many times. I couldn't risk infecting you if it turned out that piece of shit had infected me." Cool tungsten steel eyes implore me to understand his position. Smoke is nothing if not loyal and unwavering under direct orders. I mean, if it were me, I would have written it down on a scrap of paper before eating the evidence like they do in the movies. Not him, though.

"Is that why Feather went on vacation?"

"Yeah," he says, his broad palm scrubbing over his face. "We couldn't risk any of his fluids—blood or saliva, or sweat, landing on any customers he might evict from Wilds or Kittens. He went to see his sister in Ohio but came back because he was worried about his nephew. Rodin said you can't contract anything from making a kid his breakfast, but Feather was adamant he wouldn't put his family at risk either."

"Just as adamant as you were with me," I whisper. And he pulls me into his chest. My God, I've missed this man. The hard planes of his stomach muscles, the way his pecs fill his shirts so well, they almost look painted on. This man fought so hard to keep me safe when he worried he might be infected with a horrendous virus. He put distance and silence between us, because there was no other choice.

"Bedroom. NOW!" he growls, and the hairs at the back of my neck are as attentive as the rest of me. His plaintive, pleading tone from earlier has left the building, replaced by the dominant Marine who loves nothing more than to go to war on my body. In my body. He uses every weapon at his disposal—his talented fingers, his filthy, wicked tongue. His cock—oh my god, forget weapons of mass destruction; it's a weapon of mass delirium. And it's rock hard and ready to rumble under my thigh right now, causing the slick between my thighs to increase. My core is molten and needy, and ready for all of him.

"Please tell me you haven't been with anyone else," he pleads, those stormy eyes flecked with soft purples; the clouds after a thunderstorm. "You know as of today, I'm clean."

"There is no one else for me, Smoke. Only you, and you know that," I breathe, perspiration threatening. "And Max."

He stills his palm, framing my face. "Mr. Pro Max, my favorite vibe. You know, the pink one?" I clarify, and he grips my jaw to the point of pain before releasing me with a shake of his head. If a look could promise anything, that look has my ass striped pink and my pussy sore in advance.

I am scooped into one arm while he strides purposefully into the bedroom, frowning at the open suitcases and articles of clothing strewn everywhere. Smoke stands me under the hook where I pegged him the first time and sweeps the bed clear of debris with minimal effort. Tops, shorts, snow jackets and bras form a mountain of fabric on the floor next to the bed, and the mattress is bare. He wastes no more time, spinning to face me and beginning to strip me out of the hoodie and sweatpants. His moves are raw, almost rabid, a fervent need and zero patience to unwrap his prize... me.

"For a man who earned a living by mastering patience, I no longer have any," he declares. "I want my pussy right fucking now. And have two months to make up for."

"Your pussy, huh?" My words are cut off as his mouth claims mine in a bruising, brutal kiss. A kiss so primal, if we were in public, we'd be arrested. He's a flurry of methodical movements, practiced and efficient. Smoke divests himself of his clothes, only stopping our kiss long enough to remove his shirt. We've never really kissed before. Not that either of us discussed it as an issue, our agreement didn't embody slow, sensual sex with drawn-out, passionate foreplay. Now that I know how his tongue maps mine with expert cartography, I want to kiss him as often as possible.

"That's right, sweetheart. Mine. If you want my cock, save that smart mouth for later."

I'm laid on the mattress with little finesse. Smoke palms the length of his impressive erection once, twice, before diving between my legs.

"You're going to come on my tongue. Then your pussy is going to choke my cock until we both explode. After that, anything else is on the table, but right now, you and I have two months to make up for. Get comfy, darlin', it's gonna be a long and dirty night."

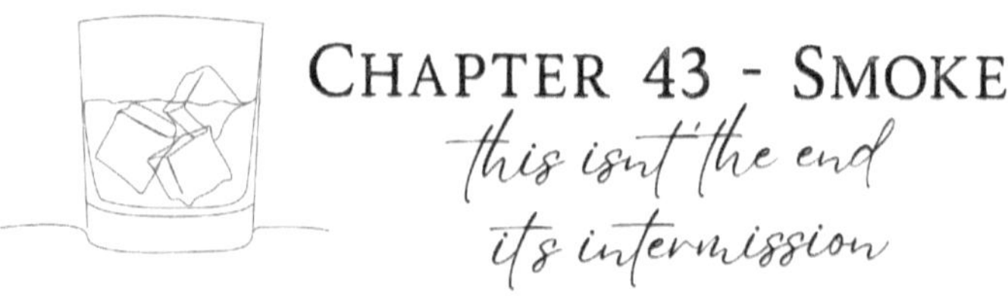

CHAPTER 43 - SMOKE
this isn't the end
its intermission

This should be the place I sleep the soundest. I'm content, sure, but the last thing I want to be doing with this woman nestled into my body is sleep. Breathing in the cotton-floral scent of her shampoo as flames fan across my shoulder and over my chest, I roll her onto her stomach with a nudge from my hip. She rolls, still dazed from slumber and no doubt spent from the animalistic sex we had when we first entered the bedroom. And the time after, and again in the early hours of the morning. As the sun threatens the last of the inky blackness, I want, no, I *need* her again.

My stirring cock nestles in her back seam as my body blankets hers. Sweeping the flames aside, I pin her hands together under the pillow she's unknowingly imprisoned them beneath, and bite the shell of her ear before soothing the sting with my tongue. Her response is to push that pert little backside right into my throbbing dick. Brat! Nudging her knees wider with my own, I rock forward while she pushes back into me, aware of the dirty little tease that she is. That, or she knows this will be the last time we fuck because she leaves in less than three hours.

Knowing that, I don't want props or costumes. This scene will be one of domination and submission, sure, but only using willing trust and the dominance of power. I can keep her compliant with one hand, and she trusts me not to abuse that power. Any bite marks can be attended to in the shower before she dresses for her journey, and I lick my metaphorical wounds. My hands snake along the mattress and under her sleep-warmed body to cup her tits. They're on the smaller side, but I've never been a tit man. I don't think I'm an ass man either, more the complete package. An artist's vision of the perfectly imperfect, the magnificent with the malevolent, the pure with the primal. Five feet, seven inches of porcelain perfection with a built-in flamethrower aimed at your heart, or cock, depending on the day and her fluctuating moods.

"Mmmmmm," she moans sleepily into the air as my hands continue to pinch and pluck at her pebbling flesh. She has the most responsive nipples, and my hands and teeth are more than ready to elicit the stiffening peaks to turgid points. Still teasing one, pulling it to a point just shy of painful, my other hand slides to her cuff, her neck. Breath play is a big part of her submission requests. Whether she's read the data pertaining to the heightening of orgasm with mild asphyxia is anyone's guess. The only thing I've even noticed her read was the labels on wine bottles and a slutty-looking romance book with some buff dude on the cover.

"Suck," I demand, sliding two fingers into her waiting mouth. She obliges like the good fucking girl I know she can be when not hellbent on being a brat to earn a spanking and a deeper fucking. Not necessarily in that order either.

Withdrawing the hand from her throat to offer her a temporary reprieve, I use it to test her readiness for my thick dick. Unsurprisingly, she's soaked the sheets already. Dirty fucking girl. Lining my cock up with her dripping pussy, I thrust inside her to the hilt in one movement, causing her breath to catch around my probing fingers. That's it, princess, take all of me. My hips jerk forward and withdraw until only the tip of my dripping crown is inside her. I rock forward again, returning to restrict her throat while her tongue laves at my stroking fingers. Her mouth is just as wet as her pussy, welcoming my fingers like her tight cunt welcomed my cock home.

The pulse in her neck thrums double time while she writhes, every thrust propelling her towards the headboard without actual contact. The pressure of my hand at her mouth has saliva pooling at the corners, dripping onto the white linens every time my dick bottoms out at her womb. I want to punish her for believing the bullshit rumor about me being involved with that Temu whore. Or for her still wanting to leave the state and work elsewhere. Most of all, I want to punish myself for letting her go.

Adjusting the grip at her throat, my opposite fingers find her clit, and she bucks at the contact. She's oil hitting the surface of a sizzling hotplate; the clash of temperature and surface too much for physics. Continuing to bite a reddened path down her ear and along her jaw, I reach the dripping mess on her cheeks, mouth pulled into a tight O.

"That's it, baby. So fucking wet for me. Everywhere. Which cock owns your cunt, hmmm?"

"Yours." It's a jumble of consonants and moaned vowels. Eyes squinted shut before her lids burst open again. I ease my hand off a touch, watching as she gulps in a welcome lungful of air.

"I didn't hear you," I tease, fingers spanning her carotid artery and jugular vein as my cock slams home again and again.

"YOURS," she chokes out, eyes blown wide, tears forming at the corner of the eye I can see. She draws in the limited oxygen through her nose, nostrils flared. So damn beautiful like this.

"That's right. No one will fuck you like I do." My declaration comes as the circles on her clit elicit the response I knew was coming from a mile away. I don't just sense her approaching orgasm, I smell the change in scent of her arousal leaking all over my thrusting cock, coating me. I want to bottle and fucking bathe in it.

"So close. So close, baby. Come for me. Before you fucking leave me. Come fucking now!" She does with a whole-body rigor. Her inner walls vice my dick in rippling waves that demand my release. Fucking her through her orgasm morphs into her milking me into mine. My cum joins hers on the sheets, her tear-stained pillow also harboring the pooled saliva. "Don't bother packing or washing these, darlin', they're coming back to the MC with me so I can inhale you all night long."

Cally's possessions packed into boxes and bags strewn about the trunk of her car send my chest void into arrhythmia. I don't know why I thought she'd stay after we worked through our communication difficulties through multiple orgasms. I'm humble enough to know that once a woman like Cally has her mind made up, my fingers, dick and tongue would have quite the task ahead of them. But they worked together as a cohesive unit, and the results were delicious and repetitive. Only the car remains crammed full of her shit, *and she's still leaving*. Her word means that, and she doesn't want to go back on it and offend a new employer. Here I am, leaning against the side of the Dark Horse, as the woman I have fallen head over heels in love with, readies to vanish from my life. To fucking Florida.

My mind drifts to greeting cards with inspirational quotes like, "If you love something, set it free. If it comes back to you, it's yours. If it doesn't, it never was." Will she come back? And a free spirit like Cally Rae will only ever belong to herself. I don't want to own her, or claim her outside of the bedroom, I only need her to understand that time apart isn't what we both need, considering the two months we survived almost killed us.

A flash of red darts from the porch, whirls around and ducks inside the cottage again. She is a Texas tornado. A whir of energy that can sweep you up and dump you back down again. Whether you land on your feet is up to her mood that day. She's unpredictable, spontaneous and spectacular in every way. And she's leaving for fucking Florida.

"I'd tell you to drive safe, but I've seen how you drive and know that is logistically impossible," I state, swatting her on the ass as she walks towards the car.

"Well, that's all on you, because you taught me how to drive," she retorts, with the usual Cally Rae sassy spice. That mouth. That goddamn smart mouth.

"I gave you the knowledge, sure. You took those lessons and ran with them. Ran into a fire hydrant and trash can. So that's not on me."

"Ran off the road, you mean!" She giggles, and the sound goes straight to my dick.

She's a terrible driver, although having her pilot an automatic car saves her chaotic mind from remembering too much at once. Forgetting to check her mirrors before she changes lanes, and on the rare occasions she checks for surrounding vehicles, she changes anyway because "they are where I need to be so I'm just advising them they need to move." What do you say to that? Nothing. You just hope she doesn't mess with any non-club motorcycles or twenty-four wheelers.

Pulling her to me by her belt loops, she molds her curves into me when she presses up against my front. Reclined like this, we're almost the same height, and she doesn't waste the opportunity to look me square in the eyes and breathe. "I'm going to miss you so, so much."

"I'm going to miss you more." Sappy? Sure, but it's true. In the week and a half since my bloodwork showed no signs of HIV or hepatitis, we have been inseparable. She worked out her notice at Wilds and Kittens; the strippers even organized a little send off party for her with balloons and cake. All the strippers except Delta, of course. If wet scraps of food in the sink were a person, that's Delta. There is no love lost between those two, and the revolting comments she made towards the departing assistant manager were not without repercussions. She was hauled into an open-door meeting with Grave, Feather and me, and put on clear notice that while she brought a good amount of money through the door, her shitty attitude would not be tolerated. If she wants more shifts, an attitude shift is warranted first, and all staff are to be respected, especially superiors.

"You'll come meet me in Chicago, right?"

Cally is breaking up the solo trip to Florida with an extended break in Chicago. She has several shoots lined up, including one for a new client. Only after her commitments there are satisfied, will she turn south and head to fucking Florida? Will I meet her in Chicago? You bet your sweet ass I will. That's the only reason I haven't chained her to her headboard and kept her as my slave. I'm even planning a trip to Florida once she gets settled there. Not with the Indian, though. I'll fly down to maximize my time with my girl.

"How is that even a question? You know I'm coming to Chicago to make you come, darlin'. I never want to be in a place where you are not."

"Oh my god, stop it. You're gonna make me cry."

"Give me all your tears, baby. You know I crave every last one. I want to be in your thoughts every minute of every day, and in your dreams at night when you collapse into bed after making yourself come with my name on your lips. This isn't the end, it's an intermission."

Thick tears track down the apples of her cheeks and drip off her chin. Fuck sugar, this is hard. You keep that up, and I'll be bawling right alongside you.

"I hate myself for thinking the worst of you when you were waiting for those test results." Her lips pull into a smile, but the pain in her voice is obvious.

"We can't change the past darlin', only the future," I add, wiping another fat tear away with the pad of my thumb before it cascades onto her sweater.

"I know. But we were robbed of so much time. And now, I'm robbing us of more by leaving."

"Ssshhhh darlin'," I soothe, rubbing soothing circles on her back as she buries her face in my neck. "We will have all the time in the world. You'll see. Just don't drive like a fucking maniac, and I'll see you in Chicago, beautiful."

Cally pushes at my chest with her palm, all faux indignation. At least the tears have stopped. While I admitted to craving each one, I meant the tears shed during gratification and pleasure. Not these sad tears on the parting of lovers. These tears can get in the fucking bin. Gripping her body to mine, I lean around her and open her driver's door. Then I stand and plant a soft kiss on her forehead, telling her to check her mirrors twice, and again for a third time before she makes any hasty maneuvers. Then we kiss passionately for as long as we dare. A kiss of promises, of passion and apologies. Of the melting snow and the bluebird sky, of the road through the mountains, and the lakes beyond. A kiss that says everything I want to right now, but can't. Because the woman I fell head over heels in love with is leaving me.

I've followed her little dot with the dedication of a pious servant. She stopped at Popeye's, gas and fuck knows what else before settling into a motel for the night. After a quick call to confirm she had run no one off the road and that she was in one piece, our call drifted into phone sex territory. Not satisfied with that, she video called me after her shower in nothing but a towel. The towel became an unnecessary prop less than a minute in, and we picked up where we had left off earlier, both of us coming to the sight of the other's loud moans and whole-body tremors. How the hell are we going to survive this, *whatever this is?* We're exclusive; sure, that's a gigantic step. I know that I'm in love with her, but haven't trusted myself to say the words aloud. Cally hasn't given me any sign that she feels anything other than deep lust and satisfaction. Then again, she gets that same look after eating Sandra's chicken fried steaks with white gravy. I need to remember she's so young, and inexperienced. Of course, she wants to discover the world and all the opportunities coming her way. It's selfish of me to only want her coming *MY* way, with me.

She needs this opportunity to cement her independence. Both were denied to her for so long by people who purported to love her. Who were supposed to raise her right, gently guiding her path and understanding right from wrong. She wasn't raised; she was robotized.

Another day, rinse and repeat. The rinse was required after I came so fucking hard, I had cum on my top lip. I could almost feel my fingers digging into the flesh at her hip, driving into her from behind while she sank back onto my cock, meeting every one of my thrusts with a clench of her own wet cunt. Luckily for the both of us, I'm heading her way next weekend. She finishes up with Sando and the new client on Sunday, then we'll have a glorious three days together before I head back to the bars, and she heads for Florida. Guess I can't hold so much loathing for the state if it will be home to my woman. Temporary home until either I join her or she comes back to me. We could toss a coin, draw straws or fuck each other senseless, and whoever came first lost the bet. Only edging and orgasm denial is a taxing process. Denying us both defeats the purpose of fucking.

After a lackluster Saturday night, one of the worst we've had since Kittens opened, Saint and I are closing the bars while Grave and Feather make sure the girls get to their rides safely. The television in the corner is playing some news station no one is paying any attention to. Wrench, Hammer and Boomer are on their last drinks. They should have stopped drinking before, but all of them are huge guys with sound metabolisms, so this last drink shouldn't tip any of them over the limit to safely get their bikes back to the club.

Only when my gaze flicks up to the breaking story, and I see an emblem I'd recognize anywhere, does my heart leap into my throat, threatening to deprive me of oxygen. A fire; unknown as yet if it was deliberately lit, has engulfed the building and threatens neighboring structures. The reporter is uncertain of any injuries or casualties at this time and will report more of this breaking story in further bulletins.

CHAPTER 44 - CALLY
turning in circles

I drove myself to Chicago! Not without incident, sure. There are all kinds of drivers on the road, Smoke once told me, and on this trip, I encountered all of them. Some people should learn how to use their mirrors more; it would make life so much safer for the rest of us.

As the scenery changed from rolling Montana ranchscapes, through pine forests and urban sprawl, only to dissolve once again into farmland that predominates the shoulders of the I-90. Had I not been driving, I know I would have taken more in, noticed how the housing estate on the other side of Rochester was all but completed since the last time I travelled this route. Red roofs raise geometric faces towards the sun as an homage; timber truss frames are now sheathed in a skin of dressed timber siding or cloaked in an ochre clay. Only today I drove this route in my car, rather than soak it up as a passenger to a dedicated MC biker. The way an unwelcome sense of melancholy cleaves through my chest as the realization settles, has me wiping more stray tears and wishing this whelm would fuck right off. I've been on my own for a good portion of my life, learning how to cope with my exclusive company so much so that when the Moonyata offered me back into their fold, mind you because there was always a catch, I shunned their requests like the plague was attempting to infect me. Keep your unhemmed curtains and I'll stay in my room, please and thank you, only for the fuck you to slip out from between gritted teeth. Pulling into a parking spot just down the road from the studio, I returned the honk and raised my finger to the prick in the Jaguar first, then made my way up the steps to another photo shoot and the real next part of my life as an independent, free and fabulous woman.

One shoot down and another to go, plus a visit from Smoke and then I'm off to the south for some sun, sex, and a shitload of money! I don't know how much money normal people make from normal jobs because I have never had one, nor do I consider myself to be normal. . When I first was hired, I put as much money away as I dared, saving like crazy for a ticket back to Texas under any means necessary. Except for hitchhiking because all the shows I've been binge-watching in my spare time have people going missing, or being carved up into chunks and littering a field when they get into some random car. How is that so different from an Uber though? At least hitchhiking is free; with Uber you have to pay them to drive you, which seems kind of dumb. Anyway, off I went on some tangent, which happens when I'm on my own for too long and all of my rambling thoughts tend to trip over themselves on their way to the dance floor. Like my mouth just opens, and a spotlight shines, and the words think it's Carnivale or some shit. I went back to my spending habits once I worked out that Texas may not be the shimmering light of hope I once thought it was.

The sex toys were free or heavily discounted. Same with the fetish wear, especially if it had cum all over it, whoops. Rubber and vinyl are easy to clean, though—just a hose down and they're as good as new. Mesh, not so much, and lace is a bitch. You need to scrub that shit with a toothbrush. But I digress. I spent more than I should have on dresses, slutty heels and other fashion accessories. I also had regular sessions at a spa and hair salon, both of which are so expensive. I now know why so many young, gorgeous things seek balding, older sugar daddies. More for the sugar, and less for the daddy, but stuff is expensive! The Moonyatas used coffee on my hair, amongst other weird shit, so keratin masks and bond repair lotions could demand a non-vital organ, and I would line up to harvest it myself. With all of this in mind, my coveted independence and a free life for the first time, why do I feel the most alone I ever have? Then I realize, a feeling bubbling up like the orange mac and cheese sauce before it sticks to the bottom of the pot and burns. I'm not alone—I'm lonely.

Four calls and two emails to Explicators have gone unanswered, and when Smoke texts to tell me he can't visit me for another couple of days because they are short staffed at work and he can't take time off, I break down. Body-wracking, honking sobs that pain my shoulders and leave my mouth dry, because every atom of moisture from my body has either run from my nose or leaked out of my eyes. Fuck this independent fabulous woman shit. I want a refund.

"Hey, beautiful," Smoke croons, lifting me off my feet in an enormous hug. His deep inhale of my freshly washed and glossed hair doesn't go unnoticed. "Christ, you smell good, woman. Good enough to eat." Which he does the moment we are inside my hotel room. It took three attempts to get the card into the slot, a task he had to take over when my fingers shook uncontrollably.

"Does your needy pussy need my cock, darlin'?" Yes, yes, it fucking does.

Throwing me onto the bed, I bounce twice before he descends like a predator, already clawing at excess clothing. My jeans shorts are yanked down while still fastened, taking my thong with them. The scrap of lace held hostage by the denim falls in a puddle with my crop top and cotton bra, his jeans and t-shirt so thin, I could see his hardened nipples through it.

"I missed you so much," I breathe into his neck, dotting biting kisses all over his jaw and neck before he slinks away from me, chuckling softly at my pout and protests.

"You're going to come soaking my face, then on my cock, hmmm?"

His long, flat tongue splayed my outer lips open before darting around my clit in the next movement. With age comes experience, I guess. As much as I used to hate thinking about all the women he'd been with, they had a part in shaping him into the man he is today, and how well he fucks is testament to lessons learned and experience earned.

"Oh, I can tell you're close, baby girl. Are you going to come for me?" I want to tell him to shut up and keep licking, but he can multitask like a fucking champ.

"Yes, Daddy," I moan, writhing under the direct pressure from his splayed palms on my lower abdomen.

"Yes, you taste like summer fruit and sin. Soak me, beautiful." It's not a challenge, nor a question. It's a demand. A direct order from this incredible man, who tunes my body like I'm a symphony to his baton. His thumbs angle lower to open me up to him more, tongue still rolling in circles before spearing a path inside me with a fervor driving me crazy. Why, why did I get into a car and drive in the opposite direction from him? I need to speak to the MC psychologist because the elevator in my hotel doesn't reach the penthouse, and my brain took vacation time.

"More, oh, right there, I'm going to—"

"Yes, you fucking are," he demands, thrusting three fingers inside my pussy right as I combust into waves of unbridled pleasure. They stroke deep before curling, dragging down my inner walls and feeding the tremors gripping me from the inside out. "You are so fucking pretty when you come apart for me."

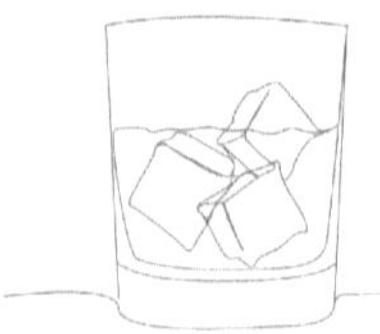

CHAPTER 45 - SMOKE
Up in flames

Before we drift into post-orgasmic slumber, we talk about anything that's on her mind, and that proves to be a chaotic place. Do I want more kids? Sure, one day. Is Daniel Craig the best James Bond? No. He's pretty good, but he's not the best. We've covered my decision to become a marine, and what direction she thought her career might take her, pre-cult of course. Then our conversation drifted to music genres, whether we appreciate musicians any less when their personal lives threaten to overshadow their music—yes Dave Grohl, your name was mentioned. Topics were swatted back and forth like a volleyball until the fire at Explicious came up.

"Have you made any other plans since the fire at Explicious?" I ask, drawing small pathways along her collarbone.

"What fire?" Oh, shit.

"The fire. About a week ago, I think it was. It came over the news at work when I was closing up."

She bolts upright.

"You didn't know?"

"No, I didn't know! I mean, they didn't respond to my phone messages or answer my emails. I thought maybe they were just busy. I didn't think their computer was barbecued!"

Panic grips her features, pulse thrumming at the side of her slender throat. She looks... lost. Moving from the covers, she retreats to the bathroom. Within three steps, I'm right behind her, pulling her body flush to mine.

"Hey, it's okay. No one was trapped inside. It's structural damage. The follow-up news reports say it was an electrical issue that ignited the insulation."

Her hands grip the edge of the vanity. She's trembling. I know this is a shock, but it's a partially collapsed building, not the loss of a relative.

"I don't have a job," she stammers, bottom lip full and slack. "I can't be independent if I don't have a job." It's a chant, a mantra. Her words might be directed at the bottom of the mirror, where the underside of her breasts almost meets the white tile, but her delivery is internal.

Hands band her waist. "Baby, you have a job. You always have a job with us."

Her head shakes, almost imperceptibly at first. "This was my opportunity. My fresh start, you know. Down to Florida for the sun and the sand." Tears pool in her thick eyelashes. "And the sex." It's almost an apology.

"It's a setback, nothing more. Please tell me you understand that."

Her chin drops, defeated. She's devastated. And I think a sex club burning down is only the tip of the iceberg. Did she equate this journey and new destination with a covenant of higher importance? She must have. Or was her escape to fucking Florida a ploy to put as many states and miles between herself and me as she could, back when she thought I'd fathered another child with my best friend's on-again, off-again fuck?

"Hey," I state, holding her chin with thumb and forefinger. "This does not define you. Don't let one setback make you think you failed. Don't do it." My reflection stares at hers, into hers. She's fighting to keep it all together, that pillowy bottom lip threatening to quiver, eyelids ready to purge any pooling tears. "What were you planning to do if you hadn't heard from HR at Explicious? Drive down there and hope?"

Her apologetic glance, all bitten lip and quirked dimples, states for the record, yes, she was. Cally, Cally, Cally. I shake my head to her reflected vision, steeling her jaw in my grasp as I continue. "You, of all people, know that one's mind can be our cruelest master, yes? Instead of speaking to me when you worried I'd broken our agreement because I was with someone else, you quit. Not to me as your boss, but to Alpha as Club President. Do you have any idea how that made me feel?"

She whirls in my hold, eyes wide. "No worse than me thinking I had no chance with you, but that fucking bitch did. When I thought you'd pulled the pin because she was pregnant, I couldn't even look at you without wanting to vomit."

A fair point made. She thinks I hurt her, so she wanted to hurt me back. This was some kind of fucked-up revenge tactic. Okay then, that clarifies nothing. "If you were so goddamn angry with me, why didn't you just leave when you found out what you *thought* was fact?" I spit back at her. Two ineffective fists push at my chest. Her wild mane of hair whips about her shoulders as she thrashes, confused.

"Why? Answer me, dammit. Why?"

"I didn't want to leave the club in the lurch. I worked out my notice because I'm principled. Even when I thought you'd royally fucked me over, I still wanted to do the right thing for the club regardless if you benefitted from the situation or not."

"Again, why? You could have told Alpha to shove his job up his ass and walked out. No one could stop you. So, why?"

"Because," she fumes, "I fell in love with you."

There it is. Fact, delivered by full lips, from a reddened, tear-stained face. The fists unfurl and splay across my chest hair, pulling gently before releasing. The swirls of inky blackness and pops of color under her palms dwarf her delicate fingers.

"We had an agreement," I counter.

"Yeah, well, I went and fell in love with you anyway. Even when I thought you were being a prick, you were still my prick. Until you weren't."

"I was never not yours," I add. "I told you as much before you drove away from the cottage. This was just," my hand flourishes in the space between us, "intermission."

"That's another thing, asshole," she fires back. "Why the hell did you let me leave? Why did you drop your bombshell news, kiss me on the forehead and tell me to drive safely? Why?"

"What did you want me to do? Throw you over my shoulder and cart you back inside the house? Get down on one knee and vow to try not to annoy the shit out of you for the rest of my life? What were you seeking that I didn't do?"

"You didn't beg me to stay," she wails, the sobs returning with gale force. "When your parents came into the bar, all I wanted was for you to tell them I meant something to you, that I wasn't just staff. But no. You walked out. Then there was all the bullshit with the paternity thing."

"Hepatitis thing, not paternity thing," I grouse.

"Yeah, that. The hepatitis thing I knew nothing about because you couldn't tell me, I know that now. Still, you standing in the yard with me, with the car packed full of my shit, you still let me leave without protest. That told me you didn't want, nor need me to stay."

"Oh, darlin', if that's all you gleaned from that morning, you were watching the wrong channel, honey."

She pushes back, pressing her hands to the vanity counter once more, her ass almost resting on it, but not quite. Noticing my slow perusal of her body and ink in the soft light of morning, she folds her arms across her chest, and pouts. Her pussy is still on display though. She eyes the stack of towels over my shoulder, her mind no doubt calculating the risk versus reward. Does she dart forward to reward herself with a large, fluffy white towel to drape around her curves and shield her body from my gaze, or will she risk brushing against me in her pursuit of the cotton?

Heaving in a huge breath, one that fills my lungs to maximum capacity and then some, I heave it out again, the action making her tap her bright blue toes on the tiled floor. She's sassing me now?

"I didn't stop you from driving away from me because I couldn't. And I don't mean physically stop you. I couldn't do it because it wasn't my question to ask."

She studies me, perplexed.

"I didn't tell you not to go, or drive out here and demand that you return with me, Cal, because you needed to *want to*. For so long you were told what to do, how to think and who to be. This is your time now. You can blaze your own trail, scorch it to cinders if you want to; that's your choice to make. No more hiding away, or covering your phenomenal hair. You burn so bright, Callista. Do you know you are saved in my phone with the initials C and R and a little chili pepper? That's because I thought you were hot. From the moment I saw you dressed in frills trying to dance in the building debris, to you trussed up in a gag and harness for your fetish work, I couldn't stop thinking about how beautiful you are, and how lucky I am to be in your orbit. C R Chaos, that's for sure. But your voice, and laugh, your spontaneity and chaotic storytelling that circles back before launching nine new sub-stories, is infectious."

Her head cants to one side, studying me further, as if attempting to discover my words are some taped recording and not from my mouth direct to her ears. Forming any emotional attachment was a nod to a currency I didn't trade in. Feelings meant you were accessible, an Achilles heel to a man more prone to playing the detached, unflappable robot. I couldn't fix cars and bikes like Wrench or Hammer, or sodder garden butterflies like Flint. I had no real skills to offer this woman, yet I wanted her to accept me for what I did have, and not focus on my shortcomings or perceived imperfections.

Dropping my tone lower, I continue, unfettered. "I think I fell in love with you a long time ago."

One hour and forty minutes later, we're both showered and freshly fucked, dressed and in a position to continue the heart-to-heart conversation we began in the bathroom. Yes, Explicious was still a charred shell. Most of the staff had been employed at sister venues in either New York or San Francisco, both options too far from Montana to be of an actual choice. As Cally hadn't started work, placing her in a position was a lower priority for management, who had dozens of long-term, loyal employees with families and mortgages to comfort. It didn't matter how many times I begged her to come home with me; her eyes still held on to a vision of emptiness. While Cally chewed her thumbnail to the quick, I came up with a plan to allay her fears and cement our futures, one I thought was genius, until the logistics of it came crashing over me like a rogue wave with no tsunami warning siren.

"You want me to marry you, and the best you can come up with is a fucking hair tie?"

I was unprepared for her reaction as much as I was unprepared for the event of requesting her hand in marriage. "It's a placeholder only. You'll get a ring, don't worry."

I hold out the decorative ebony calamari, the same thing that decorated specific areas of my Indian Dark Horse when I stepped away for a moment, or was choking the shit out of my scrotum while she pegged me for the first time. These little elastic circles are a representation of our relationship. Every surface at work is littered with these tiny things, including one of the beer taps. It was removed before the health department could come in and decree our work area unsanitary, only to join a family of others in my drawer.

"A hair tie?" She remains unconvinced.

"If we loop it over a couple of times, it will fit." I gesture to the black band.

"Fuck me," she exclaims, exasperated. "How did I know this was how my life would pan out?"

"Oh, I intend to fuck you again, baby, but I'd love an answer first. Will you, Cally Rae Chaos, do me the incredible honor of becoming my wife?"

"You're just saying this so you don't feel bad about me coming back to Montana with you."

Is she serious? I want to throw her over my knee right now and redden that fucking ass.

"Let me love you. I cared enough to let you go. That's because I knew you needed this *for yourself*. You think your future has figuratively gone up in flames, darlin'. It's a blip on the radar for what life has in store for you, crazy girl. I love you enough to realize that wherever you are, I need to be too. What's the use of inhaling a deeper breath knowing you can't exhale? Like you're only using one lung. Or being too scared to close your eyes when exhaustion pulls you under, because the dreams dissolve into nightmares that you're not with me. Waking in pools of drying sweat, wrapped in tangled sheets that draped a single occupant of a bed made for two. That's me and you, darlin'. Salt and pepper, day and night, Smoke and fire. You burn so damn hot I crave the sizzle of your caress on my skin. Let me love you, the chaotic, complicated you."

CHAPTER 46 - SMOKE
one small change

The I-90 has to be one of the most enjoyable routes in the northern states. It doesn't have the historical romance and significance of Route 66, or the Pacific Coast Highway that hems the ocean in California. Any stretch of road is enjoyable when you're in a vehicle with the love of your life, who is wearing a promise ring, also known as a looped hair tie, on her left ring finger. Sure, it's bulky and unusual, but so is she. Unusual, not bulky. I was certain she'd reject my offering, throw it to the floor and howl in protest. She did none of it. She allowed me to loop it around her elegant finger and slide it up to where it sits now. The symbolism isn't lost on me; this is our relationship personified. Perfect for the two of us, and a huge fuck you to anyone who thinks differently. Cally has found her voice now, and isn't afraid to use it. The cashier at O'Grady's found that out the hard way when she said they don't add cream to their drinks because they aren't that *other* coffee franchise. Cally stated, deadpan, that she didn't order coffee, and if she wanted cream on her iced chocolate with raspberry swirl, she would have it. Six minutes later, my coffee, and her whatever it was, appeared with a generous swirl of cream and red syrup topping.

Because Cal had packed everything she had curated since leaving the cult, the car was filled almost to the roof lining with boxes of crap. I rearranged some items in the passenger seat to make room for her before she smiled, swung the key fob around her finger and told me she was driving. My heart leapt back into my throat, the remembered panic fueling a massive cortisol spike. This situation was unplanned. I flew in expecting to fly out again. She drove here on the assumption she would work out her Chicago obligations and head south to Florida, only that opportunity had gone up in flames—literally.

"Baby, you drove all the way here, by yourself," I offer. "Let me start us off and you can take over when I'm tired, okay?" In my head, it sounded chivalrous. An opportunity for her to sit back and relax, maybe even scroll on her phone or take a photo or two.

"I want to drive," she protests. "How about you take over if and when I get tired and need a break."

"Only if I'm alive that long," I mutter under my breath, but not low enough.

Pointing to her ring finger, she pouts. "Do you want this off my finger and wrapped around your balls again, hmmmmm?"

Oh, I do, I want that more than anything. If she thinks that's a punishment meant to deter my pushback, she's mistaken. Then the thought strikes me like a battering ram to the solar plexus. When she was cuffed to the pole and I berated her about the hair ties on the Indian, I asked her a very specific question.

"Where do hair ties belong, Cally Rae?"

"In my hair."

"That's right, sweetheart. And when they are not in your hair, where do you put them?"

"On or in something that isn't yours," she recites. Good girl, you *do* listen.

On or in something that isn't yours. I was alluding to them being stored in her purse or that ridiculous tote if not encasing her hair. Seeing them litter the bar and the office, and everywhere else I fucking turned used to aggravate the hell out of me. On something that wasn't mine, and the brat wound one around my balls. She knew a long time ago that I was hers, and only now I'm playing catch up. Well played, gorgeous, well played.

"You're set on this, yeah? I can't change your mind?"

"Why would you want to? I'm a way better driver than the first time you put me in a car with a stick shift. This is automatic, and there is so much less to do, meaning I can concentrate on the important things, like the stereo, the temperature and air flow. Oh, and my lipstick."

"Fucking hell."

"But on the bright side, I'm more than happy to shift *your stick,* honey, and if I'm driving, I only need one hand on the wheel, right?"

That ass, that goddamn ass, will glow like a fucking aurora when I'm done with it.

These are memories made. The tailgating, the unnecessary lane changing and the "Oh, fuck, look! A bison!" It occurred to me somewhere between Wisconsin Dells and Sioux falls, that this isn't a hurry and get to the destination kind of trip. This is an opportunity for us to delve deeper into our actual relationship and compatibility, especially if she intends to become my wife. We need a broader understanding of each other, not just the primal, explosive sex we enjoy. This trip was my chance to step up and out of my comfort zone. To right the wrongs of her isolated upbringing and introduce the wonders of the Midwest.

I watched her mouth gape in awe at the depictions of past presidents of Mount Rushmore, the eerie scape of the Badlands with its jutting eroded rock pinnacles. As the wind roared across the buttes and rustled her crazy hair, she was a child taking in the wonderment, and I couldn't be more in love with her. If the proverbial kid in a candy store is a familiar simile, Cally Rae in Corn Palace was my absolute favorite vision of unbridled excitement. The ever-evolving wall murals made with a mixture of corn and grain to depict world wonders and seasonal scenes had her taking photos like a shutter-happy tourist.

"Do you think they called it Corn Palace because Corn Hub would be too weird? Or would that be a copyright thing?"

"I dunno," was my only response. When she told me what she'd done with some of the corn cobs during her time in Utah, I was struck dumb. She's not serious? Wait, she's completely serious! When I think about uses for corn, my mind automatically goes to mash and a smooth bourbon whiskey. Not Cally Rae, She's gone the cult dildo route. Talk about nibbed for her pleasure! No sound escaped even though my jaw must have hinged open somewhere between shock, and disbelief.

"You know I looked after the grain store, right? But let me tell you how perfect a corn cob is as a dildo. All those little grooves."

Honey, I'm going to have to take you at your word. Did anyone eat the corn afterwards? Do I want to know? Then she discovered they had a corn cam, and her raucous laugh filled the foyer and across the prairies beyond. Then we joined every other tourist, indulging in an enormous tub of buttery goodness upon leaving the building, the scent of freshly popped corn having taunted us the whole time we were inside. We'd skipped all of it on our way to Chicago the first time with Wrench in tow. He's Mr. Business, and no deviation from the task at hand. Point A, point B: move. Even on a bike opening the throttle and demanding more from the engine while it hums under your seat, rides were more about the destination and screw the journey. If I can give Cally anything, it's the experiences she was robbed of. That, I can, and will do every damn day for the rest of my life, if she'll let me, and if we survive her terrible fucking driving.

Every day had her seeking an additional attraction or local landmark on our westward journey; each night had us falling into each other, a tangle of tongues, limbs and audible moans. This was our time, and it wouldn't be rushed. If it took us a week to arrive back at the cottage, so be it. I felt bad leaving Saint in the lurch with the bar, but Alpha could suck it up. I'd taken no leave since moving to Montana, working through the wait for the blood test to project a business-as-usual set of optics. The prick had given me a nice little silvery circle on my hand as a memento and accused me of impregnating his vice president's ex, whatever she was. He could damn well wait for my return and take it up with me if he had a problem. I was returning with his precious Cally Rae after all, only she wasn't his, she was mine.

Pulling up to the cottage on day six, we emerged from her car tired, sore and sated. Cally had called her sister on our second night when we stopped near Rochester to advise her of her imminent return and to "move any of her shit out of the main bedroom" she was reclaiming. That's my good girl.

\#

"You don't answer my texts anymore, asshole?" Alpha's tone is clipped, displeased, predictable. Yes, he had messaged me repeatedly to inquire if I was planning to return to Montana, and how long it would take my lame ass to do so. I had opted to protect my own mental health and ignore every single one of his messages. Knowing that I'd be returning with his favorite employee would soften his steely stance, or at least I'd hoped. Ignoring a MC President's message is foolish. Ignoring multiple, well, you were incredibly brave, incredibly stupid, or about to be incredibly dead. While not a betting man, I'll still roll that dice.

"I was busy," I bark, moving past him and behind the bar. Feeling his gaze burn a hole in the side of my head, I inwardly plead that my planned distraction is on her way out here. Anytime now, sweetheart.

"Holy shit. You managed to do something right," he mumbles under his breath before his demeanor turns on a penny. "Cally Rae, my darling girl. Get over here!"

My fiancée, complete with placeholder ring, sashays towards the president, arms outstretched for a bear hug ready to consume the woman. Groaning, he lifts her from her feet and spins her around. "Tell me you are back for good."

"I'm back, but I can't always promise to be good," she squeals when he spins her again. "Maybe I'm back for bad," she giggles. "But I am back and hope my job is still available."

Alpha sets her down on her heels, stepping back to create some much needed distance. The sight of her wrapped up in anyone else's arms, no matter how innocent, sent my cortisol spiking through the roof again. It had only normalized after a 1400-mile road trip, a good portion of that with my ass in the passenger seat, and hand gripping the oh-shit handle.

"Oh, honey. I'm so sorry," he begins, and her face falls. "We filled the bar position already. But there may be an opening elsewhere for you."

She blinks at him, lashes fanning furiously before turning her gaze on me, and I shrug. Filled her position, un-fucking-likely. He had been the one messaging me to say Saint was run off his feet, and that Wrench had to step in and help him. Wrench may be a lot of things. A bartender isn't one of them.

"An opening..." her dejected voice dissolves as that bottom lip trembles.

"Yeah, how about you let us know the music you normally work to, and we'll see what you've got?"

A wave of remembrance washes over her face before crashing onto the sand in a foamy splash. "You fucking asshole," she laughs, shoulders visibly relaxing.

Alpha's broad grin mirrors hers. "Hey Smoke, Cally Rae, Bar. This is your last chance, yeah. Don't fuck it up."

Leaning in, he plants a chaste kiss on her cheek before backing away. Turning, he stares at me before splitting his index and middle fingers in a V motion pointed towards his eyes, then towards me and back again. It says, *I'm watching you, asshole.* Yeah, I get it. I'm watching you, too.

"You don't want me naked up there for the MC and greater county to drool over, honey?" Her words purr from her lips, all sultry seduction and sin. Watch it, sweetheart, I have a good memory.

"Woman, I'll take you over my goddamn knee and stripe that ass until you can't fucking speak. As my wife, the only pole you'll be riding is mine."

There is no point in asking Charlton Jenkins for permission to wed his daughter. In his mind, I'm a biker, and strip bar owner who wants no part of the religious outpost parading itself as a righteous brotherhood, run by a narcissistic despot. Knowing that her father and the pastor handpicked a man they wanted to tame the wild woman made me sick to my stomach. He didn't love her, nor did he put her needs above his own. It's a wonder the woman didn't dry up then and there when his chode dick came anywhere near her. That's a pussy to be worshipped, not pumped twice and shunned.

"Are you ready? You said an hour over two hours ago," I yell through the closed bathroom door. Our bathroom door. If she was going to entertain the idea of becoming my wife, she had *stipulations*, she said. At the top of that list was moving out of the MC and into the pussy palace with her, Jo and the actual pussies. Fine. Job done, in fact. I have two whole drawers for my socks and underwear, and around a foot of hanging space in the wardrobe. I'll never understand how space is so limited; the woman had Flint and Volt outfit the next bedroom as a walk-in for her plethora of clothes. They stopped short at her request to cut a hole in the wall linking the bedroom spaces. She has to take two whole steps out of the main bedroom before entering her wardrobe room; that's a cross I'm sure her shoulders can bear.

"You can't rush perfection," she mumbles from the other side of the door, and I just know she's applying mascara to her lashes with the type of shocked face reserved for horror films. I couldn't give a fuck whether her lashes were inky black and curled, or not. To me, she is perfection fresh from the shower and bundled in a towel, hair damp and hanging in deep scarlet ribbons down her back. Packaging and primping are optional.

"Hurry the fuck up," I bark again, before the door flies open, almost denting the dry wall.

"I'm worth the wait." She smirks, and she absolutely is. Standing before me in a dress that looks black, only to give off a reddish sheen as she moves, like those cars that appear one color in the daylight, and a whole new one in the dark.

The restaurant is dimly lit and full of special touches you'd expect with fine dining. Cloths drape over spread-out tables, heavy silverware bracketing each place setting. A cluster of crystal glasses snuggle on either side of a floral arrangement, tones of deep burgundy, reds and golds a perfect homage to fall. Our server pulls out Cally's chair, waiting for her to sit before rocking it forward in two movements. I wave him off, able to seat myself and wanting privacy rather than more theatrics.

"I watched YouTube videos on how this shit all works," she says brightly.

This shit being fine dining, and foreign to my gorgeous counterpart. Foreign to me, too, if I'm honest. I spent a good portion of my life eating

MRE rations on the field, and in mess halls on base. This fancy scene isn't me, but for a romantic proposal though, it would do.

"YouTube videos, hey, around all your corn cam?" Her face deepens as red as her hair. Since visiting the Corn Palace, she hadn't shut up about the place, often telling bar patrons about the corn and the pictures depicted in the murals. I've seen the cam open on her phone more than once.

"You be quiet," she mocks, before realizing her error. "I'm sorry, I didn't mean to—"

"It's fine, honey," I soothe, reaching over to hold her delicate hand. Working her mind free from the tentacles of that damn cult would take time, time we had, and time I was more than happy to spend freeing her of their power. Being told to keep quiet and shut her mouth left a lasting scar on her personality. She's talked with Rodin on more than one occasion about her time in Utah. While I don't ask him about her sessions, knowing that as a professional, he won't discuss them with me, I still inquire about her progress. "She's doing great," was his last assessment, and the reason we're now seated at this stuffy establishment waiting to order eighty-dollar entrees.

"You can do better than me, you know. There are so many others who are way less fucked up than me." Her fingers move the fork to the right and back again.

"If you're fucked up, then I love your kind of fucked up, baby. I think we're both as fucked up as each other, that's why we're perfect."

"I'm not perfect," she says.

"You are to me. Perfection is an illusion, darlin'. A veiled smokescreen or soft filter hiding a bunch of shortcomings, cosmetic flaws and personality failures. When I see you... when I feel you, I don't taste your raw chicken or watch spastic dance moves. I see ferocity. You battled years of oppression from those who should have guided and protected you. People who wanted to close your mouth to that magical voice and laugh that brings on my own. To dye or cover your hair—hair that finds its way into my ass crack, and I pull it out just shaking my head at how... HOW? I'll tell you how. Because those little elastic hair ties are everywhere but your hair!"

Her laugh is polite and controlled. Was this on YouTube too?

"When we were apart, I collected every one I could find and assembled this little shrine. I don't see flaws, Cally Rae. I see beauty and loyalty and ferocity. I see... you."

She squirms in her seat, uncomfortable with the praise. "I'm a slob. I can't cook. Fuck, I sent you to the ER with food poisoning."

"Yeah, you did. But that has its own silver lining too, princess. I know not to eat your food again, and the testing for possible appendicitis led to another discovery, one I wouldn't trade for all the raw chicken in the world."

"Excuse me, sir, madam. May I recommend the sea urchins in pomegranate foam with finger lime, or the homemade crackers with caviar and cheese curds with radicchio and micro greens with champagne gel?"

The waiter bends towards our table, cloth draped over one forearm. Sea urchin or what the fuck was the other option? Caviar with champagne? Neither, thanks. I could go a steak though. "For mains, I suggest the Japanese Wagyu with a marble score of ten. It starts at two hundred and forty dollars." He bows at the price, perhaps? I do want steak though, but holy fuck, it had better be the best damn steak I've ever eaten. When the waiter stands, topping up our water glasses before departing, the timid voice across the table startles me.

"Can we go?"

"Go? Go where? You haven't eaten anything."

"I don't want to either."

Okay, my girl is uncomfortable. Understandable. I don't think there was a YouTube video for sea urchin and caviar, or two-hundred-dollar steak. "Sure, baby. Anything you want." I slap down some cash to cover the water and a generous tip, and tell the server we will not be staying.

In the parking lot, Cally paces, agitated. Her heels click-clack on the concrete as she paces back and forth, back and forth. The trees are illuminated from hidden lighting at ground level, the lumens shooting upward providing a golden hue to the silvery bark and leaves, a deeper yellowy gold and burnt ombre. "I feel bad about leaving."

"You asked if we could go!" I say, surprised.

"I know, I felt fraudulent there. Like I was pretending to be someone I'm not. I didn't see the point in continuing the charade. Better to leave while we could."

"Is this about the steak, or something else?"

"The sea urchin. The steak. Us!" She throws her arms wide, the action showing off her hourglass figure and sumptuous curves.

"Fuck the steak. What's wrong?"

Cally ceases pacing, arms settling on her hips. "I don't see myself as a trad wife. That's boring."

"You are many things, Cally Rae. Boring ain't in your DNA."

She smiles before holding up a placating hand. She has something to get off her chest, and I need to listen.

"I would rather drink a cup of my own sick than fold and iron your clothes or plant neat rows of flowers by the path to the front door. Don't expect meals you want to photograph before you eat, or a home rippling with the scents of cinnamon and baking pie crusts. So many people wanted me to change my authentic self for their distortion. I can't do that again."

"Darlin', sometimes I'd rather drink a cup of your sick than eat your food, too. Cause if we're talking choices, that's a coin toss between salmonella and listeria."

"Rude!"

Her huff is more theater. She knows I'm right. "Factual. You burned down your sister's kitchen and a good portion of her apartment. Then you sent me to the ER with your chicken sushi. Not to mention the time you cooked steaks with the plastic absorbent pad still stuck to the underside. I get it, baby. You don't cook, and you know what, I'm happy for you not to!"

"In my defense, I didn't realize that wasn't supposed to be there!"

"Which part of the cow did you think it was?"

"No red meat in the cult, remember?" she says, head tilting to the side. "I looked after the grain store, and all those corn cobs."

Oh, I remember her dropping that little bomb. "Anyway, we're getting off topic. What freaked you out?"

"I'm not special. Everyone is always trying to fix me. And you want to know something? I don't think I'm broken. Not really. I like loud. I can't cook. Or dance. But I can suck dick, and I'm damn good at it. Just once, I want to be first, and not made to feel inferior. Y'know? I want someone to choose me the way I am and not want to fix some perceived flaw. Ugh, I don't know. I just—I want to be your second favorite C word. I want to marry you, I do, but you know how I feel about being controlled, unless I'm in a harness about to be thoroughly fucked, of course. I don't want you to propose because it's... convenient."

I don't know whether to pink up that ass, or kneel and eat it. A red haze fogs my vision; the one that fires every synapse, rockets my pulse and flares my nostrils. "Second favorite C word, hey? Charismatic. Captivating. Challenging."

Her arms wrap around herself. Oh no, we can't have that. Don't hide yourself, princess. Her body softens the smallest measure. Her shoulders were rigid, now round a little, and her breathing evens out. "I only want to change one thing, sweetheart. One."

I know the glorious eye roll is happening before I even look up. Yeah, I've had my gaze downcast, like my optimism, since she began her pacing.

A flurry of fire and ferocity. She wears a veneer of anger and apathy because she doesn't want to feel unvalued again. Not by anyone she cares about. Stepping closer, I stop just shy of her feet, one of which is tapping almost imperceptibly.

"You know I love you, right?" My statement is met with silence, so I double down. "I love your gorgeous hair and stunning smile. I love the way you laugh with your whole body, unashamedly. Like you were robbed of joy for so many years, and now every muscle, every limb is intent on making up for lost time. You are opinionated, feisty and fabulous. Unpredictable and challenging, understanding and frustrating. You see the good, the bad and the wretched, and you love it anyway because that's you, honey. Please, please baby, never change. Not for me, not for anyone."

"But you want a change." Her words creep out on tiny footsteps, all timid and unsure.

"Just the one," I confirm, reaching into the pocket of my pants as I descend to one knee.

Her pupils blow wide as her mouth settles into a perfect little O. Oh, is right, sweetheart. You changed me. A change I resisted at first because I feared it, just like you did, I guess. I'm just about done with the guesswork. I want certainty. I want her.

She had offered up her body and shared her most intimate desires with me. The kind of erotic fantasies you didn't just drop like a spoon of sugar into black coffee either. It was so much more. Her body and her trust in me to fulfil her needs while keeping our secret between the two of us only. I didn't view her as a conquest to boast about, and she didn't grease the workplace rumour mill recounting how I like to fuck her full of my cock from behind while restrained, gagged, and submissive. We mutually respected the hell out of each other, and I knew for certain that I loved her. All I needed now was her confirmation.

"Whatever you have stuffed in there better be expensive and outrageously huge."

"Outrageously huge isn't in the pocket, baby, it's behind the zipper."

Cue the grin that melts my heart and makes me want to pinch myself. Pinch myself that she's listening to me ask the most pivotal question I ever will. Those plump cherry lips turning up to showcase her perfect teeth. A face of soft alabaster, eyes of barrel-aged bourbon and fire, lashes that fan her creamy cheeks when she sleeps.

"You are perfect in almost every way. My ride or die. My reason for getting up in the morning, and heaven for falling into at night. You taught me new lessons when I was sure of my education. Your humor eked out laughter when I existed in sorrow. You are the missing puzzle piece, the flame to the smoke that we create *together*. I need you."

"Ed," she whispers as I stare back at her for a visual cue. Fuck, *FUCK!*

"Cal," I all but croak out. She's still smiling, but is it one of those serial killer smiles before they end you?

Fuck it. Go hard or go home. Pulling the pouch from my pocket, I tease the throat of the drawstring bag until the puckered material relaxes. Two thick fingers reach inside, pinching the cool circular metal. With care, I withdraw my fingers, letting the fading fall light land on the facets of the red cut stones. Her hands fly to her face again, but instead of hiding away, she's gobsmacked. Eyebrows shoot towards her hairline, and the whites of her eyes are robust and obvious.

Discarding the drawstring pouch, I grasp the ring between thumb and fingers. An offering, a promise. "One change. A small one. Your last name, baby. Let me love the shit out of you as my wife."

"You're serious?"

"As a fucking heart attack, sugar."

"You don't want me to change anything else?"

"Never. Be yourself. The authentic you I love, the you my body craves. The you that pours breath into my lungs and empties my balls."

"My balls," she corrects. "Ask me again. Properly."

This time, the rolling eyes are my own. *This fucking woman.* "Cally Rae, will you do me the absolute honor of becoming my wife? Will you marry me?"

"Fuck yeah, I will."

Epilogue - Smoke
Brace yourself

I was never one for stereotypes. What does a Marine look like? Hell, I've seen thousands of them in my lifetime, and while there are similarities in body shape and muscle definition, there are also a myriad of differences. Black, white, Asian, Hispanic, fresh grunts and seasoned strategists. And what about those exploring kink and predispositions to non-vanilla sex? Are they all a horde of drooling sex maniacs without gainful employment just waiting to get their rocks off again? Hardly. There are doctors, investment bankers, teachers, laborers, physicists, hell, maybe even paper towel sniffers and taxidermists. The point is, if you paint anyone with that fine-bristled brush; you do them a disservice. Humans are multifaceted and nuanced by nature. We long to join certain clubs and to avoid relegation. Why? Because difference rather than correlation sets us apart and breathes life into our unique souls.

If I had served Cally Rae in the bar as a customer, or pulled up next to her at a set of traffic lights, would our pull be so profound? I'm guessing we may never know. A scrawled name on a crumpled and gross, stained scrap of paper set us into an orbit we could not deviate from if we tried. And try she did. She also despised every moment.

We may have connected further over our mutual yearning to discover more about kink and BDSM, but rather than a conduit to a similar shared space, it became our tether to each other. A scene may play out for minutes or hours depending on the complexity, set up and pack down, any required aftercare and post-climax rest. Yet we craved each other like air, oxygen only absorbing through our lungs at the direction of the other. In the weeks of uncertainty surrounding the deliberate contagion episode, all I wanted was Cally Rae. If not sinking inside her hot, wet cunt, because that was off the table, then just that amiable face, the one with the smirk and subsequent, "What?" she leveled at you if you stared too long. Our connection went beyond kink and physical intimacy; we were as bound as her long red hair in the decorative ebony calamari.

She craved independence, and I handed it to her as sure as a tumbler with three fingers of Macallan slid along the bar. "I don't have a driver's license," damn near sat me on my ass. What? How? So I taught her how to drive, figuring if she at least had the skills she needed, then she could drive off across state lines as easily as recross and return. I must've aged sixty fucking years in the car with her at the wheel, but dammit she needed this, and I would do my utmost to ensure she got there. And she did–just. While I'm in no hurry to be a passenger at her mercy soon, I'm so fucking proud of every learned skill she tacked, triumphed over and kicked its ass. Pouring tap beer, making cocktails, staff rosters, bank reconciliation, product ordering, client liaison.

For a homeschooled, cult-raised young woman, she had a determination that oozed from her pores like wine. She made you want to lean forward and lick it off. Learning how to cook may be an insurmountable mountain, and I think we've both come to terms with that. Sandra and Rina both make more than enough food. Both also send me home with containers of delicious food I can reheat, and lick from her delectable body. Rather than focus on what she struggled with, what she thought her flaws were, we focused on what she excelled at. In her unorthodox acceptance speech, she stated she sucked cock well, and she was correct.

Most evenings, our scenes begin with her on her knees for me or lying on the bed with her head hanging over the edge, mouth ajar and eager to swallow me down. Bondage and discipline feature prominently; the use of props and aids offers a fulfilling lifestyle that enhances our sex life, rather than overwhelm it. We talk about what new options we wish to explore, and how we hope it may help the other towards their own pleasure.

Christmas was perfect. Waking up with her mouth on my stiff dick was the only gift I thought I'd receive. Fingers pulling and pinching my sack as if she was testing to see what was in there for her. The answer, as always, is a mouthful of salty cum, which she swallows as if it is her profession. Of all her learned skills, fellatio would have to be one of my most treasured. She sucks dick just the way I like it, with the head of my cock tickling the back of her throat repeatedly before she swallows, the rippling effect sending me into a new stratosphere. I'm more than fine to return the favor, and the scenes we kick-start in a 69 position are always high on my want list.

Christmas dinner was out at the MC. None of the club girls are allowed anywhere near the main rooms until later in the evening. This promotes a family atmosphere for members with younger children, or those in dedicated relationships, not to worry about near-naked table neighbors making them uncomfortable. Cally had been in cahoots with Rina, our cook leading up to the day, and a new tradition began; the gifting of another with a sweater they had to spend the entire day in. Feather gifted Wrench a bright green Scrooge outfit that clashed with his eyes, according to Rodin. To his credit, he wore it anyway. When I discovered Cally was my recipient, and she was mine, I knew she'd mixed up the names to ensure the scenario. Brat! She wants to play, so let's fucking go. I bought her a bright red sweater with classy argyle patterns and festive trim. On the front, a simple font says; I put the *Ho* into Christmas. She loved it, throwing it on over her black long sleeve, showing Rina how pretty it was. Rina's sideways smirk let me know this wasn't as random as I might have thought with her 'you'd better brace yourself' look.

As I plucked the tape from the top of the bag, after feeling my way through tendrils of ribbons, the dark gray sweater at first appeared bland

and uninteresting. That should have been clue number two. I removed it from the bag, held it by the shoulders as the rest of it dropped to unfurl; revealing the message, in bold, white writing you could read from a fucking space station.

Begging for a Pegging.

Fucking Brat! Ass, meet hand.

EPILOGUE - CALLY
those three words

My fiancé's tongue slides through my pussy lips from my back hole towards my clit. This is the way I like to be greeted after I enter the bedroom post-shower, unless he can join me in said shower, of course. Holding me open with a thumb at each fleshy fold, his chin carves a path through my slickness, before two fingers probe my opening and thrust inside. Holy shit, he's good. He can have me coming on his tongue and fingers inside of a minute if I am horny, which is always. The noise of his fingers, now joined by a third, is wet, squelchy heaven. Lapping at my clit with his tongue, cool eyes full of concentration and reverence meet my hooded ones. Not that he needs my permission or approval. He could make me come with his eyes closed and one hand tied behind his back. We haven't tried that yet, but it's not off the table, per se.

"Right there, right there." My fingers rouse his sandy strands. "Don't stop, don't fucking—"

"Not until you get there," he says directly to my swollen clit, fingers continuing to explore my inner walls, dragging across that spot that makes me see stars and aliens and fucking unicorns shitting rainbows. My body pulses, pleasure forming at my core before radiating outwards towards each extremity. Toes, fingers, lips, even my scalp tingle at his summoned climax. The man can wreck my body in the most insane way, knowing every ache, every need and every responding muscle like he was born to research me for a thesis, only he presents his findings to me, and me alone.

"Mmmmm, that's it," he coos, lifting my languid limbs into a position to allow his hard cock the easiest, deepest penetration. Today, it's with the backs of my knees resting on his broad, powerful shoulders as he thrusts into my soaked cunt. The man is a god, and the only one I pray to now. His taut body, rippling muscles and assortment of ink decorate the most lickable body I've ever seen. Sure, he's way older than me, but who the fuck cares? He's everything I could have asked for, and then some. A man chosen by my pastor and father provided me with a sharp-tongued, lousy lay with domestic violence tendencies. I found myself an ex-military biker MC member who manages a strip club. Who would never, ever raise a hand to me in anger, yet fucks me into oblivion when I demand it rough and dirty. I wax his tuckles; he worships the ground I walk on. The way it should be.

"I fucking love you," I say dreamily after my third orgasm. They come with such power now, one will peter out and roll into the next, leaving it impossible to tell when one stopped, and the next started building. Not that we keep score. We complement each other; we lift each other. We are each other's cheer squad, soft place to fall, sounding board and debauched fantasy. He's the Smoke to my flame, the Ying to my yang and, fuck the Feng Shui, because I know the positive energy flows exactly where it should; from my wet pussy or his squirting cock.

Returning from the bathroom, I find Smoke sitting on the side of the bed, naked, hands spread in the sheet pooled behind him. Confidence oozes from him, the knowing smirk teasing the corners of his sinful mouth.

"I love you," I say, crossing the room to the man who both saves me and satiates me in every way, every damn day, and he knows it. Smug fucker. With his eyes tracking my every move, I'm the impala caught in his leonine stare. Wetting his lips with his tongue, he utters the three words I love to hear almost as much as my other three-word declaration.

The words elevate my heart rate, pebble my skin and make my core clench and drip with need.

"On. Your. Knees."

Need more? We got you...

When the HAMMER drops is the final installment of the Meanwhile in Montana, Ponderosa Pistons series. Our happy-go-lucky biker has something to confess...

PLAYLIST

Smoke and Embers ~ *Waylan Wyatt, Willow Avalon*
I Can't See ~ *ROW, Samuel Miller*
Father Ocean Ben Böhmer Remix Edit ~
Monolink, Ben Böhmer
Take Me to Church ~ *Hozier*
Broken Halos ~ *Chris Stapleton*
Strip that Down ~ *Liam Payne, Quavo*
Strip it Down ~ *Luke Bryan*
Waste Your Love ~
Disco Lines ftg. MORGXN, Kwon
How Many Drinks? ~ *Miguel*
The Door ~ *Teddy Swims*
Not Mine ~ *Kate Garfield*
Wagon Wheel ~ *Darius Rucker*
Fuck It (I Don't Want You Back) ~ *Eamon*
Ride That Pole ~ *Florida Soul*
Give It To Me ~ *Kean Dysso*
The Bar ~ *Morgan Wallen*
I Remember Everything ~ *Zach Bryan, Kacey Musgraves*
Still Into You ~ *Paramore*
Run to Paradise ~ *The Choirboys*
Tell Me What You're Gonna Do Now ~
Joss Stone, COMMON
Fight for Me ~ *Barkaa, Electric Fields*
Hold Onto Me - Acoustic ~ *The Black Sorrows*
Tie Me Up! ~ *JELEEL!*
Slave Master ~ *Future*
Fall on Black Days ~ *Soundgarden*
They Don't Care About Us ~ *Rudimental, Yebba, Maverick
Sabre*
A Lot More Free ~ *Max McNown*
Breathe (2AM) ~ *Anna Nalick*
Whiskey Lullaby ~ *Brad Paisley, Alison Krauss*
All of Me ~ *John Legend*
I Hate Myself for Loving You ~ *Joan Jett & the Blackhearts*

Buttons ~ *The Pussycat Dolls*
Joker and the Thief ~ *Wolfmother*
Fortnight ~ *Taylor Swift ftg Post Malone*
Sex on Fire ~ *Kings of Leon*
Drowning ~ *A Boogie wit da Hoodie ftg.
Kodak Black*
Daughter ~ *Pearl Jam*
Take Me Away (Into the Night) ~ *4 Strings*
Another Hit ~ *Joel Tane*
No Church in the Wild ~ *JAY-Z, Kanye West,
Frank Ocean, The Dream*
Scar Tissue ~ *Red Hot Chilli Peppers*
Red (Taylor's Version) ~ *Taylor Swift*
I Knew You Were Trouble ~ *Taylor Swift*
Pour Me a Drink ~ *Post Malone ftg. Blake
Shelton*
Soul Man ~ *Sam and Dave*
Look Like You ~ *Gordi*
Texas (When I Die) ~ *Tanya Tucker*

ACKNOWLEDGEMENTS

A lot has to happen before a little indie author publishes a book. The planets have to align, for starters, allowing for everything else to seamlessly fall into place. Or not.

I need to thank you, dear reader, for taking a chance on my story, one I believed in with every atom I own. The MC came to me many years ago, the characters and members often popping in and out of my head, showing me their personalities and sharing their stories. Cally, well she just kind of took up residence! Their journeys are profound, the hand dealt not always an easy one. This representation is obviously a work of fiction, but if any of you reading this feels you may need to prioritize your mental health, or put yourself first in any capacity, please don't hesitate to do so. Chores can wait, and work will still be there tomorrow if you take some time out for yourself and your circle.

My own family is incredibly supportive. I couldn't do what I do without their input and sacrifice. Thank you seems wholly inadequate, yet I will scream it from the cliff tops, again and again with fervor and ferocity. We support each other and always will.

To my editors, the real heroes behind the scenes who often lament my use of commas and endashes, or lack thereof. Your careful touches and finesse with language and flow will forever humble me and keep you employed.

To my beta readers and my wonderful ARC team, my diligent PA who always answers rambling messages at midnight with typos galore. Your heavy lifting is appreciated and adored.

If you enjoyed this work, and any others in the series, please rate and review. Indie author love on multiple platforms helps spread the word that we exist, and opens up our work to a wider readership.

AUTHOR BIO

Elle J. Brae is a new author currently living in bayside Melbourne with her husband, two children and two fur kids: a Hungarian Vizsla and Weimaraner Cross. She is a devout student of the university of life, believing the most important lessons are taught *outside* of a lecture room.

Originally a chef and burnt our hospitality worker, she embraced writing again through the disruption of Covid. She wrote prolifically and sporadically, deciding to publish after a series of profound health issues affected her family in 2024.

Days are spent fueled by coffee immersed in the majesty and mystery of books, both tangible paper and audio versions. If the intent to read is a noble one, the art of listening and care of creation are fundamental to the fabric of greater storytelling.

"There is more intrinsic value in that with no cost," is a motto I wholeheartedly believe in and practice as often as possible: witnessing sunsets, gliding pelicans, swirling auroras and unfurling monstera leaves. Take the trip, drink the wine, eat the doughnut. Fuck it, eat two. And don't regret a thing.

When not writing, reading or listening, Elle is often found at the football supporting her beloved Saints, on a Pilates reformer or meticulously planning another trip away. Fit in as much as you can. Be present, be patient, and most of all, be kind...

If you have enjoyed these stories, please rate and review. As independent authors, our connection to our reader base is incredibly important,

You can find and follow Elle on social media or www.elle-jbrae.com where you can sign up to receive a newsletter about all things Elle including WIPs and upcoming novels.

9 781764 087346